BY MONICA MURPHY

ONE WEEK GIRLFRIEND SERIES
One Week Girlfriend
Second Chance Boyfriend
Three Broken Promises
Drew + Fable Forever (e-Original Novella)
Four Years Later

THE FOWLER SISTERS SERIES
Owning Violet
Stealing Rose
Taming Lily

THE NEVER SERIES
Never Tear Us Apart
Never Let You Go

NEVER LET YOU GO

NEVER LET YOU GO

Monica Murphy

 BANTAM BOOKS | NEW YORK

A Bantam Books Trade Paperback Original

Published in the United States by Bantam Books, an imprint of Random House, a division of Penguin Random House LLC, New York.

BANTAM BOOKS and the HOUSE colophon are registered trademarks of Penguin Random House LLC.

LIBRARY OF CONGRESS CATALOGING-IN-PUBLICATION DATA
Names: Murphy, Monica, author.
Title: Never let you go / Monica Murphy.
Description: New York : Bantam Books, 2016.
Identifiers: LCCN 2016000482 (print) | LCCN 2016004722 (ebook) |
ISBN 9781101967300 (softcover : acid-free paper) | ISBN 9781101967317 (ebook)
Subjects: LCSH: Man-woman relationships—Fiction. | BISAC: FICTION /
Romance / Contemporary. | FICTION / Contemporary Women. | FICTION /
Romance / Suspense. | GSAFD: Love stories | Romantic suspense fiction.
Classification: LCC PS3613.U7525 N475 2016 (print) | LCC PS3613.U7525 (ebook) |
DDC 813/.6—dc23
LC record available at http://lccn.loc.gov/2016000482

Printed in the United States of America on acid-free paper

randomhousebooks.com

9 8 7 6 5 4 3 2 1

Book design by Victoria Wong

It is better to be hurt by the raw truth rather than to be comfortably deceived.

—Anonymous

Author's Note

Dear Readers,

I'm assuming you're reading *Never Let You Go* because you read *Never Tear Us Apart* and you want to know what happens next with Ethan (Will) and Katie. Again, I must warn the reader up front that this book deals with difficult subject matter (Katie is a rape victim at the hands of a child serial rapist/killer). The story is dark, there's no way I can get around that.

But I also feel like this part of Will and Katie's story is filled with hope. These two are trying to overcome their past and find happiness with each other. Despite the way they met, despite everyone telling them they shouldn't be together, they can't resist each other. They want to be together. They're in love. And you can't get in the way of true love now, can you?

Thank you for reading their story. Thank you for not holding the cliff-hanger ending in *NTUA* against me. Thank you for understanding that this story needed to be told in two parts. A huge thank-you to my editor and publisher for believing in this story and in my writing.

Again, I'd like to thank Elizabeth Smart, Jaycee Dugard, and Michelle Knight for being brave enough to tell their stories of suffering at the hands of their kidnappers and how they survived. My Katie was lucky—her kidnapper held her captive for only a few days. Jaycee and Michelle were gone for *years*. That they survived, that they were able to so bravely tell their stories to the world, still blows my mind. They are heroes, women we should never forget.

I also want to mention the National Center for Missing and Exploited Children. They work hard to help in the search for missing children and to keep our children safe from harm. For more information, please visit www.missingkids.org.

NEVER LET
YOU GO

I cry. I can't stop. I cry at night before I go to sleep. I cry throughout the day when I should be doing something, anything to remind myself that I'm alive. I should be living.

But instead, I cry for what I've lost.

I cry for what I've found.

And then . . . one day, there are no more tears. They've dried up, like they never existed in the first place.

Gone is the girl I once was. Gone is the woman I was slowly becoming.

Now there's only this void. And there's only one person to blame for what I've become, what I've turned into.

And his name—his real *name—is Will Monroe.*

# ETHAN

She is relentless in her pursuit of me. The constant calls, the texts, the voicemails, the emails. No wonder she's one of the top investigative journalists on TV.

Lisa Swanson is a serious pain in my ass.

After three weeks of constant harassment, I give in and answer her call. She sounds surprised to hear my voice and I'm pleased that I could shock her. I don't think much gets past her.

"You answered," she says.

"It's either answer or try to ignore you for another three weeks," I tell her, sounding bored. Inside I'm a wreck. I've remained undercover since that moment Lisa texted me and Katie . . .

My heart thuds. Hard. Like it came to a complete and utter stop. How am I still alive? Just thinking about her wrecks me. Twists me up inside until I feel like I'm going to be sick.

When Katie discovered the text from Lisa and left me, I shut down. Physically and emotionally shut down for days. Only within the last week have I once again tried to pick up my normal routine. Working on projects. Talking to clients. I behave normally, move through life as if nothing's wrong, but inside . . .

Inside I'm hollow. Broken into so many tiny pieces, I don't think anyone or anything could put me back together. I've lost the only thing that matters. The only person I've ever really loved.

And she hates me. She *should* hate me. I can't excuse my actions.

"Your father's interview is set to air soon," Lisa says, her determined voice bringing me back to reality. "I've delayed it for as long as possible, but I can't put it off anymore."

"Why'd you delay it?" I know the answer. I'm just curious to hear what she has to say.

"Because I wanted to get your side of the story, Will." I flinch at hearing my name. My old name. I'm not Will any longer. I wish she would stop calling me that. "I'm going to be honest with you." She pauses.

Honesty. There's a funny concept I seem to know nothing about. Deception and lies, that's what defines me. Makes me tick. I pretend. I don't know how to be my true self. Only with Katie did I feel close to who I really am.

And now she's gone.

"Your father said some . . . not-so-nice things about you," Lisa says haltingly.

"Like what?" I sit up straighter, run a hand over my head. I'm still in bed. What's the point of getting up? I can do everything here, even work. My laptop lies discarded next to me. My iPad is on my bedside table. I'm in my underwear, I haven't eaten anything yet today, and it's already past noon. I can't remember the last time I shaved, looked at myself in the mirror. I'm afraid of what I might see, the truth in my eyes, the deception in my face.

Who said the truth hurts? Because they're so fucking right.

"Accusatory things," Lisa says, purposely being vague. Why doesn't she want to tell me? Oh, probably because she needs something to draw me in and get me to talk. "You won't like it if he goes on national television and says those things, Will. I promise you, it would be to your benefit to talk to me."

Leaning my head back, I close my eyes and blow out a harsh breath as Lisa waits for my response. I don't know what to say, how to reply. Doing a televised interview with her would expose me, when I've hidden in the shadows for far too long. Not talking to her might end up with me looking like a savage child rapist in cahoots with my father.

Either way I can't win. And Lisa knows it. She's taking a risk, hoping that I'll choose talking to her as the lesser evil.

I'm not sure if that's the right thing, though.

"Has she agreed to talk to you?" I ask, my voice tight, my muscles strained. I'm so tense I could shatter.

"Who?" Playing dumb. Lisa's good at that, too.

"You know who," I say through gritted teeth.

She sighs. "I told her I found you."

My heart fucking drops into my toes, swear to God. "What did she say?"

"She didn't say much at all, which surprised me. I thought she'd be happy to hear the news." Lisa goes quiet, then clears her throat. "Talk to me, Will. Please. You won't regret this."

I will so regret it. And she knows it. She's just trying to pretend she has my best interests at heart. "I don't know."

"Your father's interview is tentatively scheduled to air ten days from now. If you talk to me, I could get an extension. The execs would love to hear your side. And if I could somehow get Katherine involved again at one point—"

"No." The word shoots out of me like a bullet, as though I'm defending myself against a direct strike to my heart. I feel like I'm already dead with just the mere suggestion of Katie

being involved in this three-ring circus Lisa is trying to orga-
nize. My father in one ring, me in the second, and Katie in the
third, all of us alone, fighting one another.

Forget it.

"No?" Lisa's voice is brittle. She doesn't like being told no.

"She can't be involved."

"Why not?" Lisa asks incredulously. "Her perspective is
vital. I think she would rush to your defense. She spoke so
highly of you before." Another pause. A judgment. "Unless
maybe you're not telling me the truth . . ."

"Fuck you," I mutter, refusing to defend myself to her. I
couldn't give a damn what she thinks about me.

But I care about what Katie thinks. She'd hate me for talking to Lisa Swanson. I know it.

So I can't do it.

"If you talk, she might talk, too. She won't right now. She
refuses to see me. But if I offer the chance for the two of you
to speak to each other after all these years . . ." Lisa's voice
drifts, as if she's dangling a carrot and I'm supposed to jump
at that opportunity to speak with Katie.

She can't know that I've already spoken to Katie. Basked in
her presence, reveled in the sound of her voice, her laughter,
the touch of her hand. The softness of her lips, the scent of
her hair, her skin, how she tastes, how she squirms when I
touch her in one particular spot. The sound of my name falling from her lips when I make her come . . .

Not my real name, though. An imposter's name. Ethan is
no one. Will is the devil.

Again, which side do I choose? Who am I really?

"I won't put her through that. I'm not interested." I'm
about to end the call when I hear Lisa's frantic voice. I bring
the phone back to my ear.

"You should reconsider. I can put a temporary halt on this, and let you tell your side of the story. But if you choose not to talk to me, I can't be held responsible for the attack on your reputation that is bound to happen. The interview will air ten days from now, whether you like it or not."

Haughty Queen Lisa is back to playing hardball. "Let it happen."

I end the call.

I set my phone on the bedside table.

I close my eyes.

 # WILL

I cut her off. Not because my lawyer advised me to do so—though that was part of the reason. The guy wouldn't stop badgering me about it, asking every day if I was still talking to her. I lied and said no, having a hell of a time working up the nerve to tell her I didn't want to talk to her anymore. That was hard. But it had to be done. I cut Katie Watts off because I'm not good enough for her. I don't deserve to be her friend. I really don't deserve to be her hero.

Don't deserve to be in her life at all.

Despite what I did, how I saved her, she doesn't need the reminder. And that's all I am to her. The constant reminder that when she was twelve, a fucked-up asshole abducted her, raped her, and kept her chained like an animal in a hot, dirty shed in the middle of summer. I may have rescued her, but that doesn't matter in the long run. She's safe. My father is in jail and though the trial isn't over, I have a feeling I know what the outcome is going to be.

He's guilty. We all know it. He practically admitted it after he was first caught in Las Vegas, then recanted his outpouring of words and demanded a lawyer. He has charges to face there, too, though if California gets him on the death penalty, I guess those charges will end up being dropped. Hell, I don't know. I don't understand the justice system. I'm only seventeen.

I'm still just a kid. A kid with no hope, no ties, no one to help me.

Cutting Katie out of my life may have been best for her, but what about me? What about my needs? Yet again, no one gives a shit. Yet again, I'm left alone. The friends I have aren't real. I can't share with them my past, my history. It's fucked up. *I'm* fucked up. They all know who my dad is anyway. No one comes right out and says anything, but I know what they're thinking. What they're wondering.

Is Will like his dad? Did the man really rape and kill little girls? What sort of sick fuck is his father anyway? Would Will do something like that?

Those words, the rumors, they hurt. Everything hurts. All of it.

Everything.

# KATHERINE

"So." Dr. Sheila Harris's pause is heavy, full of all sorts of unspoken questions. She's watching me, her iPad resting on her lap, her expression expectant. I'd come to this appointment reluctantly, exhausted from having to constantly analyze my behavior, how I *feel*. It never stops, that *how are you feeling* question. *How are you doing?* Blah, blah, blah.

I'm over it.

"So?" I raise a brow.

Sheila's lips twitch. So happy I can amuse her. "How are you doing?"

There it is, right on time. Do I tell her the truth or lie? I'm supposed to be completely open with Sheila. She's the only one I can trust to give me an objective opinion. Mom and Brenna are on my side. They'll defend me no matter what. Forget Ethan, Will, whatever the hell his name is. He wronged me. He tricked me. Therefore, he's the bad guy. Never to be given another chance again.

It's so easy to think along those terms, especially when I don't have to see his face, hear his voice. If he were here, right now, standing in front of me, how would I react? Throw myself at him and pray his arms would wrap me up tight?

Or show him exactly how angry I am by saying horrible, awful things?

This is my daily struggle. I thought it would be so easy, to forget him, to move on, to be so unbelievably angry at what he's done to me. Most of the time I feel exactly that. His betrayal cuts deep.

But there's a secret, soft, dark spot hidden inside me that wants to forgive him. Wants to draw him back into my life. This is what happens when your heart is so thoroughly involved.

Lately, I wish I didn't have one. That way it could never be broken.

"I'm . . ." Awful. Horrible. Devastated. *Alone.* "Okay." I take a deep breath, holding it in before I slowly let it out. Trying to cleanse my mind, my heart, my soul.

It doesn't help. The ugly, crippling blackness creeps back in, wraps itself around my mind, my heart, my soul. I'm . . . angry.

No one wants to hear that, though. Not anymore. I should be getting over it by now. That's what my sister wants, and my mother.

Easy for them to say. They weren't the ones who'd been so thoroughly lied to.

"Just okay? Last we talked, you were very down." Sheila keeps her expression completely neutral. Something she's extremely good at. How I wish I had her poker face.

More like I was depressed. I've moved past that. I've focused on my anger about what happened and it's fueled me. Pushed me forward, encouraged me to do what I want for a change, even be a little defiant.

And I haven't been defiant since I was twelve.

"I got sick of crying." I shrug. I've shed enough tears to last fifty lifetimes.

Sheila smiles. "You're acting rather unusual."

"How do you mean?"

"I want to say rebellious, but I don't know if that's the

right word." She taps her finger against her lips, contemplating me. I sit in the chair, my arms crossed, my expression stony. I can feel how still I am as I watch her, wait for her to continue. I'm thinking *rebellious* is the perfect word. "Stubborn? Nonchalant? Like what Ethan did to you was no big deal."

She brings him up. Of course. My heart freaking skips a beat every time I hear his name. Tingles sweep over me. The whole romance-novel thing happens all over again and I despise it. Even though I also miss him.

It's infuriating, missing someone you're angry with. The conflicting emotions seem to be in a constant battle.

"It was a huge deal," I say quietly, unwrapping my arms so I can clutch my cold hands together.

"Have you spoken to him? Face-to-face?"

I shake my head. I received a text a week ago. That was the first and last one. Seeing his name appear on my phone screen made my heart leap into my throat. I didn't know how to react, how to respond. What could I say to him?

Please talk to me.

In the end, I didn't. I didn't reply. How can I? He lied to me. *Lied*. Over and over again, all while pretending he had my best interests at heart. More like he was concerned with his own interests.

Afterward, once I calmed down and could think clearly, I realized so many things. Like I'm a fool. An idiot. I fell for him and he knew all along that he was tricking me. Playing me.

I remember watching the old *Superman* movie with Dad when I was a kid. Before all the bad stuff, when we used to spend time together and he didn't look at me like I was tainted.

Damaged. As we watched the movie he loved as a child, I couldn't help but think Lois was a total idiot for not realizing Clark Kent was really Superman.

I've become Lois Lane. Ethan is my Clark Kent. Will was my Superman.

Frowning, I blink hard and return my gaze to Sheila.

"Has he tried to contact you at all?"

The text from Ethan came after my last weekly appointment with Sheila, so she doesn't know about it. "He texted me."

"Did you respond?"

I shake my head again. Don't say a word. I remember the sound of his voice instead. Warm and deep and steady and true, my name falling from his lips. I can hear him now.

Katie.

No one else calls me that—I don't allow them to. After everything happened, Katie was dead and gone. When I returned home I became Katherine. Until Ethan came along and started calling me Katie again and I found I didn't mind it. Now I understand why he called me that from the start.

To Will, Katie is my name.

It hurts so much to think of him, to imagine his handsome face. The way his eyes would crinkle at the corners when he smiled. The words he said, the promises he made. How he would touch me, almost reverently, as if I were fragile and could possibly break.

He was right. I feel like I might shatter at any moment.

"How about Lisa Swanson? Has she reached out to you again?" Sheila asks gently.

"Yes. She really wants me to participate in another interview. A sort of counterpoint to Aar—" My voice hitches and

I can't . . . I can't say his name. Having that problem to this very day says a lot I'm sure. "To *his* first interview from prison."

"His only interview," Sheila interjects.

"Right." I take another deep breath and release it slowly. "He's never spoken to the media until now."

"Are you curious to hear what he has to say?"

"No. Not really." A tiny part of me *is* curious, but mostly I'm repulsed that he'd think now is the appropriate time to talk. Is it because of my earlier interview with Lisa? It has to be.

What does Ethan think about this? I shouldn't care, but I'm still having a hard time wrapping my head around the idea that Ethan is in fact the son of Aaron Monroe. Spending time with Ethan, I never caught even a glimpse of violence or hatred within him. He wasn't mean. He was always kind, always sweet and respectful.

The brief, harrowing time I spent with Will, and during our contact afterward, when we would write and call and text each other, he was always sweet to me then, too. Though with an almost resentful edge, as if he needed the contact with me yet hated it all the same.

It's hard to remember the Will I knew before, without letting the Ethan I know today shadow my memories—to the point of changing them completely. I know what happened between us when we were kids. There's no forgetting it. My tortured mind won't let me.

But Ethan, my current history with him, invades the past, meshes everything together. Confuses things, which makes me angry—and my anger blinds me to everything.

No tears threaten and I'm proud. Sadness leaves me feeling useless. I'd rather clutch hold of the anger. It makes my thoughts, my intentions, clearer.

"It must be very difficult to know that people are so eager to listen to whatever he has to say," Sheila says.

"It is." I huff out an irritated sigh. "Why people are fascinated with him . . ." I hesitate, breathe in deep as my anger threatens to permeate my every pore. "I don't ever want to hear him, see him, to . . ."

"Remember?"

I press my lips together, my eyes watering. I refuse to cry. I *refuse*.

"Is that why Ethan's betrayal hurts so much? It makes you remember?"

I nod before I can catch myself, swallowing back the lump that's formed in my throat. I wipe at the corners of my eyes, blinking away any moisture. "I felt used. For the first time, there was hope that I could start over and be normal, you know? But I hadn't realized I was starting over with . . ." I catch myself before I say "Will." Ethan.

They're the same person. Interchangeable.

Mind blowing.

I had a nightmare last night. I was back in that room, the chains heavy on my wrists and ankle, trapped with the smelly mattress, the hot, stifling air. I was alone. No scared boy to come and save me. Will never appeared, but I knew he was there. Somewhere. I cried and cried, my fate clear. I was going to die.

Thankfully, I woke up before that happened.

I change the subject and talk about my sister and my mother, avoiding Sheila's probing gaze, playing along like a good little patient would. I don't want to talk about Ethan and Will and Aaron Monroe and Lisa Swanson and interviews. I'm so tired of that. That isn't all I am.

I read somewhere recently that your life is your choice. If

I choose to be sad and miserable, I will be. If I choose to be happy and strong, then that's what I am. I've been choosing wrong for the last eight years. Yet I finally catch a glimpse of happy, of something real and solid and tender and . . . loving, and it ends up ruined. Ripped from my hands and thrown away.

Lies. Deception. All of it.

As I leave Sheila's office forty-five minutes later, I blink against the light drops of rain that fall from the gloomy sky. My car is parked close by and I dash toward it, unlocking the door quickly and sinking into the driver's-side seat, the familiar scent of my own perfume and body lotion lingering in the air.

Closing my eyes, I take a deep breath, searching for calm. For strength. I need to remember that *I* get to choose. Only I have the power to find inner fulfillment. That sounds like a crock of crap, but it's true. If I choose to be unhappy, I'm unhappy.

If I choose to be angry and let my anger push me, then that's my choice, too.

For once in my life . . .

I choose me.

ETHAN

The text came on a late Tuesday afternoon, the familiar ding ringing loudly from across the room. My phone sits on the coffee table. I'm sitting in my recliner, tapping away on my laptop as I answer an email from a client.

When I finally send off the email, I get up and go to my phone, hitting the button to see who the text is from.

And proceed to drop the phone on the floor, I'm so startled by the name flashing on my screen.

Katie.

What do you want to talk about?

It's been a week since I sent that one text during a weak moment, when I was feeling particularly low and sad. I've taken care of myself my entire life. I don't remember my mom. Dad was rarely around and didn't care. I coped. I dealt with shit on my own and I preferred it that way.

Katie reenters my life and she's like a bright light I can't resist. Her warmth, her sweetness, the way she made me feel like a goddamn hero every time she so much as looked at me, I'd never experienced anything like it. I began to crave her. Need her. And once I lost her . . .

I've never been so utterly alone, felt so incredibly lonely as I do now that she's left me.

You're willing to talk to me?

I hit send and wait anxiously for her reply. Within seconds I get it.

Yes.

Running my hand through my hair, I realize I'm sweating. *Shit.* How are we going to do this? Like two civil adults who can barely speak to each other? Will she want to meet me in public? If it's somewhere private, at her place or mine, forget it. I'm done for. I won't be able to keep my hands off her.

Do you want to meet me somewhere?

It's best to be in public, I tell myself. That way I won't do something stupid and risk freaking her out, causing her to leave.

How about the coffee shop you first took me to?

Her suggestion is perfect. It had become our meeting place. Close to the amusement park—which is closed for the season. Near the ocean. In a public place, where I have to be on my best behavior. My fingers literally itch to touch her and I clench them into fists before I straighten them out and type an answer.

That sounds good.
Tomorrow at three? Or is that too soon?

I smile at her response. Is that too soon? It's never too soon to see Katie again.

Tomorrow at three is perfect.

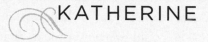# KATHERINE

I tell no one that I'm meeting with Ethan because it doesn't need to be said. Mom would freak out and Brenna would barricade herself in my house and forbid me to leave. I made the mistake of telling them immediately after I found out the truth, and their shock and horror over who he really is reaffirmed my decision to run from him.

I needed that affirmation. The doubt that plagued me after everything happened left me so confused. I barely functioned, in a fog for days afterward. It took my overwhelming, nearly suffocating anger to put everything into crystal-clear focus.

There's some regret in telling my family what happened between Ethan—Will—and me. They'll hold this against him forever, not that I can blame them. But there's telling your family things that are happening in your life in order to gain their comfort and sympathy, and then there's telling your family too much.

I went the too much route and it was a mistake. But what's done is done. There's no turning back now.

Nerves eat at me as I make the drive and my mind races. Am I wearing the right thing? Do I look pretty? Do I *want* to look pretty?

Yes. I want him aware of me. I want him to feel that same dull ache in the pit of his stomach that I feel. I want him to hurt, knowing that I'm so close but he can't have me.

But am I trying too hard? What do I say to him? What will I do when I first see him? Will I be able to face him, look into his eyes, find my voice and actually speak to him? Or will I want to run away? Worse, will I want to lash out and hurt him? Never physically—he could overpower me in an instant.

With words, though, I could hurt him. Say all those horrible things I know would tear him up inside. Do I want that? Is that what I truly seek in meeting with him right now?

The realization scares me.

It can never be the same between us. I know this. Yet despite my anger, I'm still sad that what happened is too large of an obstacle for us to overcome.

For *me* to overcome.

Somehow, I end up at the coffee shop. I hardly remember parking the car, walking along the street, and entering the warm, fragrant building, so many people inside buzzing with energy, chatting excitedly as they sip their coffee. I look around, my entire body quaking as my gaze searches for him, but he's not there.

Disappointment makes my heart drop and I tell myself to shake it off. I'm early. Glancing at my phone, I see I'm here a whopping fifteen minutes before our planned meeting time, so I go back outside, the cool, salty air like a balm to my overheated, overstimulated body.

A park bench sits out in front of the building and I settle on it, my shoulders hunched against the cold, my head bowed so my chin dips into the soft infinity scarf around my neck. I wore black leggings and an oversized charcoal-gray sweater, my hair up in a bun, my scarf a bright red color that probably draws too much attention. Pearl earrings that my grandma gave me for my twelfth birthday, minimal makeup, black flats.

I didn't want to stand out, so maybe the red scarf was a mistake? I look up and glance around, hoping to spot Ethan making his approach, but so far he's nowhere in sight.

What if he doesn't show?

Get a grip. You're worrying over nothing.

Pulling my phone out of my tiny cross-body purse, I open it up. Check my email. Boring. Just endless sale messages. I'm not on Facebook, not on Instagram, not on anything. I check my text messages, though I don't have any unread ones. I reread the chain of messages between Ethan and me, my fingers hovering over the keyboard. I'm tempted to say something, but what?

I'm here!

Too eager.

Are you coming?

Way too anxious.

Where are you?

Too demanding.

Sighing, I shove my phone back into my purse and zip it closed. I'm being ridiculous. The more I wait, the more I want him to appear, whereas on the drive over, I had contemplated that his not showing would be a good thing.

Clearly I make no sense.

"Katherine?"

The familiar female voice causes me to jerk my head up, my eyes widening when I see who's standing before me.

Lisa freaking Swanson.

"What are you doing here?" I breathe, glancing around, hoping like crazy Ethan doesn't choose this particular moment to appear. If he does, we're done for. Lisa will jump on this like a shark smelling blood in the water. She'll grab hold and never let go until we're both dead.

She sends me a look, one I can't decipher. "I could ask you the same question."

I gape at her. Is it really any of her business? "Having coffee."

Lisa's head dips, her gaze locked on my empty hands. "Hanging out first before you go get a cup?"

I say nothing. There's no point in defending my actions. I'll just scramble and trip over my words and look like a liar—exactly what I am.

"Interesting choice of location, too," Lisa continues, looking left, then right. As if she's trying to find someone. My throat goes tight and I press my lips together. "So close to the—scene of the crime. Are you trying to confront all of those inner demons, Katherine? This would make great TV, by the way."

Irritation fills me. Fuels me. I rise to my feet, causing her to back up a step. I realize in that instant I'm taller than her—and I'm of average height, so this isn't saying much. I look down at her, dredging up any scrap of strength I can find within me. "Do you consider every life moment TV-worthy?"

She tilts her head back, smiling up at me. "Yes. It's what makes me so good at my job."

Realization dawns and I step away from her, thrusting myself onto the sidewalk. A couple headed straight for me has to dodge around me and I mumble an apology to their quickly retreating backs before I return my focus on Lisa. "Are you following me?"

Lisa blinks, the personification of innocence. "Why would you think that?"

She is. Oh God, she is. How *dare* she? "You are, aren't you." My voice is flat. I don't bother waiting for a response. She could defend herself till the cows come home and I won't believe a word she says. "You have no right to follow me."

"I have every right to follow you," she says crisply, her eyebrows rising. I bet she figured I'd be my usual meek self. Well, forget that. "Agree to the interview and I'll leave you alone."

"Do you really think you'll gain my cooperation with bully tactics? I don't think so." I'm about to leave, turn on my heel and get the hell out of there, when I spot him. *Him*.

Ethan.

He's to my left, walking along the sidewalk, somehow a head taller than everyone else in the crowd. Our gazes meet. Lock. His mouth curves upward at the same time mine curves down. His brows furrow in that way he gets when he's concerned or agitated and I quickly shake my head, sending him a look that says *stay away*. My heart races as if it's desperate to leap out of my chest and chase after Ethan.

As if it knows that's where it belongs.

Enough.

I swallow hard, my gaze meeting Lisa's once more. Thank God she didn't notice Ethan making his way toward us. She's too busy talking to pay attention.

"You're being extremely difficult, Katherine, and I don't understand why. My boss says he's desperate for you to be included in this interview." *Please*. Her boss isn't desperate; she is. "Even if it's for ten minutes." At my eye roll she amends herself. "Five minutes. *Two* minutes, whatever it takes to get your opinion on Aaron Monroe and what he has to say."

I shake my head, trying my best to remain composed. "I refuse to allow you to manipulate me any further. You had your chance. Now please, leave me alone."

Without a backward glance I walk away. I can almost feel Lisa's angry gaze on me, her frustration following after me in palpable waves. But I also feel something else, something full of . . . longing and confusion. Every hair on my body seems to stand on end and I rub my hands over my forearms to wipe away the chill bumps that suddenly formed.

As subtly as I can, I glance over my shoulder to catch Ethan watching me in the near distance. Unnoticed by Lisa, by everyone but me. He's just another man in the growing crowd, his mouth tight, his eyes full of . . . so much pain.

I meet his gaze for the briefest moment and I can feel him. Feel his presence, his strengths, his weaknesses, but most of all I feel his unequivocal yearning reaching toward me. The yearning he feels for me. For this.

For us.

My traitorous body answers, everything within me growing warm and loose. I quickly turn away, my breath short, my heart thumping like a wild thing, the blood roaring in my ears. One look at him, one single moment of our gazes meeting, and I'm lost. His hold on me is so incredibly baffling, so unbelievably dangerous, I'm not sure what to do.

I don't know how to resist, even though I know I should.

Instead of going to my car, I dart into the narrow alleyway between the coffee shop and the building next to it. I lean against the brick wall to catch my breath, close my eyes for the briefest moment as I try to compose my chaotic thoughts.

Did I really think I'd be able to withstand Ethan by meeting him in public? Like that would make a difference? We just saw each other with plenty of distance between us and I feel like I've been electrified by a live wire. What might have happened if he'd actually touched me?

I don't know if I would have survived it.

"Katie."

That deep, masculine voice slides down my spine, settling low. I open my eyes, my lips parting when I see him standing directly in front of me. Panic, fear, and longing mix together and leave me breathless.

It's Ethan.

ETHAN

God, she's beautiful. I can't believe she's here, that we're breathing the same air, that our gazes are locked and I can smell her scent on the breeze, fresh and sweet. I'm so close I can touch her and I flex my fingers, eager to get my hands on her.

She parts her perfect pink lips, her eyes wide, and she finally says my name.

Immediatcly followed with, "You need to get out of here."

That was the last thing I expected to hear. Isn't she the one who asked me to meet her?

Frowning, I take a step toward her. She has nowhere to go. She's pressed against the brick wall of the coffeehouse and watching me with eyes full of wariness mixed with . . . is that excitement?

The potential excitement is what urges me on. Makes me think I have a chance. I need this chance. Need her to listen to me, to talk to me.

To go home with me.

"I'm not going anywhere," I tell her, my voice low and firm. She's not pushing me away, not when I finally got this chance. "We need to talk."

"Did you not see who was out in front of the coffee shop harassing me just a few minutes ago?" When I say nothing, she blows out an exasperated breath. "Lisa Swanson!"

"What?" I rub my hand along my jaw. The jaw I still haven't

shaved. I probably look like a damn caveman, but I don't care. "Is that why you ran away?"

I saw her shake her head, mouth something at me, and then she turned tail and ran. I didn't get it. Thought she might have panicked and considered leaving me for good. I almost collapsed with relief when I found her hiding out in the alley.

"*Yes.*" The look she sends me has *duh* written all over it. She glances toward the opening of the alley, the people passing by on the sidewalk, before she returns her gaze to mine. "You need to go."

Oh, hell no. Now that I'm actually in her presence again, no way am I leaving. "I'm not going." Reaching out, I touch her, drift my fingers down her arm. She visibly shivers, shifting away from me, and I let my hand drop. "Katie . . ."

"Stop." Her voice is shaky and she keeps her gaze downcast for too many long seconds. Like she can't stand to look at me. God, I hope that's not true. "You need to get out of here, Ethan. This was a mistake."

"A mistake?" Is she serious? Blood roars in my ears, drowning out all background noise. It's as if everything fades—the people just beyond the alley, the street, all of it. My world is only the here and now, me and Katie and nothing else.

"I should've never asked you to meet me." She shakes her head, muttering the words more to herself than me. Her gaze meets mine, completely unreadable. "What if—what if she catches you? Us?"

"So what if she does? I don't care." I don't. Let Lisa Swanson discover us together. Let her fucking film it for the entire world to see. I really don't give a shit. I can't just walk away from Katie. Not now.

Not ever again.

She lifts her head, her gaze blazing. "Maybe *I* care," she retorts. "Think about what this will do to us."

"What could it do? Force us to admit that yes, we're in a relationship now? What's wrong with that?"

"This so-called relationship only happened because you sought me out and then lied to me!" Her voice is shrill, her eyes wild, and she visibly shakes. She's angry.

At me.

"I never meant—" I clamp my lips shut when I see her hostile expression. She looks ready to pounce. Christ, maybe she's right. Maybe we shouldn't have met today. Our hurt feelings are still too close to the surface, too raw and painful.

"Do you really think meeting me today was a mistake?" I need to know her answer, though I might not like it.

Katie watches me, pressing her lips together. I wait for her response, air lodged in my throat, my heart tripping over itself in my chest. I feel like it's all come down to this. "This won't work," she whispers.

"What won't?"

"Us. The two of us . . . together. We need to accept it." Her face almost crumples but she somehow keeps it together, all while she slaughters my heart with her words. "We shouldn't be seen together in public. If anyone recognizes us, it will become this—thing, and soon the media will be talking. About us and our sick relationship. And I don't want that. I don't think you do, either."

My spine stiffens involuntarily and I slowly back away from her, holding my hands up in front of me in pure defensive mode. As if my position can ward off the blow only her words can deliver.

I thought my father knew how to pack a punch, saying just

the right thing to make me internally bleed. A few choice words from Katie Watts and I feel like I'm near fucking death.

"You want me gone? I'm gone," I tell her, but I don't budge. I'm hoping she'll stop me. Despite the pain she's causing, I don't want to walk away from her. Even though it feels like my heart is about to crack into a million tiny pieces. I swear she already broke my heart when she first found out who I really was and ran, exiting my life like she was never in it.

Now she doesn't want to be seen with me in public. Doesn't want Lisa to know. The rational side of my brain understands why she might feel that way. But the irrational side, the emotional side, is screaming in agony over her rejection, demanding that I hurt her back.

My vengeful side makes me think of my father.

Fuck. I rub a hand across my chest to ease the radiating ache, but it doesn't help. The way Katie watches me isn't helping, either.

"It's for the best," she whispers. "The minute she spots us, she'll tell . . . everyone. And then we're in trouble. They'll twist our relationship into this weird, sick thing, and I can't. I can't bear it, Ethan. I've already suffered through too much and so have you. This—we're not worth it."

My mouth drops open. We're not worth it? She's the only person in my life who's worth anything.

"I'm—I'm sorry." The choked words leave her and I can't say anything in return.

She turns and leaves, her steps hurried, her flat black shoes slapping against the pavement as she scurries away. I watch her go, don't stop her, don't say her name. I don't do a damn thing, as if I'm paralyzed, and I wonder for one crazy moment if I might be.

But I'm not. I'm just struck numb by her words, by her

worry. She's right. I know she's right. The media will turn our relationship into a fucking train wreck, and with good reason. We *are* a train wreck. We shouldn't have happened, but we did. No one else knows what it's like to be me. No one understands what we went through together except her and me. But she has walked away from me yet again. Practically ran, and I did nothing about it.

Breathing deep, I tell myself to stay strong. Either this will work or it won't—but I want it to. I'm desperate to keep that connection between us.

Yet I need to understand and respect her feelings. Forgive her for walking away from me so easily. It's damn hard. That tiny, vulnerable part buried deep within me, that little boy who never felt wanted, the one who spent his entire life moving through it essentially alone . . .

He is devastated.

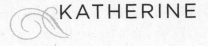KATHERINE

The restaurant is packed, full of people chatting loudly, mostly large families dealing with rambunctious children who tend to run around the tables like they're on speed or something.

Me? I sit alone. Waiting. My phone rests on the table in front of me, unchecked. I fidget in my seat, smoothing the front of my dress, pressing my lips together, the unfamiliar stickiness of the lip gloss I'm wearing making me worried I might have smeared it.

I'm all dressed up, waiting for my date. Well. Not a real date, more of a negotiation meeting. Something clicked when I was in the shower last night. An idea. Crazy and rebellious, but that's how I feel right now. I'm sick of being everyone's puppet, of always wanting to please everyone. I'm taking control now. I'm so convinced this idea will work, I made the phone call first thing this morning.

No surprise, she was eager to meet and hear what I had to say. And the moment she enters the restaurant, it's like I feel her presence. Glancing up, I see her being led toward my table by the host who greeted me earlier, a serene expression on her face as if she is the queen and we're all nothing but her indentured servants.

"Katherine." I stand when she stops by my seat, turning my cheek to accept her air kiss. So weird. The complete opposite from the almost hostile behavior I witnessed a few days ago. She'd been on edge then, I guess. I'm not sure what to think, but I do know this—I can't read this woman. She flips and she flops constantly.

It's annoying.

"Lisa." I offer her a tight smile and gather the full skirt of my dress as I sit down, scooting my chair closer to the table. The host pushes Lisa's seat in and she smiles up at him, dazzling the poor young guy. He's starstruck.

Fortunately enough, I am not.

"I was so happy to receive your call." A waiter appears, reaching for the empty water glass in front of Lisa, and he fills it expertly. She waits for him to leave before she continues talking. "I'm thrilled you're willing to discuss an interview with me."

She wastes no time and I prefer it. I really don't want to sit and have a casual lunch with her. I came dressed to impress, putting on my new outfit as some sort of armor, ready to fight. Ready to get what I want.

"I have conditions," I say, leaning my folded arms against the edge of the table. She watches me as she takes a sip of her water, her gaze never leaving mine. "Things I need you to agree to before I'll do this interview."

"Of course." Like she never expected anything less.

I smile, though it feels forced. "I won't talk to Aaron Monroe." I repeated his name over and over again all morning to ensure I'd be able to say it without a waver in my voice. I'm proud of the fact that I sound so normal. "Don't try and trick me by setting up some crazy chat between us. I will get up and walk out if you pull something like that."

The flicker in her gaze tells me—ha!—that she was considering it. Unbelievable. "Of course not," she says smoothly.

"I don't want my interview to be too long. Ten minutes. That's it. That's the most I can do. I have no idea what else you'd want me to say."

"Well, it's mostly going to be a response piece." Lisa leans forward, her expression, her demeanor, eager. I get the sense she's been dying to discuss this with me for days. Weeks even. "Monroe's interview was conducted almost a month ago. I can ask you questions related to what he told me."

"Do I have to listen to him?" I don't want to hear his voice. I don't want those clips from his interview repeated back at me so I have to sit there and watch him, listen to him, see him with that arrogant look on his face as he trashes me. Tries to ruin me.

"No. I'll read the questions to you. We already have them formatted and ready to go. We plan on running the clips from his statements during the actual interview, but if you don't want to see any of it, you don't have to." She smiles, takes another drink of her water. Her menu remains untouched and so does mine, because I'm figuring neither of us is here to order food.

I know I'm certainly not.

"I have one other condition." This is the one that makes me the most nervous. I don't know how she's going to take it. I'm not even sure if I'm making the right choice, but I feel like this is what I need to do in order for this stupid television appearance to happen.

I swore I wouldn't do this again. But here I am, agreeing to an interview with Lisa Swanson about Aaron Monroe. About to say something that is insane. Truly nuts.

"Name it. I'm sure we can come to an agreement."

"I won't do this interview unless Will Monroe is involved. If he won't participate, then neither can I."

Gotta give her credit, Lisa remains completely calm. Not one crack appears in her impassive veneer. "He's been very—reluctant to talk to me so far."

I know Ethan. He's probably refused to speak with her.

The waiter magically appears, wanting to know if we have any questions, are we ready to order, do we want something else to drink? Lisa orders a dirty martini. I say water's fine. The restaurant may have a family-friendly vibe, but they also have a giant bar covered with TVs, all of them tuned to ESPN.

"It's important that he's able to tell his side of the story," I say when the waiter leaves. "There are three sides to this experience. Mine, Monroe's, and Will's. I think Eth—Will must have a lot to say." I wince at my near slip, but she doesn't seem to notice. I push forward so I don't give her a chance. "I'm guessing he's reluctant because he's probably afraid he'll look guilty."

Lisa's gaze is steady as she watches me. "Is he guilty?"

I hate that she asked that question. It infuriates me, how so many people automatically assume he's a monster like his father. "No," I say vehemently, shaking my head. "He is one hundred percent innocent. He *saved* me. I told you this before."

"Have you searched his name online? Seen what people say about him on crime forums?" Lisa asks.

My irritation grows. Of course I have. It's hard to believe, but there are forums for anything you could ever think of. There are entire sub-forums dedicated to Aaron Monroe and his crimes. Discussions abound about his son's involvement, whether he's innocent or not. Most of the chatter had died down over the years, but with my recent television interview and the upcoming interview with Aaron Monroe himself, the interest has resurged.

Especially because William Monroe hasn't been found—until now.

"I know what they say. But none of it is true." I lean forward, desperate to get my point across. "He saved my life. I don't know how many times I can say that. The only reason I'm here, that I'm alive, is because of Will Monroe. And I will only do this interview if he participates. Otherwise, it's not going to happen."

The dirty martini is set in front of Lisa and she thanks the waiter before he leaves. She reaches for the olives skewered on a toothpick, pulling them out of the glass and popping one in her mouth. She's contemplating me. Possibly trying to make me feel uncomfortable with her interview stare—we've all seen it on television at one time or another, but it's different to actually face it.

But I'm not falling for her tactics. I'm standing firm on wanting Ethan involved in this interview. I don't know how he'll feel about taking part in it, but I don't really care.

He needs to be there.

Last time I saw him I pushed him away, yet here I am, dragging him back in. There's a method behind my madness, though. A plan to set into motion, and I hope it works. I think it will, but as always, I'm unsure.

When does anything ever work out in my life?

"I'll see what I can do," Lisa says after she swallows the olive. "I'd love to have both you and Will participating in this interview. It would be the coup of a lifetime."

Her blatant admission doesn't faze me. I rise from my chair, my purse slung across my shoulder once more as I smile down at her. "Call me and let me know how it pans out."

I start to walk away when she calls my name, halting my progress. Slowly I turn to find her coming toward me, right there in the middle of the restaurant, seemingly not giving a crap whether anyone recognizes her or not. Me? No one knows who I am. It's amazing how even after appearing on a national network, no one seems to recognize me. Ever.

I prefer it that way.

"Do you realize that he doesn't live that far from you? Will," she says when I look at her blankly. "That's really why I'm here. To chase the both of you down."

Her honesty is admirable. I purposely keep my expression as neutral as possible. "One down, one to go?" I ask.

"Exactly." She smiles, pleased that I'm not upset, I'm sure. "I'll give Will a call, tell him you want to see him. That you want to thank him for all that he did for you." Lisa pauses, gauging my reaction no doubt. "Do you mind if I say that?"

I'm frozen, unsure of how to react, what to say. Come on too strong and I look suspicious. No reaction at all and she'll suspect something's up, too. "I don't mind. But tell him . . . tell him that I miss him."

Lisa tilts her head to the side, contemplating me. "Rather strong words, don't you think? Were you really that close to him? You spent what, a couple of hours together total? Almost ten years ago, during a very traumatic and life-altering time of your life. How can you even remember him?"

She's already digging. But she's always digging, so I shouldn't be surprised. "I'm closer to him than anyone else I've ever met," I tell her before I turn and head for the front door of the restaurant.

Lisa doesn't follow, doesn't say another word, and I make my escape, thankful for the fresh breeze that washes over me when I emerge outside. My plan is in place.

Now I can only hope that Ethan will agree.

# ETHAN

The restaurant is small, a breakfast house that's mostly empty because it's close to noon. They serve lunch, too, but that's not what people come here for.

Not that I have an appetite. I'm too damn nervous to consider eating.

I walk inside, see her in the last booth that bumps against the wall, sitting so she faces the doorway. She lifts her hand in greeting, but otherwise there's no expression. She looks stiff. Worried.

The slightest bit annoyed.

I make my way toward the back of the restaurant and slide into the seat across from her, my head turning when the waitress stops before us, her gaze on me and a silver pitcher covered with condensation clutched in her hand. "Something to drink?"

"Just water, please," I tell her, and she pours me a quick glass before she takes off.

"You're late." Her voice is sharp, accusing.

I meet her gaze. "By only five minutes." I'd left fifteen minutes early but was delayed by unusually bad traffic, not that she deserves to hear my excuse. She'd just shit on it anyway.

"I thought you weren't going to show up." The smile she flashes me is brittle. Fake. "You have a bit of a reputation for disappearing at times, according to my sister."

Brenna Watts faintly reminds me of Katie. Same face

shape, same eyes. Even their voices are similar, but otherwise, that's it. There's an edge to this woman that Katie doesn't have. A sort of weariness hangs over her, implying that she's tired of . . . everything. "What did you want to talk about?" I ignore her dig, which I'm sure infuriates her further.

She leans across the table, her bluish-gray eyes steely. "You need to stop trying to contact my sister."

I raise a brow. I haven't reached out to Katie since our messed-up meeting at the coffee shop, and that was days ago. I was trying to let her cool off. Trying to get my head straight. "Are you dictating who she can or cannot see?"

Brenna slaps the edge of the table, the sound so loud the both of us jump. "You don't get to ask any questions. You don't get to act like you know what's best for her or that you *care*. You continually tear her heart out and rip it to shreds, and I hate the way you toy with her. Leave. Her. Alone."

Taking a sip of my water, I try to calm my own racing, bruised heart. I don't want a screaming match to explode between us and I can tell she's dying for one. Once that happens, Brenna will run and tell Katie everything. I'll look even more like a bad guy. "She's an adult. If she wants to see me, she'll see me."

"Please. Katherine doesn't know what's good for her half the time. She's lived scared for most of her life and doesn't know how to do it any other way. Her blind decision to start a relationship with you proves that her judgment isn't sound. She came to me crying about you and she was such a wreck. She told me everything, all that you've done to hurt her. Betray her. Yet I don't think she's over you, even after everything that's happened. I've had enough. Katherine's had enough." Brenna pauses, her gaze never flickering away from mine. "You're nothing but a monster, toying with her emotions, her body. Her heart." Another pause. "You're just like your father."

The insult is a direct hit, stabbing me in my already battered heart, and I have the sudden vision of myself bleeding out all over the chipped Formica table between us. Taking a deep breath, I let my head hang for a moment, my arms propped on the edge of the table. "You don't know what you're talking about."

"I know exactly what I'm talking about, you prick. Your father *destroyed* my family. Ruined my sister, devastated my parents, and turned me invisible." I lift my head to find her glaring at me, her eyes full of fire. "Then you come along years later and it happens all over again. My father's dead. My mother doesn't know how to help her and no one gives a shit about what I think. What sort of sicko are you?"

"I'm in love with Katie," I tell her, my voice low. Quiet.

Brenna gapes at me for a moment, just before she starts to laugh. Though the sound isn't filled with a lick of humor. "I don't think you know what love is. How could you? Look who raised you." I part my lips to answer but she cuts me off. "You're *obsessed*. You've been obsessing over her since you two first met, when you were both children. It's messed up."

"No one else has experienced what Katie and I have," I tell her vehemently. "The trauma we suffered together bonded us."

She raises a brow. "I sometimes can't help but wonder if you did participate in her kidnapping. Did you hold her down while your father raped her? Did he let you abuse her, too?"

Anger penetrates my skull, white hot and nearly blinding. "Take that back."

"Katherine's denied it all along but there are too many unanswered questions, especially with you back in her life, sniffing around her." Brenna's gaze turns dark. Heavy. "Did you want another taste? Was that it?"

Clearly she's trying to provoke me. I refuse to take the bait. "You wouldn't understand."

"You're damn right, I wouldn't understand. I can't fathom why you would want to reconnect with Katherine. Date her. Kiss her. Have sex with her—to the point you're now claiming that you're in love with her." Brenna tilts her head to the side. "What did you see next, hmm? If this would've worked between you two, did you really envision a future with her? Did you see marriage? *Babies?*"

Swallowing hard, I reach for my water glass and drain it. I have no answer. And I have a feeling I know what she's going to say next.

"Don't you think you've fucked with her head enough? A future with you is impossible for Katherine. Marrying the son of the man who raped and almost murdered her is *insane*. Having his babies is even worse. Aaron Monroe would be their grandfather. Can you imagine?" Brenna grimaces. "That's disgusting. Your children wouldn't stand a chance."

Her words chip away at my soul, one by one, bit by bit. Worse, she's saying things I've already thought myself. I may be in love with Katie, but what's the point? How can we carry on when everything between us is so fucked up? "Is that what Katherine thinks?" I ask tightly. I need to know.

"What?" Brenna frowns.

"Is that what Katherine thinks about us? About our relationship." I curl my fingers around the edge of the table, so tight I'm afraid I could snap it right off. "Does she think I'm a monster?"

Brenna leans back in her seat, a smile playing at the corners of her lips. "Well. You're the son of one."

I'm paralyzed, waiting for the rest of her verbal attack, but nothing else comes. Deep down inside, I know I deserve to hear every horrible thing she has to say to me. About me. Brenna Watts will gladly tear me down. Tear me apart.

But she says nothing more. And it's in those deathly still minutes when I realize her single statement hurts far more than anything else she could have said.

You're the son of one.

I can't change who my father is. I'm stuck with that burden no matter how much I try to ignore it. I can change my name, change my looks, and move to another country, but the fact still remains.

I'm the son of a monster.

"Is that all you wanted to say, then?" I ask when she remains quiet.

She blinks, seemingly shocked. "Yes. I suppose so."

I slide out of the booth, Brenna never taking her gaze off of me. Like she expects me to make some random threatening move toward her and she needs to be on the defensive. "Then we're done," I tell her before I exit the restaurant, never once looking back.

It's not until I'm outside in the parking lot, rounding the driver's side of my car, that the nausea crushes me in its grip. I bend over, retching back up the water I drank, my throat raw, my eyes watery. I walked in with an empty stomach and the muscles spasm, trying their damnedest to expel nothing. Resting my hands on my thighs, I hang my head, spit onto the ground, and close my eyes against the onslaught of Brenna's horrific words still spinning in my head.

The truth is hard to face. Everything Brenna said is true and I can't deny it. When it's stated so boldly, laid out before me in all of its unflinching glory, her worry for her sister is validated, as is her disgust.

Memories come at me, one after another. The memory of when I first found Katie. When I ran from her. When I came back and she didn't believe I wanted to help her. The fear I saw in her eyes, the hesitation. She didn't trust me. In her eyes I was a monster.

I'm still a monster. I've just taken on a different form. I don't hurt her physically, just emotionally. And how fucked up is that?

There's nothing else I can do.

I need to leave Katie alone.

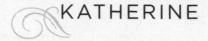KATHERINE

He said no.

I stare blankly at the email Lisa Swanson sent me. Subject line: *Interview.* One sentence within the email and that was it.

He said no.

Hitting reply, I type out my response and click send, hoping that's it, once and for all.

Then I refuse to participate.

And what would be the point? What would it get us? What did I believe I'd gain by forcing Ethan to participate in this interview? It's not like I could spill the truth and confess our darkest secrets. Baring my soul to the millions who'd watch us on national television would be the dumbest move ever.

Even I eventually realized that.

My refusal won't make Lisa happy, but I really don't care. Mom and Brenna will be relieved. They regret standing by my decision to do the original interview in the first place. It's brought me nothing but trouble and heartache since it happened, and I regret it, too.

But why did Ethan say no? I grab my phone from where it sits on the side table and stare at the screen, tempted to text him.

Tempted to tell him that I miss him.

Closing my eyes, I wait for the decision to come to me, but it doesn't. I'm hopeless. Helpless.

Lost without him, as much as I hate to admit it.

There's a quick knock on my front door before it opens and Brenna breezes in, a smile on her face, her hair streaming behind her as she whirls around and shuts the door, snicking the lock into place. "What are you up to?" she asks as she heads toward the couch and plops down on it.

I knew she was coming over—she'd called earlier this morning to let me know. For some reason she's not at work today and I don't get why. Seeing her now, she seems agitated. Anxious, and that's totally unlike her. She's my calm, cool older sister. The one who can manage a classroom full of rowdy children and never bat an eyelash. I have always envied her calm.

"Homework," I say, closing out my email program, keeping my laptop open. "I'm behind."

"Why? Because you let what happened with that asshole mess with your head?"

I blink at her, surprised at the venom in her voice. "Excuse me?"

Brenna rolls her eyes and sinks deeper into the couch. "Don't give me that innocent act, Katherine. I'm talking about Will Monroe. Or Ethan—whatever the hell his name is."

I unloaded the entire sordid story on my sister because she's truly the only friend I have, the only one I can trust. Mom just worries, not that I can blame her. Brenna offers sound advice and a shoulder to lean on. What more could I want?

But my anger fueled hers. To the point that mine has eventually dimmed while hers is still burning bright.

"I thought we agreed we wouldn't talk about him," I murmur, closing my laptop and setting it on the coffee table in front of me.

Just the mention of his name upsets us both, for different reasons.

"I talked to him today."

The sentence is like a bomb that's been dropped into the center of the room and detonated on impact. I gape at her, my throat dry, my brain scrambling to come up with the right words to say in response.

"You talked to him?" I finally say breathlessly. "When? Where?" *Why?*

She shrugs and glances down, plucking at an invisible thread on the inside seam of her jeans. "I sent him a text and asked him to meet me at a restaurant. He agreed. I saw him earlier and let him know how I feel."

My mouth is still hanging open and I snap my jaw shut. How did she find his number? Did she somehow . . . sneak into my phone and get it? "I don't understand."

"I warned him to stay away from you."

That's all she says. I still can hardly wrap my head around the fact that she actually went and talked to him. "And what are you going to do if he doesn't?" I ask carefully. I'm so torn. I want to see him. Then I don't. I hate him. I love him. But mostly, I love him. I just hate what he did, how he kept his secrets. Those secrets hurt.

They're also the reason I was so drawn to him, why we share such a deep connection. He's embedded in my heart, in my soul. I'm so conflicted. I don't want him to go. I want him to stay. I'm driving myself crazy.

Clearly, I'm driving my sister crazy, too.

"Call the police. Then tear his balls off with my bare hands." My God. She sounds so . . . *furious.* No wonder Ethan turned down the interview. I'm assuming Brenna scared him away from me.

"The police? He hasn't broken the law, Brenna. You didn't have to do that," I start, my voice small, but she cuts me off before I can say anything else.

"Oh, but I did. You've told me *everything*, Katherine. Just because you're not talking to him now doesn't mean he won't try and reach out to you eventually. You'll start talking to him again. Or worse, you'll meet him somewhere, he'll ply you with lies, and the next thing we know, you're having sex with him." She visibly shudders. "You *can't* let that happen. You *can't* continue to be weak your entire life. You'll only end up being taken advantage of, again and again."

"You think I'm weak?" There's an unfamiliar hard edge to my voice. "You think I let people take advantage of me?"

"I *know* you're weak, Katherine. And I *know* people take advantage of you on a constant basis." She touches my arm and I flinch, her hand falling away. "You want proof? I have three perfect examples. First, when you let Aaron Monroe take you out of the park. Next is when you let Lisa Swanson somehow convince you it was a good idea to do that stupid interview. And now we have Will Monroe, who somehow wormed his way into your life and into your bed."

"Brenna!" I'm shocked by her words, at the anger behind them. "Are you implying that I asked for all of this?"

The look she sends me is accusatory. "It's always been about you. Can't you see it? You disappeared that day and they forgot all about me. All they could focus on was *you*. You were gone and I may as well have disappeared along with you, not that they would've noticed."

Never in the eight years since it happened has my sister ever expressed any resentment. We became closer. I thought we still were close. She'd always been my rock when I needed her.

But now . . . I don't know. Has she carried this resentment and anger all this time? Was it growing and festering deep inside her until she couldn't contain it anymore?

Confusion makes my head throb and I lean forward, my elbows propped on my thighs, my head in my hands. It's mind-boggling, how one small choice causes a ripple effect throughout the rest of your life. I had to go to the bathroom that sunny afternoon at the park. That one seemingly inconsequential decision forever changed everything.

It killed my father's spirit and most likely sent him to an early grave.

It turned my mother into a sad, lonely woman.

It made my sister angry. Resentful. Bitter.

It made me afraid of my own shadow.

It also brought Will Monroe into your life.

I'm not so sure that's a good thing anymore.

"I may be the older one, but I will forever remain in your shadow because of what happened to you," she spits out as she rises to her feet. "So if you can't tell that asshole to back off, then I will. We don't need the Monroes doing anything else to destroy our family. I refuse to let you see him again."

Dropping my hands, I stand and look her right in the eye, my gaze calm. Unflinching. "I won't allow you to tell me what to do, Brenna."

She returns my stare, equally calm. Unflinching. "And I'm not going to stand by and watch you go back to him, Katherine. If you do, that's your choice. Just know that I won't be a part of your life as long as you're with him."

My heart stalls and I exhale raggedly. "Are you actually going to make me choose?"

Brenna shrugs. "It should be easy. It's either your family or the son of the man who raped you repeatedly when you were a child." She pauses. "I know what my choice would be."

If only it were that easy.

. . .

After Brenna left, the house felt too quiet. Cold. I thought about calling my mom, but I was afraid she'd only take Brenna's side and I didn't want to deal with it.

So I remain alone. Missing Ethan despite my anger toward him. All of the conflicted emotions come rushing back. It's hard to hold on to anger. It eats at you, chips away at your happiness, making you miserable. And I miss him. And when I'm alone with my thoughts, I miss him even more.

And right now? I feel horribly alone.

Lonely.

Giving in to the unease that's wrapped itself around me, I creep around the rooms of my tiny house, checking all the locks on my windows, tugging the curtains closed, sealing the blinds shut. All the doors are locked, the garage is shut, and my nosy neighbor, Mrs. Anderson, is sitting on her front porch watching the world pass her by as the sun fades into the horizon. Yet I still can't let the feeling go.

The feeling of being watched.

I go to my kitchen, which faces the backyard. The tiny window above the sink has no curtain or blinds on it. It's small, sits very high, and I like that it lets in so much natural light. I stare out the window now, at the darkening forest just beyond the fence, and wonder if someone is out there, watching me. Waiting.

Shaking my head, I tell myself it's my overactive imagination. The memories of what happened to me messing with my head. There's no one out there. The bad guy is in jail. He can't touch me.

No one can.

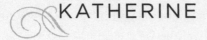# KATHERINE

I remember feeling very, very small after it happened. Insignificant. The media frenzy scared me. The attention was terrifying. Daddy didn't want me talking to anyone and he wouldn't talk, either. He eventually quit his job and found a new one.

He was ashamed.

Of what happened to me.

Of me.

Mom cried so much I was afraid to approach her.

So I didn't.

Brenna stayed away from the house. She went and lived with a friend for a while, to keep out of the fray. Daddy didn't want her victimized, too.

I heard him say that to Mom one night, while I crouched on the other side of my bedroom door, my ear pressed close to the wood as I eavesdropped on them talking about me.

Their favorite—and not so favorite—subject.

I couldn't count on them. I tried, but I couldn't open up. They looked at me like I was an open bloody wound they couldn't stare at for too long, always looking away with the tiniest shiver.

Always, *always* I noticed that little shiver. It's what hurt the most.

There was only one person who was there for me those long, lonely months after everything that happened. When I tried to get back to my everyday life, when I tried to move on and pretend that I was a normal teenager with normal wants and dreams and wishes and ambitions, there was Will.

Will.

I was fourteen the first time he called me. My parents had finally relented and let me get a phone. Will and I were still writing letters to each other and when I mentioned my new cellphone, he sent me his number and told me to call him.

I sent him my cell number back, too afraid to be the first one to call.

So we set up a specific time and he called me. Hearing his voice for the first time after so long . . .

I clutched the phone tight to my ear, so tight the phone left an imprint on my cheek. Hearing his deep, much more manly voice gave me hope.

He gave me light, when all I'd ever felt was darkness.

We talked about nothing. About everything. The calls were always short, no more than fifteen minutes long, and that was never enough. I was afraid my parents would figure out I was talking to him and I didn't want to take any risks. I didn't want to get cut off from him.

Until one day, he cut me off. I called him one last time, from another phone. My sister's, though she never knew. He answered, told me it wasn't a good idea that we talked any-more, and that was it.

The end.

Will and Katie were finished.

He was the only one who could call me that. Katie. I was Katherine to everyone else. Will was the only one who made me feel like it was okay to be Katie. Katie was strong. Katie survived. Katie saved herself.

Thanks to Will.

ETHAN

The morning dawns crisp and cold. I know this because I'm sitting out on my back porch when it happens, a mug of steaming hot coffee in my hands, wearing my thickest fleece jacket and sweats, thick socks and boots on my feet, a hat on my head. I bet I look fucking ridiculous, but I don't care.

I couldn't sleep; I tossed and turned in my bed until the sheets were practically torn off the mattress. Giving up around four, I went and made a giant pot of coffee, sucking down two cups while I focused on a work project, losing myself in the mindless tasks for a while.

Until I saw the grayish-pink dawn stretch its beams across my floor, gently filling the dark room with light. I refilled my cup and went outside, watching the sun slowly rise. The ratty grass in my backyard was covered with frozen dew, and it gleamed like little sparkling diamonds when the sun finally shone upon the ground.

It's deep into fall. The trees have started to turn and the nights and mornings are cold. The breeze brings with it chilly air plus a hint of salt from the ocean and I breathe deep, taking with it the scent of my coffee, too.

This is a morning for sharing contentment. When a man wakes up with his woman, brews them a pot of strong coffee, and they sit together in the hushed morning light, smiling secret smiles at each other while their loyal dog lies at their feet.

Frowning, I glance down at the empty spot by my feet. I

think I need a dog. Something to keep me company. The loneliness in me that Katie filled so perfectly stretches wide and black, a void deep within my soul. A dog would make me feel better. A dog would give me companionship.

I've turned into a pitiful mess.

I take another sip of my coffee, going over yet again what Katie's sister said to me yesterday. She hurled the same accusations at me that I've thought of many times. Brenna tapped straight into my own deepest insecurities and unrelenting worries, things I've tried to avoid.

Things I can't avoid any longer.

Katie expressed some of those same concerns when I last saw her. Knowing that if anyone found out about our relationship, they would think it twisted—and it is. One man links us together forever—my father, who raped her and tried to kill her. I can't deny that he's my father. I can't deny that he's the one who kidnapped her, either.

I shouldn't have these feelings for Katie. They're wrong. I know they're wrong but I can't stop them. Just like I couldn't stop looking for her. I couldn't stop following her. And once we made contact, spent time with each other . . .

I couldn't stop that, either. I've tasted her. I've seen her naked. I've been inside her body. And I want that again.

Yet she doesn't want me.

Being with Katie makes me feel complete. Whole. Comfortable in my own skin, when I've moved through my life uncomfortable as hell with just about everything I've ever done.

There's something to be said for forbidden fruit, wanting what you can't have. Is that why I want to be with her? Because I shouldn't be? If that's the case, then that's sort of fucked up.

Really fucked up.

If we were to try and make this work, our past, our connection, would have to be kept a secret. And if the truth were discovered, no one would understand. The public would think we're sick. If Lisa Swanson caught wind of us being together, she'd blast the story everywhere.

Talk about a scandal.

Sighing, I scrub a hand across my face, along my jaw. My skin is like ice, prickly with stubble since I finally attacked it with a razor a few days ago. At least my near-beard would have kept my face warm.

My phone buzzes in my jacket pocket and I reach for it, surprised that anyone would text me this early on a Saturday morning. I freeze when I see the name flashing on the screen. Even wonder for a moment if I'm dreaming.

Katie.

I miss you.

I close my eyes briefly. This . . . is the last thing I need. I'm trying to do the right thing. But she texts me out of the blue on an early Saturday morning and I want to cave in. Text her back. Unload how I feel all over her.

I shouldn't but I do.

The second text comes in on top of the first and I can almost hear her say the words in her soft, sweet voice. Christ, I miss hearing her talk, seeing her smile. The strands of wild blond hair that always seem to wisp about her face. I'd tuck them behind her ears, my fingers grazing her soft skin . . .

My phone buzzes again.

You're probably asleep, which is good. If you were awake I might be tempted to invite you to breakfast.

I sit up straight, nearly dropping the coffee mug on the ground. With a shaky hand, I set the mug on the wide armrest of my chair and furiously type out my reply.

I'm awake. Couldn't sleep.

Nerves eat at my gut as I wait for her answer. It's damn cold outside yet my palms are sweating.

Me either.

Her simple response leaves me confused. How should I respond? What do I say? Do I wait for her or is it my turn to play true confessions? I wish she were here, looking right at me. Sitting in the empty chair to my right. I could stare into her eyes, feel her calming presence and know that I'm safe. I could say anything to her.

And she could say anything to me.

I miss you too. And I shouldn't either. I'm not good enough for you. I never will be. You deserve better.

I hit send before I can second-guess my reply.

Do you want to meet for breakfast?

She ignored what I said and I'm—glad. My heart is racing. Feels like it could leap out of my chest. She's giving me another chance. I don't deserve it, but something must have happened for her to feel this way, to make this gesture. She's reaching out to me, when the last time we met face-to-face she pushed me away. Seemed almost angry.

Not that I could blame her. What I did, the enormity of my lie . . .

She shouldn't give me another chance.

Where? I ask.

Rising to my feet, I grab my mug and walk into the house, locking the door behind me. I'm already dressed. Only need to grab my keys and wallet and then I'm gone. Wherever she wants to meet, I'll be there.

My house? You can pick up doughnuts and coffee.

I frown at the screen. She . . . she can't be serious. She wants me in her *house*? How can that be? I broke her trust, the most important thing to Katie in the world. She trusts hardly anyone and after what I've done? She should trust no one.
Especially me.

Are you sure?

I stuff my wallet in the pocket of my sweats and grab my keys. Heading out the door toward my car when I get her next message.

I'm positive. I just—I'd like to see you. Talk to you.

Her honesty is cracking my heart wide open. Another text buzzes through.

Chocolate with sprinkles is my favorite doughnut, by the way.

The smile I'm wearing can't be contained. There's a bounce in my step that I haven't experienced since . . .
Ever.

How many?
   A dozen.

I'm climbing into my car when I receive the next text.

Oh, and get whatever you want too. ☺

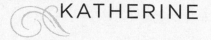KATHERINE

I wander around my little house, feeling anxious. A little lost.
Excited. Nervous.

Sleep eluded me completely last night. I tossed and turned,
my thoughts full of my sister. My past. Looking for clues that
she was unhappy, feeling neglected, full of resentment. Wrack-
ing my brain, I couldn't find a one. Not that I'd paid much
attention to her. I was too focused internally. Consumed with
my own pain, my suffering, to worry about anyone else's. And
throughout that turbulent time, Brenna had done nothing but
give me support.

Yes, our relationship before the kidnapping had been a
wreck. She was fifteen and an irritable, moody teenager. I was
her pain-in-the-butt little sister who wanted nothing but acceptance. I didn't get it—Brenna wanted nothing to do with
me. She treated me horribly. I was the one oozing resentment
before everything happened. The day at the amusement park I
was so mad at her, and I know she was mad at me.

Well, not necessarily mad. We were just . . . annoyed with
each other. It was a constant state in our house. Drove our
parents crazy.

The one thing that kept me awake long into the night was
the realization that maybe I was the selfish one. I never gave
anyone a second thought. It was always about me.

Me, me, me.

I never considered what Brenna had to go through, or my

parents, or even Will. I was too overwhelmed with my own pain to notice anyone else's. And I feel terrible for that.

I feel . . .

Ashamed.

That Brenna barged into my house and essentially told me I couldn't see Ethan any longer riled me up. Who is she to tell me what to do? I'm an adult, allowed to make as many mistakes as I want. I refuse to let her boss me around. If I want Ethan in my life, he'll be there. She can't stop me.

Feeling defiant, I'd texted him. Just to see if he'd respond. Deep down inside, I knew he would. And he didn't disappoint me. That I was brazen enough to invite him to my home says I'm not thinking clearly. But I don't think Brenna's been thinking real clearly lately, either.

So. Is Ethan turning into a case of wanting what I can't have?

Quite possibly.

We don't live in the same town, yet he's willing to drop everything to come see me. Am I testing him? Seeing just how far he'll go to see me, help me, spend time with me?

I take a quick shower and painstakingly do my makeup, though I don't want it to look too obvious. I blow-dry my hair straight, making a face at my reflection when I'm done. I am totally trying too hard.

I'm halfway dressed when there's a knock on my door. Glancing around my bedroom, I grab my leggings and tug them on, yelling, "Just a minute!" when Ethan knocks again.

By the time I make it to the door I'm a flustered, breathless mess. I undo the locks and pull the door open to find Ethan standing on my doorstep, a pink box in one hand and a tray of . . . four coffees balanced in the other. He smiles when he sees me, a slow, sensuous curve of his perfect mouth, and my stomach flutters with anticipation.

"Your breakfast," he says, his voice deadly serious, the complete opposite of the twinkle in his gaze.

I hold the door open wider for him. "Come in."

He hesitates before crossing the threshold. "Are you sure, Katie?" His voice is low, his expression solemn. That he's double-checking touches something deep within me and I nod, my cheeks flushing when he murmurs, "Thank you," as he walks past me.

I shut the door and turn to watch him as he heads for my kitchen. I follow him, my gaze eating him up. Last time we saw each other, I'd still been angry. Panicked because Lisa Swanson was nearby. So unfocused I couldn't appreciate having him close. Heck, I wasn't appreciating his closeness. I was too mad at him.

Now, I let my gaze linger on his perfect dark gray sweatpant-covered butt. He has on a thick black fleece zip-up jacket and a beanie that covers almost all of his hair. Only a few wild strands peek out from the bottom. He turns to face me as he sets the food and drink on the kitchen table and I take in his familiar, handsome face.

All at once, it hits me. That this man, who's so completely invaded my life, is also attached to my past. That this is Will. *My* Will. The boy who saved me has grown into an attractive, thoughtful man. He may have tricked me to get back into my life, but I'm starting to realize that maybe it wasn't because he wanted to play a cruel game.

More like he wanted to find a way to be close to me.

"You look good," he says as I approach the table. I don't return the compliment, suddenly feeling shy.

"Extra thirsty this morning?" I point at the four to-go cups sitting in the cardboard tray. "Or am I having unexpected company?"

He smiles. "I wasn't sure what you might want."

"So you brought a variety?" I raise my brows.

"Two for you, two for me." He looks sheepish. "Though I'm probably hopped up on enough coffee already. I've been guzzling it since four."

"In the morning?" I reach for one of the coffees and pull it from the tray, reading the side of the cup. "A vanilla latte. One of my favorites."

Ethan nods toward the pink box. "Check out what I brought you. Make sure it meets with your approval first."

I set the latte down and pry off the pink lid, sucking in a breath when I see what's inside. Nothing but chocolate doughnuts with sprinkles, but such a wide variety of them my heart actually skips with delight when I take them all in.

Three are Halloween-themed ones with black and orange sprinkles and doughnuts with a fall theme with orange and yellow sprinkles. Others are either solid pink, or white, and a few rainbow sprinkle–covered ones are in there, too. I count the doughnuts, realizing we definitely have over a dozen. I glance up at him, my gaze meeting his once more.

"A dozen and a half," he tells me, like he can read my mind. "I wanted to cover all my bases."

"This is . . ." My voice drifts and I shake my head. "Amazing. Thank you."

"Thank you for letting me come over." He hesitates, shifting on his feet. "Truth? I figured I'd never see you again."

"I don't think we can fight it any longer," I tell him quietly as I pull a chair out and settle in. Grabbing a doughnut out of the box, I snag a napkin from the nearby holder and set the doughnut on top of it. "Plus I wanted to talk to you."

"What about?" He sits across the table from me, grabs a doughnut, one with orange sprinkles on top, and takes a big bite out of it.

"My sister. She told me she talked to you yesterday."

He pauses in his chewing, then swallows. "Yeah." His voice is raw. "She did."

I almost don't want to ask, but I have to know. "What did she say?"

"She's watching out for you. That's all."

"That's not enough." I shake my head, frustrated. "Tell me what she said."

The pain that fills his gaze tells me she said awful, horrible things. Things he probably doesn't want me to know about. "Let's just say that Brenna doesn't like me very much. And the truth—it hurts."

I can say nothing in return.

We're quiet as we eat our doughnuts, separately contemplating the conversation with Brenna. I have no idea what was said, while Ethan knows that she said too much, took it too far.

"I didn't ask her to do that," I say after what felt like hours of uncomfortable silence, but was most likely only a minute.

"I know you didn't. But she said some things we have to consider."

I was contemplating having a second doughnut, but my appetite evaporates at his tone. "Like what?"

"Like the fact that we probably shouldn't be together."

"Then why are you here?" I lift my gaze to his, rubbing my thumb under the plastic lid of the to-go cup, flicking it back and forth.

"Because you call or text and I will always come running, Katie," he admits, his dark gaze locked with mine. The air expels from my lungs in one solid exhalation, taking with it my heart, my soul. The way he says that, the look in his eyes, tells me he's sincere.

He would do anything for me, regardless of whether I wanted his help or not. He'd just . . . be there.

"I know," I whisper. "And that's not fair of me, taking advantage of you." I pause, then decide to go for it. "What happened with the interview?"

"With Lisa?" He makes an irritated face, his mouth drawing into a thin line. "I don't want to talk to her. We're just opening old wounds, Katie."

"You want to move on?"

"I've always wanted to move on. It's never been about the past, not for me. The connection we have is real and was formed all those years ago, but there's more to us than what we suffered through together. You have to realize this," he says, his gaze pleading.

His words touch me deeply. I know he's right, but it's still hard for me to put together that Will and Ethan are one and the same.

"Do you want another doughnut?" He nudges the box toward me and I stare at it. His abrupt change of subject is startling. Clearly he doesn't want to talk about this.

Slowly I shake my head. "I think I'll wait for later. Thank you for bringing them. They're beautiful."

He smiles. "I've never heard doughnuts described as beautiful before."

"Well, they are, with their variety of colors." I lean back in my chair, admiring him. "I like the hat."

"Ah." He rests his hand on top of it, then tugs it off, leaving his dark hair an adorable mess. "I forgot I had it on. It was cold this morning."

"Yeah, it was." I tilt my head, cross my arms in front of my chest. "What did you have planned today?"

He looks startled by my question. "What do you mean?"

"It's going to be a beautiful Saturday. I wondered if you had any plans." I shrug, hoping he thinks my question is casual.

It's not.

"You know what I really want to do?"

"Definitely."

"I wanted to go see about a dog."

I frown at him. "A dog?"

"Yeah. Go to the local animal shelter and find one to bring home. Not a cute puppy, though. Everyone gets one of those. I'm looking for a dog who's like a year or two old and doesn't have a chance in hell of getting adopted." His eyes grow dim. "I want to save the one nobody else wants."

Of course he does. Because he thinks of himself as the one nobody else wants.

"But it's just an idea," he says with a shrug. "I probably won't go through with it."

"You should," I tell him quietly.

"You think so?" He raises a brow. "You should probably get one, too."

"Oh, I don't know about that." I've thought about having a pet, but I never manage to get around to finding one. A dog might be too high maintenance. I'd probably do better with a cat.

"A dog would make you feel safe. Warn you if there was

someone coming to your door or hanging around your house at night." He pauses, his gaze intense. "I don't like thinking of you here all alone, Katie."

Last night's uneasy feeling comes back with a vengeance. "I'm fine."

"You lock your doors, right? I don't mean just at night, but all the time."

"Of course." Why is he asking me these questions now? It's as if he knows I was quietly freaking out last night. That's probably why I couldn't sleep. Plus I have a lot on my mind. It never seems to stop spinning; it doesn't matter what time it is. "I'm beyond cautious."

"Good," he says with a finality that sounds very possessive and makes me feel fluttery and nervous. Which is stupid, because I should not be aroused by his protectiveness over me.

But I am.

"Consider a dog, though. There's no such thing as having too much protection," he continues.

I nod, sitting forward so I can grab my coffee and finish it off. "I could go with you today to look at dogs, if you want. Help you pick him out." I need to lighten the mood. I don't like thinking I *need* a dog to keep me safe.

"A him, huh?"

"Or a sweet, sweet girl. Whatever you prefer." I tap my fingers on the table, liking the idea of Ethan with a dog. He doesn't have anyone. No family, no friends. I hate thinking of him moving through his life alone. He's already done it for too long. "It would be fun."

His expression turns somber. "You want to go with me and help me pick out my new dog, Katie?"

"Yes," I whisper, my gaze dropping when I see him reach out and rest his hand on top of mine. His fingers skim across the back of my hand, sending a scattering of tingles in their wake, and I marvel at the power his touch has over me.

And how I always crave more of it.

"Then let's go." His hand drops away and he stands, as do I, fighting the disappointment that swamps me at the loss of his touch.

There will be more opportunities, I tell myself. This isn't the end.

This could be just the beginning.

# ETHAN

I've never seen a nicer day. The sky is so blue it almost looks fake, with only the occasional fluffy white cloud floating by. The sun is bright but the breeze is cool, and somehow I convinced Katie to come back with me so I could go to my local animal shelter rather than hers.

I wanted to find a dog from my area. Some left-behind, kicked-when-he-was-already-down beast of a mutt. With friendly eyes and a wagging tail. I'll know when I find the right one. It'll be a dog that will snag my heart the moment I lay eyes on it.

Sort of how Katie snagged my heart. From the moment I saw her, I knew I had to take care of her. In some inherent way, I knew she belonged to me.

It just took me years to find her again.

Is it wrong of me to want her to forget the past and focus on who we are now? Probably. I know she's still having a hard time processing that I'm Will. Though I don't like thinking of myself with that name anymore. I've moved on. It was easier that way, leaving the old me behind and never looking back.

"The ocean looks beautiful," she murmurs, her head turned toward her partially opened window, her hair flying everywhere. "The sun is so bright it's making the water sparkle like diamonds."

I try to keep my eyes on the road, but it's hard. I'd rather stare at Katie, or look at the ocean to the west of the highway, just beyond the low rolling hills and the town spread out before it. Gripping the steering wheel tighter, I force myself to face forward.

We've made small talk for most of the drive. Nothing too serious, nothing personal; it's easier that way. But I want to talk about more. I want to talk about us. I just don't know if I can.

I don't even know if there really is an "us."

We talk about our favorite breeds, Katie googling various types of dogs and flashing her phone at me when she finds one she likes. It feels good; it's so normal, acting like this. Just another Saturday between two people who like each other. No pressure. No heaviness.

I need that right now. I think Katie does, too.

"You might not be able to take the dog home right away," Katie says, her brows scrunched low as she reads something on her phone. "It might even take a few weeks."

"That sucks." I wanted to bring the dog home today. Go to a pet store and load up on treats, supplies, and a toy or two. I need the distraction. I need to focus on something else for a change.

"Or maybe you will." Katie tucks her hair behind her ear, most of it flying around her face once again since she has her window cracked. "I guess we'll find out."

Within ten minutes of arriving in town I find the animal shelter. It's busy, the parking lot full of cars, and we venture inside together, going to the front desk to say we want to look at the dogs.

The woman behind the counter smiles at the two of us and hands us a sheet of paper explaining the steps to adoption, along with an application.

Frowning, I meet the woman's gaze. "Application?"

She nods, her smile never faltering. "We have to make sure you can provide the proper living situation for your future pet. For example, if you live in a tiny apartment, we wouldn't recommend you adopting a German shepherd."

"Makes sense," I murmur as I look over the application. The woman hands me a pen and a clipboard, then waves her fingers toward the chairs lined up against the wall.

"Have a seat, fill out the application, and when you're done, someone will show you to the back."

Katie sits right next to me, her thigh pressing against mine as she reads over the adoption process instructions while I fill out the form. The questions are simple, asking about my living situation, if I work, if there are any other pets in the house, if there are any other people. I look like one lonely dude when I fill out all of my stats on the application.

A door creaks open and an older man and woman enter the lobby area, a small dog with wiry white hair dragging them by its leash. Clearly, they have no control over the animal, but they don't seem to mind. The woman laughs as the man tries to calm the dog down by kneeling and speaking low. But the dog won't have any of it, leaping up so its front paws are on the man's knee. The dog licks the man's cheek, making him laugh as well, and I can't help but smile.

"You want a dog like that?" Katie murmurs as she leans in close.

So close, I can smell her. Feel her. I want to take her hand in mine. Pull her even closer and kiss her.

But I don't. Instead, I just smile and stare into her pretty blue eyes. "I don't know if I want one that hyper."

She nudges my knee with her own. "Well, hurry up so we can go search for your future dog."

I finish up the application and then we're led to the area

where the dogs are kept. It's a cavernous room with row after row of dog runs, the fenced-off areas holding one, sometimes two dogs within. Katie keeps by my side as we slowly walk down the first aisle, scanning each dog carefully. Some are bold and come right up to us, barking playfully. Others cower in the back, too scared to approach. There are even a few that bark ferociously, looking ready to tear our heads off.

A little sigh escapes Katie when we finish walking down one aisle. "This is so depressing. All of these unwanted animals," she murmurs.

Yeah. It is depressing. If I could take all of them home, I would. But that would be impossible.

The next aisle over, I come to a stop about halfway down. The dog is medium-sized, with black and brown longish fur, a white spot on the chest. I kneel down, keeping my distance but still wanting to get close. The dog sticks its nose against the fencing and I reach out with tentative fingers, letting it smell me first.

"Her name is Molly," Katie reads from the sign that's posted. "They estimate her age at around a year."

"She's sweet." Molly licks my fingers, then sits on her haunches and pants at me. Her warm brown eyes are expressive and I feel like she's talking to me.

Take me home with you, she says.

"I think I want her," I say as I rise to my full height, spotting one of the shelter employees and waving him over.

"They don't know exactly what type of dog she is," Katie says. She's still squinting at the information sign as the employee unlocks the gate and allows me inside the dog run.

Molly hops around my feet when I enter, offering a little bark in greeting. I pet her head, scratch behind her ears, and feel her warm, solid weight press against my legs. Kneeling once more, I hold her face and stare into her eyes as the employee reassures me that she's gentle and friendly.

Yeah. She's definitely friendly. Her tongue lolls out the right side of her mouth as she pants at me and I scrub her beneath the chin, drifting my fingers down to scratch along the white scruff of fur at the center of her chest.

"She'd be great with kids," the employee continues, and I glance up at him.

"I don't have kids."

"Oh. Well. Someday, when you have them. I bet she'd be great with them." The guy, who appears around my age, maybe a little older, seems embarrassed.

"Can I come in and pet her?" Katie asks, standing at the partially cracked-open gate.

"Sure," the employee encourages, and Katie does, shutting the gate behind her before she comes over to where I am, and kneels beside me.

Molly turns her attention to Katie, coming at her with enthusiasm. Katie pets her, running her hand over the length of her back just before Molly sneaks a lick on her face.

"Oh God," Katie laughs, holding Molly away from her face. "That was gross."

"It just means she likes you," I tell her.

She smiles, her gaze still on Molly as the dog comes back my way and practically tries to climb into my lap. "I think she likes you more."

I pet the dog, my hands lingering, feeling her size. She's not too big, but I wouldn't consider her a little dog. She's solid, but trim, and kinda wiggly. Her tail won't stop whipping around, like her excitement level is at warp speed, and she continually nuzzles my hands, forcing me to keep petting her. "What do you think?" I ask Katie.

Her eyes widen the slightest bit, as if she's shocked that I want her opinion. "I think she's sweet. She has a good disposition."

Molly looks up at me with those deep brown eyes and I'm a goner. "I always wanted a dog," I admit, my voice low, only for Katie.

"You never had one?" she asks just as quietly.

I shake my head. "He wouldn't let me have any pets."

The sadness on her face makes me feel bad, like maybe I shouldn't have made that confession. I even feel a little angry. I don't want her pity, and I can tell in this moment that she feels sorry for me. Hell, *I'm* feeling sorry for me. I didn't have what anyone would consider a normal childhood. I'd watch shows on TV about a mom and dad, brothers and sisters and maybe an annoying grandma who's hanging around, putting her nose in their business. Plus there was always the rowdy dog that won't stop chasing the cat or whatever, and I remember eating it up. That shit was just pure fantasy for me.

I couldn't imagine a life like that. I had the furthest thing from it. A mom who ditched me, a fucked-up dad who was hardly ever around—and when he was, I didn't want to be around him—and a shitty, dark, and decrepit house. I found a kitten once. Out in the backyard, wandering aimlessly through the overgrown grass and weeds, meowing nonstop. It was soft and cute and cuddly, and I wanted to keep it. I brought the gray kitten into the house, tried to give it some milk, but my father found me in the kitchen, yelling and carrying on about how that kitten caused too much fucking racket.

Direct quote.

He snatched that poor yowling thing right out of my hands, threw open the front door, and tossed it outside. Reared his arm back, the kitten clutched like a ball in his hand,

and then threw it with all his might. I heard the kitten make this weird screaming noise as it hit the sidewalk and I started to cry. I was eight.

I never tried to bring an animal into our house again.

Taking a deep breath, I glance over my shoulder at the shelter employee. "I'll take her."

He nods and smiles. "She's had most of her shots, so she can go home with you today if you wish. Unless you need a few days to prepare for her arrival—get your place pet ready."

"I can take her home now," I say, looking back down at Molly's face. I swear she's smiling at me. I can feel Katie watching me, too, and I wonder what she's thinking. Whether she regrets coming with me today and helping me pick out my dog. "I can't leave without her," I say to Molly.

But I'm saying it to Katie, too.

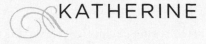# KATHERINE

It's been a long, exhausting, crazy day, but I wouldn't trade it for the world. Ethan and I didn't talk about our past, our troubles, his deceit, my anger—none of it. Instead, we acted like two regular people—two friends—who made Saturday plans together to find him a dog.

And we did. After choosing Molly and going through what felt like endless paperwork, Ethan paid for his new dog and we left the shelter with her walking in between us on the very short leash the shelter provided. She kept jerking hard against it, her feet scrambling so much she nearly tripped. Like she was trying her hardest to break free, and I could relate to her.

I was always yearning to break free from myself throughout the years. I just couldn't ever figure out how to do it.

After we loaded up Molly in the backseat of Ethan's car, we went and grabbed a quick lunch, sitting outside a local hamburger spot—both of us feeding Molly fries, though Ethan insisted this was a one-shot deal—before we ended up at a chain pet store. Where Ethan proceeded to load up an entire cart with everything his new pet could ever want or need.

Molly is going to end up one spoiled dog.

On the drive back to my place, with the sun slowly sinking into the ocean and Molly still with us, curled up sleeping in the center of the backseat, I marvel at how easy our day had been. How we got along so well, laughed together, made decisions together. There was never any tension, no arguments, no uncomfortable silences. It was . . . nice.

When we'd first started seeing each other, there was always this whisper of nervousness running through me, and I couldn't shake it. I'd never been interested in a man before, and spending time with Ethan made me feel unsure. He seemed a little on edge, too. Always on his best behavior, treating me as if I were a delicate little flower he didn't want to bruise or break.

Today, there was none of that. We finally seemed to find that comfort level we were always searching for but could never quite capture. Is that because Ethan's not hiding from me anymore? Because I know he's Will and so I feel more at ease with him?

I don't know. I'd love to discuss it with him, but I don't want to ruin the moment. So I keep the thoughts to myself.

"Do you regret not leaving her at your house?" I ask. The radio's playing softly and I can hear an occasional snort come from Molly in the backseat. Otherwise it's quiet, the late afternoon darkening at a rapid pace, lulling me, making me sleepy. My eyelids are heavy and I have to fight to keep them open.

"Nah. What was I going to do? Leave her locked up in my house so she could potentially tear everything to shreds? I couldn't put her in my backyard, because what if she broke free and ran away? I'd never forgive myself. And I wasn't about to tie her up." Ethan glances in the rearview mirror and I know he's looking at his dog. "She's happy back there. I'm glad she's with us."

I like how he said *us.* "I wish I could be there when you set up all of her new stuff," I murmur.

He laughs, the sound soft and warm, a little rusty. I like

making him laugh. I know he doesn't do it nearly enough. "It's going to be an early Christmas for Molly this year."

We're quiet for a moment before Ethan speaks again.

"You should come over tomorrow and hang out with us. I'll be in full-on training mode by then, I'm guessing."

"Are you sure?" I ask, my chest aching at his request. He's so sweet, but . . . "I don't want to intrude."

He makes a noise. "Please. Intrude on what? Me and my dog? I think I'll need you to help us out. She might be driving me insane by the time you show up."

"I could bring the doughnuts," I suggest with a little smile.

"You still have plenty," he says wryly.

We both lapse into silence once more, and I stare out the window unseeingly before I slowly close my eyes. It's warm in Ethan's car. I swear I hear Molly snoring, and Ethan taps his fingers against the steering wheel to the beat of the music coming from the radio. His scent lingers in the air, spicy and clean, and I take a deep breath, enjoying the moment.

I don't think I've ever felt more content.

"I want to thank you for today," Ethan says a few minutes later, his deep voice startling me awake. Not that I was actually asleep, though I was definitely drifting.

My eyes pop open and I swivel my head to look at him. "Thank you for taking me with you."

"I'm glad you reached out to me this morning, Katie. I've . . ." He presses his lips together, as if struggling with what he's about to say next. "I've missed you."

"I've missed you, too," I whisper. If only I could reach out and touch him. His hair. His face. His hands. I want to feel his skin, touch his lips. Press my face against his chest and breathe him in.

But that would be asking for too much, taking too much. I don't know where I stand, how exactly I feel. I'm still hurt. That he would trick me so easily cuts deep. I want to try and heal our relationship. I'm not sure if we can take it any further than this, though.

Maybe all we can be is friends.

He sends me a quick look, but I can't see his face or read his expression. It's too dark. "I've been missing you for years. And when I finally found you again . . ."

"Maybe we shouldn't talk about it," I say, cutting him off. Though I'm desperate to hear his words, the explanation. I want to know exactly how much he's missed me. More than anything, I want to go back to the beginning. To when he first saw me at the boardwalk and rushed to my rescue from the would-be purse snatchers.

What possessed him to interfere with my life and become a part of it again? Did he hate having to continue the lie? Or was it easier to pretend to be someone else? Were his intentions pure when he first started to track me down? Or was he after something else?

And what could that something else be? I almost don't want to know.

So many questions, and only Ethan has the answers. I don't think he's ready to divulge all of that information yet. I'm not sure if I want to hear it, either.

"You're right," he says, his jaw clenched tight. I don't want him angry with me, so I hope he understands. "We should just—enjoy the day."

"Exactly."

We remain quiet for the rest of the drive back to my place, right until he pulls his car into my driveway and shuts the engine off. Molly emits a little growl, but otherwise, that's it.

When I glance into the backseat, I see her head is resting on her front paws, her eyes almost closed but not quite as she stares at me through the little slits.

"Want me to walk you to your door?" Ethan asks as he reaches for his door handle.

I shake my head. "It's not necessary. But thank you so—"

He's already got his door open, turning to look into the backseat and saying in a firm voice, "Stay, Molly. Be a good girl."

As if she has anywhere else to go.

He slams the door and I exit the car as well, tugging my purse strap over my shoulder as I follow him up the sidewalk to my front porch. He scans the area, his hands in his jacket pockets, still wearing the beanie he had on first thing this morning.

Ethan looks good in a hat. He looks good in anything.

"This is a safe neighborhood," he says as I stop beside him, my keys in my hand. "I like knowing you're here."

"I have my nosy neighbor, Mrs. Anderson, to keep watch, so I always feel protected," I joke as I insert my house key into the lock and turn the deadbolt.

"I don't like the woods, though." There's a forest of thick redwoods just beyond my backyard. At first it used to scare me, my imagination running wild and coming up with all sorts of imaginary boogeymen lying in wait for me just outside. I had a hard time going into the backyard, even in the daylight.

But eventually, I got over it. Now I love the forest that's right behind my house. There's nothing better than the scent of pine greeting you every morning. I can smell it now, fresh and exhilarating, reminding me of Christmas.

"They're fine. Nothing ever happens there," I reassure him

as I undo the second lock before I turn to smile up at him. "Thank you again for today. I had—an amazing time."

"I had a good time, too." He lifts his hand, almost as if he's going to touch me, and I go completely still, silently urging him to do it. To touch me just once, just so I can feel his hands on me one more time.

He drops his hand instead, the disappointment welling inside of me almost crushing. Why do I care? Why do I still want him so much? I should be furious with him, right? "I'll see you tomorrow, then?"

I nod, licking my lips, noting the way his gaze tracks my every movement. Heat flares in his eyes and I wish we didn't have all of these past barriers, the lies and the bullshit built up between us. I'd do what I want versus what I should.

That I can go from angry to wanting him in a matter of approximately forty-eight hours is mind blowing. I'm so confused, so torn up by this weird situation that's become our lives.

"I'll text you first, and let you know when I'm coming over," I finally say.

He nods, looking like he wants to say something else but is unsure. I wish he would keep talking, to not end this moment between us, when he clears his throat, parts his lips, and seems to go for it.

"I wish I could kiss you," he murmurs, his voice low, so incredibly deep I feel it reverberating in my bones, my blood. I wish he could kiss me, too, but we can't do that. Not yet. I'm not ready.

I'm still too damaged and fragile, and I've been in this state for what feels like forever. And I'm too hurt by his lies—and his lies dig deep. I bared my body and my soul to him all while he was too busy keeping secrets and losing track of his lies.

"You can't," I tell him, the flicker of disappointment in his gaze obvious. "I'm just—I'm not ready. I'm sorry." The last words leave me in a harsh whisper.

"Jesus, Katie. Don't apologize. I'm the one who should say I'm sorry. I wish you knew . . ." His voice drifts and he shakes his head, as if he could get rid of his thoughts.

"You wish I knew what?"

"How I feel about you." He hangs his head, as if he doesn't want to look at me. Is he ashamed of making this confession? "How I've always felt about you. I've been wandering through my life like I'm in search of a missing piece and when I finally found you again, everything seemed to click into place."

My voice has left me. There's so much I want to say to him. I feel the same way. The same exact way, but I'm scared to tell him. He could use it against me.

"It's too soon, I know it is," Ethan continues. "I get it, I totally get it, and I would never push you to do something you're not ready for." He makes a frustrated noise. "But having you so close right now, hell, spending the entire day with you, has been a slow form of torture."

"I know what you mean," I say breathlessly, snapping my mouth shut the moment the words leave me. Even the smallest admission feels like too much.

He lifts his head, his gaze imploring. Almost pleading with me to understand. "Can I at least . . . hug you? As a thank-you for your help in picking out Molly?"

We stare at each other in silence. I'm hesitant, unsure. Letting him touch me would be such a relief. Yet giving in would feel like a failure, too. I need to be strong. I need to hold on to my anger over his betrayal and make him suffer.

But when he suffers, I suffer, too.

Giving in, giving up, I walk into his arms. They close

around me as I wrap my arms around his middle, rest my hands on his back. He places his mouth on the top of my forehead, a sort of half kiss that lands right along my hairline, and I close my eyes. Clutch the back of his fleece jacket, marveling at how soft it is.

He's big and warm, and being in his strong arms makes me feel safe. Protected. He presses his face into my hair, seeming to breathe in deep, and I close my eyes, resting the side of my head against his chest so I can feel the constant boom, boom, boom of his heart close to my ear.

"You should go," I finally say, my voice muffled against his chest. I don't want him to leave. I'd rather he stay, slip into my bed and just hold me. I don't want anything else. Just to know he's with me is enough.

Though eventually he'd want more. And I probably would, too.

Slowly I disentangle myself from his grip and he releases his hold on me, his arms hanging loose at his sides. He takes a step back, appearing so forlorn and sad I almost want to ask him to stay the night at my place.

Almost.

"Yeah. I should go." He smiles, though it doesn't quite reach his eyes. "See you tomorrow?"

"I'll text you," I remind him.

"I'll count on it," he says.

I'm sure without a doubt that he will.

# WILL

I was seventeen when I went to the tattoo shop. Saved up some money I earned working various odd jobs, all of them under the table. Had a fake ID in case they questioned my age and told me I needed to get my parents' permission. I didn't have parents. The people who ran the group home didn't count. Not that they'd sign anything that had to do with a tattoo.

Not that they cared what I did with my body, either. They didn't care about me at all. I was just another number, another punk kid they had to feed, make sure he did his homework and kept his shit together.

The girl who sat at the front desk hadn't asked to see my ID, let alone mentioned a parental permission slip. She just checked her appointment book while I checked her out. She was a few years older than me, her right arm covered in a tattooed sleeve, her eyebrow pierced, as well as her lip.

Cute, but not my type. Her hair was too dark, her body too curvy, her eyes too knowing.

She looked up, her ruby-red lips curved into a sultry smile when she told me to sit and wait. The artist I made an appointment with was wrapping up his previous appointment with another client.

I fell into a skinny chair that was right next to the window and grabbed a magazine, flipping through it and checking out all the various tattoo designs. Some of them were badass, some were hideous, but most of them were pretty cool. I already knew exactly what I wanted to get. I had the piece of paper tucked into an envelope after making a copy of it at school. I wasn't too excited about letting a needle touch my skin, but I'd already suffered through enough pain in my life to know I could stand it.

What was taking a needle for a few minutes?

After waiting for almost fifteen minutes, I was finally called back into the studio. The artist ran through all the prep, I handed over the piece of paper, and the artist—his name was Otto—looked at it, then lifted his head to look at me.

"Where you want it?"

I tugged my T-shirt over my head and pointed to the spot on my side, right below my ribs. "Right there."

Otto nodded and sketched out his own interpretation of the drawing I showed him, while I hung over his shoulder watching him work. He was a great artist. The wings seemed to come alive, each individual feather perfectly detailed. Way better than the original sketch.

Of course, a scared thirteen-year-old had drawn those original angel wings, so I couldn't knock them too hard. I couldn't. That drawing came from the heart. From a girl I still missed.

So bad I never wanted to forget her.

"I don't want them to look too different from the original," I told Otto, and he nodded in answer.

In the end, the wings looked perfect. Similar to the drawing Katie had sent me, but much more detailed. The script he chose for the words below the wings was almost feminine, but without being too flowery. Not that I wanted some girly tattoo on my side. But I did want it to be a proper representation of Katie.

"You like it?" Otto asked when he was done. His steady gaze met mine. "You ready?"

It was my turn to nod my answer and he instructed me to get into place. He didn't take long, spending most of his time on the wings, etching and shading every little feather into my skin. I winced. Gritted my teeth. Never uttered a sound as I powered through it. I could handle this.

I could handle fucking anything.

When Otto was finished he shut off the needle, glancing up at me. "So tell me."

I raised a brow, waiting for him to continue.

He was cleaning off my skin, wiping at it with a white rag and making me flinch. "Are you doing this for a girl? Or for you?"

Sighing, I stared straight ahead, trying my best to look cool but most likely failing miserably. "For a girl," I admitted, my voice low.

"Yeah." Otto sighed, too. "It's always for a girl."

ETHAN

I forgot to check the mail when I came home Saturday night. I was too damn tired, physically and emotionally, after my day with Katie. When I finally manage to check it this morning, Molly following at my heels, seeing the single envelope with small, neat print on the front in the box throws me. I rarely receive mail, considering I pay most of my bills online. So when I have a handwritten letter, that's especially odd. The only ones I'd received in the past came to a different box, to a different person . . .

Unease slipping down my spine, I grab the envelope and look at the return address. There isn't one.

But I'd recognize that handwriting anywhere.

There was a movie I watched a long time ago, though I can't remember what it was called. Some eighties chick flick, I think, which is probably why I shoved it out of my mind. There's a line from the movie that stuck in my memory, one I always think of when I see anything from this particular person.

You have the handwriting of a serial killer.

The letter is from my father. Sent to my address—my Ethan Williams address. The address he's not supposed to know.

Shit.

I clutch the letter in my hand, crumpling the envelope as I make my way back into my house, shutting and locking the door behind me. As if it's that simple to keep the bad memories out. Molly runs around my feet, excited, and I absently pat her head, the envelope seeming to burn into my palm. I'm tempted to throw it away. Never read it, pretend I never even received it.

But I can't do that. I have to know what he says. I refuse to ever let him get the upper hand again. I don't care that he's in prison for life and can never get out. No one is safe when it comes to Aaron Monroe.

Least of all me.

I collapse on the couch and tear into the envelope, pulling out the single sheet of lined paper with shaky hands. His handwriting is small, precise, almost square-shaped. And since he's been in jail, it's like he's turned it into an art form, perfecting his handwriting over the years.

Taking a deep breath, I start to read his letter.

Dear Will,

Or should I call you Ethan? I find it funny that you changed your name. Not that I'm surprised really. I guess you're in hiding, afraid to be associated with me. I can understand that, yet it hurts, too. It hurts real bad. A man should be proud of his boy and a son should be proud of his father, but I guess I haven't given you much to be proud of through the years.

Lisa Swanson is the one who told me you changed your name and gave me your address. I appreciate her honesty. She's never been anything less than kind. She's been a real blessing in my life lately. It's a life that's not filled with many blessings, so hers is most appreciated.

Have you met her? She says you two have talked over the phone but it's always been a brief conversa-

tion. That's a real mistake on your part, son. You should get to know her. She's an interesting woman. One who's been very vocal in getting me what I want and understanding my desire to speak to the world. To share my side of the story. No one has ever heard my side before, beyond what's in the court records.

But right now, more than I want to tell my story, the thing I want most in this world is to see you.

I miss you, son. With much reflection, I've come to realize that I've done you wrong and I need your forgiveness. All those years you suffered living with me, it was unfair. You were just a kid and I took out all my anger and frustration on you. Until eventually that wasn't enough, and I started taking my anger out on other people.

Like that poor little Katherine Watts.

I can't take back what I've done, to you or to those other poor souls, may they all rest in peace. I want to confess my sins, Will. I want to cleanse my soul and make life right with God and my victims and you.

I've already said it in this letter but I'm saying it again: I need your forgiveness. I want Katherine's forgiveness, too. And the only way I can get that is if you both do the interview with Lisa. That way I can send my message through Lisa to each of you. And maybe eventually, I can convince you to come see me in person. That would give me so much joy, but I know these sorts of decisions take time.

It's been years since I've seen you, looked into your eyes, heard your voice. I bet you've changed. I bet I'd hardly recognize you, son, and that breaks my heart. It tears me apart, knowing that I can't be with you, that

*we can't be a family. You don't want to acknowledge
that your old man is in prison and I get that, I do. But
we're family. We share the same blood. And because as
much as I know I should, I never want to let you go.*

*You're a part of me. You are my legacy. And I want
us to have a relationship before it's too late and I'm
dead and gone. Or worse, what if something happens
to you? I could never forgive myself.*

*I want you to think real hard and consider my sugges-
tion. The girl has already talked to Lisa once. It won't
hurt to talk to her again. I think my request is pretty
simple. The least you could do is honor it. Honor me.*

After all, I am your father.

Dad

# KATHERINE

My phone rings around eight in the morning, startling me out of a deep sleep. I sit straight up in bed, frowning at the phone where it's perched on the bedside table. People don't call me. I text. I much prefer texting. That way you don't have to work up the nerve to actually make a call.

The phone stops ringing before I can grab it and I lean over to see who it was.

Ethan.

I'm about to return his call when my phone starts ringing again. I answer it this time, before the first ring is done. He doesn't even give me the chance to say hello.

"Katie, God, I uh . . . I'm sorry to call you so early." He sounds frazzled. A little out of breath. His panic bleeds through and worry grips hold of me, making my heart pound.

"Are you okay? Did something happen to Molly?" I sit up once more, brushing my hair away from my face. I'd been sleeping hard; I can feel a crease on my cheek from having it firmly pressed into my pillow.

"Happen to who? Oh. Molly. She's fine. This isn't about her." He clears his throat yet doesn't say a word. It feels like he's stalling for time and I flop back against the pillows, closing my eyes as I wait for him to say something, anything to clue me in.

But he still doesn't.

"What's going on?" I ask. "Are you all right?"

"No. Shit. I'm not all right. You won't be either when I tell you." He hesitates, and in that tiny moment my heart rate shoots up even more. "I . . . received a letter from my father."

Oh. Now it's my turn to not talk. I have no idea what to say.

"And he mailed it to me here. To Ethan Williams." He sucks in a harsh breath, then releases it in a shuddery exhale. "He knows my home address, Katie. And my new name."

"Has he ever reached out to you before?"

"He's written me a few letters over the years. I keep a post office box under Will Monroe."

Hearing him say his real name makes something splinter inside of me. Like tiny shards of glass shooting throughout my body, piercing my most vital organs. I close my eyes, rest my hand over my chest. It's still difficult to grasp that I'm actually talking to Will. That I've spent so much time with him, kissed him. Had sex with him.

"He's never written to me here. I never gave him this address or my new name. I'm not that stupid. I needed distance from him. I wanted him to believe I'd fallen off the face of the earth, you know? He said that bitch Lisa Swanson gave him my mailing address. How could she?" Now he sounds furious. "What the fuck did she think she'd gain by doing that? What's that crazy old man going to do for her while he's stuck in prison, huh?"

I try to interrupt him but he won't let me. He's too angry, and I can't blame him.

"I considered letting her interview me for all of about ten minutes and decided against it. Is this some sort of retaliation on her part? Because she couldn't get me to do what she wants? I think she's sick. Selfish. Bitch only cares about herself."

"Ethan." I say his name firmly, and he stops talking. "What exactly did the letter say?"

"A bunch of bullshit about how he wants my forgiveness and hopes to see me again soon."

My stomach cramps. He wants to see Ethan. Of course he does. Ethan is his son. They have a connection that goes beyond anything that Ethan—Will—and I share. How can I even consider being with Ethan when there's any possibility that he might reconnect with his father—my rapist—and I'd have to live with that? I couldn't deal with it. There's just no way.

No way in hell. I'd rather die than have Aaron Monroe be a part of my life once again.

But if I want Ethan to be a part of my life, then that means his father would be, too.

I close my eyes again, squeeze them tight to prevent even a single tear from falling. I refuse to cry. This isn't about me right now. This is about Will. Ethan. God, whatever he wants me to call him.

"Do you want me to come over still?" I ask. If he wants to be alone I can understand. He might need to take time and process everything his father wrote to him. But maybe he wants me there, too . . .

"If I could have you here with me right now I could probably get through this shit a lot better," he admits, sounding so incredibly tortured, so sad. "But . . . I understand if you don't want to deal with it. This is a lot for you to take in, I know."

He's right. It *is* a lot for me to take in. And it all circles back to me. To what happened to me at the hands of his father. I'm not sure I'm ready to absorb it all, deal with it. It was bad enough discovering that Ethan is really Will. That he'd tricked me the entire time we were together and like an idiot, I never caught on.

Knowing that his father is the man who abducted and raped me, held me captive for days, is hard to face. It's so hard to compare the two men, too. Ethan is nothing like his father. He's sweet and kind and funny and thoughtful. He protects me, watches out for me, only wants the best for me.

He would be the perfect, understanding boyfriend if I could just be with him. But how can I? In all reality, we both know we shouldn't be together. No one else would understand. *I* can barely understand.

I'm thinking Ethan feels the same way.

"I can't lie to you. It's overwhelming, and it's scary to imagine that he's reached out to you like this," I tell him, trying my best to choose my words carefully. "I want to be there for you. I want to help you as a friend, Ethan. I hope you know that."

"I could really use a friend right now," he murmurs.

"Give me ninety minutes," I say before I end the call.

It takes me closer to two hours before I finally arrive at Ethan's house. Traffic wasn't the best, plus I stopped off and bought us large coffees before I got to his house. I figured we'd need the caffeine boost.

By the time I approach his front door, he's already there, standing in the open doorway, wearing a button-down black-and-blue flannel shirt undone over a black T-shirt and jeans, Molly at his feet and wagging her tail furiously. She looks ready to burst with excitement. The moment she spots me she comes wiggling over, her tail whipping fast, lashing through the air as she sniffs my legs from the knee down.

"Coffee," Ethan says gratefully as he reaches out to take the small cardboard tray from my hands. "Thank you."

"And the doughnuts from yesterday. I left them in the freezer, but hopefully they mostly thawed out on the drive over," I say as I follow Ethan into the house, closing the door behind me with my foot. I reach for Molly's head and give it a rub, balancing the pastry box in my other hand. "How did she do last night?"

"She was great. Got a little whiny when we first went to bed, but eventually I picked her up and let her sleep next to me on the bed, curled up like a ball all night." He rolls his eyes, looking the faintest bit embarrassed. "I told her we shouldn't make a habit out of her doing that."

"Why not? I think it's adorable." I set the box on the coffee table and turn to look at him, purposely keeping my expression as cheerful as possible. I don't want him to think I'm worried or apprehensive over the real reason I'm here. Knowing I'm going to read that letter, or at least catch a glimpse of that man's handwriting on a piece of paper that he's actually touched, shouldn't make me so nervous.

But it so does. And maybe it's not right, me unable to be real with Ethan when I expect nothing less from him, but I can't help it. The man that is his father is a complete monster. I've suffered at the hands of Aaron Monroe and I'm one of the few who actually survived.

So did Ethan. We're both survivors.

We make nice and pretend nothing bad has happened. I grab the box of doughnuts and bring them to the small kitchen table. Ethan walks over and sits down, bringing our coffees with him. His gaze never leaves me as I putter around his kitchen like I belong here. I find plates and napkins, then ask if he might want a glass of milk when finally he tells me to come sit down and eat.

"Thank you," he says when I sit across from him and reach into the box, extracting a doughnut covered with rainbow sprinkles. "For coming over. I know—I know you probably don't want to deal with any of this. So I appreciate that you're here."

"I want to help you, Ethan. I want to be your friend," I tell him, ducking my head. I'm sure he hates that I say I only want to be his friend. Isn't that the worst way to break up with a guy? Besides, I can't face him right now. It's too hard. "We're eventually going to have to talk about everything that's happened, but I just . . . I don't know how. I don't understand exactly how we came back into each other's lives, and why you felt it necessary to keep your identity a secret."

"Would you have been happy to know it was really me, Katie? That it was Will you were talking to? Spending time with?"

If I'd known he was Will, I'm not sure how far I would have taken any of this. "I don't know how I would've reacted," I admit.

He takes a deep breath and I keep my head bent, fear and nerves and anger making me tremble. My appetite leaves me yet again, the doughnut sitting in front of me totally unappealing. I don't want to hurt him, yet I do. I want to give him comfort and I also want to hit him. Scream at him. Allow him to speak and then beg him to shut up.

I'm completely conflicted. Hopelessly confused.

"When I saw your interview, it was a total shock, to hear your voice, to see your face. You looked the same, yet different. So grown up, so beautiful. And I knew . . ." His voice drifts. "I knew I wanted to try and find you."

I wait for him to say more, refuse to allow his words to touch me. Affect me. I need to remain strong. Impassive. As though what he says doesn't mean anything.

"Do you really want to hear this?" he asks, his voice soft, the slightest bit shaky.

I lift my head, my gaze meeting his. I see the reluctance there. And the pain—so much pain. "I need to hear it. Before we can move forward, I have to know what led up to our meeting."

Yesterday was the two of us playing at normal. Pretending life was fun and carefree when it so wasn't. Our problematic past will always plague us. I don't think it's possible for me to be with him right now, not romantically, but I can't let him go, either. We've shared too much, been through too much together. To walk away after everything that's happened would be cruel.

But what he did to you was cruel, too. Don't forget it.

"After the interview, I started to search for you on the Internet. I found you through your sister Brenna's Facebook page," he admits. "I saw a photo of you there."

My mouth drops open. I'd purposely avoided social media just to stop this sort of situation, yet that's how Ethan found me.

"I'll admit I did a few illegal searches. There are ways to hack into systems, to find out information that people don't want you to know." He pauses, shaking his head once. "But I found the purchase of your house legally. Your address was right there. I knew where you lived, so I went to your house."

My heart sinks. "You did?"

He nods, his expression grim. "I never did anything else. I wanted to see where you lived. I wanted to make sure you were happy, Katie. That's it. After so much suffering, after dealing with everything all those years, I just wanted . . . hell, I don't know what I wanted. My motives were selfish, too, I can't lie."

"Selfish how?" I frown.

"I wanted to see you. See you in person, just once. I only went by your house that one time. Your neighbor called me out and questioned me, so I left. But after that I started . . . fuck, I started to follow you."

This went so much deeper than I realized. I should be terrified. I should run out of his house and never look back. "Why?" My voice is nothing but a rasp of sound.

"I was worried about you, Katie. You seemed so alone. And you were being reckless. When you went to the park where it all happened, I couldn't fucking believe it. I told myself to keep driving, to let you go out there on your own, but in the end, I couldn't. I kept pace behind you the entire time you were there that day."

"And those kids who tried to mug me?" He frowns and I wave a hand. "You didn't set that up, did you?"

"My God, *no*. I would never do something like that to you. Those kids were trying to take your purse. And I stepped in. I couldn't just stand by and let them hurt you. I could never forgive myself if something happened to you."

So he really did run in and rescue me that day. Once I discovered he was Will, my mind had gone back to that moment and I wondered if he'd set it up. Not that I ever wanted to believe it, but I wasn't sure. I was unsure of everything at that point. I'm still unsure.

"Why did you cut me off when we were younger? You just . . . quit talking to me." I need to know. That had hurt so much and I'd been so devastated. I never understood how he could just end all contact like that with me so easily.

"Aw, Katie." He makes a face and shakes his head. "I was young and stupid and listening to my lawyer, who said it wouldn't look good if I were in contact with you. I was stupid enough to tell him that we talked. I just . . . I felt bad. Figured you didn't need me in your life anymore. I was just a reminder of what happened to you."

He was the only good thing to come out of that entire situation. "It hurt, how you just cut me off."

"It hurt me, too. I thought I was doing what was best, but I was just a kid," he admits. "I never wanted to bother you again."

"But you sought me out again, all these years later," I say weakly, uneasy with the way he's looking at me. Not in a bad way. I'm aware of the attraction between us, the quiet need to feel his hands on me. I want to fight it. I *need* to fight it.

It's so hard.

"I couldn't resist." His voice is low, his gaze direct. "When it comes to you, I've discovered I can never resist."

"Yet now, you never found an opportunity to tell me the truth," I point out. I want to hear his reasons for not telling me. I need to know why he kept that secret.

"I always told myself, just one more time. I'd see you, talk to you, spend a few minutes with you just one more time and then I could walk away. But it was never that easy. The more I was with you, the more I started to fall for you." His gaze is locked on mine, intense and almost pleading. "I know we can't be together. It will never work out for us, Katie. I realize that. But for that tiny amount of time that we were together and happy, it was the best time of my life. I need you to know that. Nothing I've ever done was meant to hurt you, and I'm sorry that I did. I'm sorry that I lied, that I misled you."

I swallow past the lump in my throat. I want to hug him. I want to offer up my forgiveness and tell him I'll be there for him no matter what. I want to be his rock. He needs to know I care.

But I say none of those things. I just stare at him for a quick, agonizing moment before I bow my head, too overwhelmed by the chaotic emotions swirling within me.

"I know we can't start over," he murmurs. "But I have no one else. There's no one I can talk to about this. I don't want to put this on you or make you feel guilty, but—I need you, Katie. And I realize I'm asking for too much. You can tell me to go to hell if you want. I'd deserve it."

He's already suffered in hell for years. How can I turn him away now?

# ETHAN

Somehow she finds the courage to read the letter. She sits on the couch, holding it far away from her, as if she's afraid my father can leap from the page and attack her face. Her hands shake, the paper rattles in her grip, and she takes plenty of cleansing, fortifying breaths.

That I asked her to read this means I'm a complete dick. But I need to know if my overactive imagination is at play or if I'm interpreting his words correctly. I sit in an overstuffed chair, wrenching my hands together, anxious as hell. I'm almost scared to hear what she thinks.

The moment she's finished, she sets the letter onto the coffee table in front of her, her head averted, like she doesn't want to look at me. She rubs her arms up and down, warding off an imaginary chill, and a trembling exhale escapes her. "It feels like he's threatening you," she starts, then hesitates.

Exactly what I was thinking. "Go on," I urge.

Katie lifts her head, her gaze meeting mine. "I think he wants to use you to look like the good guy. As if your acceptance of him abolishes every horrible deed and crime he's committed. I don't doubt that Lisa put him up to writing this letter, either. It might have been her idea in the first place. She's all about the ratings. The both of them will want as much attention on his upcoming interview as possible."

"We're thinking along the same lines," I murmur. She can't

begin to understand how much it means to me, that she feels the same way I do. "I don't like the veiled threats."

"I wouldn't, either." She glances toward where the letter sits, drawing up her legs and curling into herself. Trying to get away from that piece of paper as much as she can. "It's eerie how he can sit in a maximum security prison and we can still feel him as if he's in the same room with us."

"It's how I feel every time I receive a letter from him," I admit.

The sorrow in her eyes cuts deep. Reminds me that she's suffered so much, too. More than I ever have. "Has he ever tried to call you?"

I shake my head in answer.

"Do you want to do the interview?"

I shake my head again, more vehemently this time. "I don't think I can bear it."

"I don't want to do it, either. I don't want to do any of this." Her face crumples and then she's crying. Tears slide down her cheeks, her eyes closing just before she covers her face with her hands. "All my interview did was bring us more heartache and pain," she says, her voice muffled by her hands.

Ah, hell. Her tears kill me. I never want to see her in pain. I will always do my damnedest to make sure she's safe. Happy. That's been my job since I was fifteen fucking years old and though we've been apart for most of those years in between, I vow I will never allow her to be hurt by my father again. No matter what.

Rising from the chair, I go to her, my steps tentative, my intentions true. I only want to offer comfort. Though I want more from her, too—I can't lie—but not in this moment. She needs to know I'm here for her. Just like she came running to be here for me.

"Katie," I whisper, but she shakes her head, turning to press her face into my couch as she cries harder.

And breaks my heart more.

I sit next to her on the couch and pull her into my arms. She tries to resist at first, bracing her hands out like she wants to push me away, but I don't let her. I need to hold her. She needs to be held. Slowly she melts into me, her head against my chest, her hands curling around my shoulders. She clings to me and cries hard, ugly tears. I smooth my hand over her hair, circle my other arm around her back, but say nothing. She just needs to get it all out.

Molly comes trotting into the living room, cocking her head at me like she's confused. I say nothing as she approaches us, stopping to rest her chin on top of Katie's thigh. Katie reaches out and pats Molly's head, sniffing loudly as she withdraws her hand. Molly will have none of it, licking Katie's fingers and making her laugh.

It's a nice sound, watery with tears, but still a laugh.

"She licked me," Katie murmurs.

"She likes you."

"I like her, too." She lifts her head to look up at me. Her eyes are red, as is her nose, and I reach out, brush the tears away from her face with my thumb. "Thank you."

"For what?"

"For comforting me. I've . . . cried a lot of lonely tears over the years." She smiles again and shakes her head. "That rhymed. I could probably write a perfect country song, what with everything I've gone through."

"Me too," I admit with a chuckle. I brush her hair away from her forehead, any excuse to touch her. "What are we going to do, Katie?"

She frowns. "About what?"

Shifting, I lean in close, my mouth hovering above hers. My heart is racing. Surely she can feel it beneath her palm. The way she's touching me, wrapped all around me without any inhibitions . . . I'm pushing my luck but damn it, I can't seem to resist when it comes to her. "About this. About us."

Her gaze drops to my mouth and she licks her lips. I close my eyes briefly, searching for a shred of control to cling on to, but it's hard. So damn hard. "I'm still mad at you," she admits.

"Understandable. I'll respect your boundaries." I touch her jaw with just my fingertips, drifting them under her chin. "But don't you see how the moment we get too close, it's like we're naturally drawn to each other?"

"Chemistry means nothing," she says, her voice shaky. "That's all this is."

"Chemistry is everything," I say vehemently. "You of all people should understand that."

"I'm afraid." She pauses and I wait patiently. When it comes to Katie, I can be forever patient. "I'm afraid we're not good for each other," she whispers. I lean in and press my mouth to her cheek. Her breath hitches at the first touch of my lips on her skin. "In the end, all we'll do is cause each other pain. I don't know if I can stand that again. The pain. Always so much pain in my life."

My heart aches. I've suffered way too much pain, too. It's all I know. Except for these few stolen days and nights with Katie. "But won't the moments when we give each other pleasure be worth the burn?"

She says nothing. She doesn't resist, either. I'm taking it too far. I'm pushing too hard, but I can't help myself. When I'm with Katie like this I can't resist her. The smell of her skin, her taste. The way she feels in my arms. It's too much.

Too perfect.

I'm about to kiss her when her eyes crack open, bright blue and shining. "I don't know what to call you, who to think of you as. Are you Ethan? Or are you Will? My brain . . . it's all a jumble. I want to call you Will, but I know you won't like it. It's like I don't know who you are anymore."

I stare at her and heave out a breath, my mind drawing a blank. I have no response. None. Instead I shift away from her, her body slipping out of my arms, past my fingers, and just like that, there's a vast, yawning distance between us.

And I'm scared as hell that I'll never be close to Katie again.

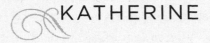# KATHERINE

I wake up early, pushing past the sadness that I'm alone. For one brief, hopeful moment yesterday I thought I might give in to my baser needs and let Ethan do whatever he wanted to me. I wanted it, too. I felt the need to be with him, in the closest way two people can be. But then my mind got muddled and I wanted to identify him as Will. My Will. The boy who saved me, who never gave up on me, until one day he just . . . did.

That's who I wanted to be close to. The one I wanted to kiss. Not Ethan. I adore Ethan, but now the name almost feels fake when it falls from my tongue. Because it *is* fake. I don't care if he legally changed his name. It doesn't feel real.

And that's me being completely unfair. He's shed his old self, yet I want that boy back. He's trying to escape his father, yet his father found him anyway. We're both trying to escape our demons, but reality continues to thrust them in our faces and we can't avoid it.

So in the end, we didn't do anything but talk through the letter, discuss a strategy on how to best avoid Lisa, and walk Molly through the neighborhood. Anything dog related has become neutral ground; it's like we need her to feel normal.

I drag myself out of bed and start the coffee, turn on the TV. It's tuned to a national morning show and I listen to the talking heads drone on. Potential political candidates, a random sniper on the loose in another state, a funny video of a disastrous wedding ceremony that has gone viral.

And then, a name. A name so familiar, so dear, that when I hear it said by the morning show host, the mug I just grabbed from the cabinet slips from my fingers and shatters once it hits the floor.

"Sources say William Monroe, the son of convicted serial killer Aaron Monroe, has been residing in the very town his father terrorized, living under an assumed name and trying to escape the notoriety of his father's crimes. For more on that story, here's Lisa Swanson."

I touch my cold lips with shaky fingers, standing amid the broken shards of my favorite mug, stunned as I hear Lisa's voice talk of the upcoming interview with Aaron Monroe, the fact that his execution date is drawing closer, and catch a quick glimpse of footage from said interview—she's always the tease, Lisa—and then grainy shots of a tall man leaving his house, climbing into his black car, which is parked in the driveway in front of his garage.

Ethan. Will.

"Since the moment kidnap victim Katherine Watts was delivered to the police station by William Monroe eight years ago, the then fifteen-year-old was a suspect in Watts's kidnapping and rape. Despite his father being found guilty in the Watts case and the murders of four other young girls, suspicion has lingered throughout the years in regard to the younger Monroe's involvement, specifically with the Watts case. Now, in my upcoming interview with Aaron Monroe, he tells the full story of what exactly happened all those years ago. And he shares with us the extent to which his son was involved in those crimes."

Her sensationalizing tone grates. She may as well have said that Will stood right next to his father and they divided the murderous duties between them.

"Ohmygod." The words are strung together, one horrified whisper. My phone starts to chime from where it sits on my kitchen counter and I step gingerly, avoiding the broken pieces of the cup on the floor before I grab my phone.

A text from Mom.

Call me when you get this message.

Another ding. This time it's a text from Brenna.

Are you up? Watching the morning news?

I text Brenna first.

I saw it. None of it is true.

She responds before I get a chance to call Mom.

We don't know what Monroe says in that interview.
For all you know, it could be true.

Thanks, Brenna, for having faith in my life choices.
I don't bother answering her. Instead, I call Mom, my gaze stuck on the mess in my kitchen. The mug shattered in what looks like at least a hundred pieces, though I know I'm exaggerating. I dread having to clean up that mess. I'm up early because I have to work on a paper that's due tomorrow. A paper I was supposed to work on over the weekend, before I got distracted.

"Katherine." Mom's voice is brisk. Efficient. She's trying to be the strong one right now and I appreciate that. "I don't know if you saw the news yet . . ."

"I did," I say, cutting her off. "She's invading his privacy, Mom. It's not right, trying to out him in order to promote her interview."

"Regardless, he's been put on national news, though thank goodness they didn't reveal his other name." She goes quiet, and I say nothing, either. It's a waste of my time to defend him, so right now I don't. If she knew I spent the weekend with him, she'd flip. "It's good you discovered the truth when you did, so you didn't get caught up in *this* mess."

"You're right," I say with a sigh. And she is. If I'd found out he was Will this way, via a morning show broadcast? I would have been beyond devastated. "Though I feel terrible that he's being exposed like this. She's only doing it to gain interest in her interview."

"And perhaps to get him to participate? She doesn't want you involved, does she?" Mom sounds anxious.

I never told her that Lisa's been trying to convince me to talk to her again. "She does," I admit. "She's tried to convince me to respond to—*his* interview." That I can hardly say his name after all these years drives me bonkers. I need to get over it.

"Oh, Katherine. You can't. You just . . . I don't want you involved in this sordid mess. It's only going to get worse. More networks and gossip sites will pick up the story. And you know how they are. They'll try to twist it into a giant mess, and that's something you don't need. Haven't you had enough of that? You're trying to straighten out your life, not make it worse."

"I know, Mom," I say wearily.

"Please tell me you're not going to do this."

If she'd asked me last night, I would have promised her I wouldn't. Even when I first woke up, I wouldn't have been tempted to agree to anything Lisa wants.

But now? After seeing her try to ruin Ethan's reputation

and expose him to the public when she knows just how private he is? That he purposely and legally changed his name so he wouldn't have to be linked to his father ever again? I want to rush to his defense and protect him. The only way I can do that is if I speak on his behalf.

It's risky and I'm scared of what Lisa could ask me, but I think . . . no, I *know* I have to do it.

"I'm not sure what I'm going to do, Mom," I say, hoping she stays calm. "But what she's doing, it's not right."

"So you're going to what? Defend him? Don't forget he *lied* to you. He tricked you, Katherine, so he could worm his way into your life and manipulate you. And it *worked*. You should hate him for what he's done."

Mom definitely hates him for what he's done to me, but I can't. Yes, I'm still hurt. I care about him too much, though, to hold on to the anger. "I can't hate him. Not after I discovered who he really is."

"You're a fool, Katherine." She spits the words out, almost as if it hurts to say them. I gasp, shocked that she would say such a thing to me. "I've tried to help you. I've stood by your side throughout the years and did my best to ensure you were safe. But if you want to put yourself into a perilous situation again and again, I can't stop you. You're an adult. So go ahead, spend time with the son of the man who almost killed you. Defend his lies. Stand by his side and make a fool of yourself on national television. Just know that if you support him, I can't support you."

She ends the call before I can say anything else.

I'm numb as I absently sweep up the mess in my kitchen, dumping the broken mug pieces into the trash. I haven't even had a cup of coffee yet, so I pour myself one in a new mug, adding creamer before I take a much needed sip.

My mother is making me choose sides. She won't stand by and let me support Ethan. If I do, I'm on my own.

I'm sure Brenna will rush to her side, too. She's already let Ethan know exactly how she feels about him.

For this battle, I'll be going it alone. No family support.

And the realization is terrifying.

# ETHAN

I try my best not to call or text Katie, but by mid-afternoon I'm tempted to give in. I told myself I could handle this new crisis on my own. And I did. I contacted a lawyer and met with him at eleven. He told me I really didn't have much to stand on. Lisa didn't reveal my address, didn't show my face, and the footage that was broadcast was grainy and distorted at best.

My legal name wasn't mentioned. As Will Monroe I'm a public figure, he reminded me. If Lisa had blasted my new name everywhere, my address, every little detail, then maybe I could go after her. Otherwise, I had to grin and bear it.

"Bet you could demand payment for an interview and they'd give it to you," the lawyer suggested gently. "Or you could probably get a book deal out of this. I'm sure plenty of publishers would love to hear your side of the story."

Yeah. He's probably right. But do I want to write a book about the bullshit that was my life? I don't think so.

When I returned home, I almost expected the media to be hanging out in front of my house, but thank God that didn't happen. Nothing happened really. I thought I'd hear from Lisa Swanson, but she hasn't contacted me so far, either.

The entire day has been surreal. I'm on the morning news, used as bait for dear old Dad's interview, but other than that, it's business as usual. I'm almost . . . disappointed. Which is fucking mental, but what can I say? I'm used to the media circus. It's been a part of my life off and on for years and I believed they'd come running.

I almost feel like this is a test. And I'm on the cusp of failing.

Molly's a comfort and I'm so glad I have her. She doesn't judge, doesn't have any expectations beyond my feeding her, walking her, and giving her affection. Why did I wait so long to get a dog? She's just what I need right now, especially since my relationship with Katie is so uncertain.

I'm about to text her when there's a knock on my door, causing Molly to go into a fit of barking. She runs toward the door, her claws clacking on the wood floor, and I ease up from my spot on the couch, approaching the door cautiously, my phone clutched in my hand. The dog won't let up; she's barking so loud it's hurting my ears, and I use my fiercest voice to make her stop.

"Molly. No." I send her a stern look and she quiets down to a low, continuous growl. Impressive little guard dog I have.

"Who is it?" I ask, pissed that I never installed that peephole I meant to get when I first moved in.

"It's me. Katie."

Oh. Shit. I hurriedly unlock the door, surprised that she's come by without letting me know. I open the door and she rushes toward me, giving me no chance to say anything in greeting.

"Are you okay?" She grabs hold of my hands and drags me back into the house, shutting and locking the door for me. She scolds Molly kindly. "Why are you barking so ferociously, girly? It's just me."

"What are you doing here?" I ask, immediately grimacing. "I'm glad you're here, but you usually call or whatever."

"Yeah, I'm sorry. I was busy all morning finishing up a

paper that's due and then I just spent the last hour on the phone with Lisa Swanson. I was so frazzled I came right over here." She makes a face, looking unsure. "I hope that was okay?"

"It's always okay," I say sincerely. "And what do you mean, you were talking to Lisa Swanson?"

She sinks her teeth into her lower lip. "You're not going to like what I have to tell you."

I drag her over to the couch and we sit, not pressed up against each other but close enough that we're in touching distance. I think this is progress. That she came over here on her own is progress, too. But talking to Lisa Swanson? I know whatever she's about to say is going to piss me off.

"Explain," I tell her.

She grips her knees, her arms extended, her expression unsure. "I saw the news this morning and I was so angry on your behalf. I knew I had to do something to help you."

"So you called Lisa?" That's not going to help anyone.

"Not at first. I told myself this was your battle to fight. I was almost . . . scared to call you and see how you were doing, and I'm sorry," she admits.

"I didn't reach out to you because I wanted to handle this shit on my own," I confess. "Instead of running to you every single time."

She smiles gently, her eyes kind. "I would've helped. I wanted to help. Still do."

"I know. Thank you. But you're not telling me how Lisa plays into this."

"Oh. Well, I was working on the paper and I couldn't stop thinking about Lisa and her wanting me to participate in the interview. We talked a bunch of times about it. I even met her in person to negotiate a deal with her."

I frown. "Negotiate a deal?"

She shrugs, looking embarrassed. "I told her I wouldn't do an interview unless you participated, too. At first, it was my way to get back at you. To force you to do an interview when I knew you didn't want to. But I hoped you would just for the chance to see me."

She's always tempting, but when you throw Lisa into the mix, that's usually a firm no from me.

"But then I realized maybe it would be good if we both did the interview, because if we could make this work between us, our supposed meeting during the interview would make sense, you know? The relationship could start after our televised re-union. And no one could give us grief for that. Maybe. Or they'd give us less grief. I don't know. It's all a big mess, really," she mumbles, waving a dismissive hand.

"This was a few weeks ago, though, right? I turned down Lisa's offer. I wouldn't speak with Lisa then, and I'm definitely not going to speak to her now. No way. She'd skewer me alive."

"Yeah, I turned her down, too, when I heard you weren't going to do it. But . . . I changed my mind."

"Katie," I start, but she holds up a hand, silencing me.

"Hear me out." She clears her throat, her gaze meeting mine. "She's trying to manipulate this entire thing and I'm sick of it. Your father is trying to manipulate it, too. Trying to gain sympathy as he's on his way to be executed. We should do the interview. We need to show them that we're not scared. We're not the ones who have something to hide. He is. Your father. He's the monster, not us. You did nothing wrong. *You* saved my life."

My chest aches. That she would do this, open herself to the possible humiliation and tough questions Lisa will most definitely dole out in order to defend me, is an honor. But it also breaks my heart. I can't let her do this. What if Lisa found out what else I did to Katie? How I lied and tricked her?

"You don't need to do this for me," I say, but she shakes her head, her lips thinning.

"It may help you, but my motives are purely selfish. We need to shut this down. I need to show your father that I'm not scared of him. That I can face my demons and defeat them." She tries to smile, but it's shaky. "I am doing it for you, too. If we can control the situation, we can control what's said. No one will find out what's happened between us recently. We won't let them."

"But what if they do find out?" My insides feel like they're shredding. The last thing I ever want to do is hurt her. "They'll tear us apart, Katie. Us being together, even as friends, will freak people out. If they ever discovered what really happened . . ."

"They won't," she says quickly. "But if they do, then that's the chance we'll have to take. Still, I'm betting they won't." She dips her head, gazing downward. "I want to do this for you. Please let me."

I don't want to go along with her plan, but I don't want to hurt her, either. "I don't want to do this."

Her shoulders go tense, but she doesn't utter a word.

"But for you, I will," I finish quietly.

She lifts her head, our gazes meeting. Sticking. She doesn't look away and neither do I. "So we're doing this for each other."

I nod. "For each other." I don't miss the unspoken meaning behind our words and neither does she.

"I took Molly to the vet," I say to fill the silence.

"Really? Already?" The small smile curving her lips is a sight to see. "That's great."

"I had to make sure she was okay." She probably thinks I'm

a softie, but I don't care. I sort of am—but only when it comes to my dog and Katie. "She's fine. Got some shots and those made her sleepy, but otherwise, she's healthy."

Her smile fades. "So. Are you going to call Lisa?"

Nice change of subject, though pretty abrupt. "Not yet." I shake my head. "I'll text her later."

"Do it now," she insists. "Or else you probably never will."

I crack a smile, though it's hard. I don't feel much like smiling when it comes to dealing with Lisa. "Have you always been this pushy?"

"No," she says simply. "I used to be. And then I wasn't. But now I'm trying to dig back up my courage."

"So I'm your test subject."

"Unfortunately for you, yes." She nods. "And by the way, the interview's happening in San Francisco. She wanted to use the local affiliate's studio there."

"When exactly is it going to happen?" Dread fills me. I don't want to do this at all. I really am doing this just for her. No other reason. I'd rather face a firing squad than Lisa and her persistent, never-ending questions.

"Wednesday afternoon, one o'clock. The entire interview, including your—father, is going to air Thursday. They bumped it. The interview was originally scheduled for next week." She pauses. "That was Lisa's intent all along, I think. To bump it up by exposing you."

"Shit, Katie. That's crazy. That's less than two days away." I shake my head. "I need to find a place for Molly to stay. The vet has a kenneling service, so I'll give them a call."

"Oh good." She literally wrings her hands together. She knows I'm not pleased with how quickly this interview is happening.

"We're falling right into her hands, you know," I tell her,

my voice low. "This is exactly what she wants. It's probably some sort of trap."

"We have to think faster than her, that's all." She shrugs. "Besides, at least we'll get it over with."

That's one way to look at it. "We'll go together. I'll drive."

"Do you think that's a good idea?"

"It's crazy to travel separately."

"And it's risky to travel together." Her point is valid, but I don't care. I want her with me.

"Come on, Katie. We can make this work. And no way am I going to let you drive to San Francisco by yourself."

"I can handle it." She actually looks offended.

"Let me do this. I don't like the thought of you going there alone," I insist gently. This has nothing to do with me believing she can't handle anything by herself and is all about needing her close to me. A purely selfish motivation on my part.

"I can take care of myself," she sniffs.

"Yeah, you can," I agree. Better than anyone gives her credit for.

Including myself.

# KATHERINE

Upon our arrival in San Francisco on Wednesday morning, we go to the hotel, where the network is putting the two of us up for the night. We checked into our rooms at the front desk, which we discovered were on the same floor, then separated so we could get ready before we left for the studio. Two cars were coming to pick us up, at two different times. Ethan is leaving fifteen minutes before me, so I guess he can arrive at the studio first and hide away before I get there.

I believe Lisa's orchestrated some big reunion for the two of us. They still don't have a clue that we already know each other, or that we traveled together to San Francisco.

Something they can never know. We took such a huge risk, riding together. One I tried to prevent, but Ethan would have none of it. He claims he just wanted me with him. I figured he was worried about me traveling alone. But I conceded, because I wanted the excuse to spend time with him alone in his car during a long drive. It gave us time to talk—about all sorts of things. Little things, though, never the big things that still divide us.

Like his lies. His deception. My family's hatred and disapproval. I don't know if I can trust him. I know what he wants, but I'm scared it could ruin us completely.

We circle around those frightening topics, afraid to approach them for fear that once we do, there's no going back.

The hotel is nice, my room large, old but elegant, with a

king-sized bed and a fantastic view of the entire city. I stare out the window for a while, knowing Ethan has the same view, and I wonder what he's thinking. Is he as nervous as I am? He'd seemed pretty at ease during the drive, but he's pretty good at hiding his emotions.

I'm not good at that trick at all.

Giving up on the view, I throw open my suitcase on the bed and hang the three outfits I brought as options in the closet, then take a step back to examine each one. I'm already a tangle of nerves, unable to decide what to wear, which is silly. I want to look pretty but strong. Confident. I know I'm not talking to Aaron Monroe live or anything crazy like that, because if that were the case, I wouldn't be able to go through with it. But we're going to be shown clips from Monroe's interview and I'm not sure if I'm prepared to see him.

What if I get sick? I'm nauseous just thinking about it. I can pretend I'm strong all I want, wearing my new outfit as armor, but deep down inside, one look at him and I'll be rendered back to the scared twelve-year-old girl I once was. Lisa will probably love every minute of it, too. I'm starting to think she's heartless.

To say Lisa was beyond ecstatic to hear from Ethan/Will would be an understatement. From the moment he texted her, I knew she believed she'd won. She got exactly what she wanted and for a brief, terrifying moment, I wondered if what Ethan and I agreed to do was a mistake.

But I realized quickly that we can handle this, as long as we are in it together. That's what I tell myself at least.

I take a shower and blow my hair dry until it's nice and straight. Carefully apply my makeup, though I figure a makeup artist is going to be there, so why I'm wasting my time I'm not sure. I finally decide on an outfit, choosing the charcoal-gray, long-sleeved dress that I'll wear with black tights and knee-high boots. Sort of a kick-ass look for me, one I'm hoping I own when I walk into the room.

I'm rolling on the tights when my phone chimes with a text message. It's Ethan.

> You'll need to pretend you haven't seen me in years when we first set eyes on each other at the studio. Don't forget.

I'm glad he texted me. I did sort of forget. That would have been awkward.

I text him back.

> Thanks for the reminder.

I'm still struggling with the stupid tights when he finally texts again.

> Are you ready for this? Do you need anything? Moral support? A stiff drink?

I need him to hold my hand and tell me it's going to be okay. I need him to remain calm so I'll be calm, too. I need so much from him, probably more than he can ever give, so instead I tell him nothing at all.

> I'm fine. How about you?

His response is quick.

> I'm good. A little nervous. I'll be glad when it's over.
> Me too.

"Thank you so much for doing this," Lisa gushes the moment I walk into the hushed studio. She's the only one there. Not even the cameramen have arrived yet, which I find strange. Her assistant is the one who escorted me to Lisa after they touched up my makeup and shellacked my hair with too much hairspray. The woman, who was probably around my age or a little older, couldn't stop gushing over what an "honor" it was to meet me.

I wondered if Lisa put her up to that.

"I know it wasn't an easy decision," Lisa continues. "But I'm thrilled you're giving me another opportunity for you to tell your side of the story."

"Did you really give me a choice, Lisa?" I cross my arms in front of my chest, trying to tamp down my anger. But it's hard. She's manipulated this entire situation from the start.

"We always have choices," she says cheerily, ignoring my stormy mood. "And I'm so excited for you to meet Will again after all of these years. He's here, you know."

My heart starts to pound, so hard I'm afraid she can see it through the material of my dress. It's almost like this really *is* the first time I'm seeing him after going for so many years without any contact. "He is?"

Lisa nods. "He arrived about twenty minutes before you. We just conducted his interview." She pauses as my mind tries to play catch-up. They already had his interview? Wow, that was fast. And I thought we were going to be interviewed together. "He looks great, by the way."

I raise a brow. What is she trying to say?

"He's so handsome, well spoken, successful in his chosen career," Lisa continues, her eyes sparkling like a mischievous child's. "Quite the catch."

Okay, yeah, she's saying exactly what I thought. "Are you trying to make a love connection between us, Lisa?"

She starts to laugh and waves a dismissive hand. "No.

Don't be silly. As if that would ever happen. You two would have way too much baggage to deal with if you ever started seeing each other romantically. I can't *imagine* how difficult that would be."

I say nothing. She's totally right. We are a disaster waiting to happen.

"Besides, he mentioned there was someone special in his life." Lisa smiles mysteriously. "He wouldn't name names or anything like that, but I could tell by his reaction that he has a girlfriend or, who knows, maybe even a boyfriend? Though he did mention a 'she' . . . "

Her speculation is a sight to behold. And could Ethan be referring to me? Or did he say he was in a relationship to ward Lisa off? I'd think that sort of admission would open up an entirely new line of questioning. "I'm glad he's found someone," I tell her. "Everyone deserves someone to love."

"Including you, my dear. I think of you often, drifting through your life alone." Lisa makes a *tsk*-ing noise, while I'm standing there with my hands suddenly clenched into fists, wanting to punch her right in her stupid mocking face.

How dare she?

"Oh, I'm fine," I say through clenched teeth. "It's not like I'm an old maid put up on the shelf yet." I remember reading that line once, and automatically thinking of myself. That had been a few years ago, though, when I had a different attitude.

I'm only twenty-one, which is still pretty young. I have plenty of years ahead of me to find a lasting relationship. Why would she imply I'm a lonely loser who'll never find love?

" 'Put up on the shelf,' such a quaint saying." Lisa sounds amused. Of course, she would. I never realized before just how mocking she can be.

"Are we ready to do this or what?" I ask irritably.

She clasps her hands together, appearing almost as if in prayer. "Let's get started."

The cameramen enter the small studio as if they knew they were being summoned, as well as Lisa's assistant. They arrange the chairs so that we'll be seated facing each other and a large television is brought into the room on a rolling stand, situated behind Lisa and just to her right.

My nerves immediately flare up, performing a tap dance in my stomach. That TV represents Aaron Monroe. I told her the last time I agreed to this interview that I wouldn't listen to what he had to say, but this time, I gave in, as did Will. She promised it would be brief and I believe her. But knowing I'll see his face flash on the screen . . . hear his voice . . . I'm testing myself on virgin ground. Will I be able to stand seeing him? Hearing him? Or will I lose it completely and do something horrible . . . like vomit all over Lisa?

Oh God, if I do something like that I'll be forever mortified.

"I'm not going to talk for long," I tell her the moment she sits in the chair opposite mine. "We agreed to ten minutes."

Lisa nods, her expression betraying no emotion. "That's fine."

I felt the need for a reminder. "If I don't feel comfortable with the questions regarding Monroe, I'll put a halt to the entire interview."

Her lips shift into an almost sneer. But as quickly as it appears, the expression is gone. "I wouldn't recommend that."

"Of course you wouldn't," I retort. Lisa's eyes widen the slightest bit. I'm not acting like the scared girl who she spoke to only a few months ago. I'm a little savvier, a lot fiercer.

"Let's just get this started." She glances over her shoulder. "Are we ready yet?"

Within minutes, we are. The cameras are pointed directly at us, the lights bright, making me sweat along my hairline, just like last time. I'm nervous, my hands clutched in my lap, and I will them to relax, forcing my tense shoulders to fall. I don't want Lisa to know I'm anxious.

Though knowing her, I'm sure she can sense it.

The formalities are gone through. The usual introductory questions, the meaningless answers. She segues into the tough questions right off the bat like the pro she is, her expression neutral, her gaze full of that wide-eyed acceptance she's so good at.

"What was your first reaction when you heard that Aaron Monroe agreed to do an interview?" She blinks at me, her lips curved into a pleasant smile.

"Disgust." I let the word drop like a bomb in between us. She doesn't even twitch. I have to give her credit. "What could he possibly say that anyone would want to hear?"

"Quite a lot, actually." Lisa leans forward, as if she's about to deliver a particularly juicy tidbit. "More than anything, he wants your forgiveness."

Right on cue the television screen lights up and there he is, clad in his white prison uniform, his head shaved down to nothing so that he's bald. He's fleshy. Pale. Like he doesn't get much time outside, which I'm sure he doesn't. His eyes are dull and so dark, just like I remember. He'd been strong then, too much so for me to fight off.

I lean back in my chair, as if I need the distance. But I can't look away, my gaze locked on the man's face.

The very same man who thrust his face in mine, screaming filth. I remember those eyes, almost black and full of so much rage as he called me horrific names. Tore my clothes off. Choked me until I almost passed out.

His voice spills from the TV speaker and I cringe, my hands automatically going to the chair's armrests, fingers curling tight. I haven't heard him speak in a long time and I preferred it that way.

Hearing him takes me right back. The memories assail me, one after the other.

"What I did was wrong," he says, his cigarette-roughened voice even scratchier than I remember. "And I wish for Katherine's forgiveness, though I know I probably won't get it. But it would mean so much if she could dig deep and find forgiveness in her heart for what I've done. I've already found my peace with Jesus. I'd like to find my peace with Katherine Watts, too."

The screen goes black.

As do my thoughts.

"So, Katherine. Can you find it in your heart to forgive Aaron Monroe for what he's done to you?"

# KATIE

Then

It was hot in the shed, but I felt so cold. I couldn't stop shivering, and I was scared. So scared. I closed my eyes and prayed to God that someone would find me. We're not a religious family, though it's not like we're atheists, either. We never really went to church, but I'd gone to a few services with my best friend, Sarah, mostly holiday-themed stuff. It had been nice. Sometimes even comforting.

Right now, I desperately needed that comfort. I needed God to tell me it was going to be okay. It didn't feel like it was going to be, though. I hurt everywhere. My head, my neck, my chest, between my legs . . .

Would he let me go? Or would he kill me? I'd been here at least a day, but maybe less. I was losing track of time. I think it was the morning, not much past noon if at all, and I wondered where my parents were. Looking for me? Had they called the police? They had to have by now. But would they ever find me?

Did I even want to be found, after everything the man had done to me?

The door cracked open and I turned away from the bright light shining from outside. The light was immediately snuffed out, the door slamming shut, and shuddery little breaths escaped me, making my chest ache, my head dizzy.

He was here, in the shed with me. God only knew what he had planned.

"Not dead yet?" He sounded amused. Pleasantly surprised. The word *dead* crushed my heart, my soul. I wished I were dead.

Then I wouldn't have to be subjected again to this.

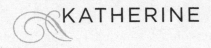

KATHERINE

I release my grip on the armrests and lean forward, as if I, too, am about to impart a juicy little secret. "No. I can never find it in my heart to forgive him and what he did to me. He *raped* me, Lisa. He almost *killed* me. The only reason I'm alive has nothing to do with him."

"So you believe his asking for your forgiveness is wrong?"

Nodding, I lean back into my chair, surprised at how light my heart feels after saying those words. I don't know how many times I have to prove that Aaron Monroe spared me nothing. The only reason I'm here is because I escaped—with the help of Will. "How can I forgive him, Lisa? I can never forget what he did to me, what he did to my family. He almost killed me. His request is quite frankly ridiculous."

Lisa's eyebrows go way up and I'm . . . thrilled. I shocked her. And I love it. "So you're going to hold on to this bitterness for the rest of your life? Do you really think that's wise? After all, he did allow you to live."

Oh, now I'm all fired up. He *allowed* me to live? Please. It's like she's purposely trying to rile me. "Do you really believe that? That he's the one who 'allowed' me to live?"

Lisa's brows are still halfway up her forehead. I'm sure she doesn't like that I just challenged her. "I suppose not. Are you going to insist yet again that Will Monroe is the one who saved you?"

"Come on, Lisa. You know the story. Have I ever deviated from it? He *is* the one who saved me. Not his father. *Will*." I stress the last word. I'm trembling, I'm so full of righteous anger, and when I see a sudden movement to the right, it surprises me. I turn my head.

And there he is. My Will. Gone is Ethan. All I see is Will Monroe standing in front of me, strong yet unsure. Friendly but wary, which is how he should act, considering we supposedly haven't seen each other in years. Wearing black trousers and a blue button-down shirt, his hair neatly combed, the beard, the stubble, all of it gone so he looks fresh-faced. Young. He's not even wearing his glasses. His handsome, masculine features are on raw display, his mouth strained, eyes incredibly dark as they watch me.

For the briefest, most fleeting moment, those eyes remind me of his father's. They're the same. The exact same color, shape, size. The only difference is that when Will looks at me with those eyes, it's with kindness. Warmth. Never cruelty.

The shock—some of it feigned, the rest genuine—must show on my face because Lisa doesn't say a word. She doesn't stop the cameras from filming, either. They keep rolling. She wants to capture this moment forever.

So I let her.

Slowly I rise to my feet, my gaze never leaving his. I take a few steps toward him but he takes the rest, his long stride bringing him to me that much faster.

We're standing toe to toe. Face to chest, since he's so much taller than me. I tilt my head back, our gazes meeting, his warm and full of so much tender emotion as his eyes roam over my face, I almost want to cry.

In fact, I do. The tears form but never quite slip from my

eyes and he sends me a look. One that says *please don't torture me,* but it's too late. I blink, hold my eyes closed for a moment to ward off the tears, and when I reopen them, he's already reaching for me, my name falling from his lips in a hushed breath. He wraps me up in his arms and I hug him in return, squeezing him tight.

He feels good. Strong. He smells good, too. I'm glad I didn't see him before we left separately for the studio. The transformation seems real. It's so weird, but no longer do I feel like I'm in the presence of Ethan. I'm with Will, the hero from my past. The boy from my dreams, my letters, my texts, my phone calls. Those stolen moments when I watched him on TV during the trial, he'd looked so different then.

And here he is now. All grown up and holding me close. I'm being foolish, thinking like this. Delusional even. But I need to keep up the illusion, so I'm wallowing in my imaginary state. The pretense has become reality.

"You two are adorable," Lisa says, her smug voice causing the two of us to remember where we are, and we spring apart from each other. My cheeks are warm. Will offers me a sheepish smile. "Stop taping." She turns to the cameramen, and they do as she bids before she returns her attention to us. "That was perfect. I couldn't have orchestrated it better! We need to get a chair for Will and then we'll start the interview with the both of you together."

I chance a glance in Will's direction to find he's watching me, a closed-mouth smile curving his lips. I smile in return, feeling shy, which is ridiculous because this man has seen me naked. He's seen me in my most vulnerable moments, yet I feel like I don't know him at all.

In reality, I guess I don't. Ethan only allowed me glimpses

into his life, but never the whole truth. Never the real him. What are his struggles? His dreams? Does he have a hard time sleeping at night? Do his memories haunt him? Is he happy? Does he want more?

I want to know everything I can about him.

Not Ethan, but Will.

Lisa's busy directing her poor assistant in moving the chairs around the set and Will approaches, his expression full of concern. "Are you all right?" he asks, his voice low, for only me to hear.

I nod, not wanting her to think we're sharing secrets. Speaking intimately will spark her interest and I really don't want Lisa paying any more attention to us than is necessary. "I'm fine," I whisper out of the side of my mouth.

"We were convincing, huh?" He looks proud of himself. I can't blame him, but he probably should tone it down.

"Very." I turn to smile at him, unable to stop myself from reaching out and running my index finger down the front of his shirt. His chest is firm and hot, and something mysterious swirls low in my belly. "You dress up really nice."

"So do you." His gaze roams over me once again, starting at the top of my head and wandering a path along my entire body, until I feel warm and flush, a little shaky. "You look beautiful, Katie."

The air shifts, changes. Becomes heavier, charged with some unknown force. I'm caught up in the romanticism of it all. Two kids reunited after all this time, the connection between them just as strong as it was before, made stronger by what they've shared as adults.

"Thank you," I murmur, my gaze cutting to where Lisa stands. She's now yelling at her assistant and I wince. I would never want to feel the wrath of Lisa Swanson. She's on her best behavior in front of us, so I can only imagine what she's like behind closed doors. "We should probably be careful."

"Why? This is exactly what she wants." He leans in closer, his mouth by my ear. "She talked you up to me, before she started our interview. Told me how beautiful and poised you are, how genuine and sweet. I could only silently agree, though I did tell her I watched your earlier interview."

"She acts like she wants to set us up." Fear twists my insides. I'm terrified of the public reaction if people found out what we've shared. I'm also concerned for my sanity if we were to pick up where we left off. It's so troubling, how easily he lied, if I let myself think about it. It means he could do it again.

"Doesn't that work out with our plans?" He leans back when I turn to look at him, his expression impassive. Only the slight lift of his eyebrows indicates he wants an answer.

"You look different without your glasses," I say instead, changing the subject. If he objects, he doesn't say a word.

"I thought it best to keep them off for the day. It keeps our façade going," he explains, squinting a little.

"Can you even see?" He usually wears his glasses all the time.

"I got contacts a while ago and just never got used to putting them in." He smiles down at me. "Thought I'd bust them back out and give it a go. Poked my eyeballs twenty times each, but I eventually got them in."

I smile in return, getting a little lost in his deep brown gaze, when I hear footsteps approach. A throat clears.

Lisa.

"Well, aren't you two cozy?" I look at her, my smile fading while hers stretches wide. "Sharing secrets already?"

"Just catching up," Will says easily, standing up straighter and taking a step toward Lisa. "Are you ready for us?"

I watch him, admiration running through my veins. He just took command of the entire situation and I'm sort of . . . turned on? No, that's not the feeling I'm experiencing.

Or is it?

"I am." She looks at the two of us, her gaze going from him to me. "Are you ready?"

"As we'll ever be," Will says smoothly.

ETHAN

Katherine is being . . . odd. Not like her usual self, and I can't quite put my finger on it. I know we're playing a part and pretending that we haven't seen each other in years, but still. She's looking at me in this sort of dreamy way, her gaze full of longing. Like I'm her Prince Charming who just burst into the room, sword drawn and ready to fight for his princess till the death.

I sort of feel that way myself. I'm here to protect her, something I will always do. My one-on-one interview with Lisa wasn't as bad as I thought it would be and I was fully prepared for the worst. She asked a few general questions before getting to the meat of it, her curiosity apparent as she asked if I'd talked to my father, if I was prepared to go see him, if I'd ever be able to forgive him.

The answer to her questions was pretty much all no. I have no desire to see him ever again. I've had enough of Aaron Monroe to last twenty lifetimes. I don't need to see him. It's like he doesn't even really exist anymore. He's going to be executed soon. I don't know how many appeals and stays this man can get. When does he run out of chances?

Sometimes I wish he were already dead, so this nightmare would be completely over.

A terrible thought. I feel guilty every time I have it, but does he ever feel guilty for the lives he took? The lives he ruined? He claims he does, with his crocodile tears and false pleas for forgiveness. But I see his tactics for what they really are.

A cry for attention.

"Sit down, please," Lisa says, pulling me from my thoughts. She waves a hand at one chair, saying, "Take that one, Katherine."

I take the other, Katie and I sitting next to each other. Lisa smiles at us, the makeup artist appearing out of nowhere and patting her face with powder, then coming over to Katie and patting her cheeks and forehead as well.

When the makeup artist turns toward me I shake my head. It's bad enough I let her brush my hair and tame my freaking eyebrows. My man card is in serious peril right now.

"Before we start, I wanted to discuss with you both the questions I'm going to ask. I want to focus on what happened that day, when you took Katherine to the police station, Will." Lisa pauses, her expression grave. "Are you both okay to talk about it?"

I'm surprised she's concerned about my so-called delicate feelings. "I'm fine with it."

"And you, Katherine?" She turns to look at Katie, her expression almost . . . mocking? I think maybe Katie's made her mad and Lisa doesn't like it. "Are you okay with discussing that particular day?"

Katie nods, her posture perfect, head tilted high. She reminds me of royalty, ruling over her court. "Yes, I am," she murmurs.

"All right, then." Lisa smiles. "Let's get started."

# WILL

Then

Panic had hit me at one point during the walk with Katie. What if the police didn't believe me? What if they thought I was the one who hurt her? Who . . . raped her?

I flinched just at the thought. I couldn't stand the idea of the police believing I was the one who did that to her. Put those bruises on her, held her down, forced her to do things that revolted her, shit that revolted *me*. Things no girl her age should ever have to go through.

Hell, I was a virgin myself, not that anyone would be able to tell since I'm a guy. But I haven't had sex yet. I'd messed around a little bit but nothing serious. And I would never hurt a girl, especially one as young as Katie. I wasn't like my dad.

I clenched my hands into fists. I would *never* be like my dad.

Ever.

"How much farther?" Katie whined.

I whirled around to find her dragging along, walking slow, the too-big flip-flops nearly sliding off her feet. She looked exhausted. Dark circles were heavy under her eyes and she had my sweatshirt on, which completely swallowed her up. She looked even younger than when I'd first seen her.

"Not much longer," I reassured her, wishing I knew for sure that I was doing the right thing. This could all backfire in my face, and then where would I be? What would happen to me? Would I end up going to jail like my old man? Because he was going, there was no doubt in my mind. And the police were going to lock him up for a long-ass time.

He didn't deserve any less.

We came to an intersection and had to wait for the light to change. Katie stood beside me, shivering even though the night air wasn't that cold. I took her hand and held it, giving her fingers a squeeze. She smiled up at me, her eyes filled with so much sadness, but a hint of gratitude, too. Gratitude that was all for me.

"My feet hurt. I'm so tired," she whispered. "I know all I've done is complain and I'm—I'm sorry."

"Don't apologize." Her complaining had driven me crazy a couple of times, but I'd brushed it off. I couldn't be mad at her, not after what she'd gone through.

"I want to thank you, Will," she said, her voice so tiny I could barely hear her. "You saved my life."

"No, I did—"

She cut me off, squeezing my hand extra hard. "Yeah, you did. He would've killed me. I know he would've. You know it, too."

The shiver that moved through me had nothing to do with the breeze that just washed over us and everything to do with understanding that what Katie said was true.

It scared me, the possibility of what my father might have done to her. Would he have murdered her? Dumped her body where it couldn't be found? I most likely saved her life.

The enormity of what I'd just done almost sent me to my knees.

 ETHAN

"So, Will." Lisa clasps her hands in front of her, her elbows propped on the chair's armrests. "Tell us your thoughts when you first found Katie in the shed in the backyard of your house."

I go still, not sure how I should answer. Talk about diving right in. I knew she'd ask this, so you'd think I'd be prepared, but . . .

I'm not.

"Shocked," I say slowly. "At first I thought I was seeing things. Finding her there scared me and I . . ." My voice drifts and I swallow hard. This is the most difficult part for me to admit. I'm not proud of what I did. "I ran. I left her there."

I can feel Katie's gaze on me but I can't look at her. The guilt I still feel for leaving her when I should have done something at that very moment hurts. Negates the hero business Katie's always trying to put on me. It's why I'm so uncomfortable when she does praise me for saving her life. I got lucky. So did she. If I'd gone back to that shed the next day and she wasn't there?

I don't know if I ever could have forgiven myself.

"Why did you leave her?"

"I was just a kid. Fifteen years old, a messed-up kid. I didn't know how to act, didn't know what the hell to do. I was so afraid my dad would be mad at me if he knew that I found her. I'd get in trouble. I was always in trouble." It sounds completely fucked up, because guess what? It *was* fucked up, living in my house. Dealing with my dad. More than anything, I was scared that if he knew what I'd found, he'd lock me up in that shed, too. Make me do things I didn't want to, like watch him with . . . Katie.

Or worse, force *me* to do something with her. Hell, I didn't know the depths of his depravity. I still don't understand how he turned into such a complete monster, or when exactly it happened.

"But you went back," Lisa urges, her gaze going to Katie before returning to me. "You rescued her."

"I went back and told her I was going to rescue her," I amend. "I had to do some preparation first. Get some things for Katie. Make sure my dad wasn't around. I didn't want him to catch us because I knew if he did, the both of us—we probably wouldn't have survived." I didn't realize it then, but I do now. I'm pretty certain he would have killed us both if he caught us.

I also remember how mad Katie had been at me for leaving her. She didn't believe I'd ever come back. Not that I could blame her. But I did go back for her.

And I always would. No matter what.

"So you escaped, took her to the police station, where you fully planned on dropping her off and then leaving." The look on Lisa's face is incredulous. "Why would you do such a thing? Just . . . leave her there without trying to save yourself? That was your chance to escape, too."

Katie had been mad at me about that, too. No one can understand why I tried to run, not even me. "I didn't know any better," I admit. "My life . . . with my dad wasn't normal, but it was the only thing I knew. It was *my* normal. I didn't want to lose it."

"It wasn't necessarily a good life, though. Was it?"

I shake my head, wishing she would stop questioning me. Isn't it Katie's turn yet? "It was awful."

"Did he abuse you?"

I nod, not willing to give voice to the numerous things he'd done to me.

"But you didn't want to leave him." Lisa's voice is flat.

"It's hard to leave the only thing you know," Katie says, her voice soft but edged with steel. Look at her, running to my defense. Though really, she's always had to defend me to the press, to the police. This is nothing new for her.

And I'm guessing she doesn't like Lisa's line of questioning.

Lisa barely looks at Katie. "So you were scared of the unknown."

I shrug, feeling helpless. "Yeah." What the hell does this have to do with anything?

"As you know, I spoke with your father. We met a few times and I have hours of footage that I was unable to use for the final interview." She offers a small smile. "He wanted me to share something with you in particular, privately. This won't air. I promise." She glances up at one of the cameramen. "Shut it off."

The cameras click off and I stare apprehensively at the television screen sitting on a stand just beyond Lisa. Like magic, the TV turns on and there's my father, smiling hopefully for the camera.

I grip the armrests so tight my hands ache.

"Son, I hope you can listen to my message with an open mind and heart. I want to apologize for the hell I've put you through. And for the hell I will continue to put you through, because it's never going to end. It's not fair and I understand that, but there's nothing I can do to stop it. I just hope you realize that everything I do and say is not just for you but also for me. I have my own story, my own version of events. Whether you choose to remember those particular details or not, that's up to you. But I want you to know this up front—I love you. I hope that someday we can see each other again, face-to-face. If that moment never comes, then I hope this message is good enough for the both of us."

The TV goes black.

Disgust churns in my gut, makes me nauseous. He didn't say much, but it was enough. I have no idea what he's referring to, but it can't be good.

"You look upset," Lisa says softly. The cameras are back on, recording us. "What was it about your father's message that bothered you the most?"

"He'll twist the truth to make himself look better," I say, shaking my head. "I'm sure he's said some things to you that make me look like a monster, just like him."

Lisa says nothing and I blow out a harsh breath.

"He doesn't love me. He doesn't know what love means," I mutter, keeping my head averted so I don't have to look Lisa in the eye. This is getting way too personal. If she uses this as part of her interview I'm going to be pissed. Not that I have a choice. I'm the dumbass who agreed to this.

"He said that you were involved in the kidnapping and rape of Katherine Watts," Lisa starts to say, but Katie leaps to her feet, her body stiff, her eyes blazing.

"That's a lie," Katie all but snarls. "Will was nothing but kind to me. He took care of me when no one else would." She tears the little black mic from the neckline of her dress and tosses it onto her empty chair. "I'm leaving. I won't just sit here and let you spread these vicious lies."

I stand and grab Katie's arm, halting her from storming off. Our gazes meet, hers full of so much fury and rage I almost let her go.

But all that fury and rage isn't aimed at me. It's mostly for my father. And Lisa.

"Are you done here, too?" Lisa asks me sweetly. "I understand if you both want to go."

This went nothing like I thought it would. I figured Lisa would put together something more like a reunion piece. Katie and me reminiscing over old times, though that isn't quite how I would phrase it. Not that I want to wax nostalgic about one of the most horrific experiences of my life . . .

"I'm done," Katie says with finality, her voice flat as she gives Lisa one last dismissive glance. She lifts her gaze to mine. "Are you?"

Slowly I nod, releasing my hold on her. "You know we're just going round and round in circles, right?" I ask Lisa. "This will never end the way you or the rest of the media or even my father wants it to. You're all looking for something that's not there."

"Your father says it's there," Lisa says coldly, crossing her arms in front of her. She's pissed that we're leaving. I really couldn't care less.

"Who are you going to believe? A convicted murderer sitting on death row or me?" I tug my microphone off and toss it on my chair like Katie just did.

"He may be the convicted murderer, but he has nothing to lose. He's already in prison. You, on the other hand, do." Lisa arches a brow, silently daring me to challenge her. "You have everything to lose, Will. Don't forget, the truth will set you free."

I don't say another word. I can't. All I can see is black. So much fucking black as the anger fills me, slow and steady, my hands curling into fists, my mind full of nothing but the need to lash out. With my words. My hands. With everything I've got.

But I do none of that. I can't. Unlike my father, I have control.

Instead, I walk away, never looking back, not even waiting for Katie. The need to be alone is too powerful to ignore. I exit the building, by some miracle finding the same hired car that brought me here idling by the curb. I climb into the backseat, slamming the door behind me.

"Get me the hell out of here," I mutter, leaning my head back against the seat and closing my eyes. I scrub a hand over my face, Lisa's words running through my head again and again, like a taunt.

Like a dare.

"Back to the hotel, sir?"

"That works," I say, sounding exhausted even to my own ears. I need a drink. A nap. Or maybe something to hit so I can get rid of all of this built-up frustration within me. There's a gym in the hotel. If they have a punching bag, I plan on beating the hell out of it for as long as I can stand to.

More than anything I need Katie. We need to talk about that fucked-up interview with Lisa. What my father said about me. I have no idea what her message from him was like, but I can't imagine it was any good.

How that asshole is still able to reach into our lives and stir this shit up, I'm not sure. But I can't live like this. Not any longer. I'm done talking about him and what he did to us. Talking to Lisa Swanson only gives her more rope to hang me with. I haven't talked to anyone in years, since I was a kid and this first happened, and the moment I do, it immediately bites me in the ass.

We need to move on, Katie and I. But how can we when our trauma is what brought us together in the first place? My father is the tether that binds us to each other. Will he also be the one who keeps us apart?

Breathing in deeply, I glare out the window, watching the city pass by. I need some time before I can talk to Katie. Time to calm the seething rage inside of me. Because it seethes.

And I don't want her to see me like this.

Ever.

KATHERINE

My texts to Will/Ethan/whatever I should call him go unanswered. After the fourth one I give up, not wanting to be a nag. Not willing to be one of those crazed girls who never leave their man alone.

Not that I believe he's *my* man. Whatever we have, I can't even begin to describe it anymore. It's confusing. A bit of a mess.

Fine, it's a total mess.

The other thing that turned into a total mess? That interview we just did with Lisa. Talk about a waste of our time—and Lisa's. I'm scared to see what will air tomorrow. To say it will be nothing short of a total disaster is probably being kind.

She tried to talk to me before I left. Tried to dig for more information on Will and what happened during my time with him. Her gaze was sharp, her words succinct. She wanted to know if I was being truthful with myself, or if I'd immersed myself in some sort of hero-worship complex over Will.

Immediately offended, I walked out much like he did . . .

And haven't seen him since.

Restless, I pace around the hotel room, chewing on my thumbnail, answering a text from my sister when she asks what I'm up to and if I want to come spend the weekend with her. She has no idea I'm in San Francisco and I'm not about to tell her. I also really don't want to hang out with her and her boyfriend for two days. I make the excuse that I have school-work to catch up on and decline.

Thank God.

I change out of my tights and dress, putting on a pair of jeans and a white T-shirt, throwing on my favorite black cardigan over it. I'm hungry. Nerves killed my appetite earlier, so now I'm starving. I'd love to go out for dinner—San Francisco has some of the best restaurants—but I'm not about to go out alone.

Rummaging around the desk, I find the room service menu and am reading over my options when my phone dings, letting me know I have a text message. I pull my phone out of my sweater pocket and check who it's from.

Ethan.

Sorry I took off. I needed some time alone.

I bite my lower lip, contemplating how to answer when another text comes through.

Lisa pissed me off. Worked out my frustration by going to the gym here in the hotel.

Relief floods me. As silly as I know it is, I worried he might have been mad at me. Worse, I was afraid he'd left San Francisco for good. Not that I believe he would ditch me, but I wasn't sure. Do I even know the real him? Were those glimpses he's shown me for real? Or him playing at being what he thought I wanted?

My phone dings yet again.

I'm in my room. Just took a shower. Do you have dinner plans? Want to go somewhere?

Yes, yes, yes. I want to, but I don't want to appear too eager. Which is stupid. We're beyond playing games, aren't we?

I'd love to go to dinner. I'm starving.
Me too. Do you need time to get ready?

I'm already grabbing my white Converse sneakers to slip on and I hurriedly text him my answer.

Ready now. Want to come to my room to pick me up?
I'm in 926.
Be there in a few.

I dash into the bathroom, my untied shoelaces flying around my feet as I finger-comb my hair, then run my fingers underneath my eyes, removing any eyeliner or mascara smudges. I grab a lip gloss out of my open makeup bag and slick it on my lips, taking a step back to see if I look okay.

What does he see in me? The poor little girl who still needs to be rescued? Or does he see me as a woman, the woman I am today? Considering how intimate we became in such a short amount of time, I have to assume he sees me as a woman. But I'm guessing the line is blurred for him, and now that I know Ethan is also Will, the line has become completely blurred for me as well.

Seeing him at the studio looking so different yet the same, it was easy to fall into this . . . surreal way of thinking. Who I had in front of me, and then beside me, wasn't Ethan at all. It was Will.

It sounds completely crazy but the transformation was there, at least in my head. Maybe I'm doing this to cope. Maybe I really am going crazy. Right after everything happened, my parents wanted to put me on antidepressants.

There's no denying that I was depressed. But even at that young of an age, I didn't want to be medicated. My head was already deeply submersed in a fog. I didn't think I needed to add to it.

Though I'm thinking if I keep mixing the two sides of Ethan/Will, I might need to start taking some sort of medication to keep me steeped in reality. Or perhaps up my therapy with Sheila . . .

A knock sounds and I go to the door, my pace slowing as I take a deep breath and paste a smile on my face when I turn the handle and open it. He's standing in the doorway, wearing jeans and an open black flannel button-down shirt, a white T-shirt beneath it. His hair is damp, curling around his neck and ears, and he's wearing his glasses once more, five o'clock shadow already appearing on his cheeks. He doesn't smile in return, but his gaze roves over me almost hungrily.

An answering hunger throbs in my blood and I clutch the door handle tightly, almost afraid to let go. "Hi."

"Hey." He practically glowers, but it's a good look for him. Reminding me of the sullen Will of my youth. The boy who didn't want to help, but couldn't stop himself from saving me anyway. "You ready?"

"Let me grab my purse." I open the door wider, indicating he should come in and he does, his spicy clean scent lingering in the air as he walks past me. Taking a deep breath, I let the door close, watching him as he goes straight toward the window, peering outside at the city before us.

The sky is at that perfect moment of twilight, when it's not quite fully dark, but not really light, either. It's an almost velvety mix of blue and purple. The stars should be just making their appearance, though I really don't spot any now. The city lights are too bright.

"The sky reminds me of your eyes."

Grabbing my phone, I pause, surprised at his words. "Really?" I squeak like an idiot and I briefly close my eyes, shake my head. Thank God he can't see me.

He doesn't answer me. Instead he shoves his hands into his front pockets, scanning the city spread out before us. I start to go for my purse, practically tiptoeing behind him. He seems on edge, upset still, and I'm not quite sure what to say.

"You have a better view," he finally says, never turning away from the window. "I can almost see Alcatraz from here."

I halt in grabbing my purse, watching him as he continues to stand there. Tall, immovable, his shoulders wide, his legs slightly spread, as if he's braced and ready for battle. The anger and frustration seem to vibrate from his body, and I'm tempted to go to him and offer him comfort.

But I'm not sure if comfort is what he wants.

He glances over his shoulder, his dark, intense gaze pinning me in place. "Do you think if my father got put up at Alcatraz, he would've found a way to escape?"

I shrug, wondering where he's going with this. "I'm not sure," I say hesitantly. "He hasn't tried to escape where he's at now." San Quentin State Prison is where they hold all men who've been condemned to death in the state.

"Yes he has." He turns to face me, his expression grim. "Once, four years ago."

My mouth drops open. I would have been . . . seventeen. I don't remember hearing about this. "How do you know?"

"They notified me." He shrugs, as if it's no big deal. "He was stopped before it ever got too far. He wasn't even officially missing. They just found evidence that he was planning an escape and they wanted to keep me informed."

I wonder if they notified my parents. I'm going to guess

yes, but they never thought it necessary to let me know. But why? Were they afraid I'd freak out? Probably.

"Was he punished?"

"He was put in solitary confinement and they kept a close watch on him. I don't think they consider him a threat any longer. He's an old man, starting to panic now that his execution date is drawing near."

"What would you do if he ever escaped?" I ask, my voice low, my heart in my throat. I don't know what I would do. San Quentin is maximum security. Not many inmates have escaped or even attempted to escape that prison.

A prison that's just north of San Francisco, meaning it's not very far from here or where I live.

The thought sends an icy shiver down my spine.

"Arm myself with as many weapons as possible and wait for him. He knows my address now. He could find me easily."

"Do you think he'd try?"

"I don't know, Katie, and I really don't want to talk about him anymore." He approaches me, resting his hands lightly on my shoulders, his gaze never leaving mine. "Let's go out to dinner and talk about . . . nothing that has to do with today or our past or any of that. Let's talk about now. Or tomorrow. The future. Just nothing to do with you and me and eight years ago and my father." He grazes his thumbs along the base of my neck, a gentle touch that warms my skin, and my lips part on a soft gasp. His touch feels so good.

Too good. Too real. Making me want more . . .

"Are you okay with that?" He bends his knees a little, so he can look directly into my eyes. His hands are still on my shoulders, his thumbs still touching my throat. I'm held captive by his gaze, his touch, his voice. Everything about him grabs hold of me and refuses to let go.

I nod, unable to speak past the sudden lump in my throat. He looks relieved, pulling me close so he can press his mouth to my forehead. I close my eyes, savoring the touch of his lips on my skin, his nearness, the tenderness in his gesture. But I can also feel the restrained hunger, the need he has for me.

And I want to give in.

# ETHAN

We exit the large front doors of the hotel and start walking, in search of a restaurant nearby. We're right in the middle of downtown; there has to be quality dining around. Plus, I don't feel like driving my car through a city I'm unfamiliar with.

My mood is still dark. Going to the hotel gym helped. Taking a long shower and standing under the hot spray of water while I jerked off helped, too. But it still didn't take off the edge. Just dulled it a little bit.

"Are you in the mood for anything in particular?" I ask, glancing in her direction.

Katie's keeping pace, walking beside me, the lights shining on her dark blond head and making her hair look brighter. "Not really. Are you?"

You, I want to tell her. *I'm in the mood for you.*

I've been patient. Respectful—because I want to be, not just because I think it's the right thing to do. She needed her space. I fucked with her head; it's the least I can do.

But after everything I've endured today, for the least few days, weeks, months—hell, fucking *years*—I feel like I'm about to break. Seeing her so soft and uninhibited, being in her hotel room like I was only a few minutes ago, I wanted her. The bed called to me and instantly I imagined myself pushing her onto the mattress. But I only allowed myself to touch her gently, my fingers on her neck, my lips pressed to her forehead. All I could think was that I wanted to take.

Take whatever Katie would let me have.

"I don't care," I finally say to her. "I'm so hungry I could go for anything."

"Me too. I haven't really eaten anything today," she admits.

"You must be starving."

"I am." She smiles up at me and at that exact moment someone passing by bumps into her shoulder, sending her knocking into me. I grab hold of her, gripping her arm and keeping her steady.

"You all right?"

She nods. "I'm fine." Though she does appear a little agitated.

I think the city and all of the people who inhabit it make her nervous. She doesn't go out much, having chosen to keep herself fairly secluded most of her adult life. She keeps looking around warily, still clutching my arm, tracking everyone who passes us by.

"They're not going to jump you," I murmur close to her ear and she tilts her head toward me, a secret smile on her face.

"Too many people make me anxious," she admits.

"What a surprise."

Her head jerks up, eyes wide with shock. "You say you don't want to talk about it, so you'll just give me a hard time instead?"

"Sorry," I mutter because it was an asshole thing for me to say and she called me out on it, which I deserved.

We don't speak, the bustle of the crowd silencing us, forcing us to pay attention. We pass a few delis and coffee shops, a bakery that's closed. I don't want something quick and easy, and I don't think Katie does, either, or else she could have suggested going into any of the places we just passed.

I want to sit down and have an actual meal. Maybe with a candle on the table, casting Katie in flickering golden light, a little mood music playing in the background while we eat. If that makes me a romantic, then so be it. The only person I want to be romantic with is Katie.

The heart wants what it wants, or whatever that bullshit line is.

We stop in front of a Japanese restaurant. The crowd of people waiting outside to get a table makes me think that's a good sign. "This place looks popular."

"Mmm." She makes a noncommittal noise and lets go of my arm, heading to the open doorway where a menu is posted on the wall. I follow, stopping directly behind her. Unable to resist, I rest my hands on her shoulders lightly, reading the menu along with her.

"You like sushi?" I ask.

She shrugs, and my hands rise with the movement but I don't remove them. It's like I can't. I'm drawn to her tonight. More than usual. We feel . . . different together. Like we're not Ethan and Katherine with the heavy burden of our pasts weighing us down. "I've never had sushi before."

"Seriously?" Even with my shitty, broke-ass upbringing eating mac-n-cheese or ramen every other night for dinner, I eventually discovered sushi.

"I've tried to warn you. I'm one of those annoying sheltered kids." She turns her head, smiling up at me. "I'd like to try it."

"I'll go put our name in," I tell her.

"I'll go with you."

I take her hand as we walk inside, keeping her close as I pull her through the tight crowd. Just inside, the hostess waits behind a sleek metal stand, busily flipping through a schedule book and ignoring the ringing phone sitting directly in front of her. I don't utter a word, I'm fairly certain she's not even aware of our presence, yet she holds up one long, elegantly manicured finger. Her nail polish is bloodred, matching the shade of her lipstick. "One moment, please," she murmurs as she answers the phone.

As I wait for her to finish the call, I glance around, taking in the interior. It has a clean, modern industrial feel to it, with steel-paneled walls and giant pipes crisscrossing the ceiling. The lighting is dim, the bar near the hostess stand packed, and though I can't see beyond into the dining area, I'm sure it's full, too.

"How can I help you?" the hostess asks coolly after she hangs up the phone.

"Do you have a table for two available?"

She scans the book in front of her, her mouth turned down in a frown. "I'm afraid not—oh! We have a spot at the sushi bar." Glancing up, she grimaces. "It's crowded, though. You'll have to sit next to each other really close."

Sounds perfect to me. I turn to check with Katie and she nods her approval.

"We'll take it."

The hostess leads us to the sushi bar, where two chairs right next to each other are empty. One butts right up against the wall and I let go of Katie's hand, ushering her to that one before I sit next to her. The hostess hands us our menus, then leaves.

"What do you recommend?" Katie asks as she scans the menu. A strand of hair falls across her cheek as she reads and she tucks it behind her ear, her fingers sliding along the curve of her ear, ending up at her lobe, where she absently plays with the pearl stud earring she's wearing.

I stare at her, mesmerized. I could watch her do that all day, which is fucking ridiculous but true. It's the tiniest things I notice, those small moments I want to keep imbedded in my memory so I don't forget.

Don't forget her, or this night, here in a sushi restaurant in downtown San Francisco, sitting so close together our knees brush and I can feel the warmth from her body seeping into mine.

Realizing I'm staring, I go over the various items on the menu, pointing out a few sushi rolls I've had in the past at other restaurants.

"Do you like it hot? Spicy?" I ask her.

She scrunches up her nose and shakes her head, her mouth pursed in a cute pout. "Not really. I'm sort of a wimp when it comes to hot stuff."

"So no wasabi for you." I grab my still-wrapped chopsticks and point them at the clump of wasabi and ginger on the square white plate the waitress just placed in front of me. Katie stares warily at her own plate, a little sneer curling her upper lip.

"What can I get you two to drink?" the waitress asks.

I order sake for both of us, and a vegetable tempura appetizer and a dragon roll for us to share. Spend a few minutes trying to teach her how to use chopsticks, which she fails miserably at, and watch as she takes her first sip of sake, making that adorable scrunched-nose face again as she shakes her head.

"It's so strong." She takes a big drink of her water and I watch her. Her shiny pink lips as they curve around the glass, the elegant line of her throat when she swallows. I briefly curl my hands into fists, resting them on the table in front of me so I don't do something stupid like reach out and grab her.

"You don't like it?" I knock back my entire small glass in one swallow, then give myself a refill with the pitcher our waitress left for us. "I like the way it makes me feel numb."

She stares at me, her lips parted, her eyes full of sadness and worry. I said the wrong damn thing. I shouldn't have said that. She doesn't need to know numbing myself is the only way I can get through this night without touching her.

I don't want to feel a damn thing tonight. And being with Katie like this, all I can do is feel. The alluring warmth that seems to radiate from her body, the scent of her hair and perfume. She looked gorgeous earlier during the interview, in the dark gray dress that fit her like a glove, skimming her curves. Curves I've had my hands on, a body that I wish I could lose myself in again . . .

Within minutes our appetizer arrives and we dive in, the two of us devouring as much as we can, not giving conscious thought to the fact that we still have an entire sushi roll coming for us. Katie keeps dropping her vegetables onto her plate, still unable to master the chopsticks. The waitress reappears minutes later with our sushi roll and when Katie tries to pluck a piece off the platter it slips from her chopsticks, falling apart all over her plate.

She laughs. "I'm an epic fail."

"A cute epic fail," I amend, taking another swig of my sake. My head is buzzing. My body is warm. I'm definitely feeling no pain.

Her laughter dies. "You really think so?"

This girl . . . she's going to drive me insane. "You're beautiful, Katie." I pause and she looks down, her teeth catching her lower lip. "Has no one ever told you that before?"

She slowly lifts her head, those big blue eyes about to be my undoing. "Only you ever have."

"Well, everyone's fucking blind then." I grab my sake glass and urge her to do the same, which she does. "Let's toast to your beauty."

"Ethan . . ." Her voice drifts and for one odd moment, I want her to call me Will again. I don't feel like a worthless shit when Katie calls me Will. I feel like a better man, like Katie's fucking hero when she says my real name. Now *Ethan* feels strange.

Doesn't feel like me.

"To Katie and her beautiful face." I raise my glass but she doesn't. I keep going. "To her beautiful body. Her beautiful soul, her beautiful heart—her beautiful everything. Who despite every stupid, hurtful, horrible thing I've done to her, is still here. With me. I don't deserve her." I wave my glass, indicating again that I want her to pick hers up.

She finally does, tentatively lifting it into the air, close to mine. "Don't say tha—"

"Why not?" I ask, cutting her off. "It's true, Katie. I don't deserve you." I clink my glass to hers and then bring mine to my lips. "Bottoms up," I mumble before I knock it back.

Katie takes a delicate sip from her glass before setting it on the table. She's turned back into the prim and proper girl, unsure how to behave. "I think you're drunk."

"I hope to hell I'm drunk. Then maybe I can forget for one night." I grab the pitcher to refill my glass, but it's empty. And there's no waitress in sight.

She frowns. "Forget what?"

"That I'm not allowed to touch you, that I can't have you ever again. But I'll take whatever scraps you want to give me, though deep down, it'll never be enough." Pissed that I revealed so much, I take Katie's glass and polish off the last of the sake, pretending for the moment that I just tasted her by placing my lips on the same exact spot she drank from only moments ago.

I'm a fucked-up, pitiful mess. Hopelessly gone over a girl.

A girl who can't trust me. A girl who *shouldn't* trust me. I'll only hurt her again. It's what I do. I push everyone away, just like she does.

We're more alike than we ever want to admit, Katie and I. Moving aimlessly through life with no real purpose. Lonely. So fucking lonely. For a brief, shining moment we had each other and we thought that would be enough.

Though I always knew it would end. I'm the liar. I'm the one who fucked up on her and she can't forgive me. I've blown my chance. Blown the only chance I had at happiness.

At love.

And I don't know how to change it.

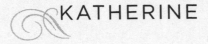# KATHERINE

His behavior is throwing me off. Making me uneasy. The sake isn't helping matters, but it's also keeping him . . . honest. Almost painfully so.

"We should order more sake." He sits up straighter, raising his arm to wave down the waitress, and I reach for him, my hands landing on his chest as I try to gain some control over him.

"We should ask for the check," I tell him, relieved when the waitress comes over to us.

"You two doing okay?" she asks sweetly.

"Just the check, please," I say at the exact moment Ethan requests more sake. I shake my head and smile at the waitress, hoping she understands. "We don't really need any more sake."

The waitress offers me a quick smile and nods. "I'll be right back."

I release my grip on his chest and sit back in my seat. The loss I feel after not touching him is strong. Ridiculous. I reach for my purse and take out my wallet.

He shakes his head. "No. I'm paying. I'm the one who asked you to dinner."

"That's fine," I agree. "Thank you."

"You're welcome." His gaze turns darker and he reaches out, resting his hand on my knee, curling his fingers around it. "I would do anything for you, Katie."

His hand slides up to my thigh and I release a shaky breath. "I know."

"Anything you want, I'll give you. Just name it."

There are so many things I could say. An entire list of all the things I want, only from him. "We should get you back to the hotel," I say softly, regretting the disappointment I see flicker in his eyes.

"So you don't want me, then. I get it." He rises to his feet, glancing around the restaurant like he wants to destroy the entire place. His jaw is tight, his eyes narrowed. He looks intimidating.

A little mean.

"That's not what I'm saying," I start, but he cuts me off with just a look.

"Don't try and make me feel better, Katie," he says bitterly. "I ruined it. This. Us. I should've never lied. Not that you'd have been with me if you knew the truth anyway. And now I've gone and fucked it all up."

The waitress appears with the check and he pulls out his wallet, handing a credit card along with the bill back to her. The minute she's gone he starts in again. The lack of sake is forgotten—thank goodness.

"I don't have a lot of regrets in my life. I can't, or else I'd believe it was all just one big regretful moment after the other, you know? But I do regret not telling you. I should've been honest with you from the beginning." He turns away from me, blowing out a harsh breath. "I'm sorry. I can say it a thousand times, but I know it won't change anything."

It changes everything. I want to say something else, something more, but what? My lips part and I reach for him, my hands catching on his shirt, clinging to him. He looks down at my hands, then slowly lifts his head, our gazes meeting.

"Say we have another chance. Please." He starts to laugh, shaking his head. "I'm going to sound like my father right now, but I need your forgiveness. I need it. I don't think I can live without it."

I tug on his shirt, hard. He can't talk like that, like . . . what? He can't live without me? I need to shake some sense into his head. "You can survive just fine without me," I murmur, not wanting anyone else to hear us. Not that anyone is paying us any attention in this crowded restaurant. "You've done it for years."

He laughs again, the sound almost painful. "It was a miserable existence, Katie. Katherine." His expression turns somber and he touches me. Drifts his fingers over my hair, tucking a strand behind my ear, touching my cheek. "I should probably call you Katherine. That's what everyone else calls you."

"I like it when you call me Katie." I like it when he touches me, too. Despite everything, I feel comfortable with him. And I feel comfortable with hardly anyone. "What do you want me to call you?"

He frowns, his fingers pausing on my cheek. "What do you want to call me? Major asshole?"

I start to laugh despite our serious conversation. I can't believe he just said that. He cracks a smile, too. "No. I just . . . with everything that happened earlier, I got sort of confused. I called you Will and I wouldn't mind if I could keep calling you that."

His hand drops from my face and he leans in close. "Is that what you want to call me?"

"Would you be offended?"

"Sort of. I don't know. I need to get used to this." He slowly shakes his head, blows out a harsh breath. "For you, I'll be whoever you need. Whatever you want, Katie."

Whatever I want. Those words are loaded with so much promise. I know he would give me whatever I wanted. If I were a mean girl, I'd take total advantage. Demand he get down on his knees and beg for my forgiveness, make him humiliate himself in order to earn my approval. He'd deserve no less. What he did to me was . . . horrible.

But his intention was never to hurt me. I realize that now. So why deny myself what I want when he could make me happy? Would I rather live a miserable existence all alone and missing him?

"Do you mean that?" I ask.

His eyes seem to glow as he watches me. "I will never lie to you again. I mean every word I say."

"Then take me back to the hotel," I murmur. Feeling emboldened, I rest my hand on his knee, that electric connection we have coming to life, sparking between us.

The moment the waitress returns with his credit card, he's grabbing my hand and practically dragging me out of the restaurant, muttering quick apologies to the people we bump into as we exit. The sidewalk has cleared and we walk hurriedly toward the hotel. I'm thankful I wore my sneakers instead of heels. His stride is long as it eats up the sidewalk and I have to walk twice as fast to keep up with him.

No words are spoken, but the urgency between us is palpable. Undeniable. We enter the hotel side by side, the hushed quiet of the lobby making me feel obvious, like I'm wearing a sign around my neck that says, *Hey! We're running to our hotel room to get naked.*

I school my expression, going for cool and collected, while inside my stomach is on a tumultuous roller-coaster ride, climbing high and dipping low again and again. My hand is clutched tightly in his as he leads us to the bank of elevators, hitting the up button, and the doors behind us automatically open as if waiting for us.

The moment we enter the car, he hits the ninth-floor button and the doors slide shut. His arms are around me, his mouth hovering above mine. "Is this what you wanted?" he murmurs just before he kisses me.

His mouth on mine is exactly what I want. What I've craved for days. Weeks. I clutch him close, my arms sneaking around his neck, my fingers playing with the soft hair at his nape. He presses me against the elevator wall, a low groan sounding from deep in his chest when I part my lips and meet his tongue with my own.

The doors sweep open silently, a soft ding indicating we're on our floor. He releases me as fast as he grabbed me, taking my hand and leading me toward my hotel room. "Is your room okay?" he asks, glancing over his shoulder to look at me.

I nod, unable to speak. My lips tingle from that too brief kiss. My entire body tingles. I want this, but I'm also apprehensive. I'm still not wholly comfortable with sex. Our first experience together was good, but I struggled to relax.

I still struggle.

We stop at my door and I pull the card key from my purse, inserting it into the slot. He stands just behind me, one hand at my waist, the other pushing my hair away from my neck so he can place his mouth there, at that sensitive little spot just behind my ear. He breathes me in, his lips parted, his teeth grazing my skin, and I shiver, pushing open the door so the two of us practically fall into the room.

The door shuts behind us and then we become a frenzy of hands and arms and legs and stumbling feet, our mouths finding each other, parting when he removes his flannel shirt, finding each other again only to separate when he tugs my cardigan from my arms. Clothes fall to the floor, shoes are kicked off, the only sounds our heavy breaths and connected mouths. I hear a clattering sound and I know he just tore off his glasses and set them . . . somewhere.

God, they could be anywhere. I'm so overcome and he is, too, both of us reaching for each other, hands sliding beneath clothes and warming cool skin. The room is dark though the curtains are still wide open, the buildings standing tall just beyond the thick glass like mighty spheres of light. They cast a soft glow within the room that renders us into nothing but shifting shadows that meld together, only to come apart.

And then drift together again.

His arms are around me, his mouth fused with mine, his hands slipping beneath the hem of my T-shirt. His fingers are hot as they brush against my skin, along my sides, igniting a restless heat that starts low in my belly. It's all happening so fast I can hardly catch my breath, can hardly think, but maybe that's a good thing. My body is running on pure, basic need and it's a wildly exhilarating ride.

"Tell me what you want," he whispers into my neck, his warm, damp lips moving against my skin and making me shiver. "Whatever you need, I want to give it to you."

I pull away from him so I can see his face, his eyes glittering in the dim light, his chest rising and falling, brushing against mine. I'm filled with the need to tear off my shirt and tear off his so we can be skin to skin. Heart to heart. "All I want is you. The real you."

"It's yours. I'm yours." He brushes the hair away from my face, his fingers drifting across my skin, his gaze hot as it roves over me. "I've missed you like this."

I suddenly feel shy, which is ridiculous because he's seen me naked. Vulnerable. At my worst times and my best. He's seen me in every way possible, he knows me better than any-one else, and I realize in this single, heart-stopping moment that he is the only person in this entire world who understands me, who knows me inside out.

And I can't deny it any longer.

I'm in love with him.

ETHAN

She whispers my name again and again as I kiss her. I don't even notice at first exactly what she's saying. I just keep my lips on hers as much as possible, my tongue sweeping inside her mouth, my hands wandering everywhere I can reach. I'm consumed with her, *consuming* her, and when I end the kiss to let her catch her breath, my forehead pressed to hers, I realize exactly what she's saying.

Will.

I don't correct her because I'm just running with it. It's a little uncomfortable, her insistence that she call me Will. And truly, she's the only one who makes it okay to be Will Monroe. But it's not who I am. Not anymore. My father has been a source of shame for so many years, the minute I could shed the name like a snake sheds its skin I went for it. Doing it legally turned into such a giant pain in the ass that I almost gave up, but it had been worth the time and money. So I could rid myself of William Aaron Monroe once and for all.

Yet here I am, allowing Katie to call me Will again. Reveling in it, really, because once upon a time, many years ago, there was a girl held captive and I was the boy who saved her. And though everyone cast their suspicions upon me, I prevailed because the girl never deviated from her belief in me.

She still hasn't. The suspicions are constantly flung at me. The enemy is the one who's now being held captive, yet his evil manages to permeate our lives.

I'm fucking sick of it.

Tonight, in this anonymous hotel room in this anonymous city, Katie and I need to purge ourselves of the memories and the pain and the bullshit once and for all.

Without a word I guide her toward the bed, walking her backward until her legs bump against the mattress. Kissing her softly on the lips, I gently push her shoulders and she falls onto the center of the bed, her mouth rounded in a shocked O. I tear off my T-shirt and let it drop to the floor. Unbuckle my belt and pull it through the loops on my jeans, dropping it on top of the T-shirt, the buckle clanking against the floor.

Laying myself bare for her.

Katie watches me, her eyes seeming to rove everywhere, all over me. She doesn't stop me from undressing, her eyes wide and full of curiosity. It's easy to forget that she's never been with anyone else, at least not in an intimate way.

I think of who else she's been with and I avert my head, clenching my jaw. It makes me sick to my stomach, what happened to her when she was only a child. If I could change anything, I would change that. What she suffered was . . . too much. That she's so strong and survived it, overcame it, leaves me in awe. Now it's up to me to take care of her. Remind her again how it can be between two people who care for each other.

If I had the chance, there's no doubt in my mind that I would kill him. Tear him apart with my bare hands, all the while making sure he knew exactly who was squeezing the very last breath out of him. I'd not only kill him for her, but I'd do it for me. For the young boy that I once was, for all the chances he tried to steal away from me. For the mere fact that he tried to mold me into himself yet it didn't work.

For that alone, I win.

I fucking win.

Taking a deep breath, I turn to look at her again, see the uncertainty on her face, and I want to ease it away with my words. My promise.

My vow to her.

"I tried to deny how I felt about you," I say, undoing my jeans and pushing them off my hips so they fall around my feet, leaving me in just my boxer briefs, and I kick them off. "I've denied it for years. From the moment we met, you touched me. I just didn't realize it then because I was young and stupid. Lost and ruined. And so fucking angry that he put me in that position. I didn't want to be anyone's hero."

She blinks up at me, her lips parting as if she wants to say something, and I shake my head, needing to get this out all at once.

"That first interview—seeing you, all grown up, so damn beautiful—made me realize I wasn't over you. I'd never gotten over you and I was curious. I had to find you. When I did, I told myself, 'I'll talk to her just once. I'll make sure she's safe.' But I couldn't stop. I couldn't resist you." I kick my jeans out of the way, kneel down to tear off my socks, and then I crawl onto the bed, until I'm right in front of her, on my hands and knees.

Fitting.

Her arms go back, her hands braced on the bed as she leans away from me, and I take a deep breath, hoping I don't mess this up. It feels like this is my last chance.

"I'm in love with you, Katie. Not just because we share a connection from our past, but because I think you're an amazing, thoughtful, giving woman. And I want to be a better man for you. I want to earn back your trust, I want to ensure your safety, but more than anything, I want you in my life. I need you." I pause, unable to read her expression. She doesn't look like she's upset, but hell, I don't know. I've never told a woman that I love her before.

I've never told anyone that I loved them before. I'm not one hundred percent sure if I even know what love is. But whatever I feel for Katie has to be the closest thing to it.

"You're in love with me."

I nod, fear strangling my insides and making me unable to speak.

She rears up on her knees and pulls her T-shirt off, tossing it over the side of the bed. "If you can bare your body and soul to me, then I should be able to do the same for you."

My heart is pounding as she reaches behind her and unhooks her bra, the cups, simple white satin trimmed with lace, loosening around her chest. I get up on my knees and practically lunge for her, stopping her from pulling the bra off because I want that privilege.

"Let me undress you," I whisper, smoothing my fingers along her bra straps, touching the soft skin just beneath. She shivers, goosebumps chasing after my touch, and I gently tug the straps down her arms until they fall at her elbows. She shrugs out of the bra and remains before me, her breasts on display, those pretty pink nipples hard and tempting.

I cup her breasts and she closes her eyes, tilting her head back. I play with her nipples with my thumbs, moving closer to her until my mouth is on hers once more and I'm devouring her.

She moans into my mouth and I'm overcome. Overcome with love and lust and need. I ease her back onto the bed, my mouth never leaving hers, fingers fumbling with the snap and zipper of her jeans. I spread the denim as wide as I can get it and touch her there, caressing the sensitive skin of her lower belly, tracing my fingers along the edge of her panties.

I wanted to take it slow. Kiss her all over her body, drive her wild until I have her begging for me. But my plan is completely waylaid by the feel of her skin, the sounds she makes, the taste of her mouth and tongue. My cock strains against my boxer briefs as I move down her body, raining her skin with hot, desperate presses of my mouth. I don't linger, I'm moving on pure, primal need, and I tear her jeans down her legs until they're stuck around her ankles and she's kicking them the rest of the way off, giggling against my lips and making me chuckle, too.

That we can laugh during sex is . . . huge. Major progress for the both of us. I was never one to linger. I treated sex almost like a job, eager to get my satisfaction and then move on.

Not with Katie. I may not be lingering this time around, but that's only because I'm so anxious to be inside her again, I feel close to blowing in my damn shorts.

"Will." She rests her hands on my head and I glance up, my gaze meeting hers, then sweeping over the length of her naked body. I study her like this, laid out before me as I lie on my elbows in between her spread legs, clad in a pair of tiny white panties and nothing else.

Meaning, she's trying to kill me.

"Yeah?" I practically croak but damn, I'm overwhelmed at having her this close, this naked, and having to actually conduct a conversation.

"I love you, too," she whispers, her eyes glowing in the near-darkness. "I just wanted you to know that."

I move back up so I'm lying on top of her, her legs between mine, my cock nestled close. We're face-to-face, chest to chest, and I can feel her heart racing.

Mine is, too.

I curl my arm around the top of her head, my fingers playing in her hair, and she closes her eyes, her lips parting on a soft sigh. "This isn't impossible, is it?"

She opens her eyes, frowning a little. Getting that crease between her eyebrows like she does when she's confused. "What isn't impossible?"

"Us." I nuzzle her cheek, inhaling her scent. I don't think I could ever get tired of smelling her. "We can make this work, can't we?"

"All we can do is try," she whispers, her arms slowly going around me as she holds me close. Her hands drift across my shoulders, her nails lightly scratching my skin, and I shift lower, resting my head in the crook of her neck. "It's not going to be easy."

"Nothing's ever easy for us," I murmur, pressing my mouth against her skin.

"That's true." She pauses in her scratching. "My mom is mad at me."

"Your sister hates me."

"So does Lisa Swanson," she adds.

"That bitch can suck it," I mutter, making her giggle. The sound warms my soul, fills me with so much happiness I could burst. Here I am nestled up close with the woman I love and suffering from a serious case of blue balls, but I don't care.

Talking with Katie, sharing with her, laughing with her . . . is this what I have to look forward to for the rest of my life?

Or will I somehow fuck this up, too?

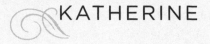

KATHERINE

I scratch Will's back, touch his soft hair, skim my fingers down his arm, tracing the line of his biceps. He's lean but muscular, heavy but keeping most of his weight from sinking me into the mattress, and he's so warm. His skin is practically on fire, and I can feel his erection pressing urgently against the front of his underwear.

"What will people say about us?" I'm voicing my biggest fear, needing him to realize that this is the thing I'm the most afraid of. I know he loves me. I know we can make this work. How can we not? We're both in so deep, there's no working our way out of it now.

And I don't want to. I'm in love with him.

"Who cares what they say?" His mouth moves against my neck when he speaks, tickling my skin, and I try to shift away from him. He only holds me closer.

"I do," I admit, my voice small. "I'm scared all the attention will ruin it. Ruin us."

He lifts his head, shifting so his hands are braced on either side of my head, his intense gaze locked with mine. "Nothing will ruin us. I will never let you go, Katie. Ever. It's like you're embedded in my very soul."

His words touch something deep inside me. I want to believe that no one can ruin what we have. I know he's strong, but am I? What if my mom and my sister turn away from me?

Can I handle the speculation and the rumors and the horrible things complete strangers will say about Will?

About me?

"I won't let anything happen to you or to us. No one can tear us apart. We belong together, Katie. You're mine." He leans down and presses his mouth to mine, a quick yet deep kiss that leaves me breathless. "Fuck what anyone else thinks. What do *you* think?"

"I think I love you." I smile up at him and he smiles in return. "I *know* I love you."

"I love you, too. It feels like I always have," he admits, his voice, his expression, so heartbreakingly sincere I kiss him before I do something crazy.

Like fall apart and cry like a little girl.

The kissing turns into touching and then my panties are gone and his boxer briefs disappear. We're wrapped around each other, skin on skin, no barriers, just us, and I can feel the head of his erection rubbing against me. Hard against soft, hot against wet.

Until he's slowly sinking inside of me, rocking back, withdrawing almost completely before he's pushing back inside, farther this time, making me sigh with pleasure. He's slow, patient, groaning low in his throat, the primal sound urging me to wrap my legs around his hips, sending him even deeper.

We both moan and he gathers me to him with one arm, holding me close as he starts to move inside of me in earnest. The push and pull of our bodies, the friction they cause, I get caught up in it. Lost to the sensation of him moving within me until I'm crying out his name on every thrust, clinging to his sweaty body, positioning myself in a way that every time he pulls out, I see sparks.

"Christ, Katie, you feel too damn good," he murmurs

against my hair, and I nod in agreement, too overcome to speak, too afraid I might say something incoherent since my brain feels like it's about to short-circuit. "Are you close?"

I want to be close. I don't know if I'm close. It feels good. The head of his erection seems to bump something deep inside that sends a bolt of sensation straight through me, but otherwise I . . . am a complete failure when it comes to knowing my body's cues sexually.

Not that I ever really wanted to figure them out. I was too damn scared for too many years, too ashamed to allow myself to have any sort of romantic or sexual feelings.

"I—I don't . . ." I shake my head, embarrassed. Frustrated.

He can sense my struggle. Lifting his torso from mine, he reaches in between us, touching the spot right above where we're joined. I suck in a surprised breath at the wave of pleasure that washes over me and my body arches toward his, like I have no control over myself.

"You like that," he whispers, sounding pleased.

I nod, not wanting to speak. Too busy concentrating on the way his fingers work their magic on my body.

"Does it feel good?" He increases his pace, his finger moving in circles as he begins to thrust again. "Are you going to come, Katie?"

Oh, his voice is so deep. I can feel his every word vibrate in his chest, every moan and ragged breath. I close my eyes and let my senses take over.

My hair rustling against the pillowcase as Will thrusts into me over and over. The gentle slap of skin on skin when he pushes in extra deep, the wet sounds of my body as he strokes me with his skilled fingers—it's too much. I'm on complete sensory overload and my muscles tense, my belly contracts just before I fall completely apart, my body shaking, my hands clutching him close. I breathe against his skin as I fall over that delicious edge and he lets out a strangled groan before he tips over that same edge right along with me.

We cling to each other. Our breaths slowly even out, our hearts, our bodies coming down, until he's rolling us to our sides so we face each other, his softening erection pulling out of me, accompanied by a gushing wetness. Shock renders me still when I realize what just happened.

"We didn't use a condom," I whisper. I didn't think of it because . . . well, I didn't think of it. *Oh my God.* So what's Will's excuse?

"Ah, shit." He blows out a harsh breath and rolls over so he's flat on his back, staring up at the ceiling. He's got his hands linked together and resting on his chest, his dark hair is a riotous mess, and he looks . . . hot. Stressed out but hot. He turns to look at me, his mouth pulled into a frown. "I'm sorry, Katie. I just . . . I don't know what happened. I forgot. Just giving you one more reason not to trust me, I guess."

"Hey." I reach for him, resting my hand on his cheek, turning his head so he's facing me. He's frowning, his eyes clouded with worry. I could be flattered that he was so overcome with need that he didn't think of using protection, but how stupid are we? The last thing we need is to bring a baby into this world. We're messed up enough. "It's okay. Nothing will come of it."

"Are you *sure*?" he asks pointedly. I know what he's referring to. I'm a woman—I get the whole cycle, period thing.

I drop my hand from his face. "I'm sure." And I sound way more confident than I feel. I've always been irregular and I'll skip a period here and there, which is normal for me. "And I trust you. I know you didn't do this on purpose."

It's a big deal, that I can trust him. I can only have faith in the fact that he won't lie to me again. If he does . . .

I have no one to blame but myself for allowing it to happen.

"Yeah, but I should be more responsible." He sounds irritated. "I don't need to put any more burden on you."

I scoot closer to him, resting my folded arms on his chest, gazing up at his handsome face. The dark stubble on his cheeks and jaw, his mouth swollen from our kisses . . . he has a dangerous look to him. I like it. "Nothing you do is ever a burden."

He smiles down at me, a little closed-mouth curve of lips that doesn't really reveal much. "You say that now. Wait until we go back home to our real lives."

"We get to go back to Molly," I point out.

His smile grows. "That's a good thing. I miss her." He's checked on her twice that I know of, calling the local overnight kennel she's staying at.

"We have to watch the interview with us and your—father tomorrow night," I remind him.

His smile fades. Not the most pleasant subject to mention, but it needed to be said. "I don't want to." He sounds like a little kid. Next he'll cross his arms and stomp his feet.

Not that I can blame him.

"We have to. I'm not going to face the potential firing squad unprepared. We have to know what he says. Besides, I'm curious to see how Lisa edits our interviews so we both look like total assholes," I mutter.

He shifts away from me, his expression full of feigned shock and horror. "Did I hear you just now? Did you just say the word *asshole*?"

"Stop." I reach out to hit his shoulder, but he dodges away from me at the last minute. "I'm serious! She's going to make us look bad."

"But like *assholes,* Katie? Such language." He's teasing. Seeing the amused light in his eyes is almost worth all the other crap we've suffered through these last few days. Weeks. Months.

Years.

"Says the man who drops constant f-bombs."

He leans in and kisses me, effectively silencing me. And then proceeds to continue silencing me for the rest of the night.

# AARON

The Bible is lying open on my lap and I try my best to read the words, but my vision is blurred. My mind is unfocused, my heart full of rage, and I wait in my cell, the resentment building, building. Always building. To the point I feel like I'm going to explode.

But I'm always ready to explode. I'm like a volcano, slowly boiling, on the verge of eruption.

Total mass destruction.

"Hey, Monroe." The guard's voice is loud, grating on my nerves, but I do my best to remain still, my back facing toward him. I'm not going to give him the satisfaction of letting him rattle me.

Fuck that.

When I don't respond, the guard lets out an exasperated breath. *Motherfucker.* "Spoke to the warden. He doesn't want you watching your interview tonight. Afraid if we leave it on the TV the other prisoners might give you a bunch of shit and you'll go nutso on them." The guard cackles like an old woman and I grit my teeth together, wishing I could snap his fucking ear off with them. Or maybe his giant, always red nose.

That would show him for making a mockery of me.

"You gonna go nutso in your cell instead, since your ass just got turned down? Better let me know now so we can prepare."

I still don't turn around and I know that makes him angry. I can practically feel his frustration radiate toward me.

Yet I remain in my position, never once looking back.

"If you'd ever give a little, you'd get a little in return, Monroe," the guard says, sounding sullen, like a child.

The sullenness reminds me of Will. My son. The boy who turned his back on me so easily and is now siding with the slut. I took the call from Lisa Swanson last evening. She told me all about their interview. How my boy walked out. How the girl stayed and defended him.

There's something odd there. I don't like it. Why is she defending him? What does she care? That punk fucked everything up. To this day I still hate him for what he did, yet I can't hate him too bad. He is my blood after all.

And you never turn on blood.

I flip through the pages of my Bible, to the spot I marked last with a photo of me and my boy. He might've been around eleven, maybe twelve. We'd gone to the amusement park that summer, lots of times. Was that the summer I worked there? I doubt it. I wouldn't want to hang out at that shit hole on my day off.

But the photo of me and Will makes that place look downright magical. Mythical, almost like a legend. Despite it being a shit hole, that was always one of my favorite places to go.

One of my favorite places to hunt. So many girls. So many pretty, pretty girls . . .

My memories of that day with Will are hazy, made supposedly clearer because of the photo. I'm grinning, my arm slung around Will's shoulders. Will's not smiling at all. He looks unhappy. During those last years together, he always looked unhappy.

Those dark eyes stare at the camera, impenetrable. His mouth a tight line, his face expressionless, stony and full of hate.

Boy always did hate me. Didn't understand he needed those lessons from me to get along in life. It's not easy. Hell, life is fucking hard. So hard, I couldn't function within society and got sent here.

I hate it here.

Barely glancing over my shoulder, I'm relieved to find the guard long gone. Good. Asshole can take a flying leap for all I care. All these dicks who work here are mean as fuck and annoying. Obnoxious. I spend a lot of time alone with my thoughts, with my Bible, and my photos and my memories.

All the memories . . .

Flipping the weathered pages, I find the other photo, the one I cut from a recent gossip magazine. They let that shit come in sometimes and I devour them. I don't know who three-quarters of those people are anymore but it doesn't matter. They're pretty. They're popular.

And there was my Katie Watts in a photo right smack dab in the middle of them, throwing me off. Sitting side by side with Lisa, the both of them smiling for the camera, though her smile isn't as bright as Lisa's, and her eyes are dim, not as sparkly. She doesn't look that happy to be there. But just looking at that stupid picture right at this very moment, I get pissed.

She's getting all the glory, all the attention. Why, because I allowed her to live? Spared her pitiful life instead of ending it? I should've ended it when I had the chance. I had plenty of chances, too. Almost choked her to death that one time. The feel of her soft bones beneath my hands, the little gasps for breath as she struggled against me. Her struggles were pointless. I threw her down on that mattress after I rendered her unconscious and then used her.

That's all they're good for. Useless, good-for-nothing little girl, gullible as all hell considering she fell for my bullshit. My oldest victim out of all of them, the most naïve, stupid little twelve-year-old I could've found. Did anyone realize that? Maybe.

I can't remember.

I look at her some more, trying to find the little girl in her grown-up features, but it's damn hard. She's all woman. Unappealing. All dirtied up now that she's most likely been fucked by some man and ruined forever.

Funny how I'm the one who did all the work and she gets to reap all the credit. Girl needs to learn her lesson. Learn her place.

I turn the pages to the back, to the spot where I cut into the pages, making a perfect skinny rectangle. It's where I keep the little shank I made out of a pen. Fuckers were stupid enough to leave it with me, so I was smart enough to turn it into a weapon. Might come in handy someday.

Might come in handy someday real soon.

Turning it this way and that, I admire my weapon, run my finger along the edge that I sharpened myself, wincing a little. It fucking stings, so it ought to hurt someone real good when I stick 'em with it.

I smile and slip the shank back into its hiding place. I've used that same little hiding spot within my Bible for a couple of years now. Most guards don't think to search so thoroughly in the book of the Lord. They flip through it quick and move on.

Dumbasses. That's all I deal with in this life. A big pile of dumbasses. If I had my way and got out of this hellhole, first thing I'd do is go find Will. He's not a dumbass. Boy is too smart for his own good, just like his daddy. Maybe I could enlist his help to find that stupid bitch Katie Watts. Would Will help me? Would he kill someone for me if I told him to? I doubt it.

But that don't mean I can't force him to do something . . . just to help out good old Pops.

 WILL

Then

Dreams were hopeless. Goals a total crock of shit. Life did nothing but show me again and again that I was wasting my time believing something good could happen to me in my life.

Nothing good ever happened to the boy whose mama had left him the first chance she got. Whose dad was a sick motherfucker who forced him to watch things no little boy should have to witness. Who grew up pissed off and hurt and defensive. Who knew there was no way he stood a chance at having something normal.

I was sitting on the couch in the dimly lit living room, zoning out as I watched TV. *Full House* was running on Nickelodeon and yeah, I was watching a channel made for a bunch of preteen girls, but there was nothing else on.

Besides, *Full House* tapped into all my favorite secret fantasies. The big, happy family who took care of one another no matter what, and even better, this particular family was unique, closer to my story.

Well. Not quite. The show might have had the single dad like mine, but that was where the similarities ended compared to my dear old dad. They had Uncle Jesse and the girls and Joey, and then Jesse married the hot Becky and everything was really coming together then. Pure fantasy stuff at that point, all those people seemingly living together in that giant house. One big, happy family.

Something I had no experience with whatsoever.

The door leading to the garage creaked open and there was my dad, standing in the middle of the kitchen and glancing around the room in disgust. "What the fuck happened in here, boy?"

I winced at the sound of his voice. He sounded drunk. I glanced over the couch and caught a glimpse of him. Red-faced and sneering, hands resting on hips as he surveyed all that he saw. Like the mighty king had come home to lord over his piece-of-shit castle.

"You didn't clean the kitchen like I told you to," he bellowed. He was always yelling. I don't think he realized that after a while, I just tuned him out. It was a lot more effective if he didn't yell as much, so when he finally did, I knew he was fucking pissed.

But my old man wasn't that smart.

"I'll clean it in a minute," I called, my focus still on the show on the TV. I needed to finish the fantasy, and then I'd wash his damn dirty dishes. Maybe pretending I shared the duty with someone else would help soften the blow. I wished like hell I had siblings. A little brother or sister or even better, an understanding older brother. One who would take me to the park along with his friends so we could all hang out. That would've been real nice. Anything would be nicer than what I had.

"Damn it, Will. You need to pay fucking attention for once!" He appeared in front of me like magic, since he was always good at sneaking around. He snapped off the TV with a vicious flick of his wrist and a snarl on his face. I gazed up at him, pissed he ended my show before it was done, but I knew my cue. Rising to my feet, I went to the kitchen without saying a word, grimacing at the piles of dirty dishes in the sink. There were flies buzzing around and everything stunk.

How the fuck long did this shit sit here before he finally asked me to help him clean it?

The door from the garage opened again, and this time a woman entered the kitchen. She looked young, early twenties, I don't know. I'm not good at judging ages. She was wearing a pair of dirty cutoff denim shorts and a raggedy old pale red T-shirt. No shoes. Dark-haired. Her eyes were big and brown and full of fear.

He probably picked her up behind the bar he liked to frequent. She looked like a damn Dumpster diver, probably some meth whore who was looking to score, and he promised her some drugs in exchange for a blow job.

Dad always knew how to pick them.

"Hey, Aaron. What's going on in here? Why you yelling?" She rested her hands on her hips, trying to look intimidating, but she couldn't fool me. I saw the way she shook. She was probably coming down off something.

"No-good boy," he muttered, waving a hand at me. "He's useless. Needs someone to keep him in line."

I barely looked at him. Didn't let his words hurt me anymore. My skin was tough, thick. My heart was like a steel trap, not allowing a damn thing inside of it. Ever.

I was only thirteen. Took me a few years, but I finally learned how to let his insults roll right off me.

"Oh. I thought you were getting in a fight or something." She wandered over to the refrigerator and popped open the door, peering inside. "Got any beer?"

Dad walked right up behind her and slapped her on the ass. Hard. She squealed. "No beer for you, bitch. You gotta earn it first."

Unease crept down my spine, but otherwise I continued to ignore them both, running the water to the hottest temperature I could stand before I started rinsing off the crusted-over dishes. I knew what my dad was talking about when it came to earning it. The women he brought home were so stupid. They seemed to fall for his lines every single time. It was unbeliev-able, how much power the asshole could hold over a woman.

Were women that stupid? Not all women could be. Were they? My mother got the hell out so that was smart, but she left me behind, which rendered her stupid in my book.

So fuck that. They were all worthless. Just like my dad said.

"Earn it how, hmm?" the woman asked, her voice low and flirty-like. I'm guessing she thought Dad liked it when she talked that way. Me? I sort of wanted to puke.

"You know how, darlin'. Now let's go to my room and you can show me all the ways you appreciate me." His head snapped up, his gaze latching onto mine. I tried to look away, but it was like I couldn't. I was paralyzed with fear. "You should come, too, Willy."

I went still, the hot water flowing over my hands, making them burn. I hardly felt it. "No." *Please God, no.* "I have to finish washing the dishes."

"They can wait." He waved a hand and glanced down at the woman, who was watching me with a mixture of fear and excitement in her eyes. I'd never seen this woman before in my life. I hoped after this was done, I'd never see her again. "Come on, Willy. We like it when you watch."

I shut off the water and followed after him, my head hang-ing down. I thought of Uncle Jesse and Danny Tanner and DJ, Stephanie and Michelle on *Full House*. They wouldn't do this sort of shit. No one would ever make them do something so awful. But I guessed all that stuff really was just fantasies.

Dreams.

# ETHAN

I sit straight up in bed, the sheet falling away from me, my chest and head pounding, my throat raw. I feel gentle hands stroking my arm, hear a soft voice calling my name, and I shake my head to clear all the ugly, dark thoughts out of it. But they linger, sinking their claws into my brain, refusing to budge.

Fuck, that had been a bad one.

I glance to my left to find Katie sitting up next to me, the sheet tucked tightly around her upper body, her fingers still stroking my arm.

"You were having a bad dream," she murmurs, her expression full of worry. "You were—you were talking in your sleep."

I fall back onto the bed, my head sinking into the pillow. My arm slips out of her grip and I immediately miss her touch. My heart gallops like the fastest horse about to overtake the race and I take a deep breath, trying to calm myself down. I'm shaky. Spooked. What I just experienced, that didn't feel like a dream.

More like a memory.

"Did you hear what I said? Could you make it out?" I ask after a few moments, surprised I sound so calm. I don't feel so calm on the inside. My heart is still thundering, my thoughts in a complete tangle.

"All I heard you say was 'don't make me watch.'" She hesitates and then rests her head on my shoulder, her hair brushing against my face. "I'm almost afraid to ask."

"You don't want to know," I agree. I'm not about to ruin what we shared tonight with a not-so-pleasant memory from my messed-up past with my dad. Screw that business.

"Have you ever considered . . . going to therapy?" she asks, her voice tentative.

"I already have." I close my eyes, enjoying the way she touches me, her fingers skimming across my chest. "Pretty much all through high school. Typical guidance-counselor-type shit. It was awful."

She's quiet for a moment and I wonder what she's thinking. That my earlier guidance counselors weren't able to work out my problems, so maybe I'm a permanent fucked-up mess? That wouldn't be too far off the mark.

"I'm talking about seeing a true professional." Katie pauses, letting her words sink in. "Have you ever tried that?"

"Nah." I keep my eyes closed, though I feel her lift her head so she can look at me. "I've never wanted to. I'm fine."

"You're not fine," she whispers. I crack open my eyes to find she's gazing at me, her expression full of pain and worry. For me. "I don't think you've worked through what your father did to you. The scab's still there, and it seems pretty easy for it to get picked off so you're left raw and open."

I grimace. "That's a disgusting way to describe it." When she doesn't say anything, just continues to watch me, I give in. "You're right. It doesn't take much for me to feel like shit over my past."

"Is that what you were dreaming of?" she asks tentatively.

"Yeah. But it was bad. I don't want to tell you what happened." I keep it bottled up inside. It's easier that way. Why share in the suffering? "You don't need to hear all that."

"I want to." She moves up so she can place a gentle kiss on my lips, and I immediately cup the back of her head, holding her in place. "I want to help you. Your pain is my pain," she murmurs against my lips.

"I don't want to hurt you, too." I thread my fingers through her hair and give it a little tug.

"That's what being in a relationship is. The two of us together helping each other out."

I stare into her eyes, get lost in them. Her breasts are pressed against my chest, her arms coming up to slide around my neck. I grab hold of her waist and pull her on top of me, her legs falling around either side of my hips so that she's straddling me. My cock comes to life, eager to get back inside her, and I run my hands up and down her back slowly, making her shiver. "You really want to know?"

She nods, her gaze never leaving mine.

"He liked to do drugs. Watching him do that shit all the time really turned me off and I was never tempted to do any of it. But he wasn't what I would call an addict. All the women he brought home? They were the addicts. He liked to make them promises and reward them with drugs," I explain, my voice low. Soft. Barely audible.

"What sort of promises?"

"He'd trade sex for meth. He had a friend, I think, who was always cooking the shit up. He'd offer them a little hit, hook them, and then bring them home and make them do—things—before he gave them what they really wanted." This is where it gets difficult. Where I don't want to admit the next part but I have to. No more lies. Only pure honesty between us from here on out. "He used to make me watch."

Katie frowns. "Watch what?"

"Him having sex with those women." I close my eyes briefly and take a deep breath. Admitting this sucks. I've never told anyone what he used to make me do. This is my secret.

My shame. "That's what I was dreaming about. Or remembering. I don't know. My life was a fucking nightmare most of the time when I was growing up."

"Oh, Will." She moves so her face is in mine, those pretty blue eyes watching me carefully. "How old were you when this first started?"

I flinch at her calling me Will. Still not used to it. Not sure I like it at this particular moment. "I don't know. Ten? Eleven?" I close my eyes again, fighting against the tidal wave of emotions that threatens to suck me under. It hurts to look at her. What if I see disgust in her eyes? "I've never told anyone this before."

"It's okay. I understand. You know I do." Her hands are soothing as she touches me, her lips on my face as she kisses me a balm to my chaotic soul. "You don't have to say anything else if you're not comfortable."

"You're the only person I feel comfortable enough with to admit it. You're the only one who knows what it's like to be . . ." I swallow hard and open my eyes. "Poisoned by him. By my father."

"He didn't poison you. He didn't." She shakes her head, her voice firm. "You're kind and sweet and fair. You respect me. You make mistakes but your intentions are never evil. You're not a monster like him. I know you're not. You have a good heart." She rests her hand on my chest, her fingers curling against my skin. "I know you do. Thank you for being honest with me. That's all I've ever wanted."

I want to be open with her. Real. This is my life, the good and the bad. It's been mostly bad, but with her in it, with Katie by my side, it can be good now. My father can't touch me. He can't touch her, either. No one can touch us as long as we're in each other's lives.

"I don't want to upset you by saying all this," I murmur.

"You're not upsetting me. Sharing with each other can only bring us closer together." She kisses my neck and I close my eyes against the swarm of emotions threatening to take over. I love this girl. I love everything about her. And if I were to lose her, I don't know what I'd do.

"I can't stand the thought of you not in my life," I whisper just before she cuts me off, her greedy lips on mine. She kisses me, soft and sweet but there's an urgency behind it, in the way she sucks my lower lip between hers, her tongue darting out for a lick. She's restless.

Hot.

Wet.

I can feel her press against me and my cock responds. I slide my hands down until I'm cupping her butt and I pull her in close, as close as I can get her. She gasps against my lips and kisses me again, deep and hot, until she breaks away first.

"That you can touch me so reverently, be so patient and kind with me when we have sex, is . . . amazing. You've been through so much."

"So have you," I remind her.

"Worse than me. You had to live with him." She kisses me again. All I can focus on is the tangle of our tongues, the taste of her, the sensation of her body sprawled on top of mine. I could slip inside her right now. It would be so easy. Too easy. "That you can show love through sex is nothing short of a miracle."

"When it's with you, it's never a struggle." I roll her over so she's on her back, making her squeal in surprise. I slide down her body, kissing her along the way. Sucking her nipples into my mouth, licking a path along the gentle curve of her stomach, kissing the inside of her thighs as I spread her wide apart, my hands braced on the inside of her knees.

I kiss her between her legs tentatively, lifting my head to

find she's watching me, her muscles drawn up tight in what appears to be tense anticipation. The questioning look I send her is enough. She grants her permission with a subtle nod and I return my attention to the spot between her legs, licking and sucking her there, and she doesn't stop me. No, she arches up into me instead when I flick her clit with my tongue. I want to make her come with my mouth. I want to show her all the many ways we can make each other come, make each other happy. Show each other how much we're in love.

Her hands sink into my hair as she makes these sexy little noises in the back of her throat. She's restless with need, her head thrown back, her fingers pulling my hair as I continue to lick her, search her with my tongue. I run my hand up her stomach and cup her breast, playing with her nipple as I try my damnedest to suck her off.

It's like I need this to wash away the filth and horror of my dream. I need the sweetness of Katie to overtake the darkness of my past.

She moans as I increase my pace, her legs coming up, her thighs practically wrapping around my head. She's squeezing me but I don't care. I slip my hands beneath her ass and hold her to me, feeling that first flutter, her body jerking in my hands, against my mouth. She cries out my name just before she comes, her body shuddering beneath my lips, her hands falling from my hair.

I don't remove my mouth from her but I slow my movements, keeping my eyes on her expressive face. She cracks open her eyes, throwing her arm over her face when she finds I'm watching her, and I move up to lie beside her, removing her arm so I can look her in the eyes.

"Don't be embarrassed," I murmur, leaning in to drop a gentle kiss to her lips.

She accepts it, a shaky breath escaping her. "I'm not."

I raise a brow. She rolls her eyes.

"Fine I am. That was just . . ."

"Perfect? Amazing? Life-changing?"

"Stop." She shoves at my shoulder but I don't move. I need to hear what she has to say. "It was good."

"Just good?"

"Do you want me to hand over a trophy? Remember, I don't have anyone else to compare you to," she says wryly.

"I'll take the trophy, then." I pull her into my arms and she nestles close, her legs tangling with mine. "You make this easy."

"What do you mean?"

"Being with you. Admitting the bad stuff, sharing the good stuff, making you laugh. Making you come." She squirms against me like she's embarrassed and I clamp my arms around her tight, keeping her immobile. "I'm being serious. This is a good thing."

"I know," she whispers. "I just hope . . ." Her voice drifts but she doesn't say anything else.

"You hope what?" Unease slips down my spine as I wait for her answer.

"I hope no one gives us any trouble for being together."

"Like who? Your family?"

"They already said they'd cut me off if I continued to see you."

I pull away from her so I can stare into her eyes. "Are you serious?"

She nods, nibbling on her lower lip. "Both my mom and sister said they wouldn't stand by and support me if we were together."

"You're willing to give up your family for me." This blows my mind. And I doubt her family would ditch her so fast . . .

would they? They love her. I'm determined to do what I can to earn their trust. I need their acceptance in order to remain in Katie's life, but what if it never comes?

That terrifies me.

"They'll come around." She shrugs, her unsure expression just about killing me.

"Christ, Katie . . ."

"Stop." She rests her fingers over my lips, silencing me. "It's not fair to make me choose. They don't understand what we share. And that's what scares me the most. If my family can't understand it, then how do we expect the general public to understand us? They'll think we're . . . sick."

"We're not," I say vehemently.

"Your father kidnapped and *raped* me. There's no getting around it. He's in jail because of it. Because he killed other little girls and I could've been one of them. And now we're together." She pauses, her expression grave. "To the outside world, we look crazy."

"I don't care what anyone thinks. I only care what *you* think." I smooth the hair away from her face and stare into her eyes. "Do you love me?"

She nods.

"Do you want to be with me?"

She nods again.

"Then that's all that matters." I kiss her forehead. Her cheeks. The tip of her nose. "That's the only thing that matters," I repeat.

"I love you," she whispers just before I kiss her. I love her, too.

I can only hope that's enough.

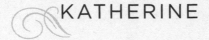# KATHERINE

I wake up slowly to find I'm wrapped up in Will's arms, his warm, naked body pressed up against my back. One hand is splayed across my stomach, the other covering my breast, and I can't help but smile.

He must have got up sometime in the night and drawn the curtains. It's so dark, save for the little beam of light shining into the room at the spot where the curtains don't quite meet. I can hear the sound of traffic. The occasional honking horn or the loud screech of brakes. Noise I'm not used to at all, since I grew up in the suburbs and now live in a small town.

Will shifts behind me, nuzzling his face into the crook of my neck, murmuring against my skin. I close my eyes and savor the feeling of being in his strong arms, his hands on my body, his legs shifting in between mine.

I never thought I could be this happy. Never believed I could find someone who accepts all of me, the broken parts, the ugly, scary parts that I can barely face. He knows my deepest, darkest secrets and they don't bother him—because he shares them with me. We can take something bad and turn it into something . . .

Wonderful.

"Good morning." He drops a kiss on my ear and I lean into him, smiling like an idiot.

"Morning." I turn my face away from his when he tries to kiss me on the lips. "I have morning breath."

"I really don't care." He grabs hold of my chin and kisses me, simple and sweet, and I smile again because I can't help myself. I've never, ever felt this happy.

Like, ever.

He lets go of my chin and I turn to face the windows, staring at that beam of light stretching across the carpet. His hands slowly wander everywhere, his fingers drifting across my nipples, down over my stomach. I can smell his skin, smell me on his skin, and I never, ever want to leave this bed. I'd rather stay right here and hide out for all eternity.

But we can't. Reality waits.

"We should get out of bed and get going," he suggests, as though he can read my mind. He doesn't move a muscle.

I don't, either.

"Do we have to?" I finally ask, sounding a little whiny.

"Unfortunately, yeah." He kisses my cheek, his lips lingering. "I have a suggestion."

"What?"

"Take a shower with me." He whispers the words close to my ear, his voice full of promise and making me shiver. "I'll get you nice and clean."

I duck my head into my shoulder, trying to stop him from kissing my ear again. "Stop. That tickles."

"Come on, Katie. I'll wash your hair," he offers. "And give you a head massage. I'm pretty good with my hands."

My cheeks heat at the implication of his words. "You are *very* good with your hands," I murmur. I should know.

"Then come on." Those skilled hands are still touching me everywhere he can reach. And he can reach pretty much every part of my body. "Let's go hop in the shower. Together."

"You don't have your clothes. Your . . . stuff." We stayed the night in my room. His bag is back in his hotel room.

"I can throw on my jeans and grab everything from my room after the shower. Don't worry about that." He pinches my butt, making me yelp. "Come on, woman. Let's go."

He exits the bed and I immediately miss him. I roll over to find his hand in my face, his fingers waving for me to get out of bed. I gaze up at him, admiring how comfortable he is being naked in front of me. I've never been one to drool over a guy's naked chest, but Will's chest is . . . drool-worthy. Lean and firm, not an ounce of fat anywhere, and with the most intriguing patch of dark hair in the center and an interesting trail of hair that runs from his navel to his . . .

My cheeks go hot just thinking about it.

"I'd give millions to know what you're thinking at this very moment to put that blush on your cheeks," he says, pushing me out of my thoughts.

I blush even harder. "You do not want to know."

"Oh, I definitely want to know. Get out of bed, sleepy-head. We gotta get going." He rests his hands on his hips and I'm tempted to giggle.

If I had even an ounce of his confidence, I'd be strutting all around this room without a stitch of clothing on. I'd wear heels and work it like I was walking on a runway.

No way can I ever see that happening. I can't imagine ever being that brazen.

"You coming or what?" He raises his brows.

I swing out of bed and take his hand, letting him pull me to my feet. His gaze immediately falls down the length of my body, lingering on all the parts that are normally covered up, and my skin prickles with heat.

Throwing my head back, I feign confidence and tug on his hand, taking the lead as we head toward the bathroom.

NEVER LET YOU GO   197

"You're really going to wash my hair?" I ask innocently, glancing at him from over my shoulder.

He grins. "I'm going to wash you everywhere," he drawls, hitting the light switch as soon as we enter the bathroom. "And I swear I won't miss an inch."

From the promise in his tone and the heat I see in his eyes, I know he'll make good on his claims.

The drive home speeds by way too fast, and we pick up Molly at the kennel before we head to my place. Will encourages me to go into the kennel with him and so I do, thankful for the chance to stretch my legs as we both pace, waiting anxiously in the lobby for the employee to bring the dog out to us.

Molly bursts through the door with a lolling tongue and a welcoming bark, lunging for Will but held back by her leash. I start to laugh and kneel down to give her a pet on the head and she licks my face, her tongue sliding over the corner of my mouth.

Gross, but I forgive her enthusiasm. I'm just as happy to see her.

"She did pretty good," the employee is saying to Will as she hands Molly's leash over. "We started on her training this morning. You'll bring her back tomorrow, right? It starts at ten."

"Yeah, I'll be here," Will tells her as he takes hold of Molly's leash. He gazes down at the dog, his voice full of affection as he says, "Ready to go home, girl?"

Molly barks in response, as if she knew what he said, and seeing the two of them together warms my heart, I swear. He needed this—something to love, something to focus on, and not just me. I can't be everything in his life. He has his job, but I don't really think he has many friends.

He's lived a solitary life, much like me. But at least I have my mom and sister.

Not anymore you won't. Not if you stick with Will.

The realization scares me. I've relied on Mom and Brenna for so long. And truly I don't know Will that well. I do but I don't. I want to know more, but we have to move at a slow pace. I can't just jump into a full-fledged relationship. I'm still worried about my family.

I need Mom's approval. She's been everything to me all these years, especially once Dad grew distant. And Brenna, too. We haven't really talked—I'm still not happy that she went to Will and basically threatened him, then got angry at me, as if what Aaron Monroe did to me were somehow my fault. I know she has her own issues she's trying to work through, but I need them both.

Worse, and it's one of my secret fears—maybe it *is* wrong for us to be in a relationship. He may have saved me, but it was his father who almost killed me. When you put it in the most basic terms, I've only been with two men—Will and his father. I can't count the rape as a real sexual encounter, but it was my introduction to sex.

And that is all sorts of messed up. To the point where I know exactly what I'm going to be talking about when I have my appointment with Sheila tomorrow.

"You okay?" he asks just before we leave the lobby.

He's attuned to my every mood. Most of the time, I like it. Right now? I'd rather keep my thoughts where they need to be—in my head.

"Fine," I say as I smile, giving his hand a squeeze.

We walk outside into the parking lot hand in hand, Will clutching the leash with his other hand as Molly tries to drag him toward the car. A steady wind blows, bringing with it fast-moving, ominous clouds and a chill in the air.

"What training was she talking about?" I ask as we approach his car.

"The basics, with a little guard-dog training thrown in for good measure," Will says. I absolutely cannot think of him as Ethan anymore and yeah, that might be messed up but I can't help it.

He releases my hand and pulls his keys out of the front pocket of his jeans, hitting the remote so it unlocks the car.

"Guard dog?" I go to the passenger-side door and open it, staring at him over the car as I wait for his response.

He shrugs, his gaze skittering away from mine. "Hey, she's small but she's mighty. I thought a little fierce training could do her some good."

I climb into the car and turn to glance at the backseat as the door swings open and Molly leaps in. She's not what I would call a little dog, but she's not big, either. And fierce? The way she's watching me with those warm brown eyes and that giant pink tongue hanging out the side of her mouth, she looks like she'd rather lick someone to death versus bite his face off.

"She doesn't look very fierce," I point out when Will climbs into the car. "She's a little too friendly if you ask me."

His gaze meets mine, hands resting on the steering wheel. "That's why she's getting trained. And I'm doing this more for you than for her, Katie."

Shock makes my mouth pop open. "What do you mean, you're doing this more for me?"

"I wanted to get her trained so she can guard . . . you." He doesn't say anything else. Just starts the car and backs out of the spot, pulling onto the road.

"Guard me how?" I ask when he still hasn't spoken.

"I want Molly to spend more time with you," he says, never taking his eyes off the road. "When I can't be there, Molly will be. And if she has some guard or attack-dog training, then I'd feel even better about leaving her with you."

"But she's your dog."

He glances at me quickly. "She's *our* dog."

Oh. I guess she sort of is. As if on cue, she pokes her head between the seats and nudges the back of my upper arm with her cold nose. I can feel it even through the thin sweater I'm wearing. Like she's saying, *Hey, you belong to me.* "You really mean that? That Molly's ours?"

"Well, yeah. What's mine is yours, Katie. We're together. I'm in love with you. That didn't happen overnight. I've cared about you for years. When it comes to us and making this work, I'm all in." We pull up to a stoplight and he grabs hold of my hand, bringing it to his mouth and kissing the back of it. "We're not going to just see each other casually. A dinner date here, a night spent over at one or the other's house there—that's not what I want. If I had my way, you'd be moving in with me right now. Today, even."

I can only gape at him. Move into his *house*? I can't imagine it. I finally feel confident enough to live on my own and now he wants us to live together. I declared my love for him last night and it's like he wants us to get engaged or married or something.

Just thinking about moving into his house makes my heart race and my palms sweat. I recognize panic when I see it. I've been going to therapy for years. I don't think I'm ready. I need time. Lots and lots of it.

And maybe he doesn't realize it yet, but so does he.

"What's wrong?"

I turn my head sharply at his question to find him watching me, his gaze narrowed. I feel like he can read my mind and I don't like that. Not now, when I'm thinking such . . . not-so-positive thoughts. "I don't know. You're giving me a lot to think about."

"You haven't been thinking about it already?"

Sort of. Not really. I haven't been giving it much thought at all. I've gone from falling for him, to devastated and hurt, to declaring my love. All in a matter of what, a month? Six weeks? It's happened so incredibly fast I'm surprised my head isn't spinning. "I don't think I'm ready to move in with you yet. That's just—moving too fast."

The light turns green, yet he hasn't hit the gas. "Moving too fast? I thought we were on the same page here."

A horn honks behind us. "I love you, Will, but I can't move in with you. Not yet. I need more time."

"Don't call me Will." His tone is sharp, making me flinch. "I don't like it."

"You were fine with it last night," I point out, hurt that he would say such a thing. He basically gave me permission and now he's taking it back?

"I just want to make you happy, but sometimes . . . I got rid of that name on purpose. I don't like the reminder of who I used to be."

His words sink in as another horn blares. He mutters something under his breath, hitting the accelerator so hard the car jerks forward, sending Molly toppling backward, grunting when she hits the backseat.

"Fine, then," I say coolly, "I won't call you Will." What can I call him? *Ethan* doesn't feel right, either. This is such a jumbled-up mess, I don't know what to do, what to say. So I remain quiet.

"You really don't want to move in with me eventually? I can't fucking believe this," he finally mutters, shaking his head.

"What do you mean, you can't believe this? What did I do wrong?" And why do I automatically think I'm the one at fault? I try to tamp down my frustration, but why is he acting this way? Doesn't he realize he's pushing me too hard? I don't like feeling out of control. And his insistence that we move in together is making me feel that way.

I don't like it.

"I thought you understood what I wanted." His voice is flat, his expression grim, as he stares at the road in front of him.

"You need to tell me what you want. I can't read your mind, Will."

"I'm ready for the next step." He frowns. "And I already asked you not to call me Will. My name's Ethan."

I press my lips together, dropping my head so I can focus on my clutched hands in my lap, not the fact that he just corrected me. I'm frustrated that the name slipped out so easily after I said I wouldn't call him that. But he's not Ethan. At least, he's not to me. He's Will. He will always be Will—Will is the one I'm in love with.

Ethan is like a ghost. A man who swept into my life just so he could play tricks on me. When I think about Ethan, I start to get mad.

"Christ, Katie, I'm sorry. I didn't mean to snap at you. I'm just . . ." He sighs, and I glance up to catch him shaking his head. "I'm tense thinking about that interview tonight. I don't want to watch it."

"We have to," I start, but he shakes his head again, cutting me off.

"You might have to, but I don't. I'd rather not."

"So, what? You're going to pretend it never happened?" I'm incredulous. Why wouldn't he want to watch it? He'd rather live in denial?

He shrugs. "I don't want to hear what he has to say. I figured you felt the same way. And I definitely don't want to see how Lisa makes me look like an idiot. There's no point in watching it. What's done is done."

"The media might want to talk to you afterward, you know." He doesn't say anything and I sigh in frustration. "You're just going to avoid them, aren't you."

"You're damn right I am. I really don't care if they want to talk to me or not. They don't know who I am or where I live. They won't find me. If I go to your house to watch it they'll definitely know where I am, and then all hell will break loose." He glances at me again and I can see the pain in his gaze, mixed with frustration. "I won't watch the interview, Katie. You can't convince me otherwise."

I'm hurting, too. Funny how we can come together so beautifully and less than twenty-four hours later, it completely falls apart. Thanks to reality. "Then take me home." I turn my head to stare at the passing scenery, not wanting to talk about it any longer. We'll just go round and round—and that's our biggest problem.

"I don't like the thought of you there alone." His voice is low, his pain obvious. But I can't give in. I have to stand up for myself, and he needs to know I don't agree with pretty much anything he's saying right now.

To give in would be giving up control. And I can't do that.

Crossing my arms in front of my chest, I keep my gaze locked on the window. I don't want to look at him. If I do, I'll cave in. Or worse, feel bad that he's suffering. I need to focus on myself. I care about him—I love him. But there are certain things I have to stand up for. Keeping myself informed is important. And slowing him down when he's dying to speed us up is important, too.

"I have Mrs. Anderson next door," I tell the window. I'm acting like a child, but I just can't face him right now. "If anything weird happens, she'll be sure to call the police first thing." Not that I'm worried. My biggest threat is locked away in a maximum-security prison.

"Having that little old lady as your neighbor isn't reassuring me," he says dryly, but I ignore him. I'm too mad.

Too hurt.

Too disappointed.

Maybe—God, I hate even thinking this, but—maybe this thing between us won't work after all.

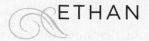# ETHAN

I ended up watching it.

And I was right. Lisa made me look stupid. Like I was some reckless idiot who didn't care about the girl. The horrible son who didn't care about his father. I was the guy who stormed off the set in a fit of rage after he was accused of doing something he claims he didn't do—and the girl rushes to my defense.

Like always.

The camera cut to Lisa after that particular moment, her expression somber, her voice hushed, as she shared almost intimately that Katie and I had a long history of doing the same exact thing over and over again. Whenever someone accuses me of being a possible partner in my father's crimes, Katie denies it vehemently. It's a known pattern. To the point that many are starting to wonder—why does Katherine Watts always defend Will Monroe so quickly?

Direct quote.

Doesn't matter that the police couldn't find an ounce of evidence to hold me—to even try and charge me with anything. There's not even any circumstantial evidence. But the truth doesn't matter.

Nothing matters. Only ratings, only views. Only getting as many hits on social media as possible. Let's titillate America and talk to the murderer.

My father sat there on camera and implied that I was involved.

"The boy was helpful," he said, that smug smile on his face filling me with dread. Nausea. *God,* I hate him.

"How so?" Lisa asked eagerly. "What did he help you with? Did he assist you with the abductions of the girls?"

Christ, she would be balls to the wall and ask him such a blatant, horrific question. I couldn't tear my eyes away from the TV screen as I watched my father make an irritated face, tipping his head, a little sound falling from his lips when Lisa asked him those questions.

But he didn't say a word, the bastard. No denial. No confirmation, either—thank Christ—though that wasn't reassuring. The damage was done. His expression was enough to set suspicion into motion yet again. Even after all these years.

Katie was wrong. I should never have done that interview. It's only made things worse.

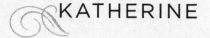# KATHERINE

"I haven't seen you in a while." Sheila smiles at me.

I settle into the couch and scowl at her in return.

She shifts in her chair, leaning forward, her hands clasped in front of her. "I saw the interview."

I still say nothing. I'm not mad at her. More like I'm frustrated with myself. I just need to figure out exactly what I'm going to say. The entire drive to her office I ran through a multitude of things I could tell her. None of them sounded good.

If I'm not going to believe in my own words, how do I expect her to?

"I was surprised that you did it." She pauses. Waiting for me to say something? So am I. "Surprised even more that you didn't tell me about it."

"A lot has happened since I last saw you," I mumble.

"Clearly." She takes a deep breath. She can also clearly sense my hesitation. "So. Why did you choose to do another interview?"

I launch into my explanation, starting with reconnecting with Ethan, picking out Molly the dog, agreeing to the interview, going with him to San Francisco, spending the night with him in my hotel room . . . all of it. Every bit. My internal struggle. The sex. The proclamations of love, yesterday's argument, and that I haven't heard from him since.

"It's a mess," I conclude miserably.

"One that can be fixed," Sheila points out.

Her optimism is usually appreciated. Not so much right now. "I don't know about that. We . . . struggle. A lot." And that's an understatement.

"You were each hurt by the same person, and that unites you both." She makes us sound so romantic. To the outside observer, maybe we are. But our story is more like a romantic tragedy.

"It also divides us," I murmur.

Sheila tips her head. "True. But the connection you share is so understandably intense. What happened to the two of you was a life-changing event. It's formed who you both are, and how you behave with others. It's natural that you're drawn to each other and you want to be together." She pauses, and I know to mentally prepare for what she says next. "You say you love him—and I believe you do, but I'm wondering if sometimes you love the *idea* of him more than the *real* him."

Her words hit home. And they scare me. What if that's true? What if I'm in love with the idea of my hero, Will, versus the man who he really is, Ethan? "I want to know the real him," I tell her. "The lines were blurred these last few days. He became Will to me—the adult Will, not young Will. Ethan seemed to disappear."

"And so that's why you started calling him Will." Sheila nods as she taps away on her iPad. I would hate to see my file. I'm sure it's full of all sorts of cryptic observations.

It always surprises me, how astute she is. "That's exactly why," I admit. "And at the end of our trip, he didn't like it. He even corrected me. And that . . . hurt."

"Did you ever think that it hurt when you called him Will? He's tried to rid himself of that name. Down to the point where he had it legally changed. That's a pretty big step for him to take," Sheila points out.

"He said he didn't mind that I called him Will. He told me that multiple times." Should I feel guilty for pushing it? Maybe . . .

Probably.

"But he didn't like that you called him Will after you told him you thought he was moving too fast," Sheila points out.

"He *was* moving too fast. I'm not ready to live with him. I really don't even know him that well." Moving in together means getting engaged, means getting married and eventually having children. I just . . . I don't know if that's possible for us. "I'm only twenty-one. He's my first relationship ever. He's moving so fast that he's overwhelming me."

"Have you told him this? Have you explained all of this to him?"

I shake my head. I'm afraid he'll shut me down and not listen to me. Or worse, think my fears are nothing but excuses. I'm terrified he'll end up shutting me out and leaving me first.

"You should. Communication is key," she suggests gently. "If you really want this to work, then the two of you need to sit down and talk. Don't hold back—tell him how you really feel. And then you need to listen to him as well."

She's right. I know she's right. But that means I have to reach out to him and I don't know if I'm ready yet. I'm still hurt and mad and . . . scared.

"How do you feel about last night's interview?"

"Not great." I sigh. That's the understatement of the year. "We shouldn't have done it. I see that now." Lisa made him look terrible. She made me look terrible, too. Last night was all about Aaron Monroe. If I didn't know any better, if I hadn't experienced his monstrous acts firsthand, I'd almost believe all the crap he says. He can talk a good game.

But I already knew that. He convinced me to go with him

so easily. Put on an innocent face and chose his words carefully, persuading me with such charm. I was so young, too. I believed there was only good in the world. That evil couldn't touch me. I lived in a protective little bubble until Aaron Monroe entered my life.

Easygoing coercion—that was his tactic. And it worked. It still works.

The minute he gets you alone, though, the mask comes off. And the monster comes out.

"What about your family?"

I startle out of my thoughts at her words, my stomach twisting into knots. Their seeming abandonment of me during a tough time in my life hurts the most. I called Mom and let her know about the interview, and she expressed her disappointment both with words and with silence. I texted Brenna, and I could feel her frustration with me through her carefully worded reply. I never heard from either of them after the interview. Nothing from them this morning, either.

"They're mad at me."

"Because of you seeing Ethan again?" she asks gently.

I nod, swallowing past the lump in my throat. It just automatically shoves its way back in there again.

"They're just worried about you," she starts, but I interrupt her.

"That's all they've ever done, worry about me. I'm tired of it." I am. Oh, how I am. "I'm a grown woman who can make her own choices. They can't seem to realize that."

"They have always feared for your safety, ever since you were twelve. Your mom and your sister's roles are to protect you."

"Brenna acts like she hates me. The last time we talked

she said all sorts of terrible things. She's so full of resentment toward me." That still stings—and surprises me.

"Understandable. You became the center of your family's attention."

"I didn't want to be!" The words burst out of me, making my lungs ache. "I never asked for this! I told Brenna that, but she wasn't listening to me." I leap to my feet and start pacing around her tiny office. "If I could take this all back I would. Lately I've made some mistakes, I know that. But I always had good intentions. Always."

"No one is accusing you of being bad or evil."

"My mother and sister act like I'm doing the devil's work by spending time with Ethan." Will. God, I can't figure out which one he is anymore and it's making me crazy.

"In their eyes, he's the son of the devil. That association is too close for comfort."

I sag back into the couch, leaning my head back so I can stare up at the ceiling. The words repeat over and over in my brain, sending a chill down my spine.

That association is too close for comfort.

In some way is that true for me, too? I don't know.

# ETHAN

I sit in my car waiting for Katie's return while parked in front of her house. Molly isn't having it, though. She whines. She paces the backseat of my car—how that is possible, I'm not sure, but she does it. When she licks my ear and drools on my shoulder, that's the final straw. Hooking the leash onto her collar, I exit the car, taking Molly along with me.

"You're back."

Turning, I see Katie's neighbor Mrs. Anderson sitting on her front porch, her keen gaze glued to me. Does she recognize me from when I first came here to spy on Katie? I hope to hell not. "Hi." I throw my hand up in a quick wave.

She slowly rises from her chair and starts for me, one step at a time from the porch, tottering carefully down the sidewalk until she's standing just before me on the other side of the waist-high white picket fence. "You're Katherine's friend."

We've waved at each other before when I've come over. Always briefly; we never really talk. I avoided her. Didn't want her to realize she's met me before.

"I am," I agree, sending Molly a stern look when she appears ready to leap over the fence and lick the poor old lady to death. "Katie's told me all about you."

Her silvery-white eyebrows go way up. "Katie, is it? Sounds like you two are real familiar."

"We knew each other a long time ago," I admit.

"Back when you used to live in her house? Oh so long

ago?" I gape at her, excuses clogging my throat, but she just carries on like it's no big deal. "I got you all figured out, you know. Recognized you from the start."

Well, *shit*. What do I say to that? I have no excuse. "I can ex—" I start, but she holds up her hand to silence me.

"Whatever you do is your business. I don't like to butt in. Though I do make it my job to watch over this neighborhood. I watch over Katherine, too. She's a young girl, living all alone in that house. Lonely, too. I like seeing her with some male company." Her shrewd eyes seem to see right through me. "As long as your intentions are true, I'm going to let our very first meeting slide."

Relief fills me and my knees go a little weak. "Uh, thanks."

"Who's this?" Mrs. Anderson steps closer to the fence and reaches over to pat Molly's head. "She's a cutie."

"Her name's Molly." She gives a little bark in greeting, her ever-present tongue hanging out the side of her mouth. "She's very friendly."

"She looks it. A real killer, isn't she?" Mrs. Anderson pats her head some more. "Katherine could do well with a dog."

My sentiments exactly. I took Molly to training yesterday and this morning, and she's already catching on to a few things. I'll be taking her all next week, too. It's eating into my work time and the training isn't cheap, but in the end, I think it'll be worth it.

"A big, ferocious dog, like a Rottweiler or a pit bull," Mrs. Anderson continues on as she keeps petting Molly. The dog's eyes are closed, meaning she's totally blissed out. "Something to protect her."

"You think she needs protection?"

"I know she does," the old woman says with a fierce nod. "Girl feels vulnerable enough in her own head. Spooky things have been happening in those woods behind us lately. I don't like it."

My interest picks up at the words *spooky things*. "What are you referring to?"

"Oh, I thought I saw someone sneaking around back there a few nights ago. I even called the cops, though they did a search and came up with nothing." She shakes her head, her tone bitter. "They never take me seriously."

"Did you tell Katie?"

"I asked her if she'd seen anything and she said one night, she felt like someone was out there, watching her. Though it was dark and she couldn't see anything, so she claims she imagined it. I got real mad at her for not calling the police. Or at the very least, she should've been calling *me*." Mrs. Anderson makes a harrumph noise that would have made me smile any other day, but not now.

Not if Katie's at risk.

"I appreciate that you're so concerned with Katie's safety," I say with the utmost sincerity. "It's reassuring, knowing she has someone so close who's always looking out for her."

"I'm nosy, I can admit it. I like to know everything that's happening around here," Mrs. Anderson says, waving her hand. "I've seen some shady dealings. Couple people have gotten robbed, but only because they're damn stupid, leaving their windows unlocked or a back door. Who does that? Maybe forty years ago we could get away with that kind of carelessness, but definitely not now."

I glance around. Katie's neighborhood is quiet. Older but clean, most of the homes have been renovated, with decent yards and nice cars parked in the driveways and garages. Kids' bikes dumped on the lawn. Fall flowers waving in the breeze, trees slowly losing all of their leaves. It's your typical middle-to upper-class neighborhood where a person could be lulled into a false sense of security. I'm always aware of that false sense, the ability for someone to barge in and smash it to bits. So is Katie.

"If something ever feels off or wrong around Katie's, would you mind calling me? It could be the littlest thing—I don't care. Just . . . can I give you my phone number?"

"Of course." She whips a phone out of the pocket of her cardigan sweater, an iPhone 6s Plus, which makes me want to laugh. The woman may be old, but she's got the latest and greatest technology. "Give me your name and number and I'll text you whenever I see something fishy."

She's going to text me. I love it. "That would be great." I give her my number and she looks up at me when she finishes tapping it in. "What's your name again?"

I hesitate for the slightest moment. "Will," I say softly, shocked at how easily the name slips out. "It's Will."

I'm sitting on her front porch when Katie pulls into the driveway about a half hour later, her garage door slowly creeping up. Molly flies from the porch, barking excitedly and following after Katie's car as it enters the garage. I don't get up from my perch on her front steps, almost afraid to approach for fear she'll tell me to get the hell out of there.

Not that I can blame her. Yet again, I'm in the wrong and I need to ask for her forgiveness. How many chances do I get to fuck up before she's done forgiving me? I hope I didn't already lose my last chance.

So I wait anxiously, tapping my foot against the concrete step, straining to catch her voice when I hear the car door open and slam shut. She's talking to Molly, petting her, and the dog is eating it up.

I'd be eating it up, too. Any bit of attention from Katie makes me feel like I can take on the world and conquer it all in one try. She's practically cooing at Molly, telling her what a good girl she is, how pretty she is, that her fur is so soft. Her voice draws closer, gets louder, and then there she is, exiting the garage, Molly at her heels, Katie's expression hesitant. Wary.

But I see it, the slightest hint of joy in her eyes. She's glad to see me. She's just pretending that she's not. There's irritation, too, and I get it. I didn't warn her, call her, or text her that I was coming by. I just sprung myself on her. Bringing Molly with me wasn't an accident. I knew the dog would soften her.

"Hi." Katie stops a few feet away from me, about midpoint up the walkway that leads to her front porch. "Um, what are you doing here?"

"I thought I'd stop by. See if we could talk," I say easily, ignoring the rapid pounding of my heart.

"Stop by? You live an hour away. There's no stopping by for us." Molly hops up on her hind legs, licking at Katie's hand, and she immediately pets her.

"Where were you?" I snap my fingers for Molly to come over here but she ignores me, too enraptured with Katie. Guess I can't blame her.

"At an appointment." She sighs and approaches the porch, climbing the stairs and settling on the top one, right next to me. Close enough that I could reach out and touch, but not close enough that I can feel her body pressed to mine. "What are you doing here really?" She sounds weary. Looks it, too. There are dark circles under her eyes and her skin is pale. Her hair is in a sloppy ponytail and I swear she looks like she might have been crying.

If I was the reason—and I bet I was, *shit*—I hate that I'm

the one who causes her tears. "If you want me to go, I will," I say quietly. "I don't want to upset you. I know you're mad at me."

"I thought *you* were mad at *me*." She sighs again and leans her head against my shoulder, staying there. I turn and automatically kiss her forehead, breathing in her fresh, flowery scent. She doesn't flinch, doesn't move away from me, and I take that as a good sign. "I was at my weekly therapy session, unloading on her everything that's happened," she murmurs, so low I almost didn't hear her.

I stiffen but otherwise say nothing. Just wait for her to continue.

"We're kind of a mess, you and me. You do realize this, don't you?" Molly comes up the steps, nosing her way into Katie's lap, and she doesn't push her away. Just pets her like she belongs there.

"I know," I agree. "But I missed you, Katie. I'm even more of a mess when I don't have you by my side."

She lifts her head to stare into my eyes, hers full of so much pain it almost hurts to look at her. "You say things like that and I can't stay mad at you."

"Good." I lean in, my lips hovering above hers. "I'm sorry for what I said. I was frustrated and worried over that stupid interview and I acted like a dick." I kiss her before she can say anything in reply. A too quick, soft kiss that I pull back from reluctantly.

"Did you watch it?" She winces, as if afraid of my answer.

I nod, exhaling slowly. "It was a complete shit show. Totally sympathetic toward my father—I don't doubt he gained some new fans and believers." The words sound bitter because they are.

"She made you look awful," she agrees.

"You didn't look much better," I add.

A watery laugh escapes her. "I know. What a mistake." She shakes her head, her hand gentling on top of Molly's head. "I'm sorry I pushed you to do it."

"You didn't push me. We pushed each other. There's nothing to apologize for." I slip my arm around her shoulders and pull her in close. She goes willingly, molding into my side and fitting perfectly, like she was made for me. "It's not going to be easy, this relationship. As long as we're aware of it, that's all we can do."

"I suppose. Or maybe . . ." She lifts her head, her gaze meeting mine once more. "Maybe we're not supposed to be together at all. When it's this hard . . ." She starts to look away but I stop her.

"Everything's a struggle, especially relationships that are worth fighting for." I slide my fingers beneath her chin, not letting her escape. "The struggle makes the victory in the end that much sweeter."

"Do you really believe that?" she whispers as she reaches up and circles my wrist with her fingers, holding on to me as if I can anchor her somehow.

I feel the same way. She's my anchor in this swirling storm that's our life. I don't want to imagine navigating through all of this without her. I need her. I think she needs me. We can survive this together, but not if we're butting heads all the time.

"I do." I curl my fingers around her chin and tip her head back for my kiss just as she lets go of me. I sink into her mouth, going slow, giving her the opportunity to do what she wants. Leave. Stay. And when her lips part and I can feel her suck in a breath, triumph surges through me. I deepen the kiss, sliding my tongue against hers, and she lets me. Move my hand from her chin to her nape and pull her in closer. Angle my head so I can take the kiss deeper . . .

Molly barks loudly, startling us both, and I pull away from Katie, laughing ruefully at my cock-blocking dog. "She knows how to ruin a moment."

"It's probably best." Katie withdraws from me, putting distance between us. "Next thing you know we might make a spectacle on my front porch and shock the neighbors."

"You think?" I don't mind the thought, but yeah. We can't get too wild on her front porch in the middle of her neighborhood.

"I tend to get carried away when I'm kissing you," she admits, her cheeks the faintest pink.

"Then let's go inside and get carried away," I tell her, my voice dropping.

She shakes her head and grabs Molly, pulling her into her lap, using her like some sort of shield. "I don't think so. We need to talk first."

Yeah. She's probably right. So we'll talk first.

And get carried away after.

 KATIE

Slipping into bed together so we can talk is probably not the best move. I'll become too easily distracted and so will he, but then again, it's almost like forced intimacy, having to face each other while in bed and not being able to escape without hurting the other's feelings. There's something to be said for being open and honest with each other while lying in bed just wearing our underwear. Molly is on the floor, sleeping on an old blanket. It started to rain after dinner and the rain is still falling, the gentle sound soothing.

We ate dinner together, keeping the conversation easy, nothing confrontational, nothing too emotional. It was nice, pretending as if everything's normal. As though we don't have this overwhelming past that we share, that always seems to rear its ugly head between us at the worst moments.

When he suggested we go to bed after watching a really bad movie on HBO, I was wary at first. A little scared. But as usual, he put me at ease and said we could talk. And I want to talk. I also want to do a lot more . . .

I'm lying on my side, facing the window, and he's snuggled up behind me, one arm around my waist, hand splayed across my stomach. I think of what I should call him and yet again, I'm conflicted. Is he Ethan? Or Will? Can I imagine him as both? Is it fair of me, seeing the divide, to want to get rid of Ethan once and for all?

"You need to work out everything with your mom and

your sister," he says out of the blue. "I think it's eating you up, how they don't approve of us."

Sighing, I rest my hand over his. "It does bother me. A lot."

"I know. That's why you can't let this go on. You need to reach out to them."

"They should reach out to me," I say bitterly.

"Be the bigger person and do it first. Tell them that you miss them."

I do miss them. More than I want to admit. But there's so much more involved now. There are my feelings for the man in my bed. The dog on the floor that belongs to me as much as she belongs to him. I'm creating new relationships, a little family of my own, and they don't approve. I need their approval.

Desperately.

"They hate you," I point out. "And I don't like that. I want it to be easy. Why can't anything ever be easy for us?"

He shrugs; I feel the movement of his chest, his shoulders. "Nothing's ever easy for anyone, Katie. We only see what others want us to see. We don't know how they suffer behind closed doors. Our pain is particularly large. And obvious. And public."

I know he's right, but I still wish I could change it.

"And if your mom and sister hate me, then I'll have to work extra hard to get into their good graces, right? If I want to be with you, I need to accept them, too. I *want* to accept them and I want them to like me, but I understand why they don't. It's only because they're concerned about you and I appreciate their concern, their protectiveness. My link to your past isn't a pleasant one. They'd rather forget I existed."

"I don't want to forget you exist," I confess, my voice soft, my fingers stroking his arm.

He squeezes me closer. "I never want to forget you exist. You saved me, Katie. Everyone always talks about how I saved you, but you did the same for me. I didn't see it then, but I know what you did for me now."

"You were mad I forced you to go to the police station."

"It's hard to leave your only home, no matter how awful it is," he whispers against my temple.

"I can be your home now." I pick his hand up and kiss the back of it. "I want to be."

"You already are," he admits.

We lie together wrapped around each other for a long time, silent and thoughtful, my mind racing, his . . . I'm not sure what he's thinking, but I wish I knew.

"I'm confused," I finally say, running my thumb back and forth across the back of his hand.

"About what?"

"What name I should call you." My voice is small. I know it doesn't make him happy when I call him Will. I need to watch myself, but it's as if I can't help it.

He sighs, and it stirs the tiny hairs grazing my forehead. "I worked my hardest to get rid of Will. I didn't want to be him. And the moment I legally changed my name, I felt like a new person with a second chance. I needed that second chance, Katie."

"I know. I know you don't like thinking of yourself as Will."

"Will represents *him*," he says vehemently, his arm tightening around me, clutching me close. "We pretty much share the same name."

"But you're not him. To me, Will was my savior, my hero. Will is the boy who understands, who knows what I suffered because he suffered it, too. I don't want to lose him, no matter how badly you want to forget."

It's quiet again and I want to say more, but what? I'll just end up talking in circles.

"For you I'd do just about anything," he says, his voice a little shaky. "And if you want to call me Will, I guess . . . I guess I can agree to that. But it won't be easy, and I might snap at you on occasion. That name—it's only associated with bad things. At least, it is for me."

"Not for me. Will is the only positive thing that happened to me that summer." I turn to face him, resting my hand against his cheek as I stare up into his eyes. Our legs tangle together and he has both of his arms around me now, holding me close. He's so warm, so solid and firm and strong, and all mine, if I want him.

And I do want him. So much, my bones ache and my blood sings and my heart races in anticipation.

"You make me want to be him again. To be Will," he admits, dipping his head so our mouths are mere inches away from each other. "That's something I never thought would happen."

"I like that." He kisses me, stealing my words, and I let him, getting lost in the taste of his lips, warm and damp, his tongue seeking mine, his hands wandering all over my bare skin. I lose myself in his taste, in his touch, my hands everywhere, too, touching as much of him as I can.

The last time I saw Sheila, she told me I needed to be patient with Will. I needed to understand his feelings about the two names, the divide of his life. He was once Will and now he's Ethan. He might never want to combine the two, no matter how much I do want to merge them.

"Katie." He whispers my name against my lips as he rolls me over so I'm lying beneath him, his hips pressed to mine. I open my eyes to find him studying me, his dark gaze roaming all over my face. "I need to know that you're with me not just because I'm Will, but because you like the man I am today, too. We can't remain stuck in our past."

"I don't want us stuck in our past," I start to explain but he shakes his head once, cutting me off.

"I need you here," he says. "Now. I want you in my present, in my future. I don't ever want to let you go."

I stare up at him, see the uncertainty in his eyes, the fear. He's scared of my answer and I'm terrified of disappointing him.

But worse, I'm even more terrified of losing him. I can't imagine doing that. Not again. Not ever.

"I'm here for you," I say, my voice strong, so loud I hear Molly offer up a little bark in answer. "Right now. And I care about you. Not just as the boy I knew in my past, but the man that you are, too. I need you in my life. I don't—I don't want to lose you."

"You're never going to lose me. I'll make sure of that." He kisses me, taking over, taking command. Raining kisses all over my skin, his fingers between my legs, spreading my thighs, pushing himself inside me, his mouth fused with mine as he rocks into me, again and again, until I'm lost. Lost in the feeling, lost in him. Ethan.

Will.

The boy of my past. The man of my future. The one I can never, ever let go.

 AARON

The phone line buzzes as I wait impatiently, tapping my fingers on the edge of the metal table in front of me. How I hate waiting for a call to go through. Takes forever with this shit phone process the prison has.

Finally the familiar click, and Lisa's voice purrs over the line.

"Aaron. So good to hear from you." Her voice is warm and inviting, like she's talking to an old friend.

My grip tightens on the receiver. She's a pretty piece, Lisa Swanson. A little old for my tastes—I'd peg her at around my age, maybe a little younger, but still. I'd fuck her. She's glamorous, with a curvy body, cold, cold blue eyes, and a thirst for blood. Those eyes, that thirst . . .

Lisa reminds me of myself.

"They wouldn't let me watch the interview," I tell her, allowing the frustration to tinge my voice. I'm fucking mad that I couldn't watch my finest moment on television last night. Fucking unfair is what it is.

"I heard; such a shame. I'll do my best to get a tape over to you so you can watch it privately. I'll talk with someone. See if I can pull some strings." She always knows just how to smooth my ruffled feathers. "The ratings were spectacular, Aaron. We had a 2.9 rating last night, and that's just with live views. Not all of the DVR and streaming views have been counted yet. I think we could jump over three when it's all said and done."

She sighs happily, like a woman who's just been well pleasured.

She starts talking all that ratings and TV mumbo jumbo and I wouldn't be surprised at all if she creams her panties. She gets off on that stuff. Me, I don't get it, and don't really give a shit, either.

"That's just great, Lisa. But I have another question." I pause, letting the crackling air fill with anticipation before I drop my bomb. "I have sources telling me my boy and that girl are in a relationship. As in, they're fucking each other."

Lisa's quiet for a moment, like she needs to digest what I just told her. Well, fuck that. She needs to listen up and tell me the truth. Fast. Just the idea of my son with that girl . . .

It turns my stomach. Makes me feel like I'm gonna puke. Why her? Why would he want my sloppy seconds?

When she still doesn't say anything I'm on the verge of exploding.

"Is that for real?" I shout into the receiver. "Is my son fucking that stupid girl or what?"

"Aaron," Lisa immediately chastises, her voice low and calm, as if she were speaking to a naughty child. "You shouldn't talk like that about Katherine Watts."

I practically growl at hearing that bitch's name. "Fuck her. And fuck that asshole son of mine, too. They *are* together, aren't they? Jesus H. Christ. Why didn't you tell me? Hell, why didn't you *expose* them so all the world could give them endless shit?"

The two of them together would flip people's crazy switches. I'm sure of it. They'd deem it unnatural. Accuse them of having a weird connection—accuse my boy of being the one who did her wrong all those years ago. Not me.

Him.

"I've been waiting for more confirmation. We're on it, but we wanted to be sure before anything was said," she murmurs. "They've been spotted together over the last week or two, but nothing has been caught on film."

I have friends—friends on the outside who are linked to my friends on the inside. One of them started spying on Katie Watts after I paid a decent sum of money. It was easy. Little bitch didn't hide herself too well and he found her with minimal digging. And what my friend saw after only a few days of watching her just about made me lose my mind.

My very own son at her house, spending time with her like they're some sort of romantic couple. It's disgusting, what they're doing. I don't understand what he sees in her. Just following in his father's footsteps, is that the deal?

I doubt it. There's more to their relationship than that. I just can't figure out what.

"You lied. You kept that from me and I don't like it," I say, my temper rising. She's done nothing but help me, but does she really want to help me? Or help herself?

Her supposed kindness makes me mad. She turned her back on me when she knew my son was banging Katie Watts. She just didn't have the nerve to tell me. I'd guess Lisa Swanson is really nothing but a no-good dirty liar.

That's probably half the reason why I like her, but I don't want her lying to *me*.

"You're right. I should've told you," she says.

"You're damn straight."

"If you want me to leak the news tomorrow, I can. I have a source who claims he caught them on camera."

"That sounds real good, Lisa." I run a hand along my chin and jaw. "Real good." *Perfect.* I breathe deep, relish the calmness washing over me. Every single thing I say to Lisa is calculated. Sometimes my emotions get the best of me. My rage. My frustration. But she seems to make it better.

Every single time.

"Perfect. So that'll be my gift to you." She hesitates once more and I eat up the quiet, the stillness on her end, the faint buzz that's always there when I talk to someone on the damn phone. Not that I take a lot of calls, but still.

There's something reassuring about talking to another human being on the outside. It reminds me that life's still happening, still carrying on. All while I sit here in my cell, pace the length of my cage, and dream of getting out. Someday it could come true.

Someday it might become a reality.

"A gift, huh?" I chuckle. "I'd like to have something a lot more exciting as a gift from you, Lisa."

She laughs, but it sounds strained. Like she doesn't mean it. "I'm sure you would. Just . . . I'll take care of this. My way of showing appreciation for you allowing me to speak with you."

"Why are you always so nice to me, Lisa?" I'm serious in asking my question. She's the only media type who's ever given me the time of day. Who's ever given me a chance to speak and let me tell my side of the story. "Why are you doing this?"

"Oh darling, because I have a heart of gold." She laughs, a throaty, sexy sound that sends a shiver through all my good parts. "And for ratings, of course—always for the ratings. You and your son earn me a shit ton of them."

I bet we do.

# KATIE

The small cluster of reporters waiting outside in front of my house early this morning was the first indication that something was up. The numerous calls on my phone from unknown numbers were another clue. Fear clawed its way up my throat as I peeked out between the blinds at the reporters milling about on the sidewalk just on the other side of my fence. They won't cross the line to come on my front yard because they know I could call the police and report them for trespassing.

I so would, too.

Mrs. Anderson is out in her yard, yelling and carrying on, trying to shoo them away as if they were annoying giant insects buzzing around. If only it were that easy to get rid of them, I'd be out there doing the same thing. I can't quite understand what she's saying—I'm only able to catch a few words, like *nuisance* and *pains in my ass*—but I can tell she's extremely irritated on my behalf. I'll need to send her a big box of candy or maybe a beautiful fall-themed bouquet as a thank-you after this whatever-it-could-be is over. I know she's a fan of the See's Candy Nuts and Chews variety box . . .

My mind is taking me elsewhere so I don't have to focus on the crap that's unfolding right in front of me. Crap I don't even understand.

"What's going on?"

I whirl around at the first sound of Will's scratchy-with-sleep voice, resting my hand on my chest, over my racing heart. Yes, I can't think of him as Ethan anymore. I really don't call him much of anything right now to his face but in my mixed-up brain, he's Will. He always will be.

"There are reporters out there," I whisper, my gaze lingering on him. He's wearing a pair of sweats and nothing else, the waistband sitting low on his hips, looking as if he makes one wrong move, they could fall and reveal . . . everything. Everything I touched last night, because our unspoken theme for the evening was exploration. As in, he let me explore to my heart's content. It had been . . . enlightening.

Electrifying.

Freaking focus!

"Why are they here?" He comes toward me, peeking over my head through the blinds, then letting them carefully snap back into place. "What the hell is going on?"

He sounds as confused as I feel. "I don't know. Should we turn on the news?"

"One of those annoying morning shows?" It's pretty early, not even eight o'clock. I'd just made coffee when I realized I could hear voices out front.

I nod mutely. "But not out here. Let's go back in my bedroom."

We both scurry down the hall and into my room, diving under the covers as I grab the remote from the bedside table and turn the TV on. Molly snoozes on the end of the bed, oblivious to any trouble outside. "She's a terrible guard dog," I point out as I enter the channel I want.

"She's still in training," he says defensively.

It's a Sunday morning. My usual morning show preference is modified on the weekend. The unfamiliar faces greet me and I lean forward, my gaze never leaving the screen as I listen to what they have to say.

Some political dustup went down; what else is new. A celebrity wedding everyone's been waiting for. Horrible storm on the East Coast, blah, blah, blah. Will stretches out his arm and starts to scratch my back, his fingers light as they skim up and down, slipping beneath my threadbare T-shirt to graze my bare skin. I shiver at his touch, wishing for the distraction, telling myself I don't need it. That I need to pay attention to the news and trying to figure out what's going on.

But he's a welcome distraction—I can admit it. He's spent the entire weekend with me and it's been amazing. No arguing, no worrying, just the two of us spending time together. Learning more about each other. After our conversation Friday night, it felt good to let my walls down and just . . . feel. Be normal. We're good together, but that doesn't surprise me. I've never felt at ease with someone the way I do with Ethan. Will. He even let me call him Will a few times over the weekend, never really flinching once, and I thought that was progress.

Real progress would be me not calling him Will any longer, but I'm not sure that's ever going to happen . . .

"Ah, shit," Will mutters, his hand dropping away from my back.

I turn to see he's staring at his phone, his brows drawn low, his mouth curved into a frown. My heart trips over itself when he doesn't look up at me.

"What is it?" I whisper.

He shakes his head, his eyes still on the screen. "They know about us. That we're together."

Now it feels like my heart just stalled. "*Who* knows about us?"

"The public. I went on a crime forum that's always talking about my father." He makes a face. "One of the members shared a link to Lisa Swanson's site. I guess she has a blog with hundreds of thousands of subscribers that's associated with her network, and she wrote a post about us. That she has confirmation we're involved in a romantic relationship. Plus there was a small mention on a morning news show."

"Confirmation? As in what?" Oh God. This was my biggest fear. This is why I should never have done the first interview, let alone the second. I'm bringing unwanted attention on myself, on the both of us. People aren't going to be happy that we're together. Not that it's any of their business, but they don't care about that. They'll pass judgment.

And what about my mother and my sister? They'll be so upset. My relationship with Will—Ethan, whatever—they're against it. Why would I want to throw it in their face? Not that I am, that's thanks to Lisa, but still. They never wanted me to be with him in the first place.

Mom had also been against the first interview. Brenna was the one who convinced her I should do it. And now the two of them are angry with me.

But if I hadn't done that interview, Will would never have seen it and we wouldn't be together today. So it's a good thing that I did it.

Right?

"There's a photo of the two of us together."

I move so I'm sitting right next to him and lean in close, squinting at the grainy photo. It was taken here, at my house. We're in the backyard with Molly. She's running around while Will and I stand together, Will's arm around my waist.

Blissfully unaware, all while someone was lurking in the woods behind my house snapping photos of us.

"That was yesterday, I think," I murmur, staring at the photo, my stomach bottoming out. We look happy. Content.

Will is smiling down at me like I'm the best thing to ever happen to him, while I'm watching Molly run around in circles like a crazy dog. It hurts my heart to know someone was spying on us, violating our privacy, taking photos of us while they hid in the forest. A forest I never really feared until . . .

"I had a weird feeling a while ago. That someone was back there," I say, glancing up at him.

"I know. Mrs. Anderson told me."

My eyes go wide. "What? When?"

"On Friday, when I was waiting for you to come home, she mentioned it. We talked for a while. About you—how we're both watching out for you." He kisses my forehead, his warm lips lingering. I love it when he does that. I feel so loved. So cherished. And I need that right now. I'm on shaky ground, any little thing rattling me, and I don't like it. "I want you to keep Molly here with you."

"I can't do that. She's your dog," I start to say but he shakes his head, the serious look on his face silencing me.

"I'll take her to training this week and keep her with me, but once she's done, she's all yours. At least, she's staying here with you, even when I'm not here." His expression is grave. "I know she's not much, but I'd feel better if she were here. At least you'd have a warning if someone is ever outside, right?"

I nod, reluctantly. I don't like thinking of someone lurking outside, but I have to be realistic. "I don't want to take your dog from you," I whisper as I slip my arms around his neck, clinging to him. "You needed something to love, to take care of."

"I have you. And Molly." He smiles, and the sight of it both breaks my heart and fills me with hope.

"But you got her for yourself . . ." He places his fingers against my lips, silencing me.

"Stop arguing with me. Besides, I think we have bigger problems right now than who gets Molly. There are reporters outside who want to talk to you." He drops his fingers from my mouth.

"They'll want to talk to the both of us, especially if they know you're here." Panic grabs hold of me and I withdraw from the bed, glancing around for something decent to wear. I can't go out there in my pajamas. "What do you think they want to know?"

"You're not going to talk to them. I refuse to let that happen." His voice is firm, but I ignore him. I'm too busy pulling on a sweatshirt, then looking for a pair of jeans.

"Do you think 'no comment' will suffice?" I ask hopefully, turning to look at him.

"I doubt it." Sighing, he drops his phone on his lap and runs both hands through his hair, his frustration a living, palpable thing. "This isn't good, Katie."

"We'll be fine," I say feebly.

"You can't go out there," he says again, sounding fierce. "I mean it. We need to call my lawyer and have him handle it."

"You have a lawyer?" Why in the world would he have a lawyer? I hate the suspicion that crawls down my spine. Only the people who do wrong have a lawyer . . . that was always my thought process in the past.

And I don't like thinking that way at all when it comes to Will.

"It's not like I keep him on retainer or whatever, but yeah. There's a lawyer I talk to when I don't know which way to go. Like with the interview a few nights ago. I thought what Lisa said was slanderous, so I met with him. But he said that because I consented to the interview, and I actually spoke to her, I wouldn't have a legal leg to stand on." He runs his hands through his hair again, making a complete mess of it. "I don't have his cell number, but I can at least call his service and they can get my message to him."

I settle heavily on the edge of the mattress, chewing on my thumbnail and watching as he climbs out of bed, his phone held up to his ear as he makes the call. He leaves a message with the weekend answering service and looks at me when he's done, trying to smile.

"It'll be okay."

"What are we going to do in the meanwhile with all those people out there?" I wave a hand toward the front of the house.

He leaves the bedroom and I trail after him, as does Molly. He's at the window by the time I'm in the living room, peeking once again through the closed blinds. I can't believe the dog doesn't bark, the little brat. She'll bark at us but not complete strangers? "There are three reporters out there and three dudes lugging the cameras. Probably the local networks."

"Should I go outside and try to get rid of them?"

"How many times do I have to say no, Katie? You should absolutely not go out there." Shaking his head, he steps away from the window. "I don't know what to do."

"I don't, either." I feel totally out of control yet again and I don't like it. I can tell Will doesn't like it, either.

We're victims of our own circumstances. We brought this on ourselves. Now we have to figure out a way to fix it.

# KATIE

"How'd you call off the reporters? I heard they were hanging out in your yard," Brenna says by way of greeting when I open the front door. "Broke up with what's-his-name?"

Ignoring her comment, I open the door wider, indicating I want her to come in. She tries to get her digs in where she can but I refuse to acknowledge them. I'm just thankful we're talking once more and she's here. Remaining patient is the name of the game. It's going to take a long time getting her to warm up to the idea of Will being a permanent part of my life.

"I have the magic touch," I tell her, making her snort as she passes by. Mom's still at the car, pulling something out of the backseat. I said I would make dinner, but I know Mom brought something. She always does. Hopefully it's something sweet. She excels at any and every dessert she's ever attempted to make.

"Seriously, Katherine. How did you get rid of them?" Brenna turns to face me, skepticism written all over her face. She crosses her arms in front of her chest in pure defensive mode. For what I can only assume is a multitude of reasons, she's still mad at me. And I don't know how to fix it. I've already told her I was sorry, but that clearly wasn't good enough.

I'm starting to wonder if it was the right choice, inviting my mom and sister to dinner tonight . . . and having Will join us. He's on his way now, and I'm praying he won't feel like he entered a vipers' nest when he gets here.

"Will knows a lawyer who helped us with the public statement," I explain, not missing the way Brenna's eyes narrow. The statement had been terse and to the point, without revealing too much information. We went out in front of my house and spoke to the few reporters who lingered there, reading the statement. Which merely stated that our friendship was of no one else's concern, that we share a connection that we cannot deny, born from a horrific experience, and that we would have nothing else to say going forward.

In other words, *none of your business, we're going to do whatever we want, so leave us alone.* I thought it was perfect, as did Will. The reporters were disappointed and tried to ask about a thousand questions all at once, but Will told them we wouldn't talk and we went back into the house. Thankfully, they abandoned their post in front of my house almost as quickly as they established it.

What helped? A new local scandal erupted between an assistant district attorney and a female judge, who were immersed in an intense affair—until the judge's angry husband waved his gun in the young DA's face, threatening to kill him. Now the judge's husband is in jail on attempted murder charges.

I've never been so grateful for someone else's problems in all my life. I know it's wrong to feel that way, but at least their story took the spotlight off ours.

"He knows a lawyer? So like what, he has one on hand whenever he needs one? Don't you find that odd?" Brenna asks.

"What does she find odd?" Mom walks into the house at that very moment, breezing past me with a pie dish wrapped in aluminum foil in her hands. I shut and lock the door, peeking out the still-open window for any unfamiliar cars parked on the street. But I see nothing.

"Her *friend* has a lawyer. That's how they handled that statement they issued a few days ago," Brenna says, her arms falling at her sides. "What twenty-three-year-old guy has a lawyer? And who issues public statements?"

"We do," I say quietly, wanting her to know that Will and I are a team. She's not going to break us up with her wild speculation. I won't let her.

"What, have you become a celebrity? You talk to Lisa Swanson a couple of times on national TV and now you need a publicist?"

"Brenna," Mom says, her voice soft but firm. "Enough."

She looks totally exasperated, but at least my sister goes quiet.

Leaving Brenna alone to stew in her anger, Mom and I go into the kitchen, where she puts the pie dish in the refrigerator before she proceeds to examine what I've prepared for dinner. She looks over the chicken dish I have baking in the oven, the rice cooking on the stovetop, and the salad that I was just finishing putting together.

"Looks good." The smile on her face is falsely bright, straining at the edges, making my own fall. She doesn't look happy and I hate that. Is she disappointed in my choosing Will? I'm starting to think it's impossible to make everyone in my life happy. "When is your friend going to be here?"

I don't even know exactly how I convinced them to come over for dinner. They were mad enough to tell me they couldn't offer their support if I continued to see Will and they proved that by not reaching out to me. Not after the Lisa interview, not after the reveal that Will and I were in a relationship. They were eerily quiet. I had to be the one to finally reach out to them.

And Will was the one who encouraged me.

"You need your family," he'd told me yet again late one

night as he was holding me in his arms, in bed and tangled up in each other. "You can't freeze them out."

"But they're freezing *me* out," I'd started to protest, and he'd cut me off by kissing me.

A wonderful way to be cut off, but still, when we were finished, I'd been irritated.

"Just call them. Start with your mom first. Ask her to talk to Brenna for you. Or just reach out to her yourself. They'll eventually come around." He'd paused then, his expression downright fierce. "I refuse to stand in the way of your relationship with them."

His words, the expression on his face, they touched me. I liked that he cared about my family relationships. He knew they were important to me and therefore, they were important to him, too.

"I'll call her," I'd promised.

And now here we are. I practically had to beg Mom to come for dinner and drag Brenna with her, but she finally, reluctantly, agreed. Now I just pray it goes well and no one screws anything up. Especially me.

Especially Will.

"He should be here in a few minutes," I tell her as she grabs a few leftover cherry tomatoes and throws them into the salad. "Mom. I want to say thank you for coming over tonight."

"Well, of course I wanted to come over. I missed you." Her fake smile fades, replaced with an expression full of motherly concern. I've seen that look more times than I can count over the years. I've given this woman so much to worry about. "I don't like fighting with you, Katherine. That's never happened before."

I wasn't the one in a fight—she was. But I decide it's best not to mention that little fact.

"I don't, either. That's why I'm glad you're here, and that you brought Brenna with you, even though I know she's still mad." I hesitate, but decide to go for it. "I really need you guys to accept him, Mom. Please." I go to her then and wrap my arms around her, and she does the same, squeezing me tight. I need this hug. I need the reassurance that my family will accept this man in my life and that we can all do this together. I need Will, but I also need Mom and Brenna.

Despite my sister's hostility and still very obvious resentment, I know eventually she'll get over it. She has to. We're too close to let something like a guy come between us and hurt our relationship.

"Brenna's in therapy," Mom admits, her voice low as she speaks close to my ear. "She's been going through some . . . stuff, and I'm afraid she's been taking it out on you. And it sounds like she's been taking it out on your—friend as well."

"What do you mean she's been going through some stuff? And why do you keep calling him my *friend*?" I withdraw from her embrace slightly, though I haven't let her go. I don't want to. It feels nice, being in my mother's arms. I need her comfort right now. These last few weeks have been so incredibly stressful and confusing.

"What else can I call him? I must say, Katherine, that this entire situation is incredibly awkward." She pulls away from me completely and starts roaming around my kitchen once more. I'm surprised she hasn't started setting the table, just to keep herself occupied. "Please don't say anything to your sister, but she and Mike broke up. She's moved back in with me."

I gape at her. "Are you serious?"

"Shh! Not so loud—she'll hear you. But yes, I'm serious. Things haven't been good between them for a while and they finally split up. She won't give me too many details, but I do know she started going to a counselor a few weeks ago." She taps her lips with her index finger, staring at my empty table. "Want me to set the table for dinner?"

Ah, there's the mom I know and love. I knew that would happen. "That would be great, thanks. Let me get the plates." I open the cupboard door as Mom goes to my silverware drawer. I grab the plates and set them on the counter before glancing toward the kitchen door. I think I heard Brenna go into the bathroom a few minutes ago, but I can't be too sure. "Wow. I can't believe it. I really thought they were going to get married."

"So did I, but apparently that didn't work out so well." Mom shakes her head, looking toward the door as well before she sets the silverware on top of the stack of plates. "We shouldn't talk about it. She'll be in here any minute and I don't want her thinking we're whispering about her."

"Why not? You two are always whispering about me." *Ouch*. That came out way snottier than I meant it to.

"Katherine. Please. Don't start that now."

I keep my lips shut, thankful when Brenna walks into the kitchen and provides the proper distraction. I stow the salad in the fridge and clean up any mess that I left on the counter, while Brenna pours herself a glass of wine from the bottle she brought with her and Mom sets the table. Brenna's going on about the kids in her class and how they drive her crazy, and all I can think about is that she's alone. Not with her boyfriend, Michael, and living back at home with Mom.

It's hard for me to wrap my head around it. I feel like I've come five steps forward in the last few months while Brenna's dropped five steps back.

My phone vibrates and I pull it out of the back pocket of my jeans to find there's a text from Will. Ethan. It says Ethan but I think Will. I'm ridiculous. Still a little confused, but trying to deal.

> I'll be there in less than five. Probably closer to two minutes.

Smiling, I slip my phone back in my pocket and start for the living room.

"Where are you going?" Brenna calls after me.

"Will is almost here," I tell her, surprised when I glance over my shoulder to find that she's following me. I glance out the front window before I turn to face her. "What's up?"

"So what are we supposed to call this guy, huh? Is it Ethan or Will?" She curls her upper lip and I hate the dread sinking like a stone in my stomach, taking my appetite, my happiness, and replacing it with worry.

"Brenna, please. Can we just . . . can you please approach meeting him with an open mind? I don't want any trouble tonight. I want us all to get along. And I really think you'll like him if you just allow yourself to get to know him." I check the window once more, thankful he hasn't pulled up yet.

"We're worried, Katherine. You have to understand that," Brenna says, her expression sincere, most of the hostility gone from her eyes. "This isn't easy for us."

"This isn't easy for me, either. But please." I pause, trying to hold back the swell of emotion threatening to overtake me. I don't want to cry. Not now, in front of Brenna before Will gets here. He'll know immediately something's wrong. "Do this for me. He makes me happy."

Brenna's quiet and I am, too. I can hear Mom in the kitchen, humming as she preps the table. It's a familiar sound, one that makes my heart ache for a simpler time, but I push that emotion aside.

I need to focus on the here and now. No more wishing for the past.

It's over.

"I'll try my best," Brenna finally says, her tone reluctant.

Relief hits me so hard I almost sway on my feet. "Thank you." I hear Will's car then, pulling in front of my house, and I turn to see it parked in my driveway, Molly's face peering out the backseat's window as she barks, though I can't hear her. I turn back to face Brenna, not able to contain the smile stretching my mouth wide. "That's all I can ask for."

# ETHAN

I enter Katie's house warily, arming myself with a bottle of wine, a smile, and Molly tugging on her leash. Brenna scowls at me from where she stands in the corner of the living room, her arms wrapped around herself as if she can ward me off. She's going to be the hardest one to thaw.

Katie gives me a kiss on the cheek in greeting and takes the wine bottle from me. Katie's mother approaches me with a tentative smile, kneeling down to pet Molly, speaking to her much like Katie does.

"Aw, such a pretty, pretty dog. Katherine's told me about you." She strokes Molly's head, and Molly settles her chin on Elizabeth Watts's knee. "Aw, aren't you sweet?"

"Mom." Katie clears her throat, shooting me a nervous smile. "I want you two to officially meet." I hope like hell she's referring to me and not the dog.

Her mother rises to her full height, smiling warmly at me and holding out her hand. "Elizabeth Watts. But you can call me Liz."

I take her hand and give it a quick shake. "Nice to meet you."

She's still shaking my hand, apprehension suddenly appearing in her gaze. "And um, what shall I call you?"

I glance in Katie's direction and see she's a little deer-in-the-headlights herself. I didn't even think of this. Katie's been switching between names, though I've noticed lately she

doesn't call me anything at all. And that's because she prefers
Will.

Fuck it, I'll run with it. It goes against everything I stood for
only months ago, but I want to make Katie happy. And though
it'll be difficult, once I say it, there's no going back. At least not
with her family. Maybe I need to embrace my former self. Katie
doesn't think he's bad. I'm the one with the problem.

"You can call me Will," I tell Liz firmly as she releases my
hand, blinking at me like maybe I said the wrong thing.

I really freaking hope I didn't say the wrong thing.

"And you've already met my sister, Brenna." Katie breezes
right over that, not that I can blame her. She smiles brightly at
both her mom and me. "Are you hungry? Dinner is just about
ready."

I follow her into the kitchen, leaving Molly with her mom
and sister, and the moment we're out of sight I pull her into
my arms and kiss her. "Did I mess that up?"

"Of course not." She shakes her head, a little breathless. I
kiss her again because I like hearing her sound that way. She
pushes at my chest to gain some distance. "It's going to take a
while to win them both over, I guess. Though Mom likes
Molly."

"Who doesn't like Molly? That would be a crime." I push
a strand of hair behind her ear, unable to stop touching her.
"Do you need help with anything?"

Katie shakes her head, disentangling herself from my embrace and going to the oven. She peeks inside and then hits a
couple of buttons, turning it off. "Dinner really is almost
ready. If you want to get yourself something to drink, that
would be great."

I go to the fridge and grab a water bottle. I'll save the wine
for actual dinner. "You made a pie?"

"My mom did. She's an amazing baker. I think it's pump-kin."

"Thanksgiving a little early, huh?" I take a drink, the water soothing my dry throat.

"Well, I'm pretty thankful that we're able to have this din-ner together in a civil manner," Katie says, making me laugh.

Unable to hold back, I go to her again, waiting until she sets the baking dish on the stovetop and shuts the oven door before I slip my arms around her waist and hug her from be-hind. "Don't worry. This will all work out."

"If I only had half your confidence," she says with a sigh, leaning her head against my chest for a too-brief moment be-fore she pulls away and starts her dinner prep in earnest.

I'm faking my confidence. I'm worried this dinner could go down in flames if I don't watch it. I plan on being on my best behavior tonight, and I have a feeling Katie's mother will be fine. Polite, though she'll search for a reason to dislike me. I refuse to give her one.

Brenna we can't count on. She's a loose cannon. A really pissed-off one, too, by the expression on her face when I first walked in. I'll have to be careful around her. I need this to work.

I need them to like me.

"So, Will." Liz smiles at me and I do my best not to wince at her calling me Will. I'm still not used to it. The only reason I offered up the name was to please Katie. "Tell me exactly what you do for a living."

We've finished our salads and Katie's brought out the vari-ous dishes that make up the main course. She's on top of her game tonight, playing the perfect hostess and doing a damn good job of it. I had no idea she had it in her. But there are still so many things for me to learn about Katie.

"Well, I'm a Web designer." I launch into my story, about how my friend was in a band and they wanted a website, but their designer ditched them at the last minute so I stepped in. "I'd been messing around with graphics and design all through high school and took a few courses in community college." Only the courses that interested me—otherwise, I hated going to college. I had financial aid and could pretty much take any course for free, accompanied by a few minor fees. But ultimately I bailed once my Web design business started to pick up.

"Did you graduate college?" Liz asks as she spoons some rice onto her plate.

I shake my head. "I took a few courses at my local JC, but otherwise, no. Most of what I learned was self-taught."

"Quite enterprising, aren't you?" She smiles, her gaze going to Katie as she nods. "She's taking courses currently. Online, though I wish she would go to an actual campus. It might be good for her, to meet new people, make new friends."

I can't quite tell if that's a dig or her just making conversation. "Katie needs to do whatever she thinks is best for her."

"Mom, don't push," Katie says as she reaches for her wineglass and takes a big swallow.

"And do you believe you're the one who knows what's best for Katie?" Brenna pipes up. She's been mostly quiet, drinking lots of wine and glaring at me from her spot at the other end of the table. "Or is that up to our mother, who's been watching out for her, oh, you know—her entire life?"

Here it is. Brenna's hostility is back in action. "She's a grown woman. I think she can make decisions for herself."

Brenna snorts and Liz eases right over it, changing the subject and talking about some social ladies' club she's a part of, telling stories about how they're donating their time around town and doing good deeds.

I tune out, eating my dinner, tossing the occasional small bite of chicken to Molly, who rests at my feet. No one's paying me any attention and that's fine with me, because that means I don't have to make painful conversation or ward off Brenna's biting commentary. She's quiet, too, staring into her never-empty wineglass, muttering responses whenever Katie or Liz acknowledges her.

Something's up with her, and I don't believe it has to do with just me.

"So, Brenna." Katie smiles at her sister as she sets her fork down on her mostly empty plate. "What's new with you?"

Brenna's shoulders tense and the smile on her face is completely over the top. "Oh, you know, I've just turned into a big loser and moved back in with Mom."

"Brenna," Liz starts, but Brenna waves a hand and laughs, though there's no humor in the sound.

"May as well tell her the truth, Mom. She'll find out eventually." Her laughter dies. "Mike broke up with me."

Liz's mouth drops open. "I thought *you* broke up with *him*."

Brenna shakes her head. "He was tired of dealing with my bullshit—direct quote. Said I have too many hang-ups about sex and marriage."

I remain quiet while Liz and Katie gasp in unison. Looks like too much wine makes Brenna overshare.

"Though he's not too off the mark," Brenna continues. "Our screwed-up family focuses so much on Katherine's problems, no one has ever given mine a second thought."

"Brenna, please," Liz starts, but Brenna barrels right over her.

"I'm in therapy and it's going surprisingly well. I can see why you keep going, Katherine." Brenna drains her wineglass and sets it onto the table with a loud thump. "I stuck it out too long with Mike. Our relationship has been dying a slow, boring death. We grew apart. End of story. No dramatic ending; no tragic event happened to split us up. Unfortunately, I don't have a romantic, star-crossed, forbidden love story like you two." She points at Katie and me.

We exchange glances. "Romantic, star-crossed, forbidden love story" isn't what I would call us, but everyone has their own interpretation.

Including Katie's sister.

# KATIE

The moment my sister and Mom leave the house, Will and I start to clean the kitchen. Me quietly putting things away while Will rinses off the dishes and sets them in the dishwasher.

"Well, that didn't go quite the way I planned," I finally say, coming to stand beside him and help rinse out the pot I used for the rice.

He says nothing for a while. Simply sets silverware into the dishwasher, his movements methodical and careful, just as is his silence. He's trying to figure out what to say, I think.

"Your sister has a lot going on," he finally says.

"That's a nice way to put it." He's just being polite.

Bracing his hands on the edge of the sink, he turns to face me. "I also think she's tired of living in your shadow."

I turn off the water, irritated. Okay, I didn't think he'd say that. "I never asked for any of this," I remind him. "If she's jealous because everyone focused on me over the years, trust me. I'd trade places with her in a heartbeat. Not that I'd ever wish what happened to me on my sister—"

"I know. I understand. But she doesn't. No one really does. All she sees is you got all the attention over the years, and she feels like she didn't get any." He dries his hands off with a dish towel, tossing it onto the counter before he pulls me into him, his arms going around me and holding me tight. I snuggle close to his chest and breathe in his warm, masculine, undeniably Will scent. "I didn't think dinner went too bad, despite your sister's outburst," he murmurs into my hair.

I agree with him. Mom was nice. Friendly. She loves Molly, but who wouldn't? Will loved Mom's pumpkin pie, having two big slices, which pleased her. Once Brenna got over her minor fit and off the wine, she mellowed out, too. Will tried his best to be friendly, but she really didn't warm to him. That'll take time, I'm sure.

He's always watching out for me and I wish Brenna could see that. He's my own personal guardian angel. I've thought that about him from the very start. My wrist still feels empty considering I never took the bracelet he gave me long ago to a jeweler. It still sits on my dresser in my tiny jewelry box, waiting for me to do something about it. After the bracelet fell off my wrist when we were on the Sky Gliders and he'd been able to find it, I never found the time to take it to get fixed. I needed to make time and do that.

"It went well," I say, smiling up at him. My smile fades when I see the intent in his gaze, the way his head lowers, and then his mouth is on mine. Gently. Then not so gently, with that hint of fire lying just beneath the surface, the hint that tells me he wants more. He'll take this further.

And I'll let him. I always let him.

We kiss like we haven't seen each other in months, standing in front of the sink in the middle of my kitchen, our arms wrapped around each other, mouths fused. My lips part the slightest bit and his tongue is there, touching just the tip of mine. A tease, a promise of what's to come, and I open my mouth wider, welcoming the invasion. Needing his kiss, his touch, to take me away and help me forget.

Everything.

The tension from dinner eases slowly from my muscles, leaving me a boneless heap in his arms. Still he kisses me, his hand moving up to cup the side of my face, his fingers streaking across my cheek, down my neck, pressing against the spot where my pulse flutters like a wild thing.

I feel a little wild with the way he's kissing me. Consuming me. Yet his mouth and hands are also like anchors, grounding me, reminding me that I'm a woman and it's okay for me to have this yearning, all-encompassing need building and growing inside of me. This need is all for him. Only him. He makes me feel alive. Like every light is extra bright, each sound is higher, louder, and his every touch is more intense, more urgent, more *now, now, now* and *mine, mine, mine.*

That's what it feels like, to be with this man. To have his focus centralized only on me. It's a delicious, heady experience, even while we stand in the kitchen, the dishwasher open, my still-damp hands clinging to the back of his shirt. We can take the ordinary and turn it into something amazing with only a few kisses, a smattering of stolen words, a whispered sign and a muffled moan.

One big hand with splayed fingers slides over my backside, staying there. Reminding me that I belong to him. And I want to belong to him. The more time I spend with Will, the more I know that this was the right choice. That *he* was the right choice.

We belong together. And no one can ever change that.

"Come on," he whispers against my lips and I frown, about to ask him what he means when he's suddenly lifting me up, into his arms. My legs automatically circle his hips and he's carrying me as if I weigh nothing, Molly padding after us. I point a finger at her, my other arm wrapped around Will's neck as I cling to him.

"Stay," I command her, making Will chuckle. Making Molly halt in her tracks in the middle of the hallway.

At least she listens to me.

He pushes open the bedroom door, walking inside, and then I'm sliding down his body, feeling every hard inch of him press into me. I land softly on my feet, my hands at his flannel shirt as I hurriedly undo the buttons. He doesn't stop me, just watches me with those dark, heated eyes, his chest moving faster and faster as his breathing accelerates.

All for me, I think. *His reaction is all mine.*

My breaths match his, my trembling fingers fumbling over the last buttons, and he bats my hands away, taking over the job. He shrugs out of his flannel, tears off the white T-shirt he wore underneath, and then there's just acres of firm, masculine skin on display. Just for me.

I touch him. Press my hands against his pecs, then slide them down, palms flat, brushing against his hot, hard flesh. He's lean, I can feel his ribs, and I run my fingers over the tattoo, the tattoo I never asked about but now understand.

The angel wings, the words *Only us.* It's me. It's him. It's us, together.

"Did you get this for me?" I press a kiss to the wings, letting my lips linger, tasting his skin.

"Yeah." He cups my nape and I gaze up at him. "Took the drawing you gave me into the tattoo shop and the artist recreated it with more detail. You said 'only us' in your first letter to me and the words stuck with me."

I frown up at him. "I did?" I don't remember, and that makes me feel bad.

He nods. "You said that no one else understood what happened. Only us."

Only us. The words stuck with him all this time. Permanently. That he would etch those words and the wings I drew him onto his skin forever . . . makes my heart feel like it grew wings and is desperate to take flight.

"I love it, that you did this. For me. For us." I trace the tattoo again, drift my fingers along his rib cage. Exploring. I was always too shy to closely examine his body at first. And once I got over that, I became too shy to say the words that always seem to clog my throat when we're together like this.

It's overwhelming, what I want to say to him. What I want to do to him. But I'm working up my courage, slowly but surely.

Without another word, I touch the tattoo again, tracing the wings, the letters, my fingers sliding down over his firm belly, the indent of his navel, the dark hair that's just beneath. I draw my index finger along that soft trail until I reach his jeans, curling my fingers around the denim and slipping them inside, my knuckles brushing nothing but warm flesh.

He sucks in a breath and I glance up to catch him closing his eyes, his expression one of pure, unadulterated torture. And pleasure. So much pleasure. He took off his glasses earlier when we started cleaning the kitchen and I stare at his handsome face, seeing his younger features, the ones that remind me so much of my Will from before, the boy who saved me. There's a tiny hole just beneath his lower lip and I reach up, touching it, knowing exactly what it's from.

His eyes open and he knows what I'm touching, too. "You remember the lip ring?" he asks quietly.

I nod, never taking my hands off his face, moving my fingers up so I can trace his eyebrow. There had been a ring there, too. Funny, how we've never talked about this until now. "What happened to them?"

"Got rid of them when I changed my name."

"And your hair?" It had been black as night when I first met him. An unnatural color that made him appear totally emo, like some of the kids Brenna had in her class back then. He'd scared me the first time I saw him. All the black, the piercings, though, it was all a façade.

A mask.

"I dyed it for years. Finally shaved it all off and started over."

"You shaved your head?" All that pretty hair, gone. He has the best hair. Thick and soft, I love to run my fingers through it.

"I wanted a complete change." He smiles, a teasing light in his gaze. "You want me to repierce my lip? Or maybe my eyebrow?"

Shaking my head, I reach for the silver button and undo it, tugging harder so that the entire button fly comes undone before I spread the denim wide only to discover . . .

Will's not wearing any underwear.

His smile grows at the precise moment I suck in a harsh breath at my discovery.

"Found out my little secret," he murmurs, his eyes sparkling.

His little secret makes me feel shy. A little unsure. I still feel somewhat anxious when it comes to sex. Sheila warned me I'd continue to feel that way for a while and here I am, panicking over discovering that he's naked beneath those jeans. Any other girl would be thrilled. Any other girl would take her opportunity and touch him. Get down on her knees for him and draw him into her mouth, reward him for his pleasant surprise.

But not me. I can't. I'm still too self-conscious. I've never given him a blow job. I wouldn't know how to do it. I'm not ready to give him one, either, too self-conscious that I might mess it up or worse, that I might freak out. Not that he's asked for one. I just think he's so glad that we're together, he'll take what he can get from me.

That sounds horrible. Like he's settling. Is he? I hope not. I know I'm not. He's all I know.

He's all I *want* to know.

"I was in a hurry after I took a shower," he murmurs, catching my chin with his fingers and tilting my head up so I have to look at him. He looks amused, even a little sheepish. "In such a hurry, I forgot to grab underwear when I picked out my clothes for tonight earlier this afternoon. So I just got dressed and left the house."

Aw, he picked out clothes to wear special for meeting my mom and sister. That's so adorable. I know he was worried about tonight, maybe more worried than I was, though he never acted like it. I envied his calm, cool demeanor.

He's being pretty cool and calm right now, considering I have my hand down his jeans, fingers brushing awfully close to his private parts.

"This would be the moment when most women would tear your jeans off and grab hold of you like they never want to let you go," I suggest, feeling immediately stupid for even saying it.

He winces. "If you're referring to my cock, then I don't know if I want a woman grabbing hold of it like she's never going to let go."

I'm blushing so furiously my cheeks feel like they're on fire. I can't believe he just said the word *cock* so casually. I'm even more surprised that I kind of liked hearing him say it. "That does sound a little too fierce," I concede softly.

"Yeah." He leans in and kisses me, lifting away to murmur,

"It does. And you're not most women. You're *my* woman. That's all that matters."

My heart flutters at his words, at the intense look in his eyes, and I melt. Giving me one more lingering kiss, he reaches for me, his hands sneaking under my sweater, and then he's removing it as well as my bra. I cover my chest when he kneels down and slides my jeans down my legs, his mouth following the same path, and then I forget all modesty, grabbing hold of his shoulders to keep myself from falling. I whimper low in my throat when he presses his mouth against the front of my pink panties.

"So sweet," he murmurs there, making me shudder. I clutch his shoulders harder for fear my legs will give out and I'll collapse on the floor.

He slowly rises to his feet, his mouth blazing a trail of damp heat along my skin before he's finally standing above me. He sheds his jeans, his movements almost awkward in his rush to get naked, and I love seeing his excitement, that he doesn't care how he looks in front of me. He just wants me.

I lie back onto the mattress and he's standing at the foot of the bed, completely naked, hard and ready, just for me. I open my arms to him and he falls atop me, his mouth on mine, his hot body pressing me deeper into the mattress. I'm blanketed by his body, his hot skin making me feel like I'm burning up from the inside.

And then he grabs a condom and he's actually inside of me, our bodies connected. I arch up against him, needing him closer, and when I open my eyes I find that he's watching me. He runs his fingers through my hair, his hips shifting slowly as he lies atop me, and I slide my legs along his, wrapping them around his hips and sending him even deeper. We both groan and he leans in, pressing his forehead against mine, his features strained.

"I don't know what I'd do without you."

I close my eyes against the sudden sting of tears.

"Thank you for allowing me into your life," he murmurs. "I appreciate you letting me meet your family tonight."

His words crack my already sensitive, barely held-together heart. I don't want to talk. Instead I loop my arms around his neck and pull him into me for a kiss, but he breaks away after the first one.

"I mean it, Katie. I love you. I've never had a real family. I've always been alone, taking care of myself. To the point where I truly believed I didn't need anyone else. Definitely not a woman." His voice breaks, and I close my eyes against the onslaught of emotions swarming inside of me. "With you, I don't ever feel alone. With you . . . I feel whole."

"That's because you're not alone, not when you're with me," I whisper, opening my eyes to see him smile in response.

"I don't ever want to lose you. I've lived without you for too long. I won't let anything get between us. Nothing." The kiss he presses to my lips is almost brutal. Ferocious. As if he's trying to prove a point. And he is. "You belong with me. We belong together."

I don't disagree because I can't. Fate pushed us together. To lose each other again would only tempt fate to tear us apart.

And I don't want to tempt fate.

# WILL

A cold nose nudges against my arm, followed by low, incessant whining, and at first I think I'm dreaming. Of a dog tugging on my arm, trying to pull me somewhere, but the both of us getting frustrated because I can't figure out what she wants.

I crack open my eyes to find Molly's face in mine and she licks my hand. Immediately I pull it under the covers, but she doesn't appear offended. No, she pants, practically smiling at me, her warm dog breath blowing across my face and making me grimace. I blow out a harsh breath, closing my eyes, wishing she'd go away.

She nudges my arm again. Then licks it, offering up a soft "ruff" to encourage my lazy ass to get out of bed. I'm not getting out of this.

"All right, all right," I mutter, keeping my voice low so I don't wake up Katie. She's nestled up close to me, warm and naked and too damn delicious to leave in this bed by herself, but I have to. I pull away from her slowly, careful not to disturb her. She murmurs something unintelligible and rolls over on her side, facing me, and I pause, watching her, waiting for her to wake up.

But she doesn't.

I slip out of bed and grab the pair of sweats I left on the chair in her room the last time I was here. Pulling them on and the T-shirt I wore earlier, I snap my fingers at Molly and she falls into step behind me, the two of us walking slowly. I lead her down the hall and through the kitchen to the door that opens to the backyard.

Molly practically flies out the door the second it swings open, sniffing around the perimeter of the backyard, pausing in spots like she's discovered something extra good, her nose buried in the grass or a bush, only for her to trot off until she finds the next spot worthy of a good sniff.

I stand on the back porch, shivering in the cold night air as I watch her. I forgot to check my phone, so I have no idea what time it is. Molly stops and pees here and there and I wait for her, knowing this is her ritual, though usually I get it handled before I go to bed. She'll come up to the porch when she's done and sit by my feet; she always does. It's just that some pee sessions take a little longer than others.

My thoughts drift, my mind still hazy from sleep and sex. Earlier with Katie had been especially good. Every time we have sex I feel closer to her. I've paid attention, learning her body's cues, what she prefers, where she likes to be touched. Kissed. Sucked.

Breathing deep, I scrub my arms with my hands to create some heat considering it's so damn cold I feel like my balls are gonna freeze off. But instead of focusing on my cold balls, I think about my girl and what gets her off. Yeah, Katie likes soft, slow kisses with lots of tongue. Gentle touches that make her shiver and shake. She especially likes it when I suck her nipples, and when I go down on her? I don't think she wants to like it, but she does.

I wouldn't mind going back inside and waking her up with my mouth all over her body. Stroking her between her legs, kissing her neck and her breasts, driving her wild before she's even fully awake . . .

A loud snapping sound comes from somewhere deep in the

woods beyond the house, and I lift my head at the same moment Molly goes completely still. She tilts her head back, nose in the air, her nostrils quivering as she sniffs again and again. And that's when she goes bat-shit crazy.

The low, scary growl she emits is immediately followed by an outburst of constant, ferocious barking, unlike anything I've heard come out of her before. She runs back and forth along the back fence, like she wants to jump over it and take off running into the dark, dense woods. I'm damn thankful she can't. I'd probably never be able to coax her back inside.

I try to get her to quiet down from where I stand on the porch, but she's too wound up now. Panting and whining in between all the barking, so loud she's probably going to wake the entire neighborhood. Reluctantly I run down into the yard, yelping when my bare feet hit the cold, wet grass. Molly's still barking uncontrollably and I grab hold of her collar, offering her a stern *no*.

She quiets down, her butt hitting the ground and her tail thumping wildly, flicking up moisture from the grass, and it lands on my sweats. She's still whining; her entire body is tense. Poised to run. Letting go of her collar, I go to the fence and carefully step onto the ledge, hoping like hell I don't get splinters in the bottom of my feet. Molly's just behind me, pacing back and forth, the low whine continuous. I peer over the edge of the wood, staring into the dark forest, but I can't see a damn thing. The moon's not even a quarter full, so the night sky is dark. Black.

Ominous.

Molly finally settles down—somewhat—sitting directly behind me, whining and fidgety, but I ignore her. Something flickers in the trees—was that a flashlight? I squint into the darkness, mentally willing that flickering to happen again when Molly gives a happy bark and dashes off toward the house.

"What are you doing?"

I turn to see Katie standing on the back porch, sleepy and disheveled and so fucking beautiful it hurts to look at her. She turned the porch light on, so she's cast in a golden glow that makes her blond hair shine. She has a quilt from the foot of her bed wrapped around her and I'd bet money she has nothing on underneath it.

Shit.

Glancing back at the woods one more time, I see nothing. No flickering of light, no movement, not a sound, not even a whisper that something was out there. Molly's totally over it; instead she's happy to see Katie's joined us for our too-early morning adventures, and I hop off the fence, quickly dashing back to the porch so I can join them.

"Molly had to go outside," I explain when I stop just in front of her.

Katie nods, her eyes barely open. She looks tired and sort of out of it. "Let's go back to bed," she whispers.

I check over my shoulder one more time, but no one's out there. I'm freaking out over nothing. It was probably a small animal that stepped on a branch. Molly caught scent of it and went crazy. I can't blame her.

"Okay," I murmur, slipping my arm around Katie and leading her back to the door, Molly right at our heels. I firmly turn the deadbolt into place and we all go back to bed, Molly sleeping on the floor while I proceed to make love to Katie one more time, quick and easy and satisfying, before she falls asleep in my arms. Yet I stay awake.

Plagued by the ominous feeling that never really leaves me for the rest of the night.

# KATIE

Will becomes consumed with a design project for a solid week straight, so consumed I rarely see him and when I do, he's usually distracted, bringing his laptop with him to my house and working on it long into the night.

"Deadline," he always mutters when he comes up for air—and coffee. Then he offers me that sweet, apologetic smile of his, the one I can't resist, and kisses me deeply, making me lose my head like usual. "I'll make it up to you when I'm done. I swear." His voice is always full of promise.

I take him at his word. He's already made it up to me in the middle of the night, when I awoke to his urgent hands pulling me toward him, his seeking lips finding mine. He makes love to me with a single-minded focus that steals my breath every single time. Until I'm a breathless mess afterward, unable to think or speak or move. I just lie there with my heart thundering and a spinning head, my limbs weak, my skin still tingling when he pulls away, a satisfied smile curling his perfect lips.

I've never seen him so distracted before, but do I really know him? No. I'm learning, though. I see that the job I thought was so easygoing is really filled with moments that are intense and can drag on for days, consuming him. I try my best not to disturb him while he's like this, staying out of his way as best I can. Instead I concentrate fully on my school-work since we're getting closer to the end of the semester. I have a paper to write, a project to work on. The semester is over mid-December and I can't wait.

I'm also contemplating taking the spring semester off. Mom will flip and tell me I'm making a huge mistake, but I need a break. I just want to live. To breathe. To be. I even want to try and get a job. Nothing major, something simple and part-time. I still have money saved from my father's death and though it feels weird to spend it on everyday stuff, I'd like to think he wouldn't mind. He'd rather see me happy and being normal, wouldn't he? Versus never touching the money and never really living?

That's what I tell myself at least.

Work-wise, I'd consider just about anything. Retail. An office. I can type reasonably fast and can write a letter or put together a spreadsheet. And I can answer a phone. I'll work at a fast-food place if I have to, slinging fries and getting zits from the grease I deal with all day. I just feel the need to be out among people and actually *doing* something.

And that's all thanks to Will. He's given me confidence, made me realize that living all by myself, holed up in my house alone every day, is not the way to live. Not that he was any better since he did the same exact thing. I like to think we brought each other out of our respective shells.

With him so consumed with work lately, I'm glad he insisted Molly should stay with me on a more permanent basis. She's excellent company. I take her out for a walk first thing in the morning and those last fifteen or twenty minutes before the sun goes down, just wandering around the neighborhood and saying hi to the people who live near me. I've gotten to know a few a little better by simply chatting them up and being friendly.

But as we get closer to winter, the night comes even faster, causing me to bump my walks earlier and earlier. Mrs. Anderson likes to accompany me during my walk with Molly if she spots me in time, which she usually does.

Wouldn't doubt for a moment that she sits and waits by her front window, leaping to her feet when she sees Molly and me go past her house. The old woman moves surprisingly fast for her age. We talk about life, about her late husband, and she allows me to ramble on about Will without making me feel like I talk too much. She encourages the conversation, telling me that since romance has left her life, she has to live through my stories. She claims it gives her butterflies when I tell her something extra sweet that Will did for me.

I have no idea if she's putting me on or not. I like to think she's not.

I'm waiting for Will to come over now and I peer out my own front window, anxious for his car to appear. It's dark outside, fog rolling in earlier, low and eerie, making the streetlights cast weird cone-shaped beams of orangey light. I let the blinds fall back into place and settle on the couch, pleased when Molly curls up close to my feet.

Will is bringing dinner with him, but he wouldn't say where he's picking up the food. I'm starving, so I hope to God he shows up soon. This living-an-hour-apart business in different towns is getting old, I swear.

He insists on knocking on my front door every time he comes over, which I think is silly, but whatever. Soon enough he'll just barge in like he owns the place, pretty much like Molly does. She'll nose through my partially closed doors like she's the queen of my house and I've finally given in to the fact that yes, she is the queen. She's comfortable here. Happy. Will always complains about how Molly is too big for his backyard, which is about the size of a postage stamp. The tiny house he lives in is a rental and his lease is coming up soon, right after the first of the year—he told me that a few nights ago.

I'm considering asking him to move in with me as a sort of Christmas present. Is that cheesy? I don't know. I do know I balked only a few weeks ago, but things have changed. We've become closer. I'm not so unsure anymore, though I was still unsure just enough not to mention it to Sheila during our last appointment. I'm almost afraid to hear her response. I don't want her to tell me that she thinks it's a bad idea for us to live together.

That's the last thing I need.

I'm so distracted by my own thoughts I didn't hear the car pull up in front of my house, so I nearly jump out of my skin when there's a loud knock on my door. Molly goes crazy as usual, barking like the ferocious dog she's not, running toward the door, her claws clicking a rapid beat against the bare wood floor. I go to the door and peek through the peephole to see Will standing there, a bag of food in his hands and his computer bag slung over his broad shoulder.

Great. Another work night.

Unlocking the door, I throw it open and he smiles, waving the bag of food at me like I'm Molly and easily mesmerized by a doggy treat. Which I sort of am, considering that I'm beyond hungry—but never for doggy treats, *ew*.

"Thai food," he says as he walks in, bringing with him the most delicious smell in all the land.

"Pad Thai?" I ask hopefully as I close and lock the door.

"You know it," he says as he heads into the kitchen. Molly trots after him, looking hopeful that he brought her a treat, too, and I head for the kitchen myself, going for the cupboard and pulling down the shallow bowls I normally use for salads, while Will empties the to-go bag of its contents. He cracks open one container, revealing my favorite Thai dish. I grab two giant spoons and a couple of forks from the drawer and proceed to scoop up the biggest amount of food I can manage.

Will chuckles, shaking his head. "Hungry?"

"Starving. I was wasting away while I waited for you to get here." I go to the fridge and open the door. "What do you want to drink?"

"A beer if you have any." He pauses. "Do you mind if we watch the football game? It's Monday and the Niners are playing."

"Sure." I grab myself a bottle of water and a beer for Will, then shut the door with my hip.

We settle in on the couch with our plates of food perched in our laps and turn on the game, the low roar from the crowd and the continuous commentary from the announcers almost soothing as I devour my dinner. Football reminds me of simpler times. When I was young and didn't have a care in the world and I would watch the games with my dad. I only pretended that I cared at the time, but really I absorbed everything he told me. To the point that I can follow a football game pretty well, though I don't know who the best players are.

After everything that happened and my father distanced himself from me, I avoided him, and slowly but surely lost my love for football.

Maybe I can gain it all back with Will. Even though my dad is gone, watching football again can make me feel somewhat closer to him, and I need that. Over the years I've been filled with so much resentment and hurt at the way he rejected me after the kidnapping, and I really haven't been able to get over it. No wonder I'm bitter toward the male species. At one time or another, all the men in my life have disappointed me.

Even Will.

We finish our food and Will never breaks out his laptop once, which makes me secretly happy. He's glued to the television, though, yelling with triumph when the 49ers score and roaring with anger when they make a fumble or the other team scores—or worse, when the ball is intercepted. I stare in mute fascination as he sits on the edge of the couch as tense as he can be, his gaze wide while staring at the TV that hangs on the wall. This is a side of Will I've never seen before. My rabid sports fanatic boyfriend is kind of hot.

"Sorry. I tend to get carried away," he tells me once halftime begins and he seems to relax somewhat. Considering the Niners are losing, I don't think he's completely relaxed. "I used to play football in high school."

"You did?" If he's mentioned that to me before, I forgot.

He nods, absently petting Molly's head, which is resting in his lap. She somehow worked her way onto the couch while we were concentrating on the game, and I didn't protest. She's sitting in between us now, sleeping contentedly. "Played baseball, too. We were state champions my senior year."

"Wow. You must've been good." I'm impressed.

"I was okay." He shrugs, brushing off his accomplishments as usual. "Never good enough to earn scholarships, though that was my secret dream. It was hard, though. My grades were just okay and I had to work a lot to earn extra cash, so I couldn't practice as much as I wanted."

How sad. He missed out on so many opportunities because of life circumstances. Then again, so did I. We're both pitiful. "I'm surprised. You've never wanted to watch football before."

"Ycah, that's because I'm usually DVR'ing it and watching it at home later." He smiles sheepishly, looking like he just got busted. "I wanted to catch tonight's game live. Thanks for being so agreeable."

"I don't mind football." I consider telling him why.

"Really? So you're like my dream woman?" He raises his brows, his smile reminding me of a little boy's.

"We already knew that." I reach over and slug him on the arm, my knuckles making contact with his hard biceps. Yikes, he's built. I decide to tell him what I'm really feeling, how football is affecting me. "I used to always watch football with my dad when I was little."

"Oh yeah?" Will's voice goes soft. "I've noticed you never really talk about him."

"There's not much to say. We were close, and then one day, we weren't anymore." It's painful, talking about my dad's rejection. I like to pretend it never happened, but that's so hard. Memories always come up. Old resentments and new, past good times that meld into voids of nothingness.

"After you were kidnapped?"

I nod, telling myself not to cry. I refuse to cry. That would be pointless. I'm tired of tears.

So tired of them.

"He missed out, then, getting to know you as you grew up," Will continues as he reaches out and rests his hand on my knee, giving it a squeeze.

I drop my head and close my eyes, exhaling slowly, trying to calm my racing heart. "He was too ashamed of me." Saying the words hurt my chest and I press my hand against it, willing the pain away. I should be over this, over my father's rejection. But I'm not. There are a lot of things that are good in my life right now that I should focus on, but I can't help this. I'm not perfect.

I'm damaged. I probably always will be. But I can at least pick up the pieces the best that I can and carry on. It's the only thing to do. Life is what you make it.

If you make it shit, it's shit. But if you make it wonderful, well . . .

"He wasn't ashamed of you, Katie. More like he was ashamed of himself. Angry that he let something so horrible happen to his little girl."

"He didn't *let* it hap—" I start, but Will cuts me off.

"He felt like he did. And that's as good as actually letting it happen. It was guilt, baby. Pure and simple." He squeezes my knee again and then nudges at Molly's side. "Get out of here, dog."

She rises slowly and hops off the couch, settling on the floor. The second she's gone, Will pulls me to him so I'm cuddled in his lap, my head nestled against his shoulder, my lips pressed against his neck and my legs draped over him. "I never blamed him for what happened," I admit softly. "Never. It was the wrong place at the wrong time. Luck and timing worked against me that afternoon. I know that now. No one's to blame." Not even myself.

"He blamed himself and that's probably worse." He runs his hand over my hair, his mouth at my temple. "I know it's hard to forgive him for his rejection, but I'd bet money that he struggled every damn day for the rest of his life. I also wouldn't doubt that he felt completely responsible."

Why does he have to be so reasonable?

I remain quiet, plucking at his soft T-shirt, secretly wishing he wasn't wearing it. I like it best when we're alone together, bare skin on skin. I wish he was over watching this football game. That he'd take me to bed instead. Or maybe he could take me right here on the couch. We haven't tried that yet.

Anything to forget the pain thinking of my father always brings me. But it's no use. He's there, front and center in my memories, never letting me forget. I remember a moment a long time ago, not long after I came home from the hospital, once I was mostly healed physically but still in tremendous, overwhelming pain mentally. I'd eavesdropped on my parents, when my dad practically broke down and cried while talking to my mom, asking how he could have let something so horrible happen to his little girl.

Despite my not wanting them, the tears come anyway. Quiet, mournful tears for what I lost with my father. What he lost with me. Will's fingers find my face and he gently wipes away my tears, but it's no use. The tears keep coming. He tilts my face up and kisses the tears away, one after another, his lips covering every inch of my skin. Until his mouth is on mine. Finally, *finally* his kisses help me forget my turbulent relationship with my father, chasing away all the bad memories.

But Will also helps me remember the good times. As strained as our relationship was till the very end, I still miss my father and what we used to have. Even when we shared nothing, at least he was still there. Still in my life.

Somehow, despite it all, I can cherish the bad times, too.

More than I ever have before.

 WILL

The call comes a week before Thanksgiving, bringing with it both good news and bad.

"Give me the good news first," Katie says to me over the phone. I'd called her the minute I finished the previous call, knowing I had to tell her what was going on. I was actually anxious to tell her since I felt the need to share it with someone—with *my* special someone.

I've never had one of those before and it feels good.

"I was offered a job that will pay really well." When I lower my voice and offer up the price, Katie sucks in a startled breath. "It's a big job. Remember my friend Jay? The singer in the band—the concert I took you to?"

"I remember." Her voice is soft. That was a night that had started out great and ended with me nearly beating the shit out of some asshole who scared her. Not one of my finer moments.

"Well, he's close friends with a lead singer from another band; they've both been on the circuit for years. And his friend's band is about to hit the big time. They landed a record deal, they're going to embark on a tour to support the album within two months of its release, and they need a new website yesterday." I pause, letting my words sink in. "That's where I come into the picture."

"Oh. So you're going to design their new website? That's wonderful! Think of all the exposure you'll get." Katie sounds enthused. This is a good thing, because she's not going to be so enthused about the next thing.

"I have to go out of town, though." I wince, waiting for the verbal blow, but it doesn't come. Not yet, at least. "Hopefully it's just for a week, maybe shorter, but they want me there. They want me to see them perform, see them in action at the studio, meet the execs at their new record company. They're big on submerging their team within the process—that's a direct quote from Jay." I chuckle, but Katie doesn't respond in kind.

Uh-oh.

"It'll go by fast." Another pause on my part as an idea forms in my brain, and it's too good not to mention. "You should come with me. We could check out L.A. See the sights. Whatever you want to do, Katie."

She sighs, the sound full of longing. "When do you leave?"

"Right after Thanksgiving." Yet that won't work for her, I can feel it in my bones.

"I wish I could go. But I'm still in school and finals are coming up. If it were the week of Thanksgiving that would be perfect, since there are no classes then," she explains.

"You sure you can't take off? Take your tests or whatever from the hotel? They've gotta have decent Wi-Fi."

"I'm sure they do, but it'll be too much of a distraction, my being there with you while struggling through the remaining homework, the studying, the final projects, and the studying." I'm thinking the studying is extra important to her right now. "I could end up distracting you, too, you know."

"No way," I scoff, but she has a point. I do need to concentrate on this project and not worry about Katie the entire time. Though I'll end up worrying about Katie anyway because she won't be with me.

"It might be what I need anyway," she continues, as if she's trying to convince herself my being away is a good idea. "Your being gone means I'll be able to study Will-free."

"You make that sound like a good thing," I say, feeling a little bit hurt, which is stupid.

"Oh, it is definitely a good thing. You're too distracting, I hope you know." There's a smile in her voice and it lightens my heart, which had been feeling pretty heavy over leaving her alone.

"Yeah?" I sit up straighter. "How distracting do you think I am exactly?"

"Very distracting. Now stop. I'm not going to go on and on about how great you are just to feed your ego," she mumbles, sounding irritated.

I chuckle. "Why not? I planned on doing the same thing to you."

"Well, aren't you sweet?" She finally laughs, too, but it dies quickly. "I'm going to miss you when you're gone."

My chest goes tight. "Good. Because I'm going to miss you, too—more than you'll ever know," I reassure her. I could go on and on about how much I'll miss her, but I don't want to freak her out.

"Sometimes I'm not sure if you're being sincere or not," she says feebly. "I'm always secretly afraid that you're exaggerating."

I can't believe she just said that. "Baby, my feelings for you are never exaggerated. I love you. And I mean it. You need to believe in me." I pause. "You do believe in me, right?"

"Sometimes it's just . . . it's hard." She sighs. "These are my hang-ups messing with my head. It has nothing to do with you. Not really."

"I don't want to leave you." Shit, I can't believe I'm going to say this, but here I go. "Maybe I should turn down that job."

"Oh, no way. You're not going to give up on the opportunity of a lifetime because I'm feeling insecure about you leaving me. I won't let you."

Okay, good. I would give it up if I had to. I'd do anything for her. But I'm glad to see she's willing to sacrifice for me, too. "Thank you for saying that." I lower my voice. "You know once I leave I'll be counting the days until I can see you again."

She laughs again, but she sounds sad. "I'll be doing the same. Probably more than you, considering how busy you'll be."

"You'll be busy, too, finishing up school," I remind her. My chest aches at the realization that we'll be apart. I'll be down in Southern California and she'll be here, all by herself for at least five days, maybe more. She'll have Molly and Mrs. Anderson, but will that really be enough?

No.

"So hey, I keep meaning to ask you this, but do you want to come over to my mom's house for Thanksgiving dinner? I can't promise there won't be any drama, but I can guarantee a delicious turkey meal. And you already had Mom's pumpkin pie."

"I thought you'd never ask." I'm being one hundred percent sincere. I was afraid she wasn't going to ask. Or that her mom might hate me so much she wanted me nowhere near her prized turkey, let alone her daughter.

But somehow, some way, I must have done something right. I must have impressed that woman to cause her to open up her home to me.

"It's nothing formal or anything like that. It's always a simple affair," she says. "Sometimes my uncle and his family are there, but I don't know if that's the case this year. I hope so. I think you'd like him."

"I've never been to a Thanksgiving dinner," I blurt out. *Damn,* why did I say that? I sound pathetic.

It's quiet on the other end, as if Katie needs the time to absorb what I just said, which she might. "Are you serious?" she finally asks.

I nod, then realize she can't see me. "Yeah. I mean, I've had the crappy Thanksgiving lunches in a school cafeteria and they weren't so bad. But nothing like a real home-cooked meal. Uh, we never really celebrated the holiday." I swallow past the burning lump in my throat. That was hard to admit. We weren't big on Christmas much, either.

Our last one together, he threw me a carton of cigarettes and wished me a happy holiday before he bailed on me and went to a bar. I spent that Christmas alone.

A common occurrence. I've never been a big fan of the holiday season.

"Well, then we'll need to make this Thanksgiving extra special," she says. "I'll tell Mom to make twice as much pie as she normally does."

I start to laugh, glad she didn't dwell on the sad part of my admission. "Should I bring anything?"

"Just yourself. Now that I think about it, Mom might invite a few of her friends. She mentioned there was a widower who lives in the neighborhood and they've become friendly recently. Brenna's usually with her boring boyfriend but since she broke up with him, that's a done deal, thank goodness. Though maybe she'll bring another guy."

My girl is rambling now. And I rarely hear her talk like this. I like it. She sounds excited. Happy. Maybe she could turn around my sour feelings about the holiday season and make me see the good in it.

Katie has a way of making me see the good in everything.

# KATIE

She won't stop calling, and I've never been so glad in all my life that I entered her name in my contacts. Now I know when Lisa Swanson is reaching out to me.

And I can ignore her.

Nothing good can come from taking that call and I've had nothing *but* good things happening these last few days—minus Will's news that he's leaving for a week the beginning of December. I'm okay with it. I know he has a job to do and I can't expect him to spend all of his time with me. I have Molly now. I can go stay with Mom if I get too freaked out, which I might. I'm so used to having Will with me, it'll be weird when he's gone. If I do decide to go spend time with Mom, she'll be glad to have me visit. We haven't had a chance to talk and catch up in a long time. I've become so caught up in Will, I haven't had much time for anything else beyond school.

The phone starts ringing again—Lisa. Again. She's called four times in a row. Left one voicemail that I haven't checked yet. Ignoring the call, I wait for the ringing to stop before I go into my voicemail and listen to her message.

"Katherine, it's urgent that you call me. I think I've discovered something about Aaron Monroe that you need to know. Please call me right away."

I delete the voicemail, my mind reeling. She sounded frantic. Almost . . . scared? No. Nothing scares Lisa Swanson. That's part of her on-screen persona. She takes on the tough subjects and never backs down. Viewers love her fearless attitude.

Will would definitely tell me not to call her. He'd probably delete her number from my contacts list and block all of her calls if he could. She brings nothing but bad news. He's said that time and again.

Deciding against my better judgment, I call her back, startled when she answers on the first ring.

"Katherine, thank God. I'm so glad you called. There's so much I need to tell you." The words rush out of her and apprehension has me in its grip at the sound of panic in her voice. I fall onto the couch before my legs decide to give out.

"I shouldn't give you the time of day after everything you've done," I tell her, and she starts to say something but I interrupt her. "But I'm giving you five minutes. So talk."

She takes a deep breath, as if she needs to calm herself down. "I've remained in contact with Aaron Monroe over the last few weeks, after the interview. He's been acting rather . . . unusual lately."

"How so?" Of course he's been acting unusual. The man is crazy, and I don't use that word lightly, especially when it's in reference to him.

"He's been talking a lot about being on the outside. What he would do if he were free." Her voice lowers, and I swear I hear a tremor run through her words. "He claims we would make a perfect couple."

"You and him?" I ask incredulously.

"Yes. He's been mentioning it more and more, to the point where it was creeping me out and I stopped calling him. But he keeps reaching out to me, calling me collect at the office. I don't think I want to talk to him any longer. He makes me too nervous."

I don't feel sorry for her. This is what she gets for showing him even an ounce of kindness. He takes advantage of everyone in his life, even a famous reporter who was only using him to improve her ratings. Now she's been sucked into his sticky web and finding it hard to get away from him.

She sort of deserves it.

"He's not happy that you and Will are together." Lisa's voice lowers. "He's not happy about that at all."

What a surprise. "And thanks to you, now everyone knows about it," I retort, tempted to end the call right now. She's not telling me anything new.

"He asked me to make that reveal," she says defensively. Like that's going to make a difference.

Whatever. I don't really believe her. Maybe he pushed her to do it, but she was going to let the world know about us regardless. It's what she does. What she enjoys. She's the one who controls her news reports, not Aaron Monroe.

"Right, because you do everything a convicted killer tells you to. Listen, Lisa, I need to go," I say, but she stops me.

"He has someone on the outside who's spying on you. Who is monitoring your every move."

I go completely still. Completely silent. Is she serious? Who could he have watching me? And why? Why does he still care? Because I'm the one who got away—or does it have to do with Will and me being together now? "Who is it? Did he say?" I ask after I swallow past the scratchiness in my throat. As if a name would matter—I wouldn't know who he was talking about.

"He said . . . he said it's Will." She pauses. "That the only reason Will is with you is because he wants to get close to you and then . . . hurt you. To exact revenge for his father by getting back at you."

My heart flips over itself at her words. Impossible. "No. That is absolutely not true."

"How do you really know, Katherine? Do you know Will Monroe very well? You only just reconnected. He's been this . . . enigma for years. No one knows much about him or what he's been doing. He could be working with his father. It's not too far out of the realm of possibilities. What is he really capable of?"

Lisa's questions only confuse me further. I refuse to believe what she's saying. She doesn't know Will, not like I do. Not even his father knows him like I do. He's a good man. He's thoughtful and kind, without a cruel bone in his body.

I think of the few times I've seen him act violently, and always it was in defense of me. He's protective. Protective of me. He would never hurt me.

Never.

"I know exactly what he's capable of. He wouldn't work with his father. He hates him." I stress the word *hate*. "If you're smart, you'll steer clear of Aaron Monroe like we do."

"Katherine, I'm serious. Watch out for Will. Pay attention. If he offers even a tiny clue that he could be talking or working with his father, get away from him fast. Don't hesitate." Lisa pauses. "I'm sorry for playing a part in this mess. I just wanted you to know that."

An apology. I'm in shock. But it's too late for that. She's trying to convince me that I'm in danger by being with Will and that's the most preposterous thing I've ever heard. "Thank you. But I'd prefer it if you never called me again," I say firmly before I end the call.

And then proceed to delete her name from my contacts.

# AARON

Thanksgiving. A holiday I normally don't give two shits about, but this year, I'm feeling thankful. Thankful for the opportunities this year has brought me. I was able to tell the truth about my crimes. I was able to get messages to my son, even a message to that bitch Katie Watts.

How I hate her. I'm not thankful for her, not at all. Wish that little snitch would hurry up and die once and for all.

I'm also thankful for Lisa Swanson being in my life. Ah, now there's a woman I'd like to keep around, though she's been acting strange lately. Not able to take my calls and when she does, she doesn't talk for very long, always claiming she's busy. I know she's a successful businesswoman, a celebrity in her own right, like me.

But she should make time for me. We're important to each other. We're going to continue being important to each other, too.

Life is odd—such a beautiful yet cruel thing. It brings with it opportunities. Some should be taken. Some absolutely should not—yet I took them anyway, and got myself in grave trouble. I've paid for my sins. I've done my penance. It's time for me to rise again. To become the man that I know I can be.

I just need to be patient. Take my time. Plot and plan.

Carefully put it together. I've been working on the plan for months. Dreaming of it for years. Because when I'm finally free, I'll make sure that everyone knows I'm out, and that I'm ready to be seen. To be known.

To be heard.

KATIE

Lisa's words never leave me despite how much I want to banish them from my brain completely. Her warning about Will, about his father—they linger within me, always nagging. Throughout the week, when I try to focus on anything else, like cleaning my house, purging my closet, messing around with a paper that's due the Monday after Thanksgiving. But I can't get into it. Any time I try to engage my brain, my thoughts circle back to what Lisa said.

So I'm constantly doing something mindless. Reorganizing my kitchen. Bagging up all the stuff I banished from my closet and delivering it to Goodwill. I cleaned out my extra bedroom, at one point thinking it would make a great office for Will, but then my thoughts turned dark. Heavy.

Ominous.

Do you really want him to move in with you after all? What if it's true? What if he's talking to his father and your relationship is really some big, crazy plan for them to get their revenge against you?

It sounds crazy. It *is* crazy. But I can't help it. We don't spend much time together Thanksgiving week, since he's so busy preparing for his trip to Southern California and the new Web design project it's going to bring. Plus, he's wrapping up another project that he wants done before he leaves, so I give him his space, needing some for myself. Processing Lisa's words, trying to spot any clues on Will's part.

But there are none. Not a one. I mention his dad and he clams up, saying he doesn't want to talk about him anymore. I can't blame him for that. I don't want to talk about Aaron Monroe ever again, either. I casually mention Lisa, see if I can work our talk into the conversation, but he's even more resistant to talking about her. His hatred for her is bigger than ever.

So I let the subject drop. It's not worth pursuing. All Lisa did was put doubt in my head. Will hasn't given me one reason to doubt him. Not a one. This is something I need to get over on my own.

We spend Thanksgiving together at my mom's house and the day turns out better than I thought it would. Brenna brings a friend with her, a fellow teacher who's new to the area and whose family lives across the country. My sister didn't want to come alone for the holiday. The widower down the street stops by for dessert, and I think I detect a hint of flirtation between him and my mother.

Interesting.

Will takes everything in stride. He did his best to help Mom in the kitchen, though she shooed him away most of the time, accusing him of wanting to get close to the pumpkin pies. He never denied it, just played along like he was some sort of pie thief, and I think Mom enjoyed it way too much.

I did, too. He's adapted to my family so well and they seem to be accepting of him. Even Brenna, who was ready to scratch his face off the last time they saw each other, is now joking and laughing with him like they're old friends. I should be reassured by their acceptance. It's Thanksgiving—everyone should let bygones be bygones and get along. I think my mom and sister are embracing that way of thinking, Brenna a little more reluctant than Mom, but I expected that.

So why am I skeptical? Why am I watching Will's every

move throughout the day, waiting for him to do or say something awful so I can immediately think, *Look at him. Lisa was right?*

I hate that I'm thinking this way, that I'm so suspicious. I regret talking to Lisa. She's filled my head with so much doubt that I can't differentiate from it anymore. She's shaded my entire outlook on Will. And that's not fair to him.

It's not fair to us.

He's kind to my mother, praising her pumpkin pie to the point that he embarrasses her, and I wonder if there's a motive behind his actions. He's so over-the-top happy, so friendly to everyone, I can't help but think it feels fake. Phony. Like he's putting on an act.

My doubt is like a disease slowly eating at my insides and I hate it. I need to talk to Will. Ethan. Tell him how I feel, what Lisa said. He'll be angry, but he needs to know the truth. I need to unload that truth on him and get rid of this guilty feeling. But will me telling him this only upset him?

It's the risk I have to take.

We drive back to my house Thursday night, both of us quiet. Will's going to stay through Saturday before he leaves first thing Sunday for Los Angeles, and I'm hoping these next few days with him will remind me why my rampant thoughts are ridiculous. I need to remember the good things between Will and me. My suspicions are just that—there's no proof behind Lisa's words.

But is it a sign that there's something wrong with our relationship that I'm so quick to suspect him with no proof? I'm almost afraid it is. And that thought alone terrifies me. Worse, I haven't been able to discuss anything with Sheila. She's out of the office all week, so we skipped my weekly appointment. She would be the perfect one to spill my fears to.

Instead I have to keep them bottled up inside, all to myself.

"You've been quiet all day," he says as he takes the off-ramp that leads to my house.

"There was so much happening, I'm surprised you noticed." I clamp my lips shut. That sounded bitter—and a little bratty, too.

We come to a stop at a red light and Will looks my way. "Are you upset with me about something?"

I shake my head. "I'm just tired and a little grumpy. Spending too much time with my family has a way of doing that." And that isn't a lie, though it's not necessarily the truth in this case, either.

He nods and looks away, staring straight ahead at the mostly abandoned road as we wait for the light to turn green. It's late, past nine o'clock, and I'm ready to collapse into bed. "I had a great time today," he says. "Thank you for inviting me."

"You don't have to keep saying thank you." The words come out harsher than I intended and I soften my tone. "I'm glad you had a good time." And I really am. I hate that his father didn't treat the holidays as special. It was pretty much just another crappy day in the Monroe household and that's terrible.

Whereas my mother celebrated any and every little thing, decorating the house for St. Patrick's Day even, and we aren't Irish. It drove my Scottish father crazy.

I smile at the fond memory.

"You've opened up your heart and your family to me and I appreciate it. That's why I keep saying thank you." He sounds hurt but he won't look at me, and I feel bad, too. I'm taking my worry over what Lisa said out on him. Should I tell him about our conversation? Or will he be too angry, too defensive?

It's probably best forgotten. Yet I can't seem to forget it . . .

"I spoke to Lisa. She said . . ." I hesitate, then decide to just spit it all out. "She said that your father has someone who's spying on me and reporting back to him. And that someone is you."

He's silent for a moment, his fingers curling around the steering wheel tight before he swivels his head in my direction. "That's the most ridiculous thing I've ever heard." His voice is flat, no emotion, and I part my lips, ready to say more when he beats me to the punch. "Are you really going to believe her over me, Katie? After everything we've been through? After everything I've done to protect you? Seriously? I hate him. You know this. I hate him for what he did to me and I especially hate him for what he did to you."

"She said she was worried about me." My voice is small. Saying the words out loud proves Will is right. They do sound ridiculous.

"The only person Lisa Swanson is worried about is herself. Don't let her get in your head and fill it with doubt. I love you, Katie. I would never hurt you or betray you like that. Ever." He sounds weary, his expression grim. I feel bad for saying it, for even bringing up the topic, but I had to get it off my chest.

Definitely not the way I wanted to end Thanksgiving. But I can't talk about it anymore. I just want to get home and crawl into my bed and sleep.

We pull up in front of my house minutes later, Will parking his car in my driveway. The neighborhood is quiet, a few houses already lit with Christmas lights, and I shut my car door, tilting my head toward the house. I fully expect to hear Molly barking in greeting since we left her outside. We bought her a new doghouse a few days ago and Will had assembled it this morning before we left for my mom's. When we left her in the backyard Molly had been curled up in her new house, looking terribly pleased with herself.

"I don't hear Molly," I tell Will after he exits the car.

He frowns but otherwise doesn't appear too disturbed. "She's probably in her new doghouse snoozing." We did put a new bed inside the doghouse, so maybe she is.

Or maybe she's not.

We start toward the house, the downright eerie silence sending a chill down my spine. I hurriedly unlock the door and sprint through the dark house, heading straight for the back door and unlocking it with shaky fingers. I burst out into the backyard, anxiously prepared for Molly to emerge from her doghouse, panting and smiling at me as she runs across the lawn.

But she doesn't come out of the doghouse. It's empty. Molly's not in the yard at all. I think of the suspicious activity in the neighborhood, how Mrs. Anderson called the cops. But why would someone want to mess with my dog?

I turn to face the back porch at the exact moment Will walks through the door, closing it behind him. "Did you find her?" he calls.

I shake my head and burst into tears.

# WILL

I do my best to comfort Katie, but the tears don't stop coming. She goes over to Mrs. Anderson's house to see if she noticed anything unusual but her neighbor was gone most of the day, spending the holiday at her son's house. We walk the neighborhood, calling for Molly, but we can't find her.

She's gone.

"I knew I shouldn't have let her stay in the yard for that long," Katie says with a sob, burying her face against my chest. I hold her close, offering murmured words of encouragement, but my heart feels like a stone, heavy and gray.

Guilt swamps me, too. It was more my idea to leave her out there than Katie's. I tested the fence, figuring it was in decent shape and she couldn't bust through any of the boards. She's not that strong of a dog. There weren't any holes beneath the fence, either, and she's not much of a digger. She had the back porch, her new doghouse, and her food and water dish. There was food still left in her dish, making me think she's been gone for a few hours at least.

That realization doesn't give me much hope that we'll find her.

"Do you think someone took her?" Katie asks a few minutes later.

I think of the night when I thought I saw someone out in the woods behind the house. Mrs. Anderson calling the cops. If there were thieves in the neighborhood, what would they want with a mutt like Molly? It makes no sense. She just got out. That had to be it.

"I don't know, baby." I wish I could offer her comfort, but she's inconsolable. Hell, I wish I could break down and cry like a baby, too. I love Molly. I don't like the idea of her being out there alone. What if she was hit by a car but she's still alive, suffering on the side of the road? What if she's stuck in someone's backyard? The possibilities are endless.

Endless.

"Maybe she just ran away," I suggest, wincing at the incredulous look Katie shoots me. She shakes her head, her lips thinned into a tight line.

"No way. Why would she leave? She had it made with us. Anything she could ever want."

"She's still young, just around a year, according to the vet. She might be inclined to take off if she was tempted," I point out.

"Who would tempt her?"

"It doesn't have to be a who. More like a what." Maybe a cat taunted her and she decided to somehow get over the fence and chase it. I've seen stranger things.

Hell, I don't know. I'm just scrambling for suggestions.

"What if . . ." Katie pauses and licks her lips, her eyes full of so much sadness the sight makes me ache to comfort her. But how? Nothing I can do will make her happy unless I can conjure up Molly, and that's not happening. I wish it would. "What if she got hit by a car and she's on the side of the road? What if she's still alive but hurt?" The tears come back, harder this time. She put my very fear into words.

"Let's go look for her," I say, and Katie silently agrees.

We drive around the neighborhood, along the busier streets surrounding Katie's house, but there's no sight of Molly whatsoever. I suggest making a missing poster, glad that my laptop is back at Katie's so I can work on putting one together as soon as we get home. But all the while Katie is quiet, tears continuously running down her cheeks accompanied by muffled sobs. She's cried so much, rubbed at her eyes again and again, that her tears no longer streak black with mascara. She's cried all of her makeup away.

We arrive back at her house over an hour later, both of us exhausted and sad. She turns to look at me, her expression suddenly filled with fierce determination as she clenches her hands into fists and rests them on her knees.

"What about the woods?" she asks quietly.

"What about them?" I glance toward her house, hoping to see Molly curled up on the front porch waiting for us, but she isn't.

"Maybe she's out in the woods. We should go look." She unclenches her fists and reaches for the door handle. I reach for her instead, stopping her mid-action. She glances down at my hand on her arm, then looks up at me, frowning so hard that little furrow is between her brows. "What?"

"Slow down. Let's make a plan first."

"Plan for what?" Good question. I just think she needs to calm the fuck down. "Our dog is out there somewhere, Will. We need to find her. She could be out in those woods, hurt and defenseless, and a wild animal could come upon her. She'd have no way to win a battle like that, especially if she's injured." She jerks her arm out of my hold and opens the car door, practically jumping out of it.

I follow after her as she reenters the house and goes to her bedroom. She's changing out of her clothes with grim determination, kicking off the black flats on her feet and stepping out of the skirt she's worn all day before pulling on a pair of jeans that were left draped across a chair. "What are you doing?" I ask her.

"Wearing something better for searching through the forest." She snaps her jeans closed and then grabs a pair of socks out of her dresser drawer. "Are you going with me?"

"Do you want me to go with you?" She's been acting weird all week, but now I know why. *Thanks, Lisa Swanson*. And now that Molly is missing—granted, I'm not happy about this, I'm just as torn up as she is—she's acting like a woman possessed.

She sits on the edge of her bed and slips a sock on each foot. "Yes. I'll need your help, Will. I can't go out in those woods alone."

"Katie." She doesn't acknowledge me, just bends down to grab a pair of black Nikes and puts one on her foot, tying it into a stranglehold of a knot. "Katie, listen to me."

But she doesn't. She's so caught up in her worry, in her mission to search, she's unable to focus on anything else. I go to her, falling onto my knees in front of her and reaching for her face, cupping her cheeks with my hands and forcing her to look at me.

"Take a deep breath," I tell her, my gaze never leaving hers. Her eyes are wide, damp and red from all the crying, and she looks like she's barely holding it together. "We're going to find her. But you need to calm down. You're so frantic you're not thinking straight."

She closes her eyes and takes a deep breath, letting it out slowly. I press a kiss to her lips and she reaches for me, clinging to me as I wrap her up in my arms. We hold each other silently, her tears dampening my shirt, and then I slowly withdraw from her, holding on to her shoulders and giving her a little shake. "Do you want to do this? I can go by myself if you're too tired . . ."

"No," she says firmly. "I want to do this. I have to help you."

We put on heavier coats and cut through the space between two houses where there's no fence. It's the path kids take to go into the forest, where they smoke or drink or do whatever it is that teenage kids like to do in secret. I know I went to many a party when I was a teen in woods very similar to this.

I have a flashlight that Katie keeps in her bedside drawer and she has a bigger one that's stashed in the kitchen. We call Molly's name, our voices echoing among the towering pines. The light wind that's blowing ruffles the branches, making me turn every time one of the heavier branches snaps and weaves, but otherwise we hear nothing.

We see nothing.

Katie's determined to go farther in, but after about an hour I tell her we need to stop. It's too late and we need to get rest before we start our search again in the morning.

"I need time to make the missing poster, too, so we can start distributing that in the morning as well," I tell her as she reluctantly turns around and heads back toward her neighborhood.

She nods, but it's like she's not really listening. "What if we can't find her?"

"We will," I say firmly, but she stops in the middle of the trail, reaching out to shove at me.

"But what if we *don't*?" She's yelling, her voice is shrill, and I take a startled step backward, shocked that she would push me. "What are we going to do then?"

"If we don't find her, then we mourn her loss," I say carefully. "And maybe, eventually, we find a new dog to replace her."

"God, what are you? Some sort of heartless monster?" She's crying again. Hysterically this time, looking so ravaged, so destroyed over her lost dog. Our lost dog. I love Molly and I've felt close to crying a time or two tonight, but Katie's acting like this is a life-or-death situation. Like everything hinges on us finding Molly and our entire world is going to fall apart if we don't.

I try to ignore the pain her words cause me. She's just upset. Worried over Molly. "Katie, seriously, you need to calm down."

"I don't want to calm down. I want to find my damn dog! Now!" She takes off, running down the trail, headed deeper into the woods, and I chase after her, confused by the way she's behaving, scared that her overreaction could hint at a deeper, more internal problem she's experiencing.

"Jesus, Katie, you need to stop! Come on! Be reasonable!" I yell. I pick up speed and run after her, catching up to her quickly. Snagging her around the waist from behind, I pick her up so her feet are dangling in the air. She kicks them against my shins, struggling against my hold, but I grip her with all my might.

She's not going to get away. Not again. She needs rest. A good night's sleep so she can calm the fuck down and think rationally again.

"Put me down." She fights to get loose, even smacks her balled-up fists against my forearms, but I won't let her go. "She could be out there all alone, you know? Crying and begging for someone to find her. I know what that's like. I know how scary that is and I can't stand the thought of her being alone. I can't . . . I just can't stand it."

Realization dawns. I'm an idiot. This is partially about the dog, but more about Katie. How she felt when she was alone, locked up in that disgustingly hot and smelly shed. How scared she was. What my father did to her. She's putting herself in Molly's place and freaking out all over again.

"Hey," I whisper against her cheek. "Hey, I'm here for you. I've got you, okay? You're not alone. We're going to find Molly. I promise."

She slowly relaxes within my arms, her head leaning back against my chest, her hands and arms going lax. I turn her within my embrace and clutch her tight, holding her to me, her face pressed against my chest, her arms around my waist. I let her get it all out, every last tear and sob and exhausted sigh. We stand in the middle of the trail in a dark, quiet forest, the only sound the wind whispering in the trees high above us as Katie once again purges her tattered soul for all she's lost.

And all I can do is helplessly comfort her as best I can.

# KATIE

We walk back to my house in silence, Will clutching my hand like he's never going to let it go, and I let him. I need the comfort, the solid feel of his long fingers curled around mine, reassuring me that he's always going to be there for me no matter what.

How could I have doubted him? How did I let Lisa Swanson and her stupid worries get into my head like that? He loves me more than anything in this world. If anyone has my back, it's Will. No one else does, not like him.

But right now he can't take my sad feelings away. No one can, unless they're the ones who bring Molly back to me.

I can't believe she's gone, and it doesn't look good. Where could she have gone? How did she get out of the backyard? So many unanswered questions. And it's not like if we do find Molly that she'll be able to tell us where she went. For the first time in my life, I wish I could speak fluent dog.

If I weren't so upset I'd almost find that thought funny.

We draw closer to my house when I see Mrs. Anderson standing out in front of hers, wearing a thick, bright blue robe, her arm raising when she spots us and waving frantically.

I let go of Will's hand and run toward her, my heart racing, hopeful that she has Molly. Mrs. Anderson's hand flutters over her chest and when I get even closer, I can hear her voice as she yells, practically hopping up and down.

"I found her, I found her!"

I stop and turn my head toward where she's pointing to see Molly sitting in Mrs. Anderson's front yard, her expression wary as she keeps licking at her bloody hind leg.

I gasp at first sight of her leg. It looks like someone . . . tore it apart? The fur is gone, and I swear I can see muscle and flesh and bone. "Oh God," I cry out as I start toward her.

Will is there, grabbing my arm and stopping me from going to her. "Hold on," he whispers. "She might be seriously hurt and on the defensive. We need to approach her carefully."

Since when did he become such a pet expert? I listen to him, though, letting him go to Molly first. She is, after all, his dog.

He kneels down in front of Molly, talking low, his voice even and soothing. Molly doesn't flinch, just leans into his offered hand, and he pets her, his head bent as he checks out her wound. I wait with Mrs. Anderson, holding my breath when Will tries his best to examine the horrific wound on Molly's leg. When he tries to touch it she whines, baring her teeth in a little growl. Will immediately retracts his hand, rising to his feet and turning to look at us.

"Is there an emergency vet in the area? I know it's a holiday, but we should really try and take her in. This wound is beyond what we can do for her," Will says, his voice shaky.

"What do you think happened to her?" I ask as Mrs. Anderson whips her phone out of her robe pocket and no doubt starts the search for a twenty-four-hour vet clinic in town.

The expression on Will's face is grim as his dark gaze meets mine. "It looks like she was . . . shot."

# AARON

The phone call comes on my smuggled-in cellphone. It's a constant problem within the prison system, and half the time it's brought to us by one of the prison guards. It's harder for death-row inmates to gain access to a phone so freely, but every once in a while one falls into my hands, and when that happens, I kind of go ape shit.

As in, I call everyone I know on the outside. They're never shocked to hear my voice and I appreciate that, but then again, anyone I tend to call is someone who used to be on the inside like me. I've made a few friends during my time here, and some of them have gone on to be released.

I've always made friends real easily. It's just part of my charm.

My phone is on vibrate and I answer it quickly, nestled deep in the darkest corner of my cell. Luckily enough, the guard made his almost hourly passing just a few minutes ago, so I'm good for a while. Unless something crazy happens and he's called out to break up a fight or some stupid shit like that.

But that rarely happens.

"What happened? How did it go?" I ask by way of greeting, eager for details. I had this guy, a cousin of one of my fellow inmates, do a particular job for me. And I want to know how it went.

"Fucked up, man. That damn dog bit my hand," the guy—

his name is Bruce—mutters irritably. "Hurt like a mother-fucker."

"So what exactly did you do to that damn dog?" Bruce has been watching Katherine Watts's house, spying on her from his perch deep in those thick woods behind her house. He's even taken photos and sent them to my phone. It's been quite interesting, getting that taste of Katherine and my son to-gether. The stupid dog they seem to dote on. Bruce noted that from the start.

So I told him he needed to take care of that dog as a little Thanksgiving present. When he'd texted that they left the dog alone in the backyard, I couldn't have asked for a better gift to be thankful for.

"Little bitch got away from me so I shot her. Hoped to kill her, but she's fast and took off running," Bruce explains. "I don't know where she ended up."

"Did you hit her?"

"In the leg. Didn't slow her down, though." Bruce coughs, the sound wet and disgusting, making me wince. He's a shady character, but he's all I've got right now so I have to settle. "They were looking for her."

"Who?"

"Your boy and his girlfriend. They were searching all around the neighborhood for that stupid-ass dog when they got home. When they headed for the woods where I was staked out, that's when I had to run," Bruce says.

"So you have no idea if they got the dog back yet or not," I say, my voice flat, my irritation on a low simmer. Fucker was supposed to end that dog once and for all. I paid him already, though I knew there were no guarantees.

"I was going to head out there in a bit but it's raining like a son of a bitch. I don't much reckon you want me to sit out in the cold rain just to see if they found their fucking dog or not, do you?" Bruce asks.

"Don't bother, asshole. Thanks for nothing." I end the call, shoving the phone back in its hiding spot.

Inside I'm simmering with anger. I can't believe he didn't kill that damn dog. Oh, she might be dead; maybe she wandered off somewhere deep in those woods to die alone. Dogs do that sometimes. But that isn't what I wanted. Not by a long shot.

No, I wanted to rub their faces in their precious dog's death. I wanted them to see her strung out, hanging from a tree in the front yard, the carcass cut up, disemboweled, with blood everywhere. I wanted them both to remember what it feels like to love something so deeply, only for it to be torn away from you, and then torn apart.

I wanted them to suffer and feel pain. Like I've suffered and felt pain since I was locked away in this fucked-up prison for life.

Well, fuck that. I've sat inside here for too long, relying on others to do my dirty work for me. I've plotted. I've planned. This weekend is when it'll happen. I've been working toward this day for months and no one knows. Not a soul. Won't they be surprised?

It's finally my time to break free.

WILL

"I don't leave until Sunday, but I can still change my flight if you want," I tell Katie as she buzzes around the kitchen, going to the sink and filling the coffeepot with water from the tap before she sets about making us a fresh pot. "If you need me to stay here with you and help take care of Molly I can fly out first thing Monday morning."

"I can handle it." She smiles at me from over her shoulder before she resumes her coffee making. "Don't change your flight. You don't want to start off this project on the wrong foot. Go. We'll be fine here."

I'm sitting at the table, my laptop in front of me. It was an exhausting last couple of days, but everything's turned out okay. Molly's going to survive—but she's now a three-legged dog, which is the craziest thing ever. We were reassured that she'll have a completely normal and long life. She's still at the vet hospital, racking up a bill that is sure to be huge, but I can't worry about it now. If I have to put it on my credit card, I will. Molly's worth it, and so is Katie's emotional well-being.

"They'll call us when she's ready to be picked up." It's Saturday morning, early. We spent most of Friday in a haze, worried over Molly, hanging out at the vet, then going home to worry some more as we waited for a phone call from the doctor. Katie cried tears of relief when we were told that Molly would make it, then tears of sorrow when she realized that she'd be minus one leg.

I told Katie that just makes our Molly that much more unique.

We still don't understand why someone shot Molly. The vet mentioned she could have upset a neighbor. There is a home on a large piece of acreage with cows on it just beyond the woods behind the house—maybe the owner shot her for coming around his property? We have no clue. No one heard the shot, which is weird. Katie mentioned again last night what Lisa told her, how someone is spying on us and that it supposedly is me. She wondered if maybe it was someone else, hence the photos of us? Was my father behind it?

I find that hard to believe. I think it's one of Lisa's minions taking photos of us. Who could my father convince to do his dirty work and spy on us? That's the craziest thing I've ever heard. This entire so-called spying situation is ludicrous.

All I know is I've cut my time down in Southern California by two days. If I work damn hard, I can get everything handled in a shorter amount of time. I want to get back to Katie as soon as possible so I can be by her side and help her care for Molly.

"I want to go buy her a new bed," Katie says as she turns to face me, leaning against the counter. "Something thick and fluffy so she'll be comfortable."

"That sounds good." I get up from the table and go to her, resting my hands on the edge of the counter as I bend over her and drop a soft kiss to her lips. "Are you okay?" I murmur. "Tell me the truth."

A sigh escapes her. "A little rattled over the fact that someone shot our dog on Thanksgiving, but otherwise, I'm fine." She offers me a shaky smile and I try to kiss her worry away. "Maybe she wandered into someone's yard and they got mad at her when she wouldn't leave?"

"Maybe," I say distractedly. She can't stop coming up with multiple reasons since it was confirmed Molly had actually been shot. It's like Katie's brain is a jumble, just one excuse after the other falling from her tongue, and I don't know what to think. Why would someone shoot a sweet dog like Molly? Yeah, I took her to dog defense class for a week straight, but she's no killer beast. She's not really even a threat. She's pretty much a softy and too friendly for her own good.

Clearly, considering she approached some asshole with a serious case of dog rage who shot her, who was probably trying to kill her. If I ever find the dick who did this to her . . .

I'll want to choke him with my own bare hands.

Katie reaches out and runs her fingers down the buttons of my flannel shirt, rubbing the one in the center of my chest back and forth. "Well, I'd like to say it doesn't matter what happened, but it does. I don't like to think it might've been one of my neighbors. I'll never want to leave Molly alone if that's the case."

I don't want her alone here, either, if one of her neighbors is a gun-toting nut job. "You're not staying here by yourself when I'm gone. I'm serious, Katie. I want you to go to your mom's."

"That was already the plan." She smiles tremulously and I kiss her again. I want to kiss and touch her as much as possible, because I leave tomorrow and won't see her for a solid six days. I fly home Friday night. That's too damn long to be away from her, but I have to do it. The timing is for shit considering what happened to Molly, but at least they can go to Liz's house and I know they'll be safe there.

Fuck, I hope they'll be safe there.

"When will you leave for your mom's?"

"Probably not until Monday morning. I want to make sure

Molly's adjusting okay before we go over there. I don't want to be too far away from the vet's in case something goes wrong," she explains.

"So you'll stay here and risk being close to a crazed neighbor." My voice is flat. I don't like this plan.

"Hey." She touches my cheek and our gazes meet. "I have Mrs. Anderson. Do you know she's already called the police seven times because she saw some 'shady characters,' as she calls them, hanging around the neighborhood?"

Of course she did. "How many of them were legit?"

Katie laughs. "One. Turns out a woman in the middle of a divorce had a restraining order on her estranged husband. He was caught lurking around. Caught, I might add, thanks to Mrs. Anderson."

"What's her first name anyway? Do you know?"

"Lillian I think? No wait, Vivian? I can't remember." Katie shakes her head. "That's awful. I'm a terrible friend."

"Yeah, you are. Look at her mail next time. Find out what her name is. I'd rather call her Vivian or Lillian or whatever than Mrs. Anderson." I brush my hand against Katie's hip and she nudges closer, like she wants more. I'll give her as much as she wants. We'll have to pick Molly up soon and then we'll be consumed with doggy care for the rest of the day but right now, it's just us.

And I want to take her back to bed.

"I appreciate all that she's done for me. For us," Katie says, her voice soft. "She's very overprotective."

"So am I. Over all three of you." I kiss her forehead. "But especially you and Molly."

She tugs on the front of my shirt, bringing me closer so our torsos brush against each other. "You should take me back to bed," she whispers.

Hmm, bold Katie is a pleasant surprise. "I was just thinking the same thing," I murmur against her lips just before I kiss her. My hands go to her waist and I step closer, our bodies meshed as she parts her lips beneath mine and I slide my tongue into her mouth.

It's been so off for us lately, we haven't been able to fully connect. I've missed that. I've missed *her.*

But now, all I want is to connect. Get her naked and kiss her all over her soft, smooth body. Get her into bed and push inside her, fuck her hard until we're both coming . . .

Yeah, I need that. Right now. I think she does, too.

She breaks the kiss first, a sly smile on her face as she takes my hand and leads me to her bedroom. "Let's go," she murmurs, and I follow her, like I always do. I can never say no to Katie.

We fall onto her bed, me on top of her, helping her shed her clothes. She's naked beneath her pajamas. No bra, no panties, just Katie. I run my hands and lips all over her skin as she clutches me close, her body arching everywhere my mouth is, as if seeking more. I rear up, unbuttoning my shirt, and tear it off and she reaches for me, her fingers tracing over my tattoo. It's like she can't stop touching it, like she needs that reminder. That she meant so damn much to me even when we were kids that I had her permanently inked into my skin.

"I love this," she murmurs, her gaze lifting from the tattoo to look into my eyes. "Even when we were apart, you thought about me."

"Always." I dip my head and kiss her, one hand on her breast, the other between her legs. She opens to me, her thighs parting, a sigh falling from her lips when I touch her in a particular spot. "You were always in my heart, Katie. And on my skin."

She kisses me, her mouth frantic as it moves beneath mine. I remember the gift I wanted to give her for Christmas, how I have it stashed in a secret spot in her closet where she'd never look. I don't want to wait for Christmas. The gift would have more meaning now.

"I'll be right back," I whisper against her lips as I pull away from her. She frowns, her brows lowered, eyes dim.

"Where are you going?" she pouts.

I stare at her, momentarily entranced. Her skin is rosy, her nipples hard, and she's so damn pretty I have to remind myself that yeah, she belongs to me. She's mine. "I have something for you."

Ignoring her protests, I go to her walk-in closet and flick on the light, going for the heavy coat she has hanging in the farthest, deepest corner. I pull out the tissue-wrapped present I stashed inside one of the coat's pockets and rejoin her in bed, handing over the gift. "Merry early Christmas."

She stares at the red tissue, then looks up at me. "What is it?"

"Open it and see."

Carefully she unfolds the tissue, her breath catching when she sees it. The old guardian angel charm I gave her, polished and gleaming, now hanging from a silver chain. She holds it up, letting the charm dangle. It spins and twirls, my symbolic gift to her all those years ago. Even when I wasn't with her physically, at least she had an angel watching over her.

And now she will once again.

"Oh, Will." She blinks away the tears and clutches the necklace in her fist, pressing it against her chest. "I love it so much. Thank you."

"I love you," I whisper, kissing her again and again, telling her just how deeply I feel for her. With my words and lips and tongue. With my hands and body and soul.

This girl is it for me. We've been through too much, have seen and done too much together. No one can ever take her place in my heart.

She belongs to me.

# AARON

When you set your mind to it, you can do just about anything you want. I discovered this a long time ago, when I was a teenager and realized I could have any girl if I just overpowered her a little bit. Oh, they struggled and fought me off as best they could, but they were always weak. I'd hold down their arms, press myself on top of them, and eventually they'd give up.

Then they'd give it up. They always did that.

As I got older, my tastes changed. Some of the girls gave in too damn easily, and that took all the challenge out of it. Then there was my good-for-nothing wife—why I married her I don't know. More for the fact that she was pregnant with my child than anything else, and I was trying to do the right thing, I guess.

That bitch didn't want to do dick. The moment she had my son, my namesake, a boy I wanted to be proud of, she lost interest in the both of us. Was always yelling at me, nagging at me about meaningless shit. I was glad when she left. Willy was sad, but he got over it. As long as a boy has his father, he'll be fine.

I'm a firm believer in that.

The games with women weren't too much fun after a while. They always gave in. I could buy them off with drugs, which always turned them into limp rag dolls, and I got off on that for a while. Fucking a woman while she's semiconscious was a turn-on. But soon I grew weary of that, too.

That's when they got younger. The ones that put up a fight

got the shit beat out of them. The ones who lay there and just took it, too terrified to fight back?

They were my absolute favorites.

Maybe that's what my Will likes about Katherine Watts. The girl just lay there and took it. Is he like his old man after all?

I'll never know. He won't talk to me.

Well, he'll talk to me now, won't he? I chose this weekend on purpose. Holiday weekends are always understaffed here. They're all distracted anyway, with thoughts of family and bullshit and the upcoming Christmas season and how much pressure it is, to spend all that money only for those ungrateful shits they call children to hate their presents and bitch the entire time they're on winter break.

Children. They're a great blessing. Yet they also fucking suck.

I know for a fact Lisa Swanson is in San Francisco for the weekend, being a good little girl and spending the holiday with her family. I even did a little searching and discovered where her parents' house is. Google Earth is the greatest invention ever made. Coincidentally enough, they live in Marin—not too far from where I am.

The reunion is in place. Won't she be surprised? I think so.

I sit on the edge of my bed, waiting for the guard to make his hourly pass. I can hear his footsteps as he approaches and I stand, walking to the bars so I can cling to them and look extra pitiful. I know I'm pale. I feel real hot, too. I have some tricks. I know what I'm doing.

He stops when he sees me, a wary expression on his face. "What's your problem, Monroe?"

"I'm real uh . . ." I draw in a ragged breath, let it out shakily, and it sounds like I have a damn death rattle in my chest.

All those years smoking produced that. A few bouts with pneumonia helped it along. "I'm not feeling so good."

He squints at me, looking skeptical. "You fucking with me, Monroe? This is, like, the worst time for you to feel like shit. No one's manning the infirmary tonight."

I nod, rubbing my chest nice and slow. "My chest aches. And I swear to fucking God my arm is all tingly and weird feeling." I shake it out for good measure, and I'm pleased with how weak and wobbly it appears.

He steps closer, his hand on his belt, close to whatever weapon he thinks he needs to draw, the asshole. I'm a sick man, weak and feeble. The more I believe it, the more believable it'll be. "You want some aspirin?"

I laugh, the sound raspy, and I turn it into a horrific cough. This is real. I bet my lungs are as black as can be. Not that I care. I'm all in now. It's do-or-die time. "I don't know if that's really gonna help. I think I'm beyond aspirin." I cough again, covering my mouth a little late. The guard dodges out of my way so he won't get my germs, a grimace on his face.

Pussy.

"Listen, I'm serious. If you're in a bad way, I need to know now. We'll have to call an outside service or drive you to the local emergency room." He's starting to sweat at that idea—I see the little beads of perspiration form at his hairline. Poor fucker. I'm really gonna blow his mind here in a bit. "The doc is off the entire weekend."

I almost want to shout *I know, asshole,* but I keep my lips clamped shut.

And proceed to collapse on the floor, my hand still clutching at my chest. The guard starts to shout and I can barely contain the smile on my face. So easy.

Too easy.

# LISA

The house was quiet while she sat in her parents' living room, listening to the patter of the rain falling outside as she finished her fifth glass of wine of the evening. She would fly back to Los Angeles first thing in the morning since she wanted to extend this holiday visit as long as possible. Headed back to reality didn't sound like much fun. She'd rather hide away a little longer. But as usual, work called.

She leaned her head back on the couch and closed her eyes, aiming for a Zen-like attitude, the stem of the glass still clutched between her fingers. The last five days in her hometown of Marin had been about family, old friends, and reconsidering her future. Did she still want to be doing the same thing ten years from now? She wasn't getting any younger. She'd be forty years old next year, and there were a bazillion young blond bitches dying to take her spot.

It wasn't that she was ungrateful for what she had. A successful career, a lot of money in the bank, and some celebrity status—but her personal life suffered from too much ambition. She couldn't remember the last time she went out on a date. She'd always envisioned herself becoming a mother one day and used to play with baby dolls all the time when she was a little girl.

But she didn't think children were in the picture after all. She could adopt, but what kind of mom would she be, working all the time? And did she really want to keep working like this? It had become such a grind.

There was a soft knock at the door and at first she thought she imagined it, sitting up straight, her entire body still as she listened for something, anything to indicate someone was outside. But no, she heard it again. A gentle rap against her parents' grand wooden front door, three times.

Knock, knock, knock.

She placed the empty wineglass on a nearby table, her fingers shaking. No one knocked on the door at—she checked her phone—11:17 p.m., especially in her parents' affluent neighborhood.

It came again. Harder this time, a little more insistent.

Knock, knock, knock.

Slowly she rose from the couch, pushing the hair away from her face, straightening her sweater. She tiptoed as she approached the door, thankful the curtains were drawn tight on the giant front window that faced the street. She could hardly breathe, barely made a sound when it came again, startling her since she was so close.

Knock, knock, knock.

And then she heard a voice, soft and coaxing. Masculine. Familiar.

"Lisa . . . I know you're in there . . ."

She frowned at the front door, trying to ignore the uneasy feeling slithering down her spine, the sudden goosebumps that raced across the back of her arms. Damn her sleeping parents for not wanting to ruin the aesthetic of their medieval-style door by putting in a peephole. She'd at least know who was on the other side of that stupid behemoth door right now.

Pressing against the cool wood, she rested her hand on it and whispered close to the crack where the door meets the frame, "Who is this?"

"Open the door and you'll find out."

She reared back, her mind scrambling, trying to place the voice. A few nights ago she'd run into an old ex-boyfriend from high school at a bar while out with a friend. He looked good. Incredible, in fact. Recently divorced, a couple of kids, successful real estate broker with a Rolex on his wrist and a too-white smile. She could handle that. Saw them all the time in L.A. He gave her his number and she immediately texted him so he could have hers.

Wouldn't he text first before he came over? And would he really come over this late on a Sunday night? But who else could it be? She hadn't seen anyone while she'd been here, not beyond a few female friends she grew up with. No one knew she was here, not really. She kept her whereabouts fairly private.

Stiffening her spine, she reached for the door handle. It was curiosity that made her so damn good at her job. Fearlessness was another trait. She wasn't scared of shit. Certainly not some guy she went to high school with who was creeping on her parents' front porch. Maybe it wasn't such a good idea giving him her number after all.

Oh well. She'd scare him off and send him on his way with his tail tucked between his legs.

Still clutching the door handle, she reached with her other hand and turned the lock as quietly as possible, undoing it before she threw open the door, hoping to surprise him.

But she was the one who was surprised. Her mouth fell open when she saw who was standing there, a leering smile on his dirt-streaked face. His eyes were wild and bright, his clothes soaked from the incessant rain, and she tried to scream but no sound came out.

He rushed toward her, his hand going to her mouth, fingers clamping over her lips so tight she started to panic, her arms flailing as she reached for his hand to pull it away, her bare feet scrambling against the slick tile floor.

"Shut the fuck up," he whispered harshly, thrusting his face in hers, his eyes huge, pupils dilated. "Keep quiet and no one else gets hurt. You got keys to one of those cars out there?"

Hanging on the rack only a few feet away, yes she did. She nodded furiously, trying her best not to inhale too deeply. Too afraid he might smother her. And she could almost taste him—salt and sweat and dirt. His fingers tightened, his smile grew, and she screamed beneath his hand, trying to kick at him. He lifted his knee, fast and hard, jamming it in her stomach, and she bent over, trying to suck in breaths, her head spinning from the pain.

"Let's grab those keys and get the fuck out of here." He jerked on her hair with his other hand, pulling so hard the sting was unbearable. It felt like he was pulling her hair out of her scalp. "Now, bitch."

She did as he said, trembling almost uncontrollably. How did he get out? When did it happen? Did they know he's gone? And how did he find her?

He smiled when she pointed out where the keys were and he grabbed the set with the Mercedes key fob. "Fancy car for a fancy girl?" His hand moved away from her mouth and she sucked in a breath, but it wasn't enough. Her lungs seized, shrinking smaller and smaller, as if she couldn't draw a breath, and she knew she was going to have a panic attack.

"Get your shit together. We gotta go." He hooked his arm through hers and led her to the still-open door. Her parents slept like the dead. Her mom always put in her earplugs and her dad used a white-noise machine. They couldn't hear her.

No one could.

"I-I don't have any sh-shoes," she stuttered, indicating her bare feet.

Aaron Monroe threw back his head and laughed. "That's what you're worried about? Funny how all you bitches freak out over the smallest things." His laughter died, and there was an eerie gleam in his eyes. "Let's go."

Fear slid over her, chilling her skin, her bones, her soul.

She was as good as dead.

# KATIE

I'm in bed with Molly snuggled against me, curled into the spot where my knees are bent. She's warm and solid, a comforting presence in my otherwise empty bed. But I can't sleep. I toss and turn, tempted to take the sleeping pills I keep in my bathroom drawer in case of an emergency. Not too long ago I'd been somewhat addicted to them—well, more like dependent on them. I finally went off them cold turkey, not liking how I felt when I took them. It was a strange feeling. Almost suffocating.

But right now, I'm tempted. Anything to quit worrying about being alone and get some actual sleep. I have a busy week ahead with plenty of schoolwork to keep me occupied. Yet I already miss Will. It's stupid; I shouldn't be so dependent on him, either, but I am. I like having him lying next to me, always with an arm around my waist or my head resting on his shoulder. He's a comfort, always grounding me, always making me feel safe and loved.

Reaching up, I touch the guardian angel charm, my fingers slipping over the wings' ridges. I love that he took the broken bracelet and added the charm to a necklace for me, that I can wear it closer to my heart. He promised he would come back to me in one piece and I know he will. He never breaks a promise.

But will I remain in one piece while he's gone? I already feel like I could shatter, and I hate that. Where's confident Katherine? I'd been trying so hard to become her. To become the woman I wanted to be. Yet the cracks in my surface first appeared when Molly disappeared.

Actually, those cracks appeared even sooner, when Lisa told me what Aaron Monroe said about Will using me. It still upsets me that I could doubt Will, though he has given me reason to not believe in him. I understand his reasoning behind the deception and I'm mostly over it.

Mostly.

I can hear the rainfall outside and I roll over on my side, careful not to disturb Molly too much. She's doing so well, seeming to find her balance rather easily despite losing her leg. I'm proud of her, and so thankful we didn't lose her. She was so happy to see us when we went to pick her up.

"We're going to leave first thing in the morning," I tell Molly as I reach out and pet her head. "I'm too spooked here, girl. We need to go spend time with your grandma."

I sound ridiculous, referring to Mom as Molly's grandma. Irritated with myself, I slip out of bed and go to the bathroom, opening the drawer and pulling out the bottle of prescription sleeping pills. I pop the lid and shake one capsule into the palm of my hand, then dry-swallow it, grimacing when I finally get it down. I go back to bed, pulling the covers up over my head.

Within minutes I can feel the pill already working. My head feels like a cloud, soft and hazy, and there's a giant moth fluttering over my face, its wings buzzing, brushing against my cheeks. I roll over on my back and let the moth take me, swallow me . . .

My phone dings and I sit up so fast my head spins. I turn my head as if in slow motion, seeing my phone lit up where it sits on my bedside table.

A text from a number, so someone I don't know? But it's one I faintly recognize. What if it's Will? What if he somehow lost his phone and had to get a new number?

Grappling for the phone, I almost drop it, my fingers squeezing around the edges to keep it from falling on the floor. I squint at the screen, trying to make out the words.

Are you home? I need to talk to you.

I frown and send a reply.

Who r u?
    It's me. Lisa.

Wait, what? I frown even harder.

Swanson?
    Yes, are you home? Can we talk? I'm at your house.

I glance toward the hall, blinking hard, my heavy lids wanting to shut. I am not in the proper frame of mind for company. More like I'm ready to pass out.

Can't we talk another time? I'm in bed.
    No. It's urgent Katherine. I have something I really
    need to tell you.

Okay, this is some straight-up bullshit, as Will would say. I get out of bed, thankful I'm wearing thick socks because the bare floor is cold. I shuffle toward the front door, peering through the peephole to see that it's completely blocked.

I back away from the door, startled. So weird. I send a text to Lisa.

Are you out on my porch? I can't see you.

"I'm here," she calls from the other side of the door. She sounds strange. Her voice is shaky. I wonder if she's been crying.

Carefully I open the door to see Lisa standing on the doormat, wearing only a thin sweater and jeans, her hair a mess, her makeup streaked all over her face like she'd been crying. There's a bruise around her neck, a red mark across her cheek, like someone hit her.

And she's not wearing any shoes. Her feet are completely bare.

"I'm sorry, I'm sorry," she sobs, just before she's shoved out of the way and the man of my nightmares suddenly appears, looming in the doorway. Clad in dark pants and a blue denim shirt, his clothes drenched through, cheap prison-issued slip-on shoes on his feet.

That I'm able to catalog his clothes and shoes is just . . . odd. My brain is fuzzy and I blink at him, my heart seizing in my chest.

Am I having a nightmare?

"Katherine. We meet again." He smiles, but it doesn't reach his eyes. No, his eyes are dead, flat. Black as obsidian, they almost glitter in the dim light. He grabs hold of Lisa's arm roughly and she cries out, the sound echoing in the otherwise quiet of the night. This infuriates him and he backhands her, right across the jaw. I jump backward, about to shut the door on him when he thrusts out an arm, stopping me.

"You're not getting away that easily." He grabs me, his fingers curling around the crook of my elbow, and I squirm against his hold, trying to break free. Lisa actually does break free when he turns to concentrate on me, sprinting toward the car parked in front of my house. She stumbles and falls knees and hands first on the driveway but picks herself back up, running toward the road.

"Jesus H. Christ," he mutters as he withdraws a gun from his waistband and aims it right at her, no hesitation when he pulls the trigger.

I'm paralyzed, fear and unspoken screams clogging my throat as I watch Lisa collapse onto the street. Aaron grabs hold of my arm, his fingers pressing into my skin as he drags me toward a newer-model black Mercedes sedan, the gun pointed straight at my head.

"You say a fucking word, you scream, you do anything, and you're dead just like that bitch out in the street." He thrusts the gun against my temple, his face in mine for the briefest, most terrifying moment. The metal is cold on my skin. "Get in the fucking car."

He pulls open the passenger-side door and shoves me inside, then runs around the front of the car, sliding behind the wheel and starting the engine, backing out of the driveway so fast the squeal of the tires makes me wince. He races past where Lisa lies in the road and I breathe a sigh of relief that at least he didn't run her over.

I wouldn't put it past him if he did.

"Damn it!" He hits the steering wheel, then stares into the rearview mirror, his eyes wide and crazy looking. "Stupid bitch had to go and mess everything up. I wanted to keep her, damn it! She was perfect!"

He's referring to Lisa. He wanted to *keep* her? How did he get out of prison? Did she help? I can't imagine her doing that, but who knows? She was so sympathetic toward him . . .

I think of how she said she was sorry just before he pushed her out of the way, the look on her face, the utter fear I saw there. No way would she help him escape from prison. She's not that crazy.

But now . . . I think she's dead.

I stare at the road stretched out before us, hear the way he mutters under his breath, every other word a curse, his fisted hand still banging against the steering wheel. His frustration is a living, breathing thing, seeming to consume the interior of the car, and I swing my heavy head toward him, my mouth dry as I blink, trying to focus.

"What the fuck is wrong with you? You on drugs or what?"

"Sleeping pill." I lean my head against the seat and close my eyes. My head is literally spinning. This feels like a dream, like it really isn't happening, but I know it is. I can hear the low hum of the engine, Aaron Monroe's heavy, almost frantic breathing. I can smell him, sweat and fear and adrenaline. I recognize his scent. It hasn't changed in all these years.

I think I'm going to throw up.

"Where's Will? Why didn't he come out and try and rescue you? Have you got him that whipped?" he asks incredulously.

"He's . . ." I swallow, my throat like sandpaper, and I open my eyes, though I can't focus. Everything is blurry. "He's in L.A."

"Ha! Are you serious? He's not even here?" He shakes his head, his mouth stretched into a thin line. "Well, this is gonna get interesting."

What does he mean by that? I don't want to know. "Wh-what do you want from me?"

"I was looking for my son. You stole him from me, you stupid little bitch." He sneers. "Had one and then you wanted the other, just to sample us both? Is that how you operate?"

My stomach lurches. Oh God, if he keeps this up I really am going to be sick. I can't believe he said that to me.

Actually, yes I can believe it. He's a sick bastard with no regard for human life. Look at how easily he shot Lisa. He'll probably just as easily shoot me.

I reach for my necklace, my trembling fingers sliding over the charm. I close my eyes and . . . pray. I'm not a religious person. But right now, I need God. I need someone to save me. To find me. To make sure I get out of this alive. I think of Will. How this will destroy him. How guilty he'll feel that he wasn't with me, that he couldn't save me. But it's not his fault. It's never his fault.

We can't control the monsters.

# WILL

Two in the morning and I'm woken up out of a dead sleep by my phone ringing. I grab it and see the call is from . . .

Mrs. Anderson?

I sit up, answering right away, and I can hardly hear her at first. There's a garbled sound, men's voices in the background, and is that a dog barking? Swear to God it sounds like Molly.

". . . And then they think he took her! Right after he shot Lisa Swanson in the middle of the street! That's what woke me up, the sound of gunfire, like it's some sort of war zone out here," Mrs. Anderson carries on.

"Hey, slow down, back it up." I pause, push my hair out of my eyes.

"Will, your Katie is *gone*. Your father broke out of prison and they believe he kidnapped her again!" she yells.

My heart cracks into a million little pieces at her words. *"What?"* I croak, blinking hard. I need to wake up, I need to fucking focus. What is she saying?

"Here, talk to the policeman. He'll explain everything." She hands off her phone—I can hear her talking to Molly, telling her to stop barking—and a man gets on the line, identifying himself as FBI.

"Is this William Monroe?" the man asks.

"Yeah, I'm Will. Where's Katie?" Fear clutches me hard, cramping my muscles, making my stomach hurt. If she's dead, so help me God if my father is responsible for this . . . I close my eyes and hold my breath.

"Your father escaped. He complained of feeling ill and the guard was afraid he was having a heart attack. He even collapsed, but they were able to rouse him to consciousness. There was no doctor on duty since it's a holiday weekend, so they decided to transport him to a local hospital." The FBI agent pauses. "During the exchange into the vehicle he stabbed the guard with a concealed weapon, grabbed his gun, and used it to shoot at the other guard, hitting him in the stomach."

"He escaped San Quentin." I can't fucking believe it.

"He went to Marin, to Lisa Swanson's parents' house. The mother discovered Lisa was gone, along with their Mercedes, and called the police. There's an APB out for the vehicle now."

"And what about Katie? How did he get her?"

The FBI agent sighs and proceeds to explain the story as best he knows it. Somehow my father gained access to the house and took Katie. For whatever reason, Lisa Swanson was shot and left for dead in the middle of the street. Just as Mrs. Anderson said, she called the police when she heard the gunshots and once she decided it was safe—yeah, how the hell the old woman knew it was safe, I don't know—she went to Katie's house. She found the door wide open and Molly sleeping on the bed. No Katie in sight.

And a dead Lisa Swanson in the middle of the street.

"Your father shot and killed Lisa Swanson," the FBI agent reiterates. "We're fairly certain he's abducted Katherine Watts, considering she's nowhere to be found." His voice lowers. "We're going to do our best to find her. You're in Los Angeles? The neighbor told us that."

"I'm leaving." I'd already been roaming around the hotel

room as the agent told me the story, gathering up my stuff and throwing it in my suitcase. "I don't know how I'll get my ass back there but I'm going to find a way. I need to find Katie."

"Sir, we don't want you to interfere in this investigation. Your father could be in search of you. You're not safe—"

"Katie is the one who's not safe if she's with my father," I say, cutting him off. "I can't just stand by and wait for him to kill her. Because he will, trust me. He's still pissed he didn't get the chance the first time around."

I end the call, tired of wasting my time. Methodically I change into jeans and a T-shirt, tug my favorite hooded sweatshirt over my head, and slip on my shoes. I have no idea what I'm going to do, how I'm going to get to Katie.

Collapsing on the end of the bed, I bury my face in my hands and just let the fucking tears come, my chest tight, my throat raw. Why can't we ever be free? Why is my father so hell-bent on destroying us that he'll break out of prison so he can hunt us down?

I lift my head and wipe my face, reaching for my phone once more. I hit my friend Jay's number and he picks up on the third ring, sounding wide awake. Thank God for musicians staying up till all hours of the night.

"Tell me you have a connection to a private plane. Even if it's some puddle jumper that'll scare the shit out of me," I say to him in greeting. "I don't care what it is, I just need to get home. Now."

"What's going on, bro?" There's genuine concern in Jay's voice and for a quick second, I'm tempted to crumble apart all over again and spill everything.

But I need to keep my shit together. I need to form a plan and get the hell out of here.

"I'll tell you later, just . . . do you know someone with a

plane?" Jay has all sorts of connections with all the people he knows in the music business. I know he'll help me if he can.

"Give me a half hour. I'll see what I can do," he says before he disconnects, no questions asked.

Within twenty minutes he's got a flight arranged for me. It leaves in less than two hours.

I just hope that's not too late.

KATIE

I startle awake, sitting up so fast my head spins. It's light outside but the sky is gray, the early morning gloomy. Breathing hard, I slowly glance to my left to find Aaron Monroe next to me, the seat tilted all the way back, his eyes closed, mouth slack.

He's asleep.

We're still in the Mercedes and it's freezing. I look around, trying to figure out where we are. It's a giant parking lot, completely empty, and when I turn to look behind me, I see it rise into the sky like a beacon, like a symbol of my past I'd rather forget.

The roller coaster. We're at the boardwalk, at the amusement park where he abducted me.

Turning in my seat, I watch him, fighting to keep my wits. I'm still drowsy, the effects of the sleeping pill lingering, and I rub my forehead, trying to force clarity. I need to escape. He's sleeping. I could open the door and slip out of the car, but then what? Where would I go? The parking lot is abandoned, as is the park. It's early in the morning and there's no one around. The boardwalk is closed for winter.

But I can't sit in this car and wait for him to kill me. Or worse . . . rape me. I'd rather he end me and get it over with. I can't stand the thought of him putting his hands on me again.

I'd rather die than endure it.

Keeping my eyes on him, I reach out toward the door and

rest my hand on the handle. I don't move, I don't make a sound, I don't even breathe for fear he'll wake up. I turn the handle, feel the door give, and I'm about to push it open, swiveling toward the door so I can slip out into the cold morning air, when I feel a hand clamp down on my thigh and hear the click of a gun.

"You get out of this car and I'll fucking shoot you right in the head. I mean it."

I slowly turn to face him to find the barrel pointed directly in my face. I recoil from it and pull the door shut, closing my eyes so I don't have to see the gun.

So I don't have to see him.

"You're such a stupid, *stupid* girl. So drugged out from your little sleeping pill that you passed out quick. I messed around with you all night and you didn't even try and fight me off." He laughs as he brings his seat up, his voice drawing closer. The gun may not be in my face any longer but I still refuse to open my eyes. I don't want to look at him. "You just laid there and took it. Probably secretly liked it, too, you little slut."

My skin crawls and I take a deep, shuddering breath. I don't believe him. I don't . . . feel violated and I know I would if he'd touched me. That's something I can't forget no matter how hard I try, no matter how many times I scrub my skin and purge all thoughts of him from my brain. What it's like to be raped by Aaron Monroe.

"We're back here at the scene of the crime." I crack open my eyes to see his eyes full of glee, his smile downright maniacal. "I thought it would be fun for the two of us to revisit the park, just like old times."

He's clearly insane. "I-I don't have any shoes." Just the thick socks I had on when I went to bed. I'm wearing red flannel pajama bottoms and one of Will's old sweatshirts that he gave to me. It still smells like him.

That thought alone makes me want to cry.

"You women always worrying about your shoes. You're fucking ridiculous." My eyes go wider when he waves the gun at me. "Stay right there. I'm getting out of the car, and then I'm opening your door. Don't fucking move a muscle, do you understand me?"

I nod, too afraid to speak. I watch as he rounds the front of the car and then opens the door for me, making a gesture with the gun, indicating he wants me to get out.

For a split second I contemplate making a run for it, but I don't want to die. Not yet. I'm too young. I can't go like this, not at the hands of Aaron Monroe. Instead I climb out of the car and look at him, trying not to flinch when he smiles and slams the car door.

"Ready for a new adventure?" he asks, his voice low, sliding all over my skin and making me shake. "It'll be fun, Katie. Trust me."

He takes me by the hand and leads me toward the park.

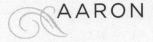# AARON

This isn't how I envisioned everything going down. Lisa is supposed to be here, standing by my side, helping me. Will is supposed to be here, too. We could've been one big happy family, the four of us. It would've been nice.

Real nice.

But Lisa had to try and run. She ruined everything. I'm most pissed at her. Damn it, she would've made an excellent accomplice, but she didn't want this. She tried to leave me.

And now no one can have her. Not even me.

I'm disappointed my boy isn't here, either. I wanted him to see this. See me with his girl. But that was just a stroke of bad luck. Any other time and I would've found him. I'm stuck alone with his stupid little girlfriend who won't hardly speak to me and she's being disrespectful. I don't like that. She hardly does anything but glare at me like she wants to take the gun I'm holding and shove it down my throat, sending a bullet through my insides.

If she doesn't watch it, I'm going to do that very thing to her.

"Did you know I used to work here?" I ask conversationally as we enter the park. Up ahead is the main ticket booth, and I know for a fact that's where they keep the spare keys that work all the rides.

When the bitch doesn't say anything I continue talking. "Yep, when Will was a kid, I worked here for the summer. Ran some of the rides. Including the Sky Glider."

No reaction. That's the very ride I asked her to take me to, back when she was twelve and gullible as fuck.

"I know where they keep the keys." I pick up my stride, letting go of her hand but aiming the gun right at her. "Don't move."

She doesn't. She just stands there and watches as I kick in the door. It caves easily, as if it were made of cardboard, and I enter the tiny, crowded booth, spotting the keys still hanging in the same spot all these years later.

"You'd think they'd take the keys with them when they close up for the winter, but they never do. They never have to. No one's fucked with these rides in all the years this shit hole has been open. Pretty unbelievable, huh." I take the keys and shove them in the front pocket of the pants I'm wearing. They came from the guard I shot. I stole his pants before I took off. Left him bleeding out in his tighty whiteys and absolutely no dignity. Wish I could've done that to every guard I had to deal with. They're all pricks.

But still she says nothing. Her silence makes me want to tear my hair out.

Instead, I ignore her, taking hold of her wrist and dragging her along with me. We turn left and head down the main walkway, past the silent, boarded-up game booths, past the various empty food booths, including my favorite funnel-cake one. The haunted house doesn't look so spooky in the early morning light. More like it looks ragged and run-down, as if it's seen better days.

I've seen better days, too.

There's no other ride I want to go on but the Sky Glider, so I decide to do a test run first. The Sea Swings are up ahead, on the right, and I nudge Katie in the shoulder with the gun. "You're gonna ride that."

She turns to look at me, her eyes wide, skin pale. "Why?"

"Because I want to make sure the keys work." I nudge the gun in her shoulder again. "Go on, get on it."

Katie pushes through the gate and goes to the swings, the clanging of the metal chain loud in the quiet stillness as she settles into one of the chairs. It sways back and forth and she wraps her arms around herself as if to ward off a chill.

"At least smile and look like you're having fun!" I yell at her. She gives me an incredulous look in return and anger fills me, making me insert the key into the control board extra hard, flipping the switches one by one. She's lucky she's not right next to me. I'd probably pistol-whip the bitch and enjoy watching her fall to the ground.

The swings slowly start to rise when I hit one switch and I smile in triumph, pleased to see it works. The ride will last three minutes, tops, and I step back to watch as the swings start to spin faster and faster, higher and higher. They fly in the wind since every one of them is empty and there sits Katie, clinging tightly to the chain that holds her swing up, her face full of apprehension and fear.

Good. I like seeing the fear. Bitch needs to know her place. We're going to have fun first. Relive the good times before we end it. Because we're going to end it, that's a sure thing. I'm a wanted fugitive who escaped from a maximum-security prison. A death-row inmate, for Christ's sake; the media must be having a field day making the wardens look bad. I'm sure they're furious I snuck past them, but I'm not stupid. The order on my head is shoot to kill—I know that without a doubt.

So I may as well enjoy my time here before I'm dead and gone, right?

# WILL

The FBI agent—his name is Woods—calls me the moment the tiny prop-engine plane touches down. His timing is impeccable, as if he knows I just landed, and I listen to him speak, fear freezing my vocal cords and making it impossible for me to answer him at first.

Until I finally hear the news I've been waiting for.

"We know where they're at and she's still alive." He pauses. "He took her to the boardwalk. Where he originally kidnapped her."

The airport is fifteen minutes away. Hell, I saw the park when we flew over the ocean, circling in preparation to land. "You have a car waiting for me here at the airport, right?"

Woods hesitates. "We don't want you here. You might prove to be a distraction."'

"You're fucking kidding me, right? I have to be there. I need to see her. I need to talk to him. Talk to them both."

"It could backfire."

"I don't think so. I know my father. And I know Katie." I take a deep breath, trying to get my emotions under control. "Even if I can't help, I have to be there. I-I need to see her."

Woods is quiet for a moment before he lets out a ragged exhale. "There's a car waiting for you. I'll radio in to the driver that you should be brought over here. We're waiting him out right now. He doesn't even know we're on to him yet."

"Seriously?" That sounds risky as shit. Why can't they just run in there and shoot his ass? End this once and for all?

"We have SWAT surrounding the place and a sniper on top of the arcade. He's had Monroe in his sights already a couple of times, but Katherine's always in the way. He can't get a clean shot."

I close my eyes, fighting the nausea that threatens. Someone is dying today. Hell, someone already died. Poor Lisa Swanson. He shot her in the back of the head and she bled out, alone in the middle of the road.

My father is a monster.

But someone else is going to die, too. My father. The man who raised me. The man who fucked me up and just about ruined me. Well, look at me now, dear old Dad. Look at me with tears in my eyes, sick as hell and worried that you're going to murder the woman I love.

That's what I should tell him, not that he cares. He doesn't care about anyone.

Just himself.

# KATIE

The idea comes to me as clear as day. I might not be able to get away, but maybe I can convince Aaron Monroe that he can't shoot me.

He's made me ride the swings, the Ferris wheel, a kiddy car ride with my knees practically bent up to my ears, and the merry-go-round. That had been the most painful so far. I could barely hold back the sobs on the merry-go-round, memories coming at me all at once, making me think of my family. My father. He loved the merry-go-round here, always riding it with us.

Thinking of my father is what gives me the idea, though I know it's a total long shot. I need to find a way to tell Monroe my news. I just pray that he believes me.

"I'm saving the best for last," he tells me as I come off the rock-and-roll ride, my head spinning from the speed of it. The cars went in circles, backward and forward, faster and faster, the music louder and louder. My ears still throb from the pounding beat.

I frown at him, not saying anything. He really hates how I don't speak and it's my only defense, so I keep up the silent treatment.

He points up at the Sky Glider. "We'll ride that last, then go down to the beach. Check out the ocean. I haven't seen the ocean in years." His voice is wistful.

The wind chooses that moment to whip up, making my

hair fly into my face, and I bat it away. He expects me to ride on that tiny seat on the Sky Glider with him by my side? I rest a hand over my stomach. I'm so hungry, but also nauseous. I haven't eaten anything in almost twelve hours and I have to pee.

But he doesn't care. He's wrapped up in his own little world, glancing around everywhere, looking for a sign that someone has discovered us, I'm sure. The longer we're here, the more paranoid he gets. And I think someone has found us. I thought I saw a man on the roof of the giant arcade about ten minutes ago, but I could be wrong.

It could be wishful thinking.

Does Will know yet? That his dad took me? That his father killed Lisa Swanson? Is Molly okay? I bet she's with Mrs. Anderson, safe and warm and missing the both of us.

I blink away the tears, wipe at them with trembling fingers, and Aaron sees me.

"You crying now? Really?" He shakes his head and squints up at the sky. "I think it's time I take you up on the Sky Glider. Our last hurrah."

He's speaking with such finality and it's scaring me. What does he mean, our last hurrah? He has to know this isn't going to end well, at least for him.

Probably for me, too.

"I'm scared of heights," I say, making my voice extra shaky. "Plus, I'm so nauseous all the time. And tired. So tired."

My plan is set into motion with that particular sentence and he perks up, his head slowly turning toward me.

"Why?"

I rest my hand on my stomach, trying to work up the courage to tell him. I've never been a good liar. I hope I can pull this off. "Because I'm—I'm pregnant with your grandchild. Will and I are going to have a baby."

He doesn't say a word, just looks at me as if I've lost my mind. I wait for him to respond, to say something, anything, but he doesn't. His gaze drops to where my hand still rests on my stomach before his gaze lifts and he sneers.

Slowly he shakes his head, stepping closer to me. My entire body shakes and I'm scared he'll touch me. Hurt me. But he just stares at me with so much disgust I feel the shame wash over me, swallowing me up.

"Unbelievable. You're nothing but a stupid whore trying to trap my son. I'll be doing him a favor by shooting you in the head." He laughs. "Did you think that bit of news would convince me to spare your life?"

I say nothing, feeling stupid. *Yes!* I want to shout at him. *Yes, I thought maybe you'd have a tiny piece of decency still left in your heart, but I guess not.*

There's no hope for me. My idea didn't work. I'm as good as dead. I don't think I can stand much more of this.

A crackling sound suddenly fills the air and I know what it is. The sound system for the entire park. I can hear the static from the speakers as they're turned on. Aaron hears it, too.

"Looks like someone's joined us, Katie. This ought to be interesting." He grins and I look away, glancing around the abandoned grounds. There's no sign of life anywhere.

"Aaron Monroe, we know you're in there. And we know you have Katherine Watts with you. If you let the woman go, give up your weapons, you'll be able to walk away from this. Just do as we say and no one gets hurt," the booming voice commands.

"Maybe I don't want to walk away from this!" he screams,

looking around wildly, the gun dangling from his fingertips. "Did anyone ever consider that? Do you think they ever thought that, Katie?" He looks at me, the gun pointed right at my chest. "Do you?"

"N-no." I shake my head. "Maybe you really don't want to walk out of here." I believe he doesn't. He'd rather die at his own hand than theirs.

"You're damn right I don't want to. What's the point? There's *no* point. None. I'm done. It's over." He waves his gun at me. "Get over here. We're riding the Glider. Now."

Disappointment washes over me as I walk over to him and we make our way to the Glider side by side, the both of us quiet. My heart is pounding so hard I swear it's going to leap out of my chest, and I feel like I'm walking to my death.

I probably am.

The voice keeps booming over the speakers, repeating the same thing over and over. Aaron's not paying attention. It's like he's tuned everyone out, even me. He's in his head, thinking, worrying . . . I don't know. All I really know is I'm afraid if I try to make one last run for it, he'll shoot me and I'll die.

I don't want to risk it. So I remain by his side.

We approach the stairs that lead to the Sky Glider and Aaron indicates he wants me to walk up them first as he falls in behind me. I climb the stairs one at a time, wincing at the cold concrete beneath my socks. They're wet and worn from all the walking and my feet hurt. My head hurts.

My heart hurts the most, though. At all I've yet to do. At the life I'm going to lose. I think of my mom and how devastated she'll be. And Brenna. Will she be mad that I stole the spotlight again? I hope not. I hope she knows how much I love her. She's the best big sister I ever could have asked for.

As I crest the top of the steps and see the ocean spread out before me, gray and majestic, stormy and endless, I think of Will. How much I love him. How much I'll miss him. That I hope he can carry on and eventually find happiness with someone else.

The tears spring to my eyes and I hang my head, stumbling when Aaron pushes past me and goes to the control panel, sticking the key into the slot and turning the ride on. I watch as the cars that hang from metal wheels start to move, one after the other, the empty cars swinging over the entry point before they take off over the park, dangling from a wire.

"Ready to get in? Have a color preference?" Aaron laughs, the bastard. "Want to ride a pink one or a green one?"

"I don't care," I mumble, but he shakes his head, waving the gun again.

"Pick a color, Katie. Yellow? Blue? Red? How about orange?"

A different voice sounds over the speaker, one I recognize. My entire body lights up with hope when I realize who it is.

"Dad. Dad, it's me."

Aaron halts in his movements, the gun going still. He doesn't joke, doesn't smile, doesn't say a word.

"Please don't hurt her, Dad. You don't need any more trouble. Just . . . surrender to the police and let this be over with. Please."

I'm crying, tears streaming down my face at the sound of his voice, how he's pleading for my life. I'm not going to make it. I can feel it. This is the end. My head is empty, my body is light, almost as if the angels have already grabbed hold of me and are preparing me to go with them.

"Get in the car," Aaron says, his voice flat. He points his gun at the cars that keep swinging by, one after the other, and he steps closer to me. "We're riding one together. That way they can't shoot my ass if there's a sniper anywhere. You're my shield. I'm not as stupid as you all think I am."

I never thought he was stupid. The man is crafty. Shady. Horrible. A monster. But he's not stupid.

"I'm begging you, Dad. You've done enough damage to her. Just . . . let Katie go. Exchange her for me. I'll take her place. Please. Please, don't hurt her."

I close my eyes against his heart-wrenching words. He can't exchange himself for me. What if his father kills him instead? How is that any better?

How could I ever survive without him?

"Meet us at the other end of the Sky Glider and then we can do the exchange!" Aaron yells toward the sky. "Did you hear that, Willy? Did you?"

My eyes slowly open to find he's crying, too. Tears fill his eyes and his cheeks are red. Does he even realize what he's doing?

There's a delay, and finally Will's voice comes over the speaker again, firm and strong. "I got it. I heard you. You'll exchange Katie for me at the other side of the Sky Glider. Deal?"

"Deal." Aaron smiles, baring his teeth at me, his eyes glittering with unshed tears. "And while we're on the Glider together, you get to watch, Willy. You have to watch."

The one word triggers what Will told me about his past. How his father used to make Will watch him have sex with women. He wants to do something to me on that Glider when we're riding together, something horrible, and he'll make Will watch the entire thing unfold.

I can't allow it to happen.

I just . . .

I can't.

Numb, my mind spinning, I start toward the cars, standing in the area where everyone in line is supposed to wait until they're called over. A car leaves and I step in front of the next one, ready to fall into it and pull the bar down so that it can take me over the boardwalk, high in the sky.

"Wait for me," Aaron starts to say but I turn on him, fast and quick. Like a whirlwind. I don't even think, I just bend my leg and kick him, making direct contact in the balls. I wish I had shoes on. That would have done more damage, but it was enough. Just enough.

Howling, he bends forward, covering his crotch, and I fall into the moving car, pulling the bar over my lap and watching him scream at me as the car takes off and up into the air, moving slowly over the park so I can get a perfect view of everything below me, spread out before me.

But I don't care about the view. I need the car to move faster. I need to get away from Aaron and make my way to Will. I glance over my shoulder to see the car right behind me is empty. Aaron's in the next car, arms straight, the gun clutched in his hand, aimed directly at me.

I duck at the precise moment the bullet goes whizzing by, and I almost slip out of the car. I cling to the metal bar in front of me, practically hanging from it, my butt almost all the way off the slick car, legs dangling toward the ground. I scramble to get back up, my hands slipping, and a scream escapes me when I hear another bullet fly by.

The ground below is a long way down. If I fall, I'm going to die. Sobbing uncontrollably, I muster all the strength I can find and somehow manage to hoist myself up, back into the seat. I drape myself across the cold hard plastic, keeping my head low so I don't give Aaron anything to aim at.

"Stay low, Katherine!" a voice shouts over the loudspeaker,

startling me, and I grip the metal bar, my sweaty fingers barely holding on. "Stay down!" the voice yells just as a hail of gunfire erupts.

I close my eyes and duck lower, as low as I can get. I'm half hanging off the Glider car and it rocks back and forth, the wire and wheel creaking above my head. I'm shaking so bad my teeth chatter and then I can tell . . . we're going lower. And lower.

Cracking open my eyes, I see we're at the other end of the ride.

And there's Will, waiting for me just like he said he would be. He's running toward me, his arms outstretched, his expression full of hope and love and fear. I fall apart in his arms, clutching him so close, like I'll never let him go.

I made it.

I survived.

# WILL

We're at the hospital. The authorities insisted Katie get checked out before they release her. They also want to question her—even though one of the FBI agents already did while we rode in the ambulance to the hospital. General questions, trying to get the timeline right, trying to figure out exactly what happened when she was in my father's captivity.

When she starts to cry in earnest I stop the questioning. She's been through too much. They could ask her questions later. We have time.

We have nothing but time.

"What happened to him?" she asks, her voice thin.

She sounds so tired, so . . . sad. We're in a private room. She's wearing a hospital gown, and there's a monitor hooked up to her as well as an IV as she lies in the bed. They didn't want to take any chances on her, ensuring that she was well hydrated and mentally stable—their words—before they let her go.

I'm dying to get out of here. I think she is, too.

"Your father," she adds. When I don't say anything she clutches my hand, her fingers tight as they curl around mine. "Tell me."

I take a deep breath and exhale roughly, my gaze meeting hers. I'm in a chair, pulled up as close as I can get it to her bed. "They shot him. He fell out of the Glider car but he was already dead before he hit the ground."

She squeezes her eyes shut, grimacing. "It sounds awful, but . . . I'm glad he's dead. He was going to kill me, Will." She starts to cry again. "I should be dead right now. I was fully prepared for it. It's like I found peace within myself that it was my time."

Her tears, her words, they break my heart. I get up from the chair and climb into the bed with her, holding her close, letting her sob into my shirt. I run my hand over her hair and breathe in her familiar scent, closing my eyes against the tears that want to fall from my eyes.

But I'm done crying for what I might have lost. She's here. Alive and in my arms. We're together. My father is dead.

He's gone.

"You're not dead, baby," I whisper close to her ear, kissing her there. My arms tighten around her and she snuggles closer. "You're alive. You're fine. You're with me. And I'm never going to let you go. Never again."

The nightmare is finally over.

# KATIE

I believe Will. I know he'll never let me go, and when I tell him the news I discovered during the series of tests they performed on me when I first arrived at the hospital, he's really going to want to keep me close by his side. His overprotective nature will kick into high gear.

Taking a deep breath, I decide to just admit everything.

"When I was with your father, I—I lied to him," I murmur against Will's chest.

He pulls away so he can look down at me. "You lied to him about what?"

"I was desperate. I came up with an idea, hoping that he wouldn't kill me once he knew." I'm shaking, so nervous to tell Will the truth. What if this isn't what he wants? I'm scared, too. What if we're both not ready? We're so young, and we've been through so much.

"What did you tell him?" His voice is soft, his gaze warm and full of so much love, I know in that instant that he won't react poorly. He'll be happy. So happy.

"I told him I was pregnant with your baby." The words rush out of me and I bend my head, not wanting to look at him. "It didn't matter. I could've had his future grandchild inside of me and it wouldn't have mattered. He wanted to kill me. That was his plan all along. I think if you'd been there, he would've wanted to kill you, too. He wanted to take all of us down along with him."

Will mutters a curse beneath his breath, but otherwise he says nothing. Just tugs me close and presses his face against my hair, kissing the top of my head. I try to fight the shivering that's taking over my body. Maybe I shouldn't say anything else. We've been through enough today. What if he totally freaks out?

"When I first got here they ran a series of tests on me," I admit quietly, my voice muffled by his chest. "I really am pregnant, Will. I don't know how it happened, but I am." I go completely still, waiting for his response, my chest aching as I hold my breath, my tears.

He's quiet for a moment, brushing my hair away from my face, his mouth at my temple. "I think you know how it happened, Katie." The quiet amusement in his voice is completely unexpected.

And the relief that rushes through me leaves me weak. He's not mad. But did I really think he'd be mad? Upset maybe, but he's already joking. "I know. I just . . . I didn't mean for it to happen."

"It's a blessing." He slips his fingers beneath my chin and tilts my face up so our gazes meet. "We'll figure this out. As long as the two of us are together, we'll always figure it out. I have faith in us."

"I have faith in us, too," I admit, blinking away my tears.

But he sees them. He leans in and kisses them away, my eyes shuttering closed at the feel of his lips feathering my skin. The relief, the pure joy that I feel at being safe and in Will's arms, is so overwhelming, it threatens to take my breath away. We're going to be okay.

"I love you," he whispers, his hand moving down to slip over my very flat stomach. "You're giving me a gift. Never think otherwise."

I won't. I swear.

"We should get married." I look up at him, see the determination written all over his face. "It's the right thing to do and we'll just be postponing the inevitable if we don't. Marry me, Katie."

I gape at him. I go from thinking I'm going to die to surviving yet another ordeal and finding out I'm pregnant and getting a marriage proposal, all in one day? I feel like I'm dreaming.

"We'll take our time. Whenever you're ready. We'll probably need to let the media speculation settle down first because everyone is already talking. You know they are." He kisses me, his mouth soft and warm. He feels like home. He feels like love. "We're in love. We're going to have a baby. Let's get married. I want you to be my wife."

Giddiness rises inside of me at hearing him call me his wife. In spite of everything that's happened, what I just went through, what I just witnessed, so much death and destruction and pure, unadulterated terror, I'm excited. My life is going to change, all for the better. All because of this man lying by my side in my hospital bed, his gaze tender and his mouth curved in the sweetest smile.

"Yes," I whisper, smiling in return when he kisses me again. "Yes, let's get married."

KATIE

Six months later

"You look beautiful." Mrs. Anderson—excuse me, *Viv*—pulls me in for a hug, her arms tight as she clamps me close. "So radiant! That dress is gorgeous. Ah, to be so young and in love. You're a lucky girl."

I pull away from her and smile, my hand going to my big belly when I feel a kick. It's amazing, how I told Aaron Monroe that I was pregnant with his grandchild and it turned out to be true. When I said it, I didn't really believe I was. More like I was pulling out all the stops to try and save myself.

Sometimes I wonder if subconsciously I knew. How, I don't know, but it's just too coincidental. And I'm not one to believe in coincidences. Not anymore.

Another kick nudges against my palm and I smile. I'm seven months along. Oh, and a married woman as of approximately ten minutes ago.

"Thank you," I tell her, leaning in to kiss her dry, wrinkled cheek. She became ordained, got certified online just so she could marry us, and I wouldn't have it any other way. "For everything."

She's become a part of my family, like the grandmother I lost when I was small. She's done so much for us, especially these last few months. Helping me out, taking care of Molly and giving her walks as I've become larger and so incredibly tired all the time. Will works a lot, too, sometimes going out of town, and Viv is my backup when he's not around.

The pregnancy hasn't always been easy. I'm exhausted a lot of the time and they discovered I was anemic. I dealt with a lot of nausea in the beginning, so the little booger was giving me trouble from the very start. But I'm close to the end now. I can't wait to hold our baby in my arms.

"My dear, you are worth it all. Every last bit." She pats my face and withdraws from my embrace, smiling. "Now go to your husband. He's waiting for you."

I turn to find he is indeed waiting for me, a patient smile on his face, his eyes filled with love, looking so handsome in black trousers and a white button-down shirt, a silver tie around his neck. I've never seen him so dressed up. My heart pangs and I think for the thousandth time today alone—I can't believe he's mine.

I go to him and he wraps me up in his arms, holding me close, his mouth against my temple. I feel him exhale, almost in relief, and I close my eyes, savoring his scent, the feel of him, warm and strong, his heartbeat steady and true. "You're beautiful," he murmurs into my hair.

"I'm wearing a tent of white lace," I joke.

"Stop. You're making fun of my bride." He kisses me, his lips lingering. "And trust me, you're gorgeous."

"So are you," I say with a happy little sigh.

"You need to get back in the house. Get some rest." His words douse out some of my happiness, just a little bit. His worry for my health touches me but also drives me a little crazy sometimes. He's beyond overprotective.

I guess after everything we've been through, I can't blame him.

"A few more minutes?" I pull back to look at him, smiling. "Please?"

He leans in and kisses the tip of my nose. "Five. Tops."

We're in Viv's backyard. That's where we had the small ceremony, with only my mom and Brenna present, as well as Viv and Molly, who has a ring of roses around her neck, made by Viv from the flowers in her yard. A few of Will's musician friends, including Jay, showed up as well, and we're all moving over to our house for a very small reception dinner put together by my mom, who brought her widower friend, Len, as her date.

They've been seeing each other since Thanksgiving and she's happy. Brenna's back in the dating game and though she loves to complain to me about the guys she meets, I think she secretly likes it. She's much more carefree, lighter. Therapy seems to have helped, too.

We are surrounded by the people who love us, and though our circle is small, we're okay with it. We don't need much. Really, as long as we have one another, that's enough.

And soon, we'll have a baby to love, too. A sweet little girl. Poor Will has nothing but females in his life, but I know he doesn't mind. He's excited. We're both excited.

For once, there's no shadow hanging over us, no ominous presence from our past chasing me, chasing him. I feel light. Happy. Free. I'm sorry that Lisa Swanson was killed, though the ratings on her show went sky high, her celebrity status firmly solidified. She'll be forever remembered as the woman who died for the story, and I like to think that would have pleased her.

But there's really no glory in that. She died alone on the street where I live. A little memorial was set up for her on the sidewalk for a while, until kids tore it apart late one night, destroying it completely. In the morning someone cleaned up the mess and it was gone.

Just like she is.

I'm lucky. So lucky. Somehow I survived. Aaron William Monroe is no longer a threat to us. He can't get me. He haunted my every thought from the time I met him, when I was twelve years old, almost thirteen, until his death. All those years, wasted. All those years, living in fear.

Life is different now. He may be a part of my husband, he will be a part of our daughter, but never again can he hurt me.

In the end, I realize Aaron Monroe *did* bring something positive into my life. He gave me Will. And for that, as crazy as it sounds . . . I will be forever grateful to the man who kidnapped me.

I am strong.

I am loved.

I am a wife.

A mother.

I am Katherine Monroe.

And I'm not afraid anymore.

Playlist

I went on a '90s music listening binge while writing this book so there are a lot of songs from that decade making an appearance. Here's my list:

"A Sorta Fairytale" by Tori Amos (Because clearly Will and Katie's story is a rather warped fairy tale).

"No Ordinary Love" by the Deftones (This was originally sung by Sade, who I adore. Again, the title is fitting because the love between Will and Katie is far from ordinary).

"#1 Crush" by Garbage (I felt like a demented weirdo loving this song in the '90s because clearly it's about someone who's obsessed with another to the point of stalker-like behavior but . . . it works for the story).

"Big Empty" by Stone Temple Pilots.

"Fall in Love" by Phantogram.

"Is It a Crime" by Sade (Whoops an '80s song and yes, I love Sade so much I added her to the playlist).

"Bloodstream" by Stateless (Best song *ever* and not the first time it's appeared on a book playlist of mine).

"Push" by Matchbox Twenty.

"Shiver" by Lucy Rose (Lyrics don't quite fit the story but such a beautiful, sad song).

"Hey Man, Nice Shot" by Filter (Uhm, this is for the villain in the story).

"The Love You're Given" by Jack Garratt (I discovered this song at the tail end of writing *NLYG* and I'm sad because I feel like this is *the* song that represents this book. Wish I could've had it on repeat as I wrote the book).

New York Times and *USA Today* bestselling author
MONICA MURPHY is a native Californian who lives
in the foothills of Yosemite. A wife and mother of
three, she writes new adult contemporary romance
and is the author of the One Week Girlfriend series
and the tie-in novella, *Drew + Fable Forever,* the
Fowler Sisters series, and the Never series.

monicamurphyauthor.com
missmonicamurphy@gmail.com
Facebook.com/MonicaMurphyauthor
@MsMonicaMurphy

About the Type

This book was set in Sabon, a typeface designed by the well-known German typographer Jan Tschichold (1902–74). Sabon's design is based upon the original letter forms of sixteenth-century French type designer Claude Garamond and was created specifically to be used for three sources: foundry type for hand composition, Linotype, and Monotype. Tschichold named his typeface for the famous Frankfurt typefounder Jacques Sabon (c. 1520–80).